USA TODAY bes
author **Caitlin Cr**
teaches her favou
classes at places li
Writers' Programm...
the MA and PhD in... ...ture she received
from the University of York in England. She currently
lives in the Pacific Northwest, with her very own hero
and too many pets. Visit her at caitlincrews.com.

Regina Kyle knew she was destined to be an author
when she won a writing contest at the age of ten with
a touching tale about a squirrel and a nut pie. By day,
she writes dry legal briefs. At night, she writes steamy
romance with heart and humour. She is a two-time
winner of the Booksellers' Best Award. A lover of all
things theatrical, Regina lives in Connecticut with her
husband, daughter and two melodramatic cats. When
she's not writing she's most likely singing, reading,
cooking or watching bad reality television.

TAKE ME

CAITLIN CREWS

DIRTY WORK

REGINA KYLE

MILLS & BOON

First Published in Great Britain 2020
by Mills & Boon, an imprint of HarperCollins*Publishers*
1 London Bridge Street, London, SE1 9GF

Take Me © 2020 Caitlin Crews

Dirty Work © 2020 Denise Smoker

ISBN: 978-0-263-27755-5

MIX
Paper from
responsible sources
FSC C007454

This book is produced from independently certified FSC™ paper
to ensure responsible forest management.
For more information visit www.harpercollins.co.uk/green.

Printed and bound in Spain
by CPI, Barcelona

TAKE ME

CAITLIN CREWS

MILLS & BOON

CHAPTER ONE

IT WASN'T UNTIL she'd landed in Sydney after the long-haul flight from London, pale from all the recycled air and a bit drunk from the mess of time zones, that it occurred to Lady Jenny Markham to worry about her welcome.

"Don't be silly," she told herself, astonished by the raspy sound of her own voice in the too-bright corridor, lost somewhere deep in the Sydney Airport. "It's Dylan."

And the one thing she knew to be true, no matter what else happened or how life kicked her around, was that Dylan Kilburn was always happy to see her. Always. That was why she always kept her visa to enter Australia current. On the off chance she might pop off down under and visit the man who'd been her best friend since their university days.

In all the years since Dylan had moved to Australia, she'd never done it. But here she was at last. Wilted straight through, but *here*.

Jenny had packed light, mostly because she'd been

in denial about what she was doing. She'd thrown a few things in a shoulder bag in her flat in Central London, that was all, because she wasn't *taking a trip*. She'd set off on a happy little lark and could as easily have simply wandered about London for a while, playing tourist. Maybe she'd pretended that was exactly what she was doing.

Though she didn't usually head off to enjoy the sights and sounds of the city with her passport in hand.

She was being *spontaneous*, and that felt weird only because Jenny was rarely spontaneous. Make that never. But she was an engaged woman now and her life was changing, and there was no time like the present to do things she'd never done before—because she never would again.

She certainly wasn't *running from* anything, she assured herself as she made it through customs and immigration and officially entered Australia for the first time.

Everyone deserved a little time to themselves before getting married. An engagement ought to come with bit of reflection and preparation, surely, before standing up before all and sundry and making vows to become legally bound forever. Some people went off to extreme yoga retreats or some such at times like these, where they could twist themselves into alarming shapes and slug down green concoctions that tasted of mud and self-righteousness. Jenny accidentally found herself at Heathrow.

But thinking about her own impending marriage was depressing, so she busied herself with finding and hiring a cab when she wasn't sure she had access to her own brain. It was possible she'd left it somewhere over the northern hemisphere.

Once she located a taxi and climbed in, she directed the driver to take her to Dylan's address. Assuming he still lived in the house he'd bought on the coast, south of Sydney proper.

Jenny doubted he would have moved without telling her. They texted all the time. When Dylan had bought this place, right after what he'd called his *wee start up* went public, he'd sent her pictures.

Just bought nauseatingly posh bachelor pad, complete with ocean views, he'd written. Guest room always available, should milady find herself in NSW.

Who wants to visit a bachelor pad? she'd texted back. That sounds medically questionable. Also, it's lovely.

She remembered white, stark, modern lines and a gorgeous view of the sea, everything sunny and sweet and bursting with vivid color. As everything Australian always was when she thought of it. That or the red hot desolation of the outback.

Sydney had always been on Jenny's list of places to see, but she'd spent most of her time before and after university filling the role of her father's hostess and companion. Her mother had died when Jenny was twelve, and she'd considered it an honor that she got to accompany her father to his business events. There was a part of her that would always be that grief-stricken twelve-year-old in a pretty dress and her mother's pearls, pretending to be grown up while her father's usually dour friends and associates acted as if it was a great privilege to meet her.

Lord Markham was not a man given to having feelings, much less expressing them. Jenny rather thought what few emotions he'd had must have died with her mother. But she always remembered those first few years. And how he'd included her when it would have been so much easier to leave her at home. She always remembered that he'd cared for her as best he could, in a way that had made them both breathe a bit better, for a time.

Maybe it wasn't surprising she felt duty bound to do the same for him, now it was her turn.

She had gone on all the dates he'd set up for her. She had smiled and had awkward conversation—or, more often, listened in appropriately reverent silence as her date banged on about himself. It was better than subjecting herself to a dating app. At least the men her father set her up with were vetted, in some form or another. They weren't pretending to be someone else—they really were that boring.

But Jenny didn't mind. Her passion wasn't for

men, it was for her work. Once she'd left uni she'd gotten a job in a worthy charity—meaning, one that supported something that wouldn't embarrass her father at a business dinner. Jenny's provided aid and care to children in war zones. And that meant that most of Jenny's trips were to places that did not glitter or attract highflyers like Dylan.

She'd always told herself—and him—that it was her work that kept her from coming down under. No matter how many times Dylan told her she was more than welcome to come and make an adventure out of it.

You're making an adventure of it now, she told herself a bit wryly as she settled into her seat, the cab lurching a bit as it headed away from the airport.

For the first time in years, she hadn't given the charity a thought. She'd simply…gotten on the plane.

It had to be an adventure because she couldn't take it back.

She blew out a breath and looked out the window. It was coming up on half six in the morning in Sydney, and the sun was only just making its appearance. Jenny was sure that once it rose, her head would feel less fuzzy. That the strange weighted feeling tugging on all her limbs, and the odd sensation that she was scraped raw, was a gift of her long plane ride. No one could possibly spend nearly twenty-four hours on two planes and not feel like an alien. Even her *feet* felt as if they belonged to someone else.

You felt equally worn out in London, a voice inside her piped up. *It wasn't the flight.*

The voice sounded suspiciously like Erika Vanderburg, her other best friend.

Erika had looked at Jenny almost pityingly the last time they'd seen each other. Jenny had been perhaps too enthusiastic about Erika's plan to return to Oxford to finish her degree course, all these years after she'd left her degree course.

Geography isn't going to cure anything but your location, Erika had said gently.

Because the new version of Erika was not the messy creature Jenny was used to, always drunk and inappropriate, scandalous and *fun.* The new version of Erika was settled in her relationship with the intimidating Dorian Alexander, best friend to Erika's older brother, Conrad. *Easygoing* in a way Jenny would not have believed possible if she hadn't seen it with her own eyes. Even having seen it, she wasn't sure she believed it. How could she? The new Erika was so self-possessed it made Jenny's lifelong pretense of self-possession look like exactly what it was. A sham.

But as the cab navigated the early morning streets, she stared down at the enormous ring on her hand that she kept meaning to get fixed so it wouldn't slide about so much, blinding unwary passersby, and wondered if it was as simple as the fact Erika was in love.

Love was something not even Jenny could fake.

Luckily, her engagement—to Conrad Vanderburg, Erika's chilly older brother, whose success in business made Lord Markham as close to giddy as a man not given to such displays could get—was practical, not passionate. No faking required.

"Dylan will sort it all out," she told herself, muttering staunchly beneath her breath so as not to alarm the driver. "He always does."

Erika had always been Jenny's most *vivid* friend, the mad one who could go out for chips and end up dancing on tabletops in a different city at dawn. She was ardently loyal, she was passionate about everything and Jenny had wanted to *be* her, some years. But Dylan had always been her stalwart. He listened. He gave good advice. He'd been keeping Jenny grounded as long as she'd known him.

If he couldn't help her, no one could.

Not that she needed help, she corrected herself as the cab continued east. She was *fine*. Her life was carrying on according to plan. Some people—Erika, for example—might think that was a bad thing, but Jenny knew better. This was life.

Dylan would take the rawness inside of her, name it and laugh at it, and in so doing, make it feel better. And make *her* feel better.

She looked around as they drove, trying to take in architecture that looked both brand new and comfortingly familiar at once. It was like looking at proper British streets, but with a certain overlay that was distinctly Australian. She couldn't have said what that was. The extra filigreed bits on the gratings and railings, perhaps? Or all the years she'd spent sneaking episodes of *Neighbours*, more like. Everything was Ramsay Street, if she squinted.

Eventually, the car went around a bend and she realized that wasn't only sky in the distance, it was the sea. And Jenny had to remind herself, with a kick of wonder, that it was the Pacific, deep and blue. Not the gray North Atlantic she knew better.

And for the first time since she'd jumped on a plane in Heathrow, on a whim, the fact that she'd taken herself off across the planet hit her.

Hard enough that she found herself quite glad she was sitting down.

She worried that huge ring on her hands instead of thinking about all the likely reactions back home, turning it around and around and telling herself that she was exhausted. Obviously. And that was why the weight of the ring, which had never been light to begin with, seemed more like a brick.

The cab wound around through narrower streets, with houses built up high on hillsides that sloped toward the sea. All of them made mostly of windows, to make the best of the view from every angle. And what a view it was, with neighborhoods clinging to rugged cliffs, and sandy beaches stretching in between. It was nothing at all like an English seaside.

The driver pulled up before a sleek white building.

The street was at garage level, and the only thing to see was the wooden door to the garage and beside it, a closed entryway. Jenny paid the driver, climbed out with her small case and stood there as the cab drove off.

There were butterflies leaping around inside her, and she told herself she didn't know why.

It was only Dylan. One of her two best friends from her Oxford days. They'd been first years on the same stair, along with Erika, and Jenny had been close with both of them ever after. She and Erika saw more of each other, it was true, but only because Dylan had relocated here, built himself a fortune and liked to call himself an *accidental billionaire*.

Before anyone else can, he'd told her when she'd asked him why. And then had texted something incomprehensible about Californian tech giants.

Jenny had spent several hours on the plane thinking about when she'd seen Dylan last. In person. She was sure it had been in Cape Town, a year or so back. She'd been at a charity ball and he'd been in town for business meetings. They'd met up at a lovely restaurant with panoramic views of Signal Hill, had a typically uproarious dinner, had laughed until Jenny had tears streaming down her face and had parted on their usual merry, friendly terms. Because that was Dylan. Always easy and fun, and the most undemanding person in her life.

Which meant there was absolutely no reason for her

to be standing there as the rising sun streaked the sky in the colors of candy floss, wracked with…nerves.

But then, though she'd seen Dylan in all sorts of places over the years, she'd never actually come to his home. Not since his home had been a room in college, same as hers.

And even then, now that she thought about it, they had spent most of their time together out and about, studying, or taking in Oxford, eating or drinking, or going on long walks.

It was funny that she'd never really thought about how intimate it was, really, to turn up at a person's house.

Uninvited.

Ten thousand miles away, without warning.

She took a deep breath, then shivered, because it was cold. It was August, which meant she'd flown out of a surprisingly warmish England straight into an Australian winter. The air was crisp, chilly and almost sweet. Dylan's house sat across from a green park that ambled its way out to the cliffs and then down to the beach, with nothing blocking the sea air. Or the views.

If Dylan wasn't home, another very real possibility she hadn't allowed herself to consider before boarding the plane, she could go down and stick her feet in the water. Then set about finding herself an appropriate hotel.

And the minute Jenny started thinking about hotels, it seemed obvious that she should have started there. She should have found herself a place to stay, had a nap and a bite to eat, maybe not in that order. And then when she got her bearings, maybe even tomorrow, she could try to figure out where Dylan might be.

Instead of appearing on his doorstep, in all her long-haul state.

She laughed, under her breath, staring out at all that gleaming, deep blue. What was she like? She'd told no one in England she was leaving, she had simply gone. She'd been sitting in her flat, supposedly looking through some or other book of wedding-related items, but she couldn't concentrate on any of it. Invitations, flowers, the lot.

She'd found herself on her mobile instead, texting Erika in Berlin. They'd been discussing one of their favorite television shows, but something Erika had said to her before Jenny's ornate engagement party had rung about inside her head, like a bell gone mad.

You've never been fucked properly.

Jenny had been mulling that over, torn between outrage and curiosity, ever since Erika had said it.

What she'd concluded was that she'd actually never *fucked* anyone at all. She'd had sex. More often, she been forced to contend with declarations and talk of *lovemaking*—a word she found deeply embarrassing. The boyfriends she'd had in the past had all been decent enough. But sex had always been

a pleasant afterthought. Never the main parts of any
relationship.

There had never been *fucking*.

And the more she thought about what *fucking
properly* would entail, the more she thought about
Dylan. Who'd had more sex—phenomenally addictive sex, if the girls who followed him around,
desperate for more of his attention, were any guide—
than Jenny had had in her entire life.

Dylan, who made women swoony. Dylan of the
dark hair, green eyes and wholly Irish, devilish grin.
It had never been hard to understand why women
got silly around him, but Jenny had always felt a bit
smug that she wasn't a part of that mess. That her
relationship with Dylan was purely platonic, always
had been and always would be.

But as her wedding date drew closer, it dawned on
her that she really was going to be expected not only
to marry Conrad in all his icy, intimidating splen-
dor, she would also be expected to sleep with him. It
would be her job to produce heirs to the Vanderburg
and Markham fortunes and whatever she might have
begun to think—or worry—about her own deficien-
cies in the bedroom, since apparently none of it had
been *proper*, she was absolutely certain of one thing.
A man like Conrad, with the personality of an iron
spike encased in a glacier, could not possibly introduce her to proper fucking.

Out there in the dawn of a new day in Sydney,

Australia, a literal world away from almost everything and everyone she knew, Jenny found herself gripping that stone he'd put on her finger.

Conrad was the man her father wanted her to marry. And luckily, Conrad was not cruel. Erika liked to pretend that he was, but Jenny knew that her friend tended toward the overdramatic. In all the time that Jenny had known Conrad, he had never been vicious. He had always been the same as he was now. Measured. Controlled. And very, very focused—on other things.

All of these things would likely make him an excellent husband. And hadn't Jenny read a thousand articles about how arranged marriages were far more stable than romantic ones? It was entirely possible that she'd fall head over heels in love with Conrad someday, since they had so much in common and he was her father's first choice for her. It was just that she would have to see if that was possible after the wedding, not before.

Something inside her shook a bit, and she pressed a hand to her belly, wishing that she'd eaten something a little more substantial than airline food.

And wishing that her first holy spontaneous action in recent recall hadn't been quite so over-the-top. Surely she could have gone out and hit up a yoga retreat, or gotten quietly pissed somewhere. Rather than leaping on a plane and flying all this way.

Suddenly, she felt foolish. Jetlagged, famished,

exhausted, a bit dizzy from all of the above and deeply silly as well.

Had she really flown all the way to Australia so she could quiz her best friend on what constituted proper fucking?

Jenny let out a laugh, and the sound of it was loud on the quiet street. The hotel idea was looking better and better. She tried to stand up straighter, wishing she hadn't sent her cab off. She raked a hand through her hair, deciding to be kind to herself and not imagine how limp and wrung out she must look. Instead, she tied it up in a knot on top of her head.

She had come all the way to Australia to learn about *proper fucking*—and to let Dylan bolster her spirits the way only he seemed to be able to do, sometimes. But she was still Lady Jenny, raised to be proper in all ways—except the one.

That struck her as funny too, and she was thinking about how she would have liked so much to horrify her strict governess, back when she'd been a girl, with questions about fucking as opposed to the manners, comportment and ballroom dancing her father had deemed so important. If she could have built a time machine on the spot, she would have.

And if there was time travel going around, she could also go back and turn Conrad down. Then she wouldn't have to worry about the long, slow dive into an ice bath that she assumed her marriage would be.

But that was disloyal. Not to Conrad so much, as

she doubted very much he thought about her much, but to her father.

She heard a sound, then. Low, male laughter. A higher-pitched, feminine voice. Then the door of the entryway next to the garage opened.

The door swung inward, and Jenny was standing right there. On the curb only a few feet away. For a moment, she couldn't make sense of what she was seeing. She was too tired, maybe. It was as if she was looking through a kaleidoscope, all bright colors and strange shapes…but then she blinked and it all came into focus.

Searing, distinct focus.

She would know Dylan anywhere, even through a cracked open door, with his dark head bent over the woman he had up against the narrow wall of his entryway. She was clinging to him, wearing extraordinarily high heels, and what Jenny thought was a tiny miniskirt, though it was hard to tell. The woman's leg was lifted in the air, and wrapped around Dylan's waist.

And they were kissing.

Though *kissing* seemed a rather tame word to describe what Jenny was witnessing.

It was too…carnal. The heat was so insane Jenny forgot it was winter. The woman was making little noises, *moans* even, and her hands snaked up to dig into Dylan's hair. Or maybe the point was to arch her body into his.

For his part, Dylan was wearing nothing but a pair of low-slung jeans. Everything else was bare skin, acres and acres of golden, perfectly packaged male beauty. It wasn't that Jenny hadn't noticed that Dylan was shockingly attractive, because of course she had. She wasn't blind. It was just that he was *Dylan*. And normally, when she saw women leaving him, she only saw the women looking starry-eyed.

She'd never seen an actual action scene before.

The kiss went on and on. Dylan's hand, which Jenny had never noticed was so big or quite so strong looking, was on the woman's ass, holding her in the perfect place for him to—

But surely that was breaking the bonds of friendship. Surely she shouldn't imagine what he was doing with that part of his body. Particularly not what was making them both make those sounds.

And Jenny felt as if she'd been cast in stone and made into a statue of foolish astonishment, right there outside his house. Because she couldn't move. She couldn't pick up her bag and slink off in shame to hide off around the corner, at the very least, until this ended.

One way or another.

The embarrassment was so great that she felt her entire body heat up, and a melting sort of sensation sink through the center of her, seeming to pool down low.

She told herself it had to be shame. Because what else could make her cheeks so hot?

He murmured something into the woman's ear that Jenny couldn't hear. It made the woman sigh a little, then nod. The leg she had hooked over his hip slid to the ground, and Jenny watched as Dylan kept a hand on her body, steadying her.

"All right, then?" he asked.

"All right," the woman said softly, then smiled in a way that made something curl around and around inside Jenny.

All that heat and the melting, too, until she wasn't sure she could breathe.

Then they both turned, and of course, Jenny was still standing right there. Her cheeks so crisp and bright they hurt.

But that didn't hold her attention. What did was the way Dylan was looking at her.

Because for a moment, she didn't recognize him.

There was something in that green gaze of his that she had never seen before. Something fierce. Hot and dark and dangerous, when Dylan was the least dangerous man she'd ever met. His face changed, too. He seemed bigger, harder, wilder—

And as long as that kiss had gone on, this moment stretched out even longer.

Jenny had the strangest notion that she had lost something. That something had shifted, permanently. It was that seismic. It was that terrifying.

Nothing will ever be the same, a voice in her whispered.

But he blinked.

Then he smiled, and was Dylan again.

"Christ, Jenny," he said, his voice filled with laughter and charm and above all, *safety.* The way it usually was. "What the bloody hell are you doing in Australia?"

CHAPTER TWO

DYLAN KILBURN WAS used to this dream.

He'd had it enough, though usually when he dreamed of Jenny appearing before him she was wearing a whole lot less.

"I should have told you I was coming," she was saying, and that was another clue that he wasn't dreaming this.

Because his fantasies weren't about Jenny sounding apologetic. Or tired.

They were far more energetic. Athletic, even.

And Dylan was only dimly aware of the woman he'd been kissing moments before. The eager Corrine, who had woken him up with her mouth on his cock, and who, if he was completely honest, he'd closed his eyes and imagined was Jenny at several points last night. Because that was how fucked-up he was. He'd been telling himself he was at a place of peace with how twisted he was, but that had been more convincing when the real Jenny wasn't…right here.

He shot Corrine a smile, turning while he did it

so he could help usher her out of his door, because he'd never been a gentleman, had he?

"You really do have a queue, don't you?" Corrine asked.

But she sounded good-natured, not jealous or upset. Dylan did pride himself on that. He liked them to leave happy, satisfied and under no illusions about the possibility of any feelings cropping up.

"Oh, I'm not in any queue," Jenny said, in that posh voice of hers that had haunted him for years now. Though it sounded a bit more frantic than usual. "To be clear. We're just friends. Old friends, that's all."

"Steady, love," Corrinne murmured, with a bawdy little laugh. She gave Dylan a wink, then stepped around Jenny and started down the street on the astonishingly high heels they'd made use of last night, in a variety of ways.

Dylan forgot her in the next breath.

Because Jenny was here. *Here.* And that probably meant something bad was happening to her or around her, but he would care about that in a minute. Right now, there was the fact of her outside his door. Jenny in the winter light, with a breeze blowing in from the sea.

You're pathetic, he told himself, but that wasn't a shock.

"I really am sorry to bust up your morning," Jenny was saying, worriedly, with that little frown between her eyes that Dylan had dedicated whole years of his life to erasing.

"No worries at all," he told her, which had the benefit of being true. "She was leaving anyway. There was nothing to bust up."

He reached over and wrapped her in a hug. And nothing ever changed. There was always that kick in him, deep and hard. His chest tight, his cock so hard it ached and that same old reaction to her he always had like a full-on wildfire, sweeping over him.

But if it was only that, he would have done something about it years ago and moved on. It was the other part that got to him even more. The sense that the world snapped back into place when he held her.

Holding Jenny was like coming home, that was the curse of it.

If Dylan knew anything in this life, it was that getting what you wanted was unlikely at best, and if it came to you, it was never in the form you wanted it. His friendship with Jenny was a prime example of that principle and he didn't care, because there was this.

Jenny snuck her arms around his waist, let out that little sound of contentment the way she always did and squeezed him back, hard.

And there it was, that moment that had haunted him almost from the moment he'd met her, and led to so many of his twisted, fucked-up nights with other women that were never her. That indescribable moment Jenny was in his arms and everything was as it should be. When she buried her head against his chest with perfect trust and he could pretend he was the man she thought he was.

Better yet, just for that moment, he could pretend that she was his.

Dylan took a breath and stepped back, because he had to let go first. That was part of the bargain he'd made with himself a long time ago to control his little addiction to this woman.

"You didn't answer my question." He grinned down at her in the morning light. "What are you doing here?"

"I don't know," Jenny said, and laughed.

That same laugh had done his head in—ruined him, if he was honest—the first week of his first year at Oxford. He could remember it so vividly. He'd come out of his room, overwhelmed that he'd made it out of his shit neighborhood and to this storied place, and there she was. She'd been talking to someone else whose face he never recalled. He'd only seen Jenny.

That laugh had gotten inside him then, and there was no getting it out.

"Better come in then," he told her.

He took her bag from her and indulged himself when she moved ahead of him, allowing his fingers to graze the small of her back.

Dylan loved sex. His appetite was intense, and

his preferences more so. He loved women. He loved the journey of it, the breathless distance between a flirtatious look and shaking, screaming woman clamped down hard on his cock while she came for the third time.

He loved every step along the way, from a naughty striptease to a sudden shock of intimacy that could change a bit of fun into a real moment in an instant—then change back.

But nothing got to him as much as Jenny Markham, and in case he kidded himself into imagining that might change, there were moments like this. Where the brush of his fingertips against the back of her jacket wiped out all memory of the night he just spent making another woman come and cry all over him, again and again and again.

Dylan came from a long line of addicts, and all things considered, he preferred Jenny to heroin.

A junkie is a junkie, he told himself sharply.

Not that it helped.

He took her inside, leading her up the stairs to the main part of his house. It was all arranged to take in the sweeping views of the coast, so he sat her down on his deck, wrapped her in a blanket to keep off the winter chill and then sorted out cups of tea. Then he dropped down in the chair opposite and let himself look at her.

Jenny. In his house. At last.

She smiled at him for a moment, then lifted her mug of tea, and that ring she wore caught the light.

That fucking ring.

"You must think I'm mad," she said after she took a slug of her tea.

She kept the mug in her hands, her legs curled up beneath her in the chair, and it turned out the Australian sun loved her as much as the English rain always had. It brought out the hints of gold in her hair, the prettiest brown he'd ever seen. It was longer now, and she'd piled it up on top of her head in a manner he knew most women spent hours to achieve. But not Jenny. Everything about her was elegant and effortless, from that delicate collarbone he could see beneath the collar of her shirt, to those cheekbones that seemed to make her dark eyes brighter.

And that mouth that had made him hungry as long as he'd known her.

"I do think you're mad," he agreed, lazily. "But then, I always have. So you turning up at my door on a random Saturday doesn't change a thing." She was flushed, he noticed, and it almost seemed as if she was having trouble meeting his eyes. "Are you embarrassed about something?"

"It's a bit cold, don't you think?" she asked, after a moment. And then, to his astonishment, fluttered her hand in his direction, as if to encompass his whole body. "Shouldn't you…put that away?"

If it was any other woman, he would have taken

great pleasure in the notion that his nakedness made her…flutter.

But Dylan had the distinction of being Jenny's friend. Her best friend, she often said, an honor he shared with only one other person on this earth. And he'd always liked crazy, reckless Erika Vanderburg well enough, but he knew full well there was no possible way she loved Jenny as much as he did. Because nobody could.

And the consistent theme in their friendship was that Jenny resolutely refused to see him as a man. He was going to remember the fluttering. And that flush.

"I'm not cold," he told her.

Which was true enough. The slap of the breeze was a good thing. It helped remind him that this wasn't one of those fantasies he'd had so many times. That whatever reason Jenny had for being here, it was not to fling off her clothes and climb on top of him at last.

His body needed to calm the fuck down.

"This really is a lovely house," she was saying, like she was at a tea party. "The pictures you sent years back really didn't do it justice. I love how it sort of flows, doesn't it, from room to room, and then of course the view must really—"

"Fucking hell, Jenny."

She blew out a breath. "I needed to get away. I need to…think about some things."

He nodded toward the gigantic rock weighing down her left hand. The symbol of what he'd known would come, sooner or later. Jenny was always going to get married, and he'd accepted that, too, hadn't he? He'd always been a realist.

But accepting it in the abstract was a lot easier than the ring in his face. And her here.

"Marriage is a big step," was all he said.

"Yes," she agreed, too quickly. "But Conrad is a good choice. Really. Some of the men my father sent me out on dates with were awful."

"Do you love him?"

He shouldn't have asked that. Because he really didn't want to know the answer.

And he didn't need to see her look of astonishment. "Love him? Oh, no." She shook her head. "Certainly not." She considered her tea for a moment, then brightened. "But maybe someday I will. They say that arranged marriages—"

"Stability isn't the same thing as love," Dylan interrupted her. He should know. It was a challenge to remain relaxed in his chair, but he did it. "And I think you'll find that friendship, however intense, is no substitute for passion."

Interestingly, that flush seemed to deepen. She busied herself with her mug of tea, once again seeming… flustered.

"You would be the expert on that," she said softly. But distinctly.

Dylan hadn't touched his tea. He thought longingly of the bottle of whiskey he had inside, aged to perfection, but he knew nothing took the edge off the Jenny effect. Nothing ever had, nothing ever would.

"You know me." He forced the easy grin that would make most of the people who knew him do a double take. Because Dylan Kilburn was edgy, not easy. But Jenny didn't know that Dylan. "As long as they leave happy."

"She seemed very happy." Jenny nodded in the vague direction of the street. "The one downstairs."

"Mission accomplished, then."

"What exactly is it that you do?" she asked, and her gaze was direct. "To her. To them. In general."

He kept the grin going. "Do you want me to draw you a manual?"

"In all the years I've known you," she said, as if she was carefully sounding out her words, "no matter how many women you sleep with or if they overlap, they always leave *delighted*. And thanking you. Why?"

"That's a bit hurtful." He lifted a brow. "Surely even you can appreciate what a piece of eye candy I am, Jenny."

A shameless attempt to get her to ogle him, he was well aware. But Jenny didn't take the bait. She kept her gaze on his, which was both disappointing and arousing, a sensation he was all too used to.

"There are a lot of good-looking men, Dylan. But with you it's something different."

"Irish charm?"

"There are a lot of Irish charmers, too. Hence the name."

Dylan had been studying Jenny for years. Today she had shadows beneath her eyes, which he blamed on the long flight. She looked tired, but it was more than that. More than travel, clearly. It was the way she was holding her head, deliberately, as if fighting back some kind of strong emotion. She seemed more fragile than usual.

Dylan had once been called a grinning bloody shark by a business associate—and it hadn't been meant as an insult—because he could smile nicely while eviscerating his opponents. Because he'd been raised up in a bleak, hard place and it was in him, too, that bleakness. That hardness. It was what made him rich. And he liked his sex the way he liked his many business deals and everything else in this life he'd built entirely with his own hands—completely under his control.

There had only ever been one shred of softness in him. Her.

And she had no clue.

It was almost funny, really.

"Did you really fly all the way to Australia to quiz me about my sex life?" he asked.

"I'm getting married," she said, and he didn't

make a face or roll his eyes at the unnecessary obviousness of that statement, because she was looking at him so intently. "And I know that many women in my position don't intend to keep their wedding vows, but I do. Or I don't see the point of being married."

He was long past the point where mentions of her boyfriends, or dates or various other relationships with lesser men got to him—but that didn't mean he wanted to sit around and talk about her marital vows.

Though he would.

"Is he planning to extend you the same courtesy?"

"He said he would." Jenny shrugged. It was a sharp, almost bitter sort of movement. "But I think we both know that's easier said than done. For him, I mean."

"A promise is a promise, Jenny."

"I don't think he cares," she said, then, and not as if it hurt her. As if it was a simple, small truth. "You're the only one I can say this to. But Conrad is a very cold man. I think if he decides to shut himself off, he will, and that's that."

"He sounds grand."

The look she sent him then was reproving, but that was an improvement, to his mind.

"Part of me thinks that this is the best it can be, given the situation." She propped her tea mug on her curled-up legs. "Most people with our sort of arrangement wouldn't dream of expecting fidelity. It's a lovely bonus."

Dylan rubbed a hand over his face. "If you say so."

"I wouldn't want to be embarrassed." She frowned down at her mug. "And you know Erika. I think that's as much embarrassment as Conrad ever wanted. I don't think *he* would cause a scandal."

"Are you trying to tell me that your man doesn't satisfy you?" Dylan asked, possibly with more edge in his voice than was needed. "Because there are books you could read, or you could have rung up, Jen. No need to go to such lengths."

"Oh, I don't know if he... I mean, we've never..." She scowled at him. "Don't look at me like that."

"You're going to marry a man who you've never had sex with." He shook his head, though it kicked at him. Or maybe that was his heart, trying to crack his ribs wide open. "I'll be honest, there's a lot I don't understand about you. But this might take the bloody cake."

"It wasn't as if the dates we went on were romantic," she protested. "And then he proposed, very quickly, which would be strange and off-putting if things were romantic—but this was never about that. So why not go along quickly? And what's the point of trying it out ahead of time? It isn't going to make a difference. Good or bad, we're stuck with it either way."

He wanted to break something. "For fuck's sake."

"I didn't come all this way to debate whether or

not I should marry Conrad. I've already agreed to do it. It's a done deal."

"You do know what year it is? Fathers don't get to go around selling off daughters. You have a say."

"Of course I have a say." Dylan beat down his temper enough to notice she didn't look upset. She looked annoyed. At him. "If I didn't want to get married, I wouldn't. It's not as if my father would force me down the aisle with a gun to my back. You've met him. You know he's not like that."

Dylan certainly had met Lord Fuckface, who had sneered down the length of his nose at the likes of Dylan Kilburn, Irish trash, anywhere near his precious daughter.

Or that was how Dylan assumed the man had felt. It was how he imagined he'd feel if he had a daughter—especially a daughter like Jenny.

"Sure, and he's a real peach."

"It's just that once I get married, that's it," Jenny said, ignoring his comment on her father. Having lectured him more than once on how shit it was to dislike people simply because they were richer than him—not an issue he had much any longer. "It will be however it is with Conrad, and I've already made my peace with that. We'll have children and a good life. I'm sure of it."

"As long as you're sure."

He didn't point out that her presence on his deck suggested otherwise.

She glared at him. "It's something Erika said. It's something she's always said, actually. But I guess it feels a little more urgent these days."

"I'm not sure I would take advice from the likes of Erika," Dylan said mildly. "Unless you have a hankering to go clubbing. For a year."

He had no quarrel with Erika. She was a gorgeous little mess and always had been. The only reason Dylan hadn't tried it on with her back in Oxford was because she'd been so close with Jenny. And Dylan was never going to do anything that might create a wedge between him and Jenny—especially her friend.

"She settled down," Jenny told him. "Quite seriously, actually."

Dylan laughed. "Are we talking about the same Erika?"

"I know." Jenny grinned. "But yes. She's even going back to Oxford to finish her degree."

"Is she now." Dylan laughed, and it wasn't forced. "I'll be damned. I wouldn't think it would matter to a trust fund princess if she finished a degree or not."

"I told you. She's turned over a new leaf."

"I can't abide people with every advantage in the world pissing it away. Good on her." He eyed Jenny more closely. "Do you feel you need to turn over a new leaf too? I don't even know what that would look like. Saint Jenny, queen of good works, got a first, as I recall."

"I understand academics," she was saying, with that passion in her voice that made his cock ache, though it was never directed where he wanted it. "And I love the charity. It makes me feel good to help, if I can. To be honest, I still love the role I played for my father. We're all we have."

The way she said that tore at him, and kept him quiet. He didn't understand the bargains she made with her father. Dylan's contact with his own relatives was limited to their semiannual attempts to extort money from him, which they'd started during his time at Oxford, so he could only assume that having a family member he loved would be a transformative experience that could possibly lead to arranged marriages. Or something.

But they'd spent years comparing and contrasting their families and upbringings without Jenny turning up in Australia. This didn't quite seem like the time to continue that conversation.

"It's beginning to feel like you're leading up to something here." And it was harder to keep his voice mildly lazy. To produce that friendly grin. "Better get to it. The suspense is killing me."

"Sex," she said.

For a curious moment, Dylan thought something must have plummeted from the sky above and hit him in the head.

His ears rung. He was almost light-headed.

But no. He wasn't imagining it. His Jenny, forever his friend and decidedly off-limits, was sitting opposite him talking about sex.

Not having a laugh about his revolving bedroom door. Not rolling her eyes at his conquests. She was staring at him with what looked like naked sincerity in her eyes, and...blowing his mind.

"Did you just say *sex*?" he asked, because he had to make sure.

He expected her to laugh. To roll her eyes at him and call him a pervert for hearing sex everywhere.

But instead, she nodded, her eyes big. "Erika says I've never been fucked properly."

Very seriously, God help him.

And Dylan would never know how it was that he stayed where he was. Lounging back in a chair on his deck on a lovely Saturday morning, while joggers ran heedlessly by on the coastal walk, seabirds careened about in the air and Jenny Markham had flown all the way down to Sydney to talk to him about *fucking*.

He would never know how he remained calm.

"Well?" he asked, casually. As if this entire conversation didn't feel, suddenly, as if he'd sustained a series of knockout blows and was reeling about blind. And wanting things he couldn't have. "Have you?"

CHAPTER THREE

THERE WAS SOMETHING about that intent look on Dylan's face, the patience in his green eyes. The way he asked her a question and then waited. Like he could wait forever, if that was what it took.

It made Jenny feel safe. But then, he always did. She could tell Dylan anything.

Even things she was afraid to tell herself.

"I think maybe I'm bad at it," she confessed.

Something flashed over his face then, some dark gleam, that reminded her of that moment out in front of his house. When she'd stared at his familiar face and hadn't recognized him at all.

Deep inside her, something clicked. Then flared into life, but she ignored it. Because she was here, in his house. With him. And wherever Dylan was, she could depend on him to keep them inside his bubble. Where everything was always okay.

And if it wasn't, he would fight it off.

"Not possible," he told her, a strange note in his voice.

"You don't know that it's not possible," Jenny argued. "Because here's the thing. I've never staggered off after having sex with someone giddy and filled with joy the way that girl did today. And I certainly don't leave anyone in that state."

She expected him to leap in, to contradict her, but he didn't. Because Dylan let her tell her own story. How had she forgotten how freeing that was? How he allowed to her relax and really, truly say what she felt?

Then again, she was here. Maybe she hadn't forgotten.

"Everyone talks about sex like it's a compulsion. Passion and desire. Need. This *hunger* that takes them over." She shook her head, and frowned at him. His legs were thrust out before him, highlighting the powerful muscles in his thighs. How had she never noticed his *thighs* before? Because she doubted they'd cropped up overnight. "Is that what it's like for you?"

"I wouldn't bother otherwise, would I?"

"It's never that way for me." Jenny took a breath, flipped over that ugly little stone she'd never wanted to look beneath and reminded herself that this was Dylan. That she could say anything to him. "I think maybe I really am frigid. Or broken, somehow."

He didn't sit with that in a solemn, concerned silence, as she'd expected he would. He rolled his eyes and didn't look the least bit shaken by her declaration. "For fuck's sake. Because that wanker told you so? A hundred years ago now? Real men don't berate women for their own piss-poor performance in bed."

Jenny had dated Christopher for two months that had seemed like a lifetime during term time their third year. A relationship—such as it was—that had ended after they'd slept together, he'd informed her that she was crap at sex, and he'd moved on to manipulate a wide-eyed first-year into his bed instead. A real charmer, that Christopher.

But.

"Christopher was renowned for being good in bed, Dylan," Jenny argued. "You like to pretend you can't remember, but girls used to go around swooning left and right every time he smiled."

"When he smiled, sure. After he embarrassed himself in their beds? Not near as much swooning, as I recall." Dylan crossed his arms, which should have made him look angry. But when Jenny studied his face, his expression was bland. Maybe too bland. "It was his job to make you come, Jenny. Everything else was a load of shite mixed with mind games to disguise the fact he was a selfish prick."

Dylan had growled the same response at her during their final year at uni, but she couldn't remember all this…prickly heat.

"No one is good or bad at sex unless they try," Dylan continued, sounding even more growly. "It's sex, not surgery. Sometimes people have mad chemistry, which takes it all to a different level. But you don't need astonishing chemistry to have good sex, Jenny. You can have good sex if you want it. It's that simple."

"I can tell you that it is not, in fact, that simple."

"It isn't a spot of calisthenics," Dylan said, and again, there was something about how relentlessly bland he looked that made the back of her neck prickle. Even more than before. "Supposed skill or experience matters far less than what I'd call…" And he smiled then, in that friendly way he had that made her want to smile, too. "Observant enthusiasm."

She wanted to smile, but she didn't. "I have no idea what that means."

His expression didn't change and yet…there was that strange flickering thing inside her again. "Do you pay attention, Jenny? Do you think about something other than getting yourself off when you're naked with someone else? I'm betting you do."

There was no reason for her to be…breathless.

But Dylan didn't give her time to respond, even if she'd managed to find breath. "But I'd also bet that if you're finding sex lacking, it's a commentary on your partner, not you. It was true years ago and it's true now."

Jenny frowned and tried to look stern, not prickly and strangely overwarm though she sat beneath a cozy blanket and was bundled up nicely against the cool breeze—unlike some people, who were bare chested and barefoot. "That's a bit sexist, isn't it?"

"I've seen the men you date. So, no, it's not sexist. It's an informed opinion." He did something with his face that made him look harder. Flintier, even. "And it's not hard to make a man come, Jenny. That's why it's on him to make sure you do, or why bother to have sex with another person? He could just have a wank and be done with it."

All of this suddenly seemed a lot less *safe* than it had before. Maybe it was the exhaustion messing with her, but he kept talking about *coming* and now she was imagining him handling his own cock, that same fierce look on his face she'd seen outside while he—

Stop, she ordered herself.

She was so horrified she was afraid she might spill her tea all over his lovely deck, so she took great care to set it carefully to the side on the table there.

And maybe that wasn't precisely *horror* that coursed through her veins then, making her shift beneath the blanket he'd draped over her. Making her aware of her own pussy when normally, she saved such awareness for the privacy of her own bed.

"Don't get me wrong," Jenny made herself say in as dry and unaffected a voice as she could manage. "I like sex. Sometimes I quite like it."

"Damned with faint praise."

"Let's talk about you, Dylan."

She concentrated on him then, and the whole golden sweep of him that she'd been trying her best not to gape at. Without much success. There wasn't an ounce of fat on the man. He was nothing but ridiculously lean muscle wherever she looked, and for all that he was meant to be a CEO forever in meetings, he clearly spent time in the sun. A lot of time. And then there was the hair that arrowed down beneath the waistband of his jeans, and made her need to shift a bit in her chair. Again.

Her mouth was dry. She told herself it was the sudden immersion in winter, the lack of sleep and all the rest of this strange and endless day.

"You're doing something different," she told him, as if she'd conducted an academic study. "I've met a lot of men who sleep with loads of women, and they're all pigs. But you're not."

"Careful, or you'll make me blush."

"I can't figure out what it is. Why are all those women so happy all the time? You toss them out, but they'd all gag for another chance. I've watched it happen. You're this…magician."

"Are you asking me a question, Jenny? Or leaving a review?"

And suddenly, it didn't matter where they were. How tired she was. All the other things she'd been telling herself this whole time.

Dylan sat there across from her, and suddenly the sweet sea air between them was taut. And his gaze changed, the green of it shaded with a certain glittering thing she couldn't understand.

But she felt it. And she felt naked, suddenly.

Because the actual reason she'd come here was so clear to her, then.

All the fuss and noise she kicked up around it, telling herself this lie and that lie as she'd gotten on the plane, all the many hours she flew, and then when she'd come to find him, too. Telling herself she was safe and she wanted his advice and she wanted to *talk*.

So many lies, and all of them boiled down to this. Here. Now.

That look in his eyes like she wasn't the only one imagining things she shouldn't.

Jenny didn't want his advice.

She wanted him to show her.

And he was sitting so still, so intent, that she had the distinct impression he knew it.

Her heart pounded in her chest, so hard she was certain it had to have bruised her ribs.

But she couldn't look away.

And her mouth was so *dry*.

Everything inside her was tied in a knot, pulling tighter and tighter and tighter, daring her to open her mouth and say the thing she wanted even if it meant changing them forever—

And that was the thing she couldn't do.

She *couldn't*.

"I'm not leaving a review or asking a question," she managed to say, though there was a bitter taste in her mouth. "It's an enthusiastic observation, that's all. I hear they're all the rage."

Across from her, Dylan didn't seem to move. But he changed, again. That tension dissipated. And she couldn't help but imagine she saw a shade of disappointment in those green eyes of his.

She told herself she had to be imagining it. That she had to be imagining all of this. Because the alternative was that he was no longer Dylan and she was no longer Jenny, and that meant there was no *them*—and she could do almost anything. She could make anything work, as her engagement proved.

But she couldn't lose Dylan. She could survive anything but that.

"I think you should eat something," he said, quietly. Years could have passed, for all she knew, tangled up as she was inside. "Have a bit of a kip. Maybe even shower off the plane ride. What do you reckon?"

And for the first time in as long as she'd known him, when he smiled at her she thought it might break her heart.

But she couldn't have said why.

Because you don't want to say why, something in her retorted.

Either way, she didn't say it. Jenny only nodded, didn't quite meet his eyes again and let him lead her back into his house.

* * *

Later, Jenny was sure she'd imagined all that tension. Those strange moments out in the bright winter sunlight on the bottom of the world. They all seemed lashed together like a dream, green eyes and the memory of Dylan's smile, none of it making any sense when she tried to recapture them or think it all through.

Better to forget and move on, she told herself staunchly.

Dylan's guest room was on the back side of the house. It had its own bit of a balcony, so she could wake in the mornings and bask in all that lovely Australian sunshine. Outside her room she could inhale the fragrance of all the flowers and pretty green things as she peered down the side of the building to see the sea, like a beckoning wall of blue.

She fetched herself a cup of tea from the kitchen and sat out on her balcony quietly. In the space between the buildings, she could imagine she lived here when, of course, she didn't. And couldn't. Her life was in England.

Though you'll be living in France soon enough, the voice inside her pointed out. Still sounding entirely too much like Erika. *Conrad's base is in Paris.*

Several days into her impromptu stay in Sydney's lovely eastern suburbs, Jenny found herself pondering that potential reality. Conrad's business took him all over the world. Just because he liked to call Paris home didn't mean she needed to do the same…did it? The automatic relocation expected when people married wouldn't be expected of an arranged wife, surely. She glared down at the rock on her hand as if it might have the answers, but it was as quiet and overlarge as ever.

And thinking about Conrad and Paris and the rest of the marital decisions she couldn't quite face made her feel a bit too close to wobbly. She decided she was too restless to stay on the little balcony off the guest room, spiraling into her own unfortunate thoughts, so she padded out into the rest of the main floor of the house instead. It was organized so that the rooms were stacked one in front of the next, with a hallway down the middle that opened up into the streamlined chef's kitchen. Beyond that, the vast lounge with its spectacular view of the ocean outside ambled out to the deck. And up above, taking over the whole of the top floor, was the master bedroom.

Dylan had showed it to her not long after she arrived as part of his general tour of the house. And maybe it had something to do with those strange moments she was already forgetting, but she'd found it…unsettling up there. That big, wide bed with its four sturdy posters and what looked like wrought iron at the head. And windows all around, floor-to-ceiling high in some places, letting in what felt like the whole of this stretch of the coast and the sweep of the Tasman Sea, until it seemed as if anyone in the room was a *part* of the sea itself. Or the man who lived there.

She preferred her little balcony downstairs. Or the neutrality of the kitchen, where she headed now. She put the kettle on, and found herself staring out the window, in that half a dream state that seemed to accompany any proper gaze at all that deep, changeable blue.

Jenny should head straight back to England. She knew that. After she'd slept, eaten and showered as ordered that first day, she'd sat down and sent off a raft of emails to explain her absence to all and sundry. She told the charity she needed a bit of personal time, and laid out all the reasons why she thought her second-in-command was more than capable of stepping into the role. She wrote her second-in-command, apologizing for the short notice, but making sure the woman she'd handpicked knew that it was her very competence that had made Jenny so sure she could slip away.

It was true, she'd realized as she wrote it all out, even though she might not have thought it through before she'd gotten on that plane.

She emailed her father—or rather, his personal secretary—and felt badly about the relief she felt because she didn't have to have an actual conversation with him. Because she already knew what he'd say. Or rather, how he would sound while he said it. And he was far too good at triggering her guilt. That it was unintentional on his part, and always motivated by concern, somehow always made her feel *more* guilty.

The truth was, Jenny didn't feel guilty at the moment. She didn't *want* to feel guilty.

I've decided to take a little break, she had texted Erika.

I support this move completely, her best friend had fired back. I hope a beach is involved. Cabana boys and cocktails.

More or less, Jenny had replied. And it had still been that first night, so that strange fear had washed over her, gripping her tight. I'm in Sydney.

And she'd stared down at her mobile, watching as the three dots that indicated Erika was typing appeared. Then disappeared.

Appeared again. Then disappeared once more.

She'd been sitting in the guest room then, her feet crossed beneath her as she sat in the armchair in the corner of the room. She'd stared at her phone, nervously worrying her knuckle between her teeth.

Tell Dylan I say hello, came the reply, at last.

And that was all.

But it didn't matter. Erika knew. And if Jenny let herself think about it, it was likely that Erika knew a whole lot more than the two of them had ever discussed directly. Like those moments with Dylan, taut and strange, that Jenny had been pretending not to notice for years now. And yet none of them as intense as what had happened here.

It took her two days to remember that she ought to let Conrad know where she was, too.

Have gone off to Sydney, she wrote him, feeling as stiff as the words sounded when she stared at them on her screen. I don't expect to be gone too long.

Conrad's reply had come swiftly. Please update my assistant with return date.

Just in case Jenny had been tempted to romanticize something that had nothing to do with romance. She told herself that what she'd felt, then, staring at his message, was peace. Relief.

She told herself that was what she felt now, too.

"What are you scowling at?" came Dylan's low voice from behind her.

Jenny jumped, then turned that scowl on him. And immediately wished she hadn't.

Because Dylan worked on that marvelous body of his. There was a gym in the house, where he put in at least an hour a day, but he also liked to run. He'd introduced her to the coastal walk that stretched from Bondi Beach to the north down to Brontë in the south, and Jenny had taken to walking it on fine mornings, breathing in deep. Letting the Tasman Sea breeze and the lovely Australian sunshine dance over her face like happiness. Stopping here and there to gaze at the water or take pictures from the rocky cliffs.

Dylan ran it.

She could tell that he'd been out on the run already this morning, because he wore nothing but a pair of athletic shorts, and he was…gleaming.

Sweating, she corrected herself crossly.

She should have been revolted. But he didn't smell bad. He smelled clean. Male. And the sweat of his exertion only made him look better, somehow. It made his green eyes gleam brightly, and Jenny felt reduced to a stuttering, bumbling mess.

It happened more and more the longer she stayed here. One more reason she should leave.

"I'm not scowling," she told him, ignoring all that *gleaming.* "I was thinking about business-related things. I'm so far away I keep pretending England doesn't exist. But it does."

"Last I heard, yes." He sounded amused as he went to the refrigerator, and pulled out the makings of the shake he put together every morning. Several different powders she assumed were proteins and superfoods and whatever else it was health nuts liked to put in themselves to keep up with all the *gleaming.* Green things and antioxidants and worthy supplements packed with vitamins. The very opposite of the full English breakfast she remembered him tucking into with gusto on hungover Oxford mornings.

There was no reason for her to be here, but she leaned against the counter, her mug of strong tea in her hands and watched. Dylan fixed himself his drink then chugged it down, tipping back his head so she could hardly help but stare at the strong column of his throat. And all the lines, planes and ridges of that body he worked so hard on almost entirely exposed to her view.

She studied the tattoo on his back, the line of Gaelic down his spine and the Celtic knot he wore over his heart. Why did she want to put her hands on him so badly? To trace those tattoos she recognized like old friends, to remind herself how well they suited him and how easily he wore them.

Because you need to go home, she told herself sternly.

"I'm headed into the office," Dylan said. And when he looked at her, his green gaze swept over her the way it always did, after that first conversation. Friendly. Happy. Not complicated in the least.

There was no reason it should make her teeth ache, so hard that she clenched them.

"The housekeeping service will be in," he continued mildly, though something about the way he looked at her made her unclench her teeth. "I told them to expect a guest on the premises, so don't be put off if you wake from a nap to find someone hoovering up the place."

"I won't be here," she said grandly. And without thinking it through. "I'm going to do a bit of the tourist thing."

"And here I thought you planned to waft up and down the coastal path again." He studied her. "You should roam about Circular Quay and the Rocks. Take the ferries all over Sydney Harbour. Get a sense of the place."

Jenny had spent most of her life charging around doing this or that, but not since she'd arrived in Australia. All she wanted to do was stay tucked up in Dylan's house, or lost in her own head as she wandered up and down what had to be the most beautiful walk in the world. It hugged the coastline, meandering through the beach towns and around a haunting cemetery set into the side of a cliff, over the ocean pools, up the rocks and down again. When the sun was out it could be warm enough to feel like summer while other days it was moody. She loved it either way.

But she'd announced she was off to play tourist, so that was what she was going to do.

"I'll drive you in then," Dylan said, with a grin.

And that was how, scarcely forty-five minutes later, she found herself sitting in an outrageously flash sports car, prowling through the morning traffic toward the Sydney Central Business District.

"I have to make a confession," she said as they waited at a light. She glanced over at him, dressed in his usual uniform of jeans and a T-shirt—which should have looked ratty and casual and student-y, but didn't. Not the way he wore them. "I had no idea you worked this hard. You underplayed it."

Dylan laughed. "Maybe I wanted you to think it was effortless."

"You work all the time," she said, shaking her head. "I don't know when you sleep. No matter what time I wake up, jetlagged and victimized by the time change, you're always awake. You take phone calls night and day. And yet you still have time to go on runs and toss weights around in your gym. I thought I was busy, but you're a right superhero."

"I do run a company, Jenny," he said, in a tone of mock reproach. But she was caught up in the way he propped his arm up on the steering wheel, and it was difficult to tell which was more powerful, the car or the man. "It can't run on its own."

"It's just so…"

"Surprising?" Dylan supplied.

And he laughed when he said it, but she didn't think he was kidding.

"Impressive," she corrected him. "I was going to say it was impressive."

The look he threw her way was unreadable, but then traffic surged forward, and he put his attention back onto the road. And then, before she could ask him something, or say those things she kept biting back, his mobile rang the way it always did. And he answered it the way he always did, because he was far busier than she'd ever imagined, and he launched himself back into another business conversation.

Jenny told herself she'd imagined her reaction to

him when he pulled up to a curb on a city street some time later, told her to walk straight ahead and indicated that she should get out. But when she reached over to open the door, his hand grabbed her arm, stopping her.

It made her feel jagged inside. Scraped up. His hand was big and hard over her forearm and his eyes were so *green*. And something about Dylan looking at her so intently made her think she might shake. She wanted to, anyway.

"I'll meet you later," he told her, gruffly. "At the Opera Bar at the Opera House. Eight o'clock."

"It's a date," she said, brightly.

And immediately regretted her choice of words.

But she didn't have time to stammer about it, or take it back. Or even qualify what she'd said.

Because Dylan smiled, and it was an edgy thing, wired directly into that jaggedness within her. "I'll see you then."

And Jenny found herself out on the street, then walking, oblivious to her surroundings. Because all she could see was that *look* on his face.

Which is why it took her a moment, after she'd walked down the block and under a rail overpass the way he'd told her to, to realize where she was.

He'd dropped her a block away from a walkway that led around to the iconic opera house itself. And the Sydney Harbour Bridge. And the gleaming, beautiful water of the harbor itself, cut through by the green-and-yellow ferries. And sailboats catching the wind.

It was like standing in a postcard.

And later, Jenny couldn't have said which one of those things made the tears begin to stream down her face. Only that she cried, and she couldn't believe that a place she'd seen on television a thousand times was far more beautiful than she ever could have imagined.

And that somehow, even though she was standing there on a bright winter morning, crying her eyes out in the middle of the streams of Sydneysiders and tourists, so very far away from England and the world she knew, she had never felt quite so at home in her life.

CHAPTER FOUR

DYLAN HAD RESIGNED himself years ago to the fact that he clearly loved a hair shirt. He liked to suffer, obviously. What other explanation was there for a hopeless, unrequited love that stretched on past hope, past reason, and insinuated itself into every interaction he had with other women?

Aren't you just a fecking martyr, his older brother Dermot had sneered at him, there in their grotty flat in the tower block of the estate—now happily demolished—when Dylan had announced that he was going up to Oxford. He might as well have said he was going to the moon. Oxford made about as much sense to his sprawling, vicious family hunkered down poor and addicted in the land of saints and scholars. *The more you suffer, the better you feel about yourself.*

Dermot had talked a metric ton of shite, but that particular dig stayed with him.

And if he'd ever had any doubt, that was gone

now. Because there was carrying a torch, which Dylan had done for years now whether he liked to admit it or not. And then there was Jenny in his house. Living under the same roof. Jenny looking soft and sleepy, shuffling around his kitchen. Jenny lost in thought, gazing out over the rail on his deck.

When they'd been at university together, he'd known things about her. Intimate things that could only come from daily interaction. That she worried a lock of her hair around and around one finger while she studied. Or when she was nervous, she worked a knuckle between her teeth. The way she hummed beneath her breath, always off tune, when she was happy. The awkward, yet endearing, way she danced to the endlessly cheesy music she liked.

Since graduation, those things had faded. When he saw her now, there was always so much less time. A dinner here. Drinks there. He texted her more than anyone else he knew, combined, but it wasn't the same as those stolen intimacies. It couldn't be. And he would have said he'd accepted all that, long since.

But she'd been here almost a week and they were building up again, those encyclopedia entries that together made up Jenny. She still twirled her hair when she was miles away, lost in thought. She still bit down on that knuckle.

She no longer hummed beneath her breath, which Dylan felt like a shocking loss. But one morning, when he'd been heading out on the long, hard runs he took to keep his goddamned hands to himself, he'd found himself standing outside the door to the guest room. She'd been in the shower and he'd heard the water running, but that wasn't what kept him there, frozen still. It was Jenny, singing an egregiously bad pop song from their Oxford days, as tuneless as ever.

His cock had been rock hard and his grin had been wide, and a bigger fool could not possibly have existed on God's green earth. And the desperate notion he'd formed over these last years when he only saw her sporadically, that familiarity would breathe a little much-needed contempt...

If anything, the opposite was true. It was worse now.

Much, much worse.

Because this time around, Dylan wasn't the overwhelmed, out-of-his-depth Irish kid on cobbled-together financial assistance, lost in the Bodleian. He was no longer afraid that he might betray himself completely and start tugging on his forelock to the English overlords, or something equally horrifying. He wasn't crushed under the pressure of his own ambition and need to climb up out of that hole his family had been in for generations, not anymore. Over the years, he'd told himself that if he ever got the chance to spend quality time with Jenny again, he would see that it had only ever been a crush. He'd been a poor kid from the worst estate in Dublin, surrounded by toffs and unsurprisingly drawn to the kindest and prettiest among them.

But the truth was that he had never been much of a kid. Children in his old neighborhood grew up fast, or not at all. By the time he'd gone up to Oxford, he'd been like an old, weary man next to the soft public schoolboys and pampered Oxford dons.

Maybe that was why he still, all these years later, was as destroyed by Jenny as if he'd only just met her.

Something he was sure he would feel more bitter about later. When she left him, the way he knew she would, and fucked off back to England. And that terrible arranged marriage of hers. And bloody Conrad Vanderburg, who was as approachable as a spot of freezer burn and would crush all the joy and *Jenny* out of her.

He would enjoy this time. Jenny here, now. He wouldn't expect anything. And he wouldn't be disappointed. He would *enjoy* it, if only because he had the distinct impression that this was the last part of her life she would enjoy, too.

Dylan had been whatever she needed him to be for as long as he'd known her. He could do it this one, last time.

Because he knew that it only *felt* like it might kill him, the weight of this thing he had for her. It never *actually* did.

That was what he told himself that night, as he

dodged tourists on his way to the bar tucked up under Sydney's famous opera house. He shoved his hands into the pockets of his jeans, glad he'd shrugged on a jacket after his last meeting. He took rather too much pleasure in dressing down, particularly when the client he was meeting with expected rather more of a song and dance.

Jenny was the only member of the landed gentry he had ever bothered to dress up for.

There was a notion to make a man's blood run cold.

But it told Dylan everything he needed to know about himself—and in truth, he already knew it— that he didn't tear off the coat he wore and toss it in the harbor. And that when he saw the slim, dark-haired woman standing at a rail near the bar, her eyes on the harbor bridge lit up against the night, he walked faster.

These were the moments he liked the most. The moments right before she turned to look at him. The moments when he could almost believe that this time, when she did, she would finally see him. The real him, which would be some feat, since he'd spent the entirety of their friendship burying the real him as deep as it could go.

He slowed, his eyes locked on her, and it was as if they were all alone instead of in one of the busiest spots in Sydney. She was dressed exactly as she had been when he'd dropped her off this morning, but she didn't look tired or frazzled. She'd clearly bought a pair of heels to replace the more comfortable shoes she'd been wearing earlier. She'd secured her hair on the back of her head, though tendrils danced in the winter breeze. Because she was Jenny, she'd somehow transformed jeans and a slouchy sweater into something elegant.

She turned her head before he reached her, her gaze finding his in the soft dark.

Dylan forgot to grin the way he usually did. And so did she.

And for the space of a long, slow heartbeat, he was lost in that gaze of hers.

Usually he broke the tension, because that was safer. Because that made sure they stayed right here. On the same ground where they'd always been.

But tonight, he didn't do it. He went to the rail and bent down so he could rest his forearms on the top of it the way she was doing.

And for a long while, they stood there, not quite touching, staring off toward the bridge together.

"Did you play tourist all day?" he asked, many long breaths and jarring heartbeats later.

"I did." He didn't look, but he could hear her smile all the same. "I marched all over the place. I explored the Rocks. I got chocolate from Haigh's. And I was nearly mowed down by health fanatics jogging around Macquarie Point whilst scoffing it down."

"Best to stay out of the line of traffic with your sugar and shame, then."

"I took the ferry out to Manly to have a bit of lunch."

"A fine beach, that."

"I rode the ferries all over. Even in the rain. I think I'd quite like to live in a place where I could take a ferry to work. It feels more civilized, somehow. And wild at the same time."

"Sydney Harbour's not the Thames," Dylan said. "But it has its charm."

"This all feels like a dream." She was no longer talking about the city, or the water, he knew. "One of those dreams where you've fallen, and try to surface again, but can't. And the longer I stay here, the more it seems as if my life back in England is the dream. I don't know. Maybe everybody feels that way on holiday."

He reminded himself that it wasn't *his* dream they were discussing here. It was hers. And much as he might like to tell himself different, he knew full well that Jenny was running away from her life. Not taking a holiday. And if he was truly her friend, not just the sad sack bloke who'd mooned about after her all these years, he would take himself out of the equation, wouldn't he?

"I haven't forgotten what you said when you arrived," he said, and he had to look at the bridge because if he looked at her, he wasn't sure what he would do. Or maybe he was sure. And that was the problem. "It sounds to me that you think you're missing something. That's the long and the short of it. But if this marriage is really what you want, the way you say it is, then you're going to have to accept it. All of it. Not just the bits you can rationalize away."

"I don't need to rationalize my marriage," she said, and he ordered himself not to pay too close attention to how cross she sounded. "You and Erika can't get your heads around it, but you don't have to. I know what I'm agreeing to."

"But you haven't accepted it, have you? Or you wouldn't be here. Across the world from where you ought to be right now, calling it a holiday when we both know you're hiding."

"I just want to *know*," she blurted out. She turned toward him then, and then he was turned toward her as well, and so much for his intentions. "I think this is an act of acceptance. Radical acceptance. I fully comprehend what marrying Conrad will mean. I want one little thing to bring with me. To hold on to, through whatever comes."

"A different radical suggestion would be not to marry him."

Jenny's eyes searched his face, and she sighed a little, then she shocked the hell out of him by reaching over, and taking one of his hands in hers.

"When my mother died, my father and I were devastated," she said quietly. "My father has never been a warm man, and never will be. But he loved my mother as much as he was capable. And in the years that followed, when it was only the two of us, he made me promise that I would arrange my life with my head, not my heart."

His system was going haywire because she was holding his hand like that, between hers and up against her chest, and he couldn't think. He had to force himself to use his big head.

"That sounds like grief talking," he said, gruffly.

"Maybe so, but it's not a grief I want to repeat. That's the promise I'm keeping, Dylan. To my father, first and foremost. He wants me to be safe, not in a position to shatter."

And Dylan was only a man, after all. He shifted so he was the one holding her hand in his, and it was a kind of agony, really. Her fingers were long and elegant, and he would never sleep again, thinking of the things she could do with them.

But all he did was hold her hand there. Safely. Sweetly, even.

"That you promised your father is all very well," he said. "But you and I both know that you've always been a romantic."

She pulled her hand away, and he let her, because he had to let her. Her eyes flashed. "I don't think I'm romantic at all."

"Please. When that wanker started writing you love poetry, you cried."

"It was love poetry, Dylan. You're supposed to cry."

"It was dreadful. Embarrassing."

"It was years ago. It was one poem and you were cruel about it then, too."

"Because you wanted it to be a romance, and it wasn't. It was an Oxford swot looking to get a leg over. And using pretty words to get the job done."

"It's not you who he was trying to get a leg over, so I don't know why on earth you would care."

"I don't care," he said, and it was a lie. A very old lie, so he said it with tremendous dignity. "I'm simply pointing out that where anyone else would see a right tosser, you saw a poet. You're romantic, plain and simple."

"Even if I am, it doesn't matter, because I'm not planning to act on it. And that's not why I'm here."

"Are you ready to tell me, then?"

And he waited, a strange, new kind of energy rising in him as she turned and met his gaze. Looking uneasy, for the first time.

He couldn't say he minded.

"I don't know what you mean."

"You can hide here as long as you like, Jenny," Dylan said quietly. "You're always welcome."

"I'm not hiding."

"It's nothing to me if you wear a groove into the coastal walk while you fret over thinking yourself frigid. Though I will point out that most people, when they want to know about sex, take to the internet. I'm not necessarily advocating that you watch porn, mind. I'm not saying you shouldn't, either. Maybe you'll learn something."

Jenny rolled her eyes. "The last thing I want to do is watch porn."

"Because you're too good, is that it?" And he laughed, though he didn't find it funny. The notion of Jenny and anything pornographic was enough to turn him inside out. "Saint Jenny, Our Lady of Restraint?"

"Of course not." She frowned at him. "Porn is just fucking. I want to know what it's like to be fucked properly."

And he wanted to say something to break the tension inside him. Between them. He wanted to make them both laugh the way he usually did. That was what he should do, and he knew it. It was the only thing that would keep them steady. On even ground, where they needed to stay.

But he didn't do it.

Jenny stared up at him, and something in her face changed. Maybe it was because he wasn't grinning. He wasn't hiding himself. Maybe the truth was, he was tired of all the hiding he'd done all these years.

For a moment, here in the dark with the light of the bridge in the distance and the opera house rising like a wave behind them, he was, for once...himself.

Unfettered.

Unapologetic.

Unleashed, at last.

Jenny made a soft, small noise. Shock, perhaps. *Need,* something dark within him insisted.

"I didn't come all the way here to talk about sex," she said her voice resolute.

"Fucking," he corrected her, and he really did sound like himself then. Not the happy-go-lucky version of himself he played for her. "The proper fucking you've gone without all this time, in fact."

He watched her swallow, and the way her throat moved. And even that felt like her elegant hands around his cock, holding him. Massaging him.

Driving him fucking crazy.

"I didn't jump on a plane and fly here to talk about it," she said, a strange insistence in her words. "I don't want to talk about it. I want to do it."

He didn't help her. He only waited, his gaze on hers, so intent he was sure he must have seemed harsh to her. But she didn't back down.

"And I don't want to do it randomly," she said, her expression every bit as intense as he felt. As he was and always had been. "I want you, Dylan. I want you to show me what it's like."

CHAPTER FIVE

JENNY COULDN'T SEEM to regulate herself. Her temperature, the way she shook, her wildly pounding heart.

Because Dylan was still Dylan. But once again, she couldn't quite recognize the man she knew on the face of the man who stood there beside her.

This Dylan was dangerous.

And the voice that whispered that word inside of her wasn't Erika's. Not this time. It was some base of feminine knowledge she wouldn't have believed existed if she didn't hear it so clearly. It understood when she didn't, when she couldn't, that whatever this was—whoever he was when he changed this way—he wasn't the easy, lazy, comfortably relaxed friend she knew so well.

"Are you sure?" he asked, and there was that intensity in the way he asked it. And the way he looked at her. And the way he held himself while he did it. "You want me to show you how to fuck?"

Jenny felt her body shift. A shudder turned into a

thrill, and wound its way through her as if connected to that same dark intent she could see all over him.

She was aware of her skin, and the way the cool sea air danced over it, soft like a touch. There was some kind of emotion making her eyes feel full, and her breasts scraped against the material of her shirt, tucked beneath her long jumper. Her nipples were so hard she ought to have been freezing cold, but she wasn't. She was too hot, if anything. A new kind of furnace fanned out from between her legs, where her pussy was a great ache of need and hunger, and all of this would have shocked her if she'd had a moment to process it.

She'd thought she'd been turned on before. She really had quite liked the sex she'd experienced so far. *But you knew,* something in her whispered. *You always knew you were missing something.*

And there was no point lying to herself about that any longer. Because she'd come all the way here, hadn't she? For this. For the way he looked at her now that made her heart stutter. And everything else seem to stutter, too.

Because the Dylan she knew was beautiful, yes, but he wasn't so…powerful. Not like this. Not as if the Sydney skyline behind him might wink out at any moment, or fade into insignificance, so bright and hot did he burn, just by standing there.

Her breath kept tangling in her throat, there was a kind of weight on her chest and the thing she most wanted to avoid thinking seemed to sneak into her anyway.

Maybe this was the real him. Maybe this was the real Dylan.

She couldn't ask herself what that meant. If that was true, what that told her about the two of them. About their friendship. About everything.

"Because you don't seem sure," he said, and even his voice was different. There was a certainty there. A ferocity. And suddenly, it was all too easy to imagine him as the CEO, owner and creator of a billion-dollar company he'd started on the strength of a couple of credit cards and his charm. She'd found it so funny before, imagining her Dylan in charge of all that. Not now. "You look a bit like you've seen a ghost, if I'm honest."

And there was something drumming in her blood. Jenny still couldn't name it, but she recognized it as the same impulse that had gotten her out of her flat that night. That had led her, not on a walk from her Kensington neighborhood into Notting Hill to wander the Portobello Road, as she sometimes liked to do, but onto the Tube. And off to Heathrow.

It was what had brought her here, and the more she stared at this version of her best friend wearing the mask of some kind of sex warrior, the louder it got.

"I don't think you're a ghost," she managed to say. "Though between you and me, I haven't seen a lot of ghosts. I wouldn't know how to tell."

There was no trace of that smile of his. So friendly, so engaging. No hint of that bright laugh that put everyone at ease.

So she made it worse.

Jenny reached out across the inches between them that seemed, then, as vast as the harbor she'd spent so much of the day exploring, stretching this way and that, inland and then out to sea. She reached across the distance between them, found the opening of his coat, and slid her hand along his soft T-shirt into the hollow between his pectoral muscles.

She could feel the heat of him, as if she'd slapped her hand down on a stovetop.

And it occurred to her as she stood there, her palm spread against his hard, dense muscles, that she didn't touch him much. They hugged each other hello and goodbye, but that was usually it. There was very little jostling of shoulders. No offhanded, friendly little touches, here and there. Sometimes, if he was being courteous, he might brush his fingers against the small of her back as he guided her somewhere.

But for all the years they'd known each other, all the intimacies they'd shared, there were never any intimacies involving touch.

And as she stared up at him, she was aware for the first time how she had to tip her head back to look at him. How big he was, so tall and with such wide shoulders. And that he was remarkably beautiful for a man who seemed so rugged at the same time.

Jenny didn't bother to ask herself why.

She knew.

Because touching him like this was electric.

It surged through her to become a part of that drumming thing in her veins, a restless, insistent rhythm that flooded through her. It went right to her pussy.

She felt slippery. Red hot.

And all they were doing was standing close together, talking. With her hand on his chest, but not even flesh to flesh.

Dylan stood very still. Too still, maybe. And something in her fluttered at the thought, because suddenly she could have sworn that he was looking at her as if she was a meal. And one he intended to savor.

"Let me make sure we're both very clear about what's happening here," he said, and there was something almost gravelly in his voice then. It only made that electric touch seemed to glow. Hot and hard. "We've been friends for a long time, Jenny. I wouldn't want there to be any misunderstandings."

"I want you," she said. Again.

"To fuck you."

And she was sure she didn't imagine the light in his green eyes then, or the way it made her…quiver.

"To fuck me properly," she corrected him. "I want to leave giddy and staggering about, like all the rest. Can you promise me that?"

"I'm insulted you would ask." But he didn't look or sound insulted. He looked…*more*, maybe. More intense. More focused. More fierce. And much more dangerous. "Let's discuss the housekeeping, shall we?"

"Housekeeping?" She frowned at him. "Does that mean you have… Grooming requirements?"

"If I did, I'd expect you to comply with them," he said, and there was some kind of amusement in his gaze then, but it still wasn't the Dylan she knew. It wasn't that laughter. It was something else, something male and demanding, and she had never felt so feminine, before.

It was as if she suddenly understood the point of fancy dresses that cinched in at the waist and made a girl breathless, or high heels that made her unsteady, because she was neither tonight and felt both of those things. And it was glorious. She felt shivery and silly. Her breasts ached and her pussy was slick, and she wanted nothing more than to rub all that against him and see what he might do with it. With her.

"Is that part of the Dylan Kilburn promise?" she found herself asking. "Compliance?"

Again, there was that gleam in his green eyes, that hard amusement that made her sway a bit on her feet. His mouth was a stern line, but that only made it better. He reached over and took the thick tendril of her hair in his hand, then tugged it. Not entirely gently.

And everything inside her…*bloomed*.

Dylan's mouth didn't move from that hard line, but she still thought she could see his smile there.

"We'll get to compliance," he told her. Promised her. "But first, there's this. Us. You've never had someone turn you out, so you have no idea how you'll feel in the aftermath."

"I thought the point is giddiness. Isn't it?"

"That's part of it. Sometimes. But the girls you're thinking about didn't call me their best friend. The only thing I promised them was orgasms. They didn't know me."

"Do I know you?" She was kidding. Or she thought she was kidding when she started speaking. And then, somehow, wasn't. "I'm not sure I've ever seen this side of you before."

"Because you haven't." He studied her face as she took that in, blinking because he sounded so uncompromising. "You need to be absolutely certain you want to open this door, Jenny. Because once it's open, I don't think you can close it again."

"Why does that sound like a threat?"

He tugged on her hair again, and it was such a strange sensation. Sharp at the start, but then like a flush as it moved through her. She didn't understand how the slightest stinging sensation on her scalp could make her nipples pinch and then travel down to make her entirely too aware of her clit.

"You've gone to great lengths to set your life up precisely as you like it," Dylan said, quiet and intense. "As long as I've known you, you've never wavered from this path of yours. You say you promised your father, but I think we both know you could have fought him if you had a mind to. You don't. This is what you want. A cold fish husband who won't ask anything of you but your bloodline. Decorous, polite society sex, genteel and very seldom, until the heirs are properly sorted out. And then you get what you really want. No more demands, nothing but an empty freedom to do what you already do. Charity work. Tending to your father. Closing yourself up tight."

Her breath suddenly seemed harsh and loud there, down below the great opera house, and echoed in her like it was quiet. When it wasn't. When there were so many people about she should have found it hard to hear him.

But she heard him all too well. "I prefer to think I'm in a position to do good," she managed to say, over the mess his words left inside her. "And I plan to. I already told you, Conrad isn't a bad man."

"Conrad is the least offensive man your father could find," Dylan replied, and she might have been outraged if there had been any heat in it. But it was a statement of fact. "At least he's not geriatric. But you never had the slightest intention of choosing your own husband. You want the arrangement. You want to stay untested. Unchallenged. Because that's the thing about intimacy, Jen. It's messy."

"I came to Australia because you're the expert

on sex," she managed to say. "Not intimacy. I've never known you to keep the same woman around for more than a weekend. And that's a very rare weekend indeed."

"Sex *is* intimacy," Dylan shot back at her, his hard tone brooking no argument. "Anyone who tells you otherwise isn't any good at it. But you need to decide if you can handle that. Because the Jenny I know has made it clear, in word and deed since the day I met her, that she wants no part of it."

"I want a taste," she heard herself say.

And she wanted to step back and put some head-clearing distance between them. Knock his hand away from her hair. But she rather thought he expected her to do all of those things, and more—that it would prove his point. So she did the opposite. She moved closer, and brought her other hand to his chest. Then angled herself against him, as if they were already in an embrace.

"A taste of me might be more than you bargained for," he said, as if he could tell that she'd just gone ahead and lit herself on fire. "It will be. And then what?"

"What do you mean? Are your morning afters normally fraught with peril? Because they look very civilized. No broken crockery or rending of garments as long as I've known you."

"For starters, my morning afters don't normally occur with women who are staying with me. So there's that to consider. But even if I gave you the weekend option, or even a week, just to make sure you were well and truly fucked properly in every possible way, do you really want that?" Dylan's gaze was as hard as his chest felt beneath her hands, and twice as hot. "Because it seems to me that it would be one thing to go into your chilly little marriage with no knowledge of what you're missing. But torture if you do know."

She wasn't sure moving closer to him had been her best idea, because he felt so good. Too good. And this close, she could smell him, and that was like a wave of sensation all its own. Something deep and spicy that made her think of forests back home. And something else that reminded her of the abundant sunshine here, even in winter. And holding it all together, him. Dylan.

All the versions of him.

"It will be my torture, not yours," she said.

"Do you think I won't care about that?" He took her elbows in his big hands, and held her away from him, almost splayed against his chest. Almost. "Because as we talk about opening doors that can't be closed, sex does have a way of changing friendship. You must know that. I remember several right tossers trying their hands at befriending you, all for a chance to get in there."

"They weren't really friends." She shrugged. "There was nothing to change. Or to lose."

"We've been friends for years, Jenny. Think about that. If I give you what you want, and it's everything you imagine it to be, what do you think will happen then?"

She searched his face, trying to figure out what the right answer would be here. What he wanted. Her experience with men had been limited to either the dates her father had sent her on, with men who had hardly noticed she was there. Or the men she'd actually dated, who had been so eager to please that she'd hardly had to express half a wish before it was excessively granted. And every now and again, the odd one who thought insulting her was the right tack to take—and it was certainly different. In all cases, it had always been easy enough to simply sway close, say something sultry, and sort them out with sex.

She didn't understand why Dylan wasn't so easily led.

That drumming thing inside her got louder. Longer.

And maybe that was the secret she'd been dancing around all this time. Men who could be led didn't produce that giddy, begging for more effect. How could they? Standing at a rail looking out over Sydney Harbour as the evening ferries slid past, that answer seemed so obvious. How had she missed it all this time?

"Nothing will change," she told him. "This will be our secret. An experiment between two good friends and when I leave Australia, everything will just…go back the way it was."

"Will it now."

She laughed. "Of course it will."

Because she couldn't imagine any other option.

Dylan shifted, one of those big hands moving up to slide along the length of her jaw, as if it belonged there.

But it was like a storm. A hurricane, unleashed from every point of contact. Skin to skin, like something torrential. The heat of his palm, its faint roughness. Everything inside her…rioted.

But she didn't move. She couldn't.

"You keep acting as if we're talking about regular sex. Tepid, faintly embarrassing fumbles in the dark with men who come too soon and act like you should be grateful all the same. But what if that's not all there is?" He shook his head slightly, his gaze so hard on hers it would have hurt, if she could feel anything but his *hand*. "I know you think that there can't be that much of a difference. Not really. You've come to conduct your wee science experiment, but in the final analysis, you don't really think I can rock your world. Change your life. Show you the difference between black-and-white and full-on color. Do you?"

And his hand was on her face like a brand. And he was crowding out the night, and the city, and the whole wide world. And her heart was beating so fast she was vaguely concerned it might turn into a medical issue.

"I think if anyone could," she managed to say, "it would be you."

She thought he should look pleased at that. But he didn't. He looked as if she'd hurt him. "And what if I do everything I claim I can do, and more, and you do the very thing I suspect you think is impossible?"

Her eyes searched his, and she frowned, faintly. "I have actually had an orgasm before, Dylan. You don't have to be quite so up yourself."

"I'm talking about love, not orgasms," he said with a certain brutal directness. And once again, there was that *ferocity* stamped all over him, so she couldn't tell if he was about to laugh or shout or take over the world. All of the above, maybe. "It tells me everything I need to know about the sad sex you've had that you don't understand how they could be connected."

"You think I'm going to fall in love with you if we have sex?" she asked, astonished.

He didn't laugh. Not exactly. It was all much too intense for that. "I think that if I fuck you properly, there is almost no possibility you *won't* fall in love with me."

"Why aren't you worried that you'll fall in love with me?" she demanded. And told herself that was outrage, not panic, that leaped around inside her, then. "Isn't that just as possible?"

"No chance of that," he said, and she could have sworn there was something almost sardonic in the way he said it.

She refused to dwell on the little stab of hurt that bloomed inside her then. That panic—that *outrage*—spurred her on.

"It doesn't matter if I go head over heels, however unlikely," she told him hotly. "I'm still engaged."

"So the worst case scenario is that I teach you what it means to properly fuck." And there was definitely a sardonic little twist in the corner of his mouth then, though she was too wound up to focus on it. "There will be sobbing, in all likelihood. Begging, almost certainly."

"I won't hold it against you," Jenny said magnanimously.

His green eyes glittered. "I appreciate that. Things may get emotional. Your plan, no matter how emotional things get, is to hop a plane back to England, continue to wave that great bloody ring around the place and marry the man your father personally selected for you. Is that it?"

"You're the one who just pointed out to me that that's always been it." She lifted her chin. "And you're right. I don't believe in love, Dylan. I never have. You and Erika seem to think that I'm some great, hidden romantic—"

"Not hidden. You've made no secret of it. You read romantic books. You like romantic films."

"That doesn't make me a romantic. I like horror films and I'm not a ghoul."

"You don't believe that *you* can have a romance, Jenny," he said, and he sounded almost tired, then. As if this conversation was costing him something, which made no sense. "Or you've decided you won't. That isn't quite the same thing as not having a romantic bone in your body."

"This is ridiculous." She pushed his hand away from her face then. And the light in his green eyes changed again, but he dropped his hand all the same. "If you don't want to have sex with me, Dylan, I wish you would just say so. All this poncing about, grimly talking about doors that can't be closed and emotional states that will be forever disrupted. I'm talking about having sex. You either want that or you don't. And I won't hate you if you don't." She made herself smile. "Too much."

And the strangest expression moved over his face then. She couldn't read it. Still, she found herself holding her breath, and felt something almost like loss when he ended up somewhere…wry.

"Risk assessments are a part of what I do for a living," he told her, sounding…careful. "The part you don't like to talk about, as it's so hard for you to imagine me ordering people about. Isn't that what you said?"

"I find it a lot less hard to imagine after tonight."

"You don't think you'll fall in love with me," he

said, and surely there was no reason for her heart to turn over at that. "That's fair enough. I won't patronize you and tell you, again, that I don't think you quite know what you're talking about."

"Even if I don't, does it matter? It's obvious in the way you're talking about this that you've had it happen before. But it's obviously not real love, or the lady in question would still be here. That means it's a sexual hangover, or some such. Don't worry, Dylan. You're safe." She smiled at him, and this time, she didn't have to force it. "I'm not going to relocate to Sydney, start stalking you and scale your wall to boil bunnies on your stove. I'm getting married next spring. And Conrad might not be in love with me, nor I with him. But I don't think either one of us is interested in the kind of scandal that would ensue if I was arrested in Australia for harassing an old friend. This is about as low risk as possible to get."

He only stared at her. She sighed.

"I promise," she said.

"Right."

And again, she watched him change. There was a flash of the Dylan she knew, almost rueful. Then that intent Dylan again, edgy and dangerous. And breathtaking.

He shifted, turning her around so her back was to the rail. And his hands moved to either side of her so he was caging her there, then angling himself toward her.

"What kind of protection do you prefer?" he asked, blandly, as her whole body *ignited*.

"Uh… You mean…?"

"Yes, *I mean*. Do you have a latex allergy? Are you on the pill? Do you prefer the ease and convenience of a coil?"

She was a grown woman. An adult in all ways. And yet the clinical frankness of those questions made her blush.

"I do not have a latex allergy," she managed to say, perhaps more primly than necessary. "And as a matter of fact, I am on the pill. Thank you for asking."

His green eyes gleamed, and this time, she was absolutely certain that it was, in fact, amusement. But she couldn't tell if that was better or worse.

"When were you last tested?" And his head was lowered close to hers, but all he did was smirk. "Or do you not bother with such things, because you're Lady Jenny, impervious to love, married off for a fortune and unlikely to ever choose the sort of disreputable man who might dare approach you anything less than squeaky clean?"

"For the record, this is the most unsexy and grossly disturbing conversation I've ever had when someone wants to get me naked."

"I find that hard to believe, given the wanker contingent you've allowed in your bed."

"I get tested once a year as a part of my annual

physical," she said loftily. "But then again, I don't throw it about like some."

"I'm never unsafe," he told her. "In terms of protection, that is. But I get tested every couple of months, because I like to be both promiscuous and sure."

"Am I supposed to be turned on now?" she asked, aware that her hands were in fists at her sides, and not willing to ask herself why. She was supposed to long for open discussions like this. It was supposed to herald her maturity. And she already knew he slept around, or he wouldn't have been the perfect person for her purposes. There was no reason this should all make her feel a bit like crying. "Because I'm whatever the opposite of that is. And I feel absolutely no trace of anything resembling impending giddiness. In case you were wondering."

"I know these practicalities are so confronting," he said, and he did bend his head then. But only to put his face…near hers. As if he was contemplating sinking his teeth into her neck like some kind of vampire.

Jenny had no idea what it said about her that the very idea made her break out goose bumps. And not because the notion disgusted or scared her.

"Are you sure you're the opposite of turned on?" he asked.

And she could feel his breath in the crook of her neck. He was *so close.* He surrounded her, and there was something dominating in the way he stood there, holding her in place without touching her at all. She should have hated that, but it was Dylan.

And the fact it was Dylan made it worse. Wrong, and strange, somehow so much better.

Her pussy began to pulse, in time with that same restless beating thing inside her. And her nipples were so hard she couldn't quite tell if the sensation that washed through her from the tight points was pleasure or pain. Only that it didn't stop.

"I can't decide if you're trying to scare me off or if this is your seduction technique," she managed to say, aware that she was panting a bit as she spoke. "But I'm beginning to think that the reason all those girls look so giddy is because of some kind of head trauma. Is that your secret?"

She felt the brush of his lips. Or she thought it was his lips, there for a moment where her pulse went wild. Then gone, and it was like being walloped with another storm system.

He was wrecking her. Remaking her.

"Fucking someone through the headboard sounds fun in theory, but no one likes a concussion when all they want is to come," he rumbled against her neck. She could *feel* it when he spoke. It danced in her. "Don't you agree?"

But she was lost in a cascade of too-hot, too-bright images of him and her and that bed of his with all its wrought iron, and all Jenny could do was gape at him when he lifted his head.

"That's what I thought you'd say," he said, and even his smile was dangerous.

Then Dylan bent that last little bit and slammed his mouth down on hers.

CHAPTER SIX

THERE WERE VERY few things in life that exceeded expectations.

And it turned out, Jenny was one of them.

Dylan didn't waste time on niceties. He claimed her mouth with his, finally.

He'd been building up this particular hunger since the moment he'd met her, and he'd long since given up hope it would ever happen with them, so he didn't hold back. It didn't occur to him to hold back.

He'd warned her. He'd given her every chance to back out or change her mind. And despite all that, he knew full well he was the one who was going to have trouble closing this bloody door now it was opened.

But he couldn't care about that now. He couldn't tie himself up into knots over the future when there was still now. When there was still *this*.

Her mouth beneath his. The touch of her tongue. And her taste, better than he'd imagined—and sweet Lord, had he imagined it. Over and over again.

Dylan didn't kiss her sweetly. This wasn't a fairy tale. He ate at her mouth, holding her face where he wanted it and indulging himself.

At last.

She fit him. He'd imagined she would, year after year, but this… The taste of her surpassed every last fantasy he'd ever had.

Particularly when she kissed him back, hesitant at first, but then meeting him fully. Hot and greedy, just the way he liked it.

Deep and wet and long and perfect, and he had to fight to remember that they weren't in private. That he had to control himself when that was the last thing he wanted to do. Because it was so good. Because it was Jenny.

Dylan wrenched his mouth away, aware that he was breathing too hard as he dropped his forehead to hers.

"I told you," he growled at her, and he didn't even know what he meant. Only that he'd warned her. And there was a madness in him, bright and hot and tangled up deep, and it had her name written all over it.

She was panting and her eyes were closed, and he angled himself back a bit, dimly remembering once again that they were in public. That his cock was so hard already that he was likely in danger of scaring off the tourists, and a chat with the local police was not part of his plans for the night.

Not when he'd finally gotten his hands on Jenny. This was *Jenny*. He had her taste in his mouth, still. She was in his veins now, the fire in his blood. And God knew she'd been in his bones for years.

She was the ruin of him. But Dylan didn't feel ruined just then. Or he liked the ruin, maybe.

But her eyes were still closed. And he found himself tensing as he watched her struggle to control her breath. As he waited to see if she'd set him back on his heels the way he'd always imagined she would. That was the way it went between the lady of the manor and an upstart chancer.

It felt like an age or two before Jenny's lashes fluttered, and she opened up her eyes to look straight at him. The brown of her eyes that he knew so well was shot through with gold. There was a flush on her cheeks that made his cock feel heavy. The look on her face made his fingers itch to tear off her clothes and see where else that flush touched.

"You kissed me," she said, there was a scratchy sort of awe in her voice. "We *kissed*. You and me, Dylan."

"We did." His gaze dropped to her mouth, that mouth he'd studied, dreamed about, fantasized over. And could now taste against his own. He wasn't sure he could believe it. "I did."

She lifted a hand to touch her lips and he couldn't tell if her fingers were shaking, or if she was simply hesitant.

And he was Dylan Kilburn. He was renowned for his confidence, though his detractors used other words to describe it. Whatever it was, he had it in spades. He could walk into any room, talk to anyone, raise up empires on the strength of his handshake. And yet this slender creature with soft eyes and an elegant neck made him forget that he was one of the youngest billionaires in Australia—and the world. She made him forget that he was normally treated like a man a good ten or twenty years his senior, such was the power he exuded and the ruthless competency he brought to any given situation.

Jenny looked at him and just like that he was once again nothing more than a poor wee lad from the worst neighborhood in Dublin, out of his element at Oxford, and terrified that at any moment he'd cock the whole thing up. Absolutely certain every moment of every day that he was about to be found out and summarily sent down, because the smartest kid in a neighborhood like the one he'd grown up in didn't mean smart enough for the pampered toffs who swanned about the dreaming spires.

And in the middle of those years of anxiety and ambition, there had been Jenny, who'd been his friend.

It wasn't lost on him that lusting after her for all these years was a bit of a betrayal of that friendship. Nor was it lost on him that in kissing her the way he had, carnal and raw, he'd made absolutely certain there would be no going back. No matter what she'd said.

But then, she was marrying a man she didn't love. The way he'd always known she would. The way she'd always said she would. It shouldn't eat at him the way it did that everything was going along according to plan.

And she might think that a man like Conrad Vanderburg wouldn't care if she stayed *friends* with her old pal from her university days, but Dylan knew better. No husband in his right mind would be all right with Dylan hanging about—because a husband would see Dylan for who he really was. He was friendly, understanding, patient, endlessly supportive and undemanding only for one person on this earth. Her marriage was the end of things.

Dylan couldn't regret kissing her the way he had, no matter what she was about to say next.

But the thing about Jenny was that he could know her inside and out, and she still surprised him.

She did now. Because she smiled. That wide, faintly wicked, fully joyous smile of hers that made him feel as if it was the middle of summer, not winter. As if it was bright daylight, instead of night.

"We *kissed*," she said again. "Can you believe it?"

She leaned forward and braced herself on his chest again, tipping back her head with the ease of someone who'd done it a thousand times before. When she hadn't. Because there had always been barriers. There had always been distance.

Because Dylan had needed to maintain some level of sanity.

But he knew how she tasted now, and the hunger in him felt new. Wilder and sharper than before.

Jenny's eyes looked more gold than brown. "Would you say that kiss was a proper kiss?"

Dylan felt nearly grim with want, drunk with desire, but he laughed anyway. "It would be hard to find a kiss more proper, in my opinion."

Her smile widened. "And do you think that was representative of your work?"

There was a teasing note in her voice, and he found himself grinning in return. But not that happy, friendly, toothless grin he'd always given her in the past. Because the door was open, and he had already shouldered his way through it. That was who he was and always had been, in every scenario but this one. And now it was too late. There was no going back to pretending he was her lovable old buddy, Dylan.

Not when she was plastered against him and her lips were still damp from his. Not now.

"A proper kiss is an excellent advertisement for proper fuck, yes," he assured her, doing nothing to rein himself in. "At least when I do it. What do you reckon, Jenny? Have I scared you off?"

And her smile faded a bit as she gazed up at him, making his heart kick at him again.

Because he honestly didn't know what he would

do if she said that yes, he had succeeded at last in scaring her away from this course of action.

Cry like a bitch, mate, a voice in him said. Caustically. *You'll cry like a little bitch, and who could blame you?*

"You haven't scared me off," Jenny said, her hands still pressed against his chest and her eyes solemn. "And I appreciate your attempts, but you're not going to. The only thing that's going to stop this from happening is if you don't want to. If you've changed your mind. Or scared yourself off."

Dylan laughed again, but not because anything was funny. "Impossible."

He jerked her to him and took her mouth again, indulging himself all over again. He sank his hands into her hair, finding it silky and thick, and warm there at her scalp. He tugged her head back, giving himself the angle he wanted, and then it was on. A little rough, a little intense.

All magic.

Because this was Jenny, his Jenny, and he was never going to recover from this. And if she was going to go ahead and marry herself off, he was going to make sure she had something to remember him by.

He was going to imprint himself on her, the way she'd imprinted herself on him at first sight.

Dylan didn't think that he could ruin her the way she'd done to him, but he could ruin this. Because they fit together like a dream, and this kiss was already better than whole nights he'd spent with other women, none of whom he could ever remember too clearly. Not when there was Jenny. And he'd done his best all these years to get by without her, but he didn't have to now. Not now. Not tonight. Not for as long as she stayed here in Australia, hiding from her real life.

He could ruin her this way. He could teach her what *proper* was, and the truth was, he felt as if he'd been practicing his whole life for this opportunity. To worship this woman in every last way he knew, turn her inside out as many times as possible, and let her spend the rest of her life fantasizing about this. The same way he would be doing.

He pulled away again and liked it when she moaned out a protest.

"Come on," he said. "I'm going to feed you."

Her eyes were a bit fuzzy, which made his cock pulse. "Feed me? Is that a code for something debaucherous? Please say yes."

His hands were still in her hair, and he kept them there, because it felt good to have control of her. To hold her like this. To have her right where he wanted her.

Another subject they were going to have to cover, but he'd get there.

"That depends how you eat." He tilted his head a bit as he gazed down at her. "Are you feeling gluttonous?"

Her gaze sharpened at last, but she was looking at his mouth. "Yes. I believe that's the perfect word."

"We need to make sure you can keep up your strength," he said. Then he reached down and helped himself to her hand, threading her fingers through his.

She stared down at their hands, clasped together like that.

"You're *holding my hand*," she said, with a certain reverence. Or more of that awe, or wonder, that was one more way she was going to kill him. "*Dylan Kilburn* is *holding my hand*."

He opened his mouth to say something wicked, or offhanded. Something to dispel the tension a bit. But she gazed up at him and the words died on his tongue, unsaid.

Because even their hands fit together perfectly, and her taste was still flooding through him, and she wasn't being silly. If anything, he would have said that look on her face was sacred.

And for once, he didn't have to pretend.

For once, he could meet that gaze of hers with his own, and acknowledge this thing that was between them. This thing that had been in him, and a part of him, and a defining characteristic of his, for so long now he didn't know who he was without it.

And it was only holding her hand. But it felt like the world. It felt right. A key into a lock.

Coming home at last.

Dylan could have stood there for another lifetime, but she wasn't here for his feelings. She was here to fuck. And he had every intention of living up to his promises.

So he made himself look away, gripped her hand harder and led her away from that dark railing and the bright crowd at the Opera Bar.

He led her around the quay, climbing up into the narrow, cobbled laneways that rose up opposite the opera house, and comprised the oldest part of Sydney.

"Are we really stopping for food?" she asked as they climbed a set of stairs between two buildings. "Do I get a vote?"

He slanted to gaze down at her. "No."

"Just…no. No explanation. Just straight up, no debate, *no*."

"I don't think I stuttered, did I?"

Jenny was laughing as he escorted her toward a deceptively old-looking building that was only accessible down a long, cobbled alleyway. The door was painted a bright red, and that was its only distinguishing facet. That and the keypad next to the door. Dylan punched in the code, and the door clicked open, instantly giving away the fact that the building had been gutted and refurbished inside, though it looked quietly historic from without.

"What is this place?" Jenny breathed. Her eyes sparkled as she looked up at him, her fingers still wrapped up tight in his. "Is this some kind of secret club? For sex?"

"I don't need a secret club for sex." He shook his head at her. "Sex is a group sport for some, sure. More power to them. I'm more of a singles player, myself."

He ushered her inside. Then he led her down a set of stairs, lit up with a buttery golden light. At the bottom was a discreet welcome desk staffed by a smiling attendant.

"Good evening, Mr. Kilburn," the man said in a plummy British accent. "Will you be dining with us tonight?"

"A table with a view," Dylan replied. "And we'll make our own way up."

"Very good, sir," the man said, and typed something into the tablet in front of him.

Dylan led Jenny farther into the building, making his way through the various lounges, bars and nooks and crannies alike that made up this particular club.

"It *is* a club," Jenny said, as if she'd caught him out. "I've always wanted to spend time in an illicit sex club, populated entirely by deviance."

"I hate to ruin the fantasy, but this club is more for business connections, entrepreneurial fantasies and high profile meetings that need to remain strictly private. There are deviant sex clubs out there, and there's sex here, too, but not of the public variety. The club provides rooms for weary travelers, and doesn't much care who fills them."

"That's a lot less fun."

"The truth about highflyers is that most of them are boring," Dylan said. "Because the reason they're highflyers is that they work themselves half to death."

"And here I thought the point of making shed-loads of cash was to fling it about indiscriminately, laughing all the while."

And years ago, Dylan would have let that go. This morning, even. But everything was different now.

"The difference is whether or not you've worked for said shedloads."

He expected Jenny to stiffen, but her expression only turned rueful. "Unlike me, you mean."

"Not everyone is born rich."

"And not everyone born rich is automatically evil," Jenny replied. She squeezed his hand as she held it. "Something you're going to have to come to terms with should you create a new generation some day. Will they grow up pampered and spoilt? Or will they learn they have a responsibility to do what others can't?"

He found his thumb moving back and forth over the back of her hand. "You don't make money at what you do, do you?"

"Of course not. I'm a career volunteer. It's what makes swanning off to Australia on a whim possible."

She peered past him into one of the salons off the

hall, where a scrum of finance types were boozing it up like they were down at the local, except what they were quaffing would qualify as a mortgage payment in some places. All she did was smile, but Dylan was suddenly uncomfortable. He'd been there once, in the first flush of his first million. And the notion that Jenny might have looked at him then as *he* was looking at the pack of them made something twist inside.

"That's the trouble with money," he said darkly. "If you've never had a lack of it and don't understand what a gift that is, you don't cherish it. You grow complacent." He nodded toward the pack of idiots, but pulled her along past their room. "And you find yourself using it to help yourself feel things you wouldn't otherwise." Like entertaining the wrong women for years because the right one was permanently out of reach. But he remembered himself. "Like leaping out of planes, which the lot of them like to do on the weekends. Regularly. But no one's a thrill junkie if they can feel things on their own. They wouldn't need it."

Jenny was looking up at him again as they walked, that rueful expression turning to something more pointed. "Have you already become bored? So quickly?"

"I don't believe in boredom," Dylan told her, growling it out as if she was hitting hard into the very heart of him. "That's one more privilege I never had."

"You seek thrills for the hell of it, then."

She wasn't quite frowning at him, but there was a challenging light in her eyes. And Dylan didn't want to debate class differences with the one person who had always treated him as if there weren't any. As if he was grand as he was, always and forever.

And she was going to leave him, soon. He didn't want to tell her that she was his model for how a very wealthy person ought to behave, because he didn't want to admit how much he thought about her, felt about her, changed himself for her. Start discussing one part of it and who knew where he'd end up?

Jenny never hid her wealth, but she never flaunted it, either. She gave back quietly, without fanfare. And she was unfailingly kind. He fell short of these things daily, but she was always there as a goal. He was good at goals.

But then, there were other, more attainable goals tonight. He could work on being a better version of himself in all the lonely years ahead of him.

Dylan stopped at the next door they passed, seeing the discreet green light that indicated it was empty. He coded them in, then leaned back against the door when he closed it. And locked it.

"Does that mean you don't feel anything?" she was asking, paying no attention to what he was doing as she walked into the lounge area, then turned back to him. "And, crucial follow-up question, if you can't feel anything, are you really the best tutor when it comes to sex?"

"Jenny."

"I'm no expert myself, but I did think it had a lot to do with sensation," she said, shaking her head at him. "Feeling. All those things you just said—"

"There's only one thrill I'm after," Dylan told her.

He hauled her into his arms, where she belonged, and he got his mouth on hers once more.

And this time, in private.

CHAPTER SEVEN

IF JENNY HAD ever had the slightest idea that kissing could be like this, her whole life would be different.

Dylan was addictive.

The scrape of his tongue, the way he moved that hard jaw of his… She couldn't get close enough. Her whole body was flushed, hot, ready.

She felt needy, filled with greed, and some part of her thought that this experiment was going to take a bit longer than planned. Because she could kiss him forever. Calling what he was doing *kissing* seemed to do it a disservice, in fact. He tasted the way she imagined heroin must feel. An impossible, magical lift, and then a beautiful storm.

And she felt dizzy, but it took her a moment to realize it was because he was moving her, backing her up until something prodded her at the hips.

She pulled away from him, which made her want to cry. But she looked around, and realized they were in a sitting room of some kind. There was the door to one side discreetly marked with an embossed WC.

There was the door they'd come in, and then a third with no markings.

"Is this a hotel?"

"After a fashion," Dylan said, in a perfectly normal voice that was at complete odds with the ferocity in his gaze. The contrast made her skin feel too tight. "These are considered day rooms. They are most properly used for members fighting off jet lag when they come in on one of those early flights. A nice place to have a bit of a sleep, freshen up and then head straight to a business meeting."

"Are we having a business meeting?" Jenny asked, there where he'd backed her up against a sturdy little antique secretary.

But he only smiled. Like a wolf. And then he was shifting, going down on his knees before her.

And suddenly, she didn't care what took place in this building. All she could see was Dylan, his eyes blazing and his face set. Hungry. Very nearly feral.

She felt the same. And she wanted to ask him what he was doing, but her mouth was too dry.

Then his hands were on her. He smoothed his way over her hips, then went straight to the fastening of her jeans.

"I'm going to feed you," he told her, and his voice sounded thicker. Darker. "But first, I need to taste you or I'm not going to make it."

She wanted to laugh at that, because it seemed like the right thing to do. To make this less intense.

Less overwhelming. But he angled a look up at her when he said it, green and hot, and she was terribly afraid she might shatter.

And she didn't know if she meant she would come—or come apart. Or both.

There was a noise in her ears, some kind of ringing. And maybe that was her breath, heaving in and out of her.

Dylan unbuttoned her jeans, then worked her zipper down.

And she wanted to tell him not to bother. That she'd never cared that much about this thing that all women were supposed to find so delightful. That in her experience, it was always a bit messy and embarrassing. The boyfriends she'd had were always so proud of themselves, so bound and determined to prove something, that she'd felt nothing but enormous pressure to scream and carry on and make out as if she was *transported*. When really, a person's head was between her legs while an endless spiral of anxiety traipsed about in her head—

"Hey. Jenny."

Dylan's voice snapped her out of the cycle, and she found his gaze. There was something in the way he was looking at her, then. Some kind of charged patience. As if he knew exactly what she was thinking. His hands were busy, even as that gaze of his was still. He tugged her jeans down over her hips, and she would have protested, maybe. But his hands were so big and they skimmed over her legs easily, and it was easier somehow to let him tug one leg free.

And besides, she liked it when he touched her.

His gaze caught hers, almost stern now. "This is for me."

"What?"

"This is for me," he told her, and there was that patient thing there in all that green, and a light she didn't quite understand. "This is what *I* need. All right?"

She nodded, because she couldn't speak.

"Good." His mouth seemed stern, then, too—a word she never would have used to describe Dylan. Her Dylan, so funny and happy and bright... But she liked this side of him. Something about that hard line of profoundly male lips and his finely cut jaw made her shudder inside, and her pussy feel wet and swollen. "I want you to think about that, please."

"Think about what? What you want?"

"I told you I was hungry."

He smoothed his hands up to her hips again, and pulled one leg wide as he went, making space for himself. He kept going up her thigh, until he reached the edge of the panties she wore.

And when he flicked his gaze to hers again, she understood that both of them were feeling that same wild heat. She was *lit up* with it. With him. His palms were against her skin, and as he knelt there, she could feel his breath against the lace that covered her pussy.

"I'll buy you more," he growled, and she had no idea what he meant.

Until he tore her panties off her.

And she couldn't help but gasp at that. She even rocked forward with the jolt of it, up on her toes.

Dylan's hands moved around to grip her ass. As if he owned it. And her. Then he pulled her forward, straight on to his mouth.

He didn't seem to care what she did with herself. Where she put her hands or how she was propped up against the secretary. He dipped his shoulder so that one of her legs fell over his back, and his hands gripped her, holding her right where he wanted her.

And he ate at her as if she was a ripe fruit, and he didn't give a shit if she ran all over his face.

She tried to brace herself against the secretary behind her, but he was too intense. His tongue, his teeth, that jaw.

It was like he was truly feasting on her. Eating his fill, and so wholly focused on the task, so deeply unconcerned with her reaction, that she felt herself... unravel. Or let go, at last.

She dug her hands in his thick, dark hair, and stopped trying to anticipate which way he would rock his head, or angle that chin.

And all the while, he licked into her. He scraped at her gently, and then not so gently, too.

And it was his intensity that rocked her. His total focus, and his fingers digging into the flesh of her ass, kneading gently from time to time to increase the sensation.

Jenny didn't have to do a thing. Dylan wasn't checking to see what her reaction was. He'd told her he wanted this, and he was taking it, and she believed that he truly didn't care about anything but pleasing himself. He was hungry, she was his appetizer—

And that was what threw her over the edge.

She'd had orgasms before. Some quite delightful ones, she would have said. By her own hand, with a partner—they'd been sweet little finishes, like a cherry on top.

But this was nothing like that.

This was a gut punch.

This was a seismic event.

She felt everything in her seize, and this had nothing to do with *cherries*, and she was shaking everywhere, inside and out, and a noise was coming out of her throat that scraped.

And she heard a deep, male rumble, that she knew—though she'd never heard anything like it before—was the sound of his pleasure. His satisfaction.

That made her come even harder.

And he didn't stop.

He kept going. He sucked her clit into his mouth, making her arch and sob, and she couldn't get her head around the fact it was *Dylan*.

Or what her body was even doing. She thought her

eyes were closed, though she couldn't tell for sure, and there was moisture leaking out of them. And she could hear the sounds he made, and the sounds he made her pussy make.

And everything was bright red, muscular and physical, and she was too hot. But she couldn't seem to stop the noises she was making, or the way she lifted her hips toward him. Because she wanted more. Because she couldn't think. Because she didn't know what was happening to her, how she was expected to survive this.

Dylan was eating her alive. He was devouring her.

He'd tripped off a series of explosions, and they didn't stop. *She* couldn't stop. One led into the next, and everything was wet, hot and just this side of painful. All the places he wasn't touching hurt, too. And the hurt was an ache, and it bled straight down into the center of her, hurtling its way through her and into her clit, and he knew it.

Oh, yes, he knew it.

Because he teased her. And he took her. And he consumed her with that voracious mouth of his, making a mockery of her belief that this was something she didn't like. Because this wasn't about *like*, it was about *need*—

And she came so hard again then that she saw stars, but she couldn't make any more noise. Because everything was too bright and searing. And it was all shattered to pieces.

Jenny was only vaguely aware of him moving, pressing a kiss against her inner thigh, and then leaning her back against the secretary she'd forgotten was even there.

She had to breathe, but it was hard to make her lungs work. She had to concentrate on the act of breathing, and only when that had gone on awhile could she take notice of her surroundings. And the fact Dylan had slid her back on the secretary when he was done with her, leaving her slumped there with her jeans at her ankles, like a crumpled doll.

An image that surely should have horrified her, but instead made another spear of bright, thick heat wind its way through her.

It seemed to take an hour or so, and enough effort to climb a mountain or two, to turn her head to the side and watched Dylan as he bent over the sink tucked into the wall outside the WC. He splashed water on his face. Then he ran his hands through his hair. And when he looked at her, clearly completely aware of her and what she was doing, Jenny thought her heart stopped.

She wanted to say something arch. Amusing.

But all she could do was slump there, entirely wrecked, until the corner of his mouth kicked up a bit.

He reached down below the sink and pulled out a fresh towel, then he moved over to her. She expected him to hand her the towel, but he didn't. He cleaned her up instead, with a brisk efficiency that made her breathless. There was something about how at ease he was with her body. As if every inch of her was his. It made her a bit light-headed.

When he was done, he tossed the towel in a basket, then set her on her feet. She was boneless and useless, so she did nothing when he squatted down, fed her foot back into the leg of her jeans, and tugged them back up. And she was only aware that she'd kicked off the flashy new heels she'd found in a boutique this afternoon when he slid them back onto her feet.

"Are you with me?" Dylan stood, then buttoned her jeans. Then he held her hips there, looking down at her.

All she could manage to do was nod.

"I'm going to need a word or two, I think." He lifted one hand, and ran his thumb beneath her eye, collecting that moisture she couldn't seem to keep from spilling over.

"I'm with you," she whispered.

Though in truth, Jenny didn't know what that meant. Or where they were. Or her own damned name.

Dylan smiled, but it wasn't that friendly smile she knew so well. This one was darker. And far more satisfied.

He laced his fingers through hers again, and led her out of the room. And she couldn't seem to concentrate on anything. Not really. It was like a dream.

He was leading her down another hall, then into a lift. And all she could think about was his hand in hers, and how sensitive her pussy was now, swollen and still molten, brushing up against the seam of her jeans because he'd left her with no panties.

He ushered her out of the lift, and then to a table on a rooftop patio festooned with walls of plants, heaters and clever lighting that managed to make every table seem private—even though she was fairly certain there were other people about. And it wasn't until they sat down, and she looked out at the stunning, sparkling view laid out before them from the Harbour Bridge to the Opera House and the sky-scrapers of central Sydney, that she could place the way he touched her.

It was proprietary.

Something inside of her curled up at that, shiver-ing in delight.

Dylan didn't ask her what she wanted to eat. He had a quiet word with the waiter. Another thing she wanted to find a little outrage about, and yet when the food arrived she was not only ravenous, she couldn't have chosen better for herself.

"Good?" he asked, sounding far too entertained.

"Surprisingly, yes."

"What's the surprise, Jenny?" And he sounded like her Dylan again, lazy and careless, but she couldn't quite believe it anymore. Not when she'd seen what lurked beneath. "I've known you a donkey's age or two, haven't I?"

She ate what he'd ordered her, but she kept getting distracted by thoughts of him feasting, on her. Watching him eat food seemed like a sensual act. His green eyes seemed so amused, lit up in a new way, as he watched her. Jenny ordered herself to make clever conversation. The way she always did, in her role as her father's hostess. But for the first time in as long as she could remember, the words didn't come.

"I'm so sorry," she said, when their mains had been cleared away. Dylan picked up her hand again to toy with her fingers, and that didn't exactly help. "It's as if I lost the power of speech."

"You're welcome."

And surely she shouldn't have found such smugness appealing. She heard herself laugh. "Why would I thank you? I thought that was all for you. It had nothing to do with me."

"You can consider it an object lesson, then. I'm greedy. I want what I want when I want it."

He was playing with her fingers, making her right hand feel like an erogenous zone. She leaned closer to him, propping up one elbow on the table. "Is this it? Is this the famous speech?"

"Do I have a famous speech?"

"I figure there has to be something. Some careful line you throw out there to manage expectations. It doesn't make any sense that out of all those women, not one was ever under the impression that whatever they had with you meant more."

"I like to be clear."

And there was that ruthlessness about him then, and a hint of those hard, stern lines to his face that had undone her earlier. She squirmed in her chair, and when his gaze got that much greener, she knew he saw it. And knew why.

"Hit me with all your clarity, then," she dared him.

His smile was not reassuring. "There are only two things you need to know. I'm going to tell you exactly what I want. You don't have to worry. You don't have to wonder if I'm liking something or not liking something. You don't have to concern yourself with whether or not I'm having fun. I'll tell you."

She blinked, her mind reeling as she tried to connect that to her supposedly easygoing best friend. "Do people normally worry?"

But even as she asked that, she knew better. Had she ever *not* felt self-conscious during sex? Had she ever not tried to imagine what was going on as if she was crouched on the ceiling, looking down? And she'd certainly been guilty of checking out a partner's face to make sure he was still enjoying himself. Or to see if she could move things along.

"All you have to do is what I tell you to do," Dylan said, and his voice was easy. Almost lazy. But she could see that look in his eyes and she knew he wasn't kidding.

"That's a bit bossy, Dylan. Don't you think?"

"I'm a bit bossy, Jenny. As it happens."

She laughed, but he didn't. And suddenly her own laugh made her feel much too restless. "Oh. Well. How bossy?"

His eyes seemed greener, then. "Very, very bossy."

"What if… What if I don't like being bossed about?"

But he only smiled. "You liked it well enough when I had your pussy in my mouth."

And once again, he didn't laugh. He didn't break. This wasn't *her* Dylan, something in her whispered. This was someone else altogether, and she couldn't possibly figure out how she felt about that. Because she felt too many things at once. And her pussy was hot and wet, and it pulsed.

"This is your secret?" Her voice was far huskier than it had been before. She couldn't seem to help it. "You're… I mean, are you a…?"

"I'm a man who likes to be in charge." Another dark, stirring smile. "And I like my sex the way I like everything else, Jenny. I like it when it's mine."

"Oh," she breathed, in a sudden rush of understanding. "This is the talk."

"It is."

"So what happens if a woman says she'd rather not let you boss her around to your heart's content, thanks very much?" She frowned at him. "Is that it? Sex off the table?"

"I never take sex off the table." Again, there was that little crook in the corner of his mouth that was so different from the friendly grin she associated with him that she honestly couldn't tell if she wanted to smack it off his mouth, or put her own lips against it. Maybe both. "Usually I offer a wee challenge, to see if she likes what I have to offer."

"And what if she doesn't?"

"I wouldn't know." That little crook deepened. "It's never happened."

She blew out a little huff of something that could as easily have been outrage as lust. Or as seemed to be the case with Dylan, all of the above. And everything had already shifted between them, outrageously. Why not take it further?

"I accept this challenge," she told him, grandly. "You can try to convince me."

She didn't expect him to laugh, then, but he did. And this laugh, she recognized. It was vintage Dylan, delighted and long.

"Why is that funny?" she asked, flushing.

"I've just had my face between your legs," he replied. "And unless I miss my guess, that's not something you'd say you much enjoy, generally."

"What does that have to do anything?"

And the laughter on his face turned too quickly to stern intent. "I already know that you like to be told what to do, Jenny."

Her flush got worse. Red and hot. "If you already know, then why are we having this conversation?"

"Because you don't know what you know," he said with a shrug, as if that was simple. "Your whole life has been filled with sorry wankers who made you work to get yourself off. It took me moments."

"I'll have that challenge now," she said, trying to sound icy.

Now the laughter had moved into his green eyes, making them brighter, which didn't help. "Right. Are you sure?"

And she wanted to scream, but they were in public. Jenny leaned forward instead. "I'm beginning to think that you're stalling, actually. What's the matter, Dylan? Are you afraid that after all this talk you won't be able to handle your end of the bargain?"

She could only describe the look on his face then as pitying.

"We covered number one, which is that I'm in charge," he said by way of a reply. As if she hadn't spoken. "I wouldn't want to forget number two."

"What's that? I fling myself prostrate at your feet and call you master?"

"You can call me anything you want." There was still laughter in Dylan's eyes, and that pitying thing, as if she was already over her head and she didn't know it.

And too many things rolled through her, all at

once. Maybe that outrage she'd been reaching for all along. Or maybe something worse. Less palatable.

Maybe something like longing, something in her whispered.

"As I said, I'm a greedy fucker," Dylan told her, calmly. Much too calmly. "I'm not always gentle. I like it hard and I like it rough, and when I say that I want you to let me be in charge, that also means I want you to trust me. But that goes both ways. I have to trust that you'll tell me if something's too intense for you."

She lifted her chin. "It won't be."

"That's big talk, Jenny. But it's easy to think you'll feel one way now, then find you feel a completely different way later. You don't have to make a speech. All you have to do is tell me. Stop. No. Raise a hand. Push me off. No matter how far we've gone, or what's going on. Do you understand that?"

"I understand that once again, there's a whole lot of talking and explaining and anticipation, and yet nothing happens."

"This is nonnegotiable."

There was that kick to his voice, and the cool, certain way he looked at her. She remembered, yet again and with that same flood of awareness, that this person she was discussing sex with was not the easygoing friend she knew so well. This was the other Dylan. And the other Dylan was one of the most powerful men in the world.

And he wasn't kidding around.

"I'm beginning to think I trusted you more before all of this," Jenny said.

"We don't have to do it then," he replied, too easily for her liking. He even shrugged. "It's entirely up to you. I'm happy to go on home, sleep it off and wake up tomorrow as if none of this ever happened."

Jenny wanted to punch him. Hard, right in his annoyingly gorgeous face. She felt distinctly violent, and it seemed connected to all the other sensations dancing around inside of her. "I have to tell you, so far I don't really understand how you've managed to talk any woman into sleeping with you. Much less legions."

"Most of them aren't you," he replied. Wholly unbothered, it would appear. "I'm not the one who's stalling, Jenny."

Ouch.

"I will tell you to stop if I want you to stop," she said, very directly, and she knew that he was right. That she was the one who'd been stalling, because her pussy was still swollen, she was too wet and she couldn't get her head around what happened already. She could feel his shoulder against her thigh and his ravenous mouth, devouring her. And that flush was a part of her now, betraying her and heating her in turn. "And now I want that challenge."

A different sort of smile played around Dylan's mouth, then. "Last opportunity to keep that door shut," he said softly. "To keep it at a crack. Not throw it wide open."

"Now who's stalling?"

Dylan didn't look away. He kept that green gaze trained on her and as she watched, it grew more intense. Until she felt as if his intensity overtook her pulse, then moved through her veins. "There's a bathroom in the hall," he said quietly. "We passed it on our way in. I want you to go there. I want you to take off all your clothes, though you can leave your shoes on. I like the heel."

She was mute. Overwhelmed. But she couldn't tear her gaze away from his.

By contrast, Dylan looked perfectly relaxed, save for that glittering in his green eyes that made her clit throb.

"I'll want you bent over, bracing yourself on your elbows. Eyes closed, hair down. And I want you to wait for me."

"With the door unlocked?"

"I want you to wait for me," he said again, with that pointed patience that made her feel weak. And something like bubbly. "Can you do that?"

"I…" But her throat wasn't working properly. And her mouth was so dry she thought she might go up in flames.

Maybe she already had.

"You don't have to tell me about it, Jenny," Dylan said in that quiet, powerful way of his. It hummed inside of her. "You don't have to find the words. You can either get up from the table and make your way to that bathroom, or you can sit here. We can discuss the weather, or the football. Old stories from uni. And everything will go back to normal. It's entirely up to you."

The breath in her lungs felt too hot. It took up too much space, and was much heavier than normal breath. Jenny was shaking so hard she worried she might fly apart at the seams, but when she looked down at her hands, she wasn't shaking at all.

And she wanted to find the words, to find *something* to help her gain her footing again—

But something washed over her as she gazed into the quiet, unmistakable challenge in his green eyes. It wasn't quite peace. It was too jagged and edgy for that.

Still, it helped.

And he was Dylan. With new and surprising facets, but still her Dylan. He would keep her safe. He would keep that bubble of his around them, and whatever happened there, it would be okay. She knew without a shred of doubt that he would fight to keep it that way.

Jenny pushed her chair back. She stood and tossed her linen napkin on the table.

Then she turned, and walked off to take his challenge.

And she had every intention of acing it.

CHAPTER EIGHT

JENNY MADE HER way through the rooftop restaurant, only vaguely aware that there were other people tucked away in their own little pockets of privacy in the soft, close dark. Because all she could think about was Dylan.

All versions of Dylan.

She found the door that led into the building, then down the same hallway they'd come up—while she'd been reeling from his mouth and barely aware that she was upright and walking.

Sure enough, there was another door with a WC slapped on the front. She stood in front of it for a moment, wracked with indecision, and then swallowed. Hard. She looked around, but there was only the one. No chance that she might arrange herself fetchingly in the wrong bathroom.

She laughed a little bit at that, but when the laugh was done, she was still standing there in the hallway. Definitely stalling, and after all that big talk at the table.

"Right, then," she told herself bracingly, as if that could launch her forward.

As if what she really needed here was a stern talking to, and then what she was about to do would all seem normal.

But it was Dylan. And she'd come here for this. And even though everything that had happened tonight was so far out of the realm of what she'd imagined or anticipated, it was all right, somehow. Because it was Dylan, and if she believed nothing else, she believed in him.

She always had—but maybe this wasn't the right time to dig into her long friendship with a man who'd apparently had *all of this* inside him all the while.

She pushed her way into the bathroom. It was small, but still managed to seem infinitely luxurious the way everything else did in this place. There was only one stall, but it was behind its own full door and it was empty when she checked.

There was dim, inviting light from a sconce on the wall. The sink was ornate, with fluffy towels on the counter and a selection of not only soaps and lotions, but a variety of toiletries.

Including condoms.

And it was only when she could hear the way she was panting—actually *panting*—that she realized there was no music piped in. It was hushed and quiet here.

"There will be no hiding," she whispered, to test it. And her own voice seemed unduly loud.

She felt drunk, she realized then. That was different than shakiness, and better, in a way. It made her feel less fragile, and more liquid.

Jenny stared at herself in the mirror that took up the whole of the wall over the sink, and there was absolutely no doubt in her mind that Dylan knew it was right there. And more, that she would be doing exactly this as she decided whether or not to do what he'd asked.

And just as she found him difficult to recognize tonight, she looked like a different version of herself, too. Her eyes were wide and her pupils were dilated. Her hair was full and wavier than usual, because his hands had been in it. Her mouth felt overly sensitive, and her lips were more swollen than before. He'd done that, too.

And the Lady Jenny Markham she had always been would never do something like this. She would never so much as consider it. Lady Jenny Markham was unfailingly polite, scrupulously well mannered, and she did not create scenes. Ever. She did volunteer charity work. She facilitated conversations between the kinds of businessmen who frequented clubs like this, and made them run smoother. She was a credit to her bloodline, as her father liked to tell his friends.

But Lady Jenny Markham was the one who was going to dutifully marry Conrad and live out the rest of her glacially polite days in precisely the manner her father wanted. Quiet gentility, companionship without emotion, like well-appointed rooms in silent houses. It would be a very pretty grave she was walking into. She knew that.

Tonight, she was only a woman. And Dylan had already done things to her that didn't make sense, that she couldn't even begin to process, and that had taught her that she was more alive and more hungry than she'd ever dreamed possible.

And she wanted to take this challenge, not because she thought that she wouldn't like the things he wanted to do to her. But because she wanted him to do them. Now.

She pulled off the soft shirt she wore that managed somehow to look a lot fancier that it was. Then she shrugged out of the tighter tank she'd worn beneath it, that kept her breasts in place without too much fuss. She sighed a little as she pulled it up and over her head, because the fabric dragged against her nipples and it was like lightning stormed through her in response. And it turned out her nipples had a direct line to her clit, and she couldn't tell the difference, anymore, between what hurt and what might just make her come again.

The bathroom floor was covered in a thick, gorgeous rug, so she kicked off her shoes, then stripped herself of her jeans. Remembering all the while that he'd done it once tonight already.

And he'd already ripped her panties off, so that was it, she was naked. And the sheer illicitness of it, to stand in a bathroom, of all places—naked, in public, when anyone could walk in—

Jenny had to steady herself with a hand on the counter. She stepped back into her shoes, carefully because she kept shivering, and moved to the sink, as ordered.

As ordered.

The words seemed to take on weight and heft, and she was glad she was bending over because she could prop herself up. And maybe not topple over, that way. The heels made her hips hitch up higher, leaving her angled toward the door to the hall that was directly behind her. Whoever walked in—and God help her, it could be *anyone*—would see her spread out before them.

Her ass and her pussy were on full display, and there was nothing she could do about that. There was no hiding it, or pretending for a moment she wasn't doing exactly what she was doing.

The heat inside her leaped into a bright flame, and burned.

Hot. Long.

Jenny dropped her head, letting it droop down toward her elbows. Her hair fell all around her. She shut her eyes.

And then she waited.

And she was shivering, though she wasn't cold.

She could feel the air all around her, and she had never been naked in a public place before—because of course she hadn't. And anyone could walk in. And even if the only person who did walk in was Dylan, that was its own problem, surely, because what did he plan to *do*—

The door swung open and a flash of ice cascaded over her, dousing her with a thousand pinpricks of pure fear.

And then in the next moment, the stunning heat of shame.

Jenny was frozen. There was no sound. She heard the door swing shut, and it had to be him. Surely it needed to be him, because anyone else would react to the sight of her. A stranger would make some kind of a sound, some kind of embarrassed cough or laugh—

But there was nothing but silence.

And her breathing was beginning to sound high-pitched and labored. She couldn't tell if she was hot or cold, but she was sweating either way. Her toes were curling up in her shoes, which was making her hips lift higher, and if it wasn't him, would whoever it was think that it was an invitation—

Of course they would think it was an invitation—

"Very nice," Dylan said, and the relief that swamped her then was as sharp and thick as what had come before. It almost knocked her sideways. "I wasn't sure you could follow directions, Jenny. I'm proud of you."

And he was behind her, then. She even thought she could feel the heat he generated, though he didn't touch her.

"Look at you. That pussy is so wet. So needy. There's only one thing for it."

Jenny had lost the power of speech. She'd left it somewhere in that neat pile of her clothes, and she thought she would die… If he touched her. If he didn't. If he didn't *do something* with her, because the fact he'd even mentioned her pussy made it throb. And she could feel a surge of raw, molten need overtake her again.

Then he touched her at last, coming up flush behind her so she could feel the scratchy material of his jeans against the curve of her ass. And his hands moved, running up the length of her spine, then down again. As if he was memorizing her. Then down the length of her arms, too. One hand moved to the nape of her neck, his thumb moving in a restless sort of demand, and she didn't understand how this small a touch could undo her so completely.

She felt moisture in the corners of her eyes again, and she knew that it was tears. Though she was nothing so simple as sad. Jenny couldn't contain all the things she felt inside. They wouldn't fit.

He shifted again, and reached out. She heard him pick up something from the array beside her. He let go of her for a moment, though he still stood close behind her. He unzipped his jeans and the sound of it was like a scream, there in the hushed confines of this bathroom.

Then she felt him, silken hot and hard like steel against the curves of her ass.

And this was *Dylan*. That was Dylan's cock, huge and hard behind her, and it was Dylan who she'd come all this way to see, when she had no idea what she was asking for. Just as he'd told her she didn't.

Dylan, something in her screamed. As if maybe she should stop this.

But it only made her wetter.

She heard the sound of the condom packet ripping, and some movement from behind her. Then one of his arms came beneath her hips to angle her up higher, even farther onto her toes.

"Tiptoes, please," he said, and the fact he could sound so normal made her shudder.

And then he was *there*, the broad, wide head of his cock pushing into her folds. She was glad she was so sodden, so hot already, because he was already a stretch.

He didn't wait. He didn't let her get used to him. He pushed into her, relentless and sure.

And worse, somehow, *slow*.

Inexorable.

All she could feel was that stretch, that radical fullness. He was too big, and she wanted to panic, but all she could do was pant.

Still he pushed in, inch by inch, crowding her. Taking her over.

And when she thought she might move her hips a bit to make it better, to ease that initial penetration, she realized that he was holding her fast. He was making her take it. Forcing her to accept him, all of him, just as he liked.

She cracked, then, the orgasm walloping her, though she was not entirely comfortable, not sure she could be, and she was bent over a sink with her ass in the air and he was inside her—*Dylan was inside her*—and she was entirely full of his cock, so big and so hard she didn't understand how she'd spent all this time in his presence and never noticed that he was *huge*—

When he was fully inside her, thrust deep, he stopped. She kept clenching and shuddering around him, but he stayed still and hard.

And something flipped over inside her, some kind of awe, as it began to dawn on her that he was totally and completely in control of himself.

"Stand up," Dylan said, and his voice was huskier. That was it. "And you can open your eyes if you like."

But his arm was still tight around her hips, so as she straightened, she had to arch.

And that was what she saw as she rose. Her body arched toward the mirror, her breasts high and her nipples tight, and some other woman's face where hers ought to have been. Wild and abandoned and drunk on sensation.

While behind her, Dylan loomed dark, hard and *everything*.

His cock was lodged deep inside her, and he kept himself there as she came up, his other hand moving around to the front of her. He traced a light line down the front of her, trailing fire, then pressed hard where they were joined, letting her know without a word how well he knew her clit already. How easily he commanded it, and her.

And satisfaction glinted in his gaze when she let out a soft cry, another punch of something not quite an orgasm slamming into her. He moved his hand up over her belly, letting her feel her own moisture as he slowly dragged his way across her skin. And he held himself still, his cock hard and deep, as his hand found her breast. He weighed it in his palm, then dragged his thumb over her nipple, making her moan as the sensation punched through her again.

Still his hand rose, while his green gaze pinned her in the mirror as surely as his cock was buried inside her. His hand kept moving, until it came up to circle her throat.

"I don't want you to forget where we are, slip off your tiptoes and choke," he told her, dark and low. His hand almost a collar, but not quite. Dylan and not Dylan, all at once, and that was its own punch. "But that might take work. I want you to do that work."

And she could see herself. She could see that dazed look on her face and the way each breath she took made her breasts bounce a little. More than that, she could see the intensity in his gaze, and the absolute certainty.

It made her, if not certain on her own, willing to trust that he was.

She nodded, but she couldn't access her voice. And she couldn't keep her hands from coming up to grip onto his strong forearm.

"If you don't want my hand there, that's fine," he told her, his green gaze direct. So intense she was sure that he could see straight through her, as deep as that giant cock of his was, buried inside her. "Pull it away. All right?"

Again, she nodded, and she could feel his hand strong at her throat. Not tight, but the faint suggestion of restriction made a new kind of sensation prickle down her back. Her clit seemed to swell.

"Up on your toes, Jenny," he said again, darker this time.

And then he fucked her.

There was no other word for it, and with each deep, raw slam of his cock deep into her body, she understood the difference in a way no one could possibly have explained to her.

If there was a rhythm, she couldn't catch it. There was no way to move her hips, either with him or against him.

It was a hammering.

He held her at her hips and at her throat, and it was up to her to grip his arm. To stand up on the very tips of her toes—because if she didn't, she would collapse against him and maybe choke for a moment. Or worse, he would stop.

It was a storm. It was magnificent, it was terrifying, and he fucked her hard.

And he changed her, every time his cock slammed deep.

Because his green gaze never wavered. He kept it trained on hers, and he watched as she sobbed. As she cried out. She hung on for dear life, he hammered into her and her body exploded.

Over and over again.

And it wasn't just her clit. Her whole body seem to come, not just her nipples and her pussy, but everything. Every inch of her, a clenching and a shuddering, inside and out. He fucked her relentlessly, so hard it was like he was making her new.

He fucked her while she burned and fell apart, and he fucked her on and on until she couldn't tell the difference between the fucking and the coming, a sob and a sigh.

And when she finally drooped a little, still trying to hold on to his forearm but no longer able to make her fingers grip, he shifted. He pulled out, then tumbled her down with him onto the ground. And that was part of it, she understood—that it was

a bathroom. That no matter how nice the rug, it was
on a bathroom floor.

And she didn't care. She didn't care about anything
but Dylan coming down over her, still fully dressed,
except for the jeans he'd opened to let himself free.

She had a glimpse of it, his huge, hard cock. And
the look on his face, almost like an agony, as he
stretched out over her. He pulled one of her knees
up high, then sank deep into her again.

Then, if it was possible, he fucked her even harder.
Even deeper.

And Jenny was sure she was done, that her body
couldn't take any more, but he dropped his head to
her breast and sucked her nipple deep into his mouth.
She came, that easily. Once, then again. And when
she was positive that this time, she really was finished, he grinned at her. All wolf.

Dylan reached down between them and pinched
her clit, hard.

Jenny screamed, but his other hand was there,
covering her mouth. Taking the sound. Making it
part of her coming again, in a wild, clenching rush.

Then he was groaning too, and she could feel
him shudder as he came. His whole body shook as
he pumped himself into her, it seemed to go on forever, and that was even hotter.

For a long while, there was nothing but breath.
Both of them, breathing heavily and loud in the quiet
little room.

He was crushing her down into the plush rug, and she could feel his cock inside her, semihard still. Dylan stirred, after what seemed like another long while, and lifted his weight off her.

And when his eyes met hers, she could have sworn that for the first time in as long as she'd known him, he looked guarded.

Jenny didn't think. She lifted her hand, and took his face in her palm. She wanted to ask him if he was all right, but there was something in his face that kept her from it.

So instead, she kissed him, and not one of those carnal, impossible kisses from before.

This was sweet. Soft. It made her want to cry.

And maybe it did something to him, too, because he looked away. His breath came heavy again, but then he was rolling off her, and she had to cope with how empty she felt without his cock so deep inside her.

He moved to the sink and handled the condom, then he zipped himself up. And when he looked back at her, she could only imagine how she looked. Sprawled out naked, save for a pair of heels, utterly and completely debauched on the bathroom floor.

It was Dylan who had done this to her.

Her Dylan, and Jenny could feel a reckoning gathering around her. She understood that there was no possible way that she could process any of what had

happened tonight, maybe ever. In that moment, she
didn't care about that, either.

He looked down at her, and he had that stranger's
face on, and now she knew what it meant. Now she
knew all of him.

She lifted her arms up over her head, and she
stretched. She felt sleepy, comprehensively used in
the best kind of way, and the smile that took over
her face felt silly.

Giddy, even.

But she let it. She didn't try to hide it.

Because there might be hell to pay later, so there
was no point pretending now.

"That was nice enough, Dylan, thanks," she told
him, in a voice that sounded cracked and torn and
as thoroughly debauched as the rest of her. "But is
that really all you've got?"

CHAPTER NINE

OF ALL THE mistakes Dylan had made in his lifetime, most of them concerning Jenny, this one was the worst.

The absolute worst of all. He knew it, and there was nothing for it.

It was done.

He helped her get to her feet, unable to keep himself from grinning as she fell against him, and laughed uproariously. For all intents and purposes, she looked drunk.

On him.

"I understand you're underwhelmed, Jenny," he murmured. "But any reasonable person would have to describe your particular behavior just now as a bit giddy, don't you think?"

He was already hard again, because this was Jenny and he had years to make up for. He watched her as she pulled her clothes back on, then did nothing more with her hair than run a hand through it. And like that, she was once again the very picture of casual elegance.

"I'll concede what happened was indeed a fuck-ing," she said, as if they were back in Oxford, study-ing something boring. She even managed to look prim, as if he hadn't just been inside her. "But whether or not it was *proper*, I couldn't say. I don't have any context, do I?"

"I think your whole life until now would qualify as context," he said dryly.

"You've taught me the difference between a shag and a fuck." She sketched a little curtsy that was so cute he thought his chest might crack open. "But now I think we need to turn our attention to what makes for a *proper* fucking, which as you may recall was what the doctor ordered."

He was leaning back against the counter, near her but not touching her. Because if he touched her again, he would repeat what had just happened. And as tempting as that was, he had a powerful need to put this woman in his bed, at last. Then take his sweet time. Over and over again, until he lost track.

And before she woke in the bright light of a new day and thought better of all of this.

"Your wish is my command, as always," he told her.

She laughed at that, as if it wasn't the humbling truth of his entire adult life. His guiding star, even. His true north had always been Jenny, and he sus-pected it always would be, whether she was married or not. But that was one more thing he kept to himself.

He threw open the door, watching Jenny turn red as she noticed that he hadn't bothered to lock it. And he liked the way she blushed so much that he decided not to tell her that there was no need to lock the door when the staff was perfectly well trained to take care of any possible interlopers. Why ruin her fantasy that she could have been walked in on at any time?

Dylan led her out a different door than the one they'd come in, this one higher up the hill, where a car waited for them. Because he didn't feel like driving them home tonight, as that might require he take his hands off her.

And he might only have this one night. He couldn't let himself forget that for a second. He had to make the most of it.

But when Dylan settled in the backseat beside her, he wasn't prepared for the way Jenny melted into his side. She *snuggled* into him, then dropped her head to his shoulder. As if they'd done this a thousand times before and she knew she would fit next to him so well. As if it was normal for them to cuddle up in the backseat of a car, or anywhere else.

And what killed him was that it felt perfectly normal. It felt right. Everything with Jenny always did and always had. That was just one of the many ways she'd ruined him from the start.

Because there was no having her. There was only losing her.

He'd made a decision a long time ago to make himself over into whoever and whatever she needed, even if that meant not getting what he wanted. That meant he got a hell of a lot more than any of those idiots who'd tried to be her boyfriend.

Tonight he'd crossed every last line he'd ever drawn.

He could boss everything around as he pleased, and did, but he had no control over his own damned heart.

And he had to sit with that, staring out the window as the lights of Sydney blurred together in front of him. Jenny was a soft weight against him, her breath slow and even and her face buried against his shoulder.

For once in his life, he had everything he'd ever wanted. And more than he'd imagined was possible.

Enjoy it, mate, he told himself darkly.

Because it wouldn't last. It couldn't last.

Her hand was on his leg, and the light spilled in from the streets outside. It made her look even prettier, which shouldn't have been possible.

It also illuminated that great bloody boulder she wore on her hand. The ring that reminded him that she wasn't his. That this was an interlude from her real life. That she'd come here because she knew exactly what she was getting herself into with this marriage her father wanted, and this was her last chance to taste how the other half lived before she surrendered to it.

He knew her too well. She might come to the other side of the globe to experiment, but she was going to go straight back. Jenny was going to lock herself away in her lonely little life, by choice. She was going to stay there, getting more brittle and far away by the year. He could see it all spin out in front of him.

She was never going to give him what he wanted from her.

Everything had changed and nothing had changed.

And at least Dylan could say he'd chosen his own ruin. At least he had that.

That was what he told himself when they arrived at his house. She was still so sleepy that he had to lift her into his arms, then carry her inside, the way he'd longed to do a million times before.

He didn't take her into the guest room. He headed up the stairs to the master bedroom instead, because he could feel time slipping away from them. And he didn't want to waste any of it. He lay her out on his big wide bed and helped her off with her clothes. He expected her to wake up, but she didn't. She murmured something when she was naked, then curled up on her side, burying her face in his pillow.

Dylan didn't have it in him to pretend that he was anything but shaken.

He didn't have to pretend, because she was asleep.

And he could take the opportunity to acknowledge that for all he'd tried his best to scare her off, or prepare her, he was the one who was losing it. Who'd already lost it. Who could do nothing but sit in a chair next to his own bed, staring at this woman who was every single one of his dreams come true.

Only while she slept, unknowing, could he think about the fact that she'd obeyed him completely. That he'd fit inside her, perfectly. There had been no wincing in pain. No adjustments.

It was as if Lady Jenny Markham had been put on this earth for the express purpose of taking his cock deep inside of her.

Dylan knew that not a single one of those little wankers who'd put their hands on her before him had ever treated her like that. They'd bored her silly. They'd made her imagine she was frigid when she couldn't *stop* coming.

She was supposed to be his.

Dylan had known that from the start. And he'd already spent a lifetime seeing her when he closed his eyes, so tonight, he didn't want to.

He wanted his eyes wide open. He didn't want to miss a single moment.

The way she breathed. The way she looked in his bed.

The way her face softened. The way she trusted him this much.

Dylan wanted all of it.

Because none of it was ever going to be enough. And it was more than he deserved. It was as if he'd only just found her, and he had to let her go.

The real problem was, he didn't know if he had it in him.

How could he possibly let her go when he knew, now? Exactly how good it really was. Far, far better than he'd dared imagine. And he had an epic, detailed, innovative imagination.

So Dylan sat where he was. He didn't move. He let the night grow later and later, the hour smaller and smaller, and he didn't care when his eyes began to feel gritty and his body began to protest.

He stayed where he was, because he wanted every single second of this. Every last second.

When Jenny's eyes fluttered open, hours later, she looked around in confusion for a moment, then landed on him.

And smiled automatically, big and sleepy.

This is how you'll do it, mate, he told himself. *You'll do it for her. You'll make her smile and wave her off.*

And he'd deal with the fallout later. When she'd gone.

When she was finally lost to him forever.

CHAPTER TEN

WHEN JENNY WOKE UP a great many hours later, she was naked again.

Better yet, she was in Dylan's bed. And Dylan himself was slumped out in the chair nearby, his brooding gaze on her, while outside there was the faintest suggestion that light might come again. Someday.

"Last thing I remember we were getting into a car," she said. And that giddiness she'd been after swelled in her, sharp and syrupy and everything she'd imagined it would be. She wriggled a bit, trying to really feel it. And ignoring the other parts that threatened to swamp her with unpleasant recollections that this wasn't hers to keep. Not really. "Is that your real secret, Dylan? Are you the reason I blacked out?"

He rubbed his hand over his face, grinning. "I get that a lot. My cock is a well-known roofie."

Jenny sat up, not bothering to clutch at the sheet, and watched the way his gaze dropped to her breasts.

And more, made them react. Her nipples pinched tight, and suddenly she remembered when she'd been sprawled out on the floor of that bathroom, his cock pounding into her and his mouth moving over her. His tongue and the hint of his teeth, there on that sensitive point.

Her whole body seemed to shiver into awareness.

"I don't remember what conclusion we reached." And she was aware of everything about him, now. When he tensed in the chair, though he was still slouching there as if he thought that made him look relaxed. The way his cock pushed at the front of his jeans. "Do I only get a night? Or am I a weekender? I don't dare to hope than I might have scored longer than that. Not to mention, I'm not entirely sure it would be physically possible."

"You can have as long as you like, Jenny." The remains of his grin were still on his mouth, but his eyes were in shadow. They seemed darker now. And connected to all those things inside her that she wasn't looking at. That she didn't want to process.

Not now, maybe not ever.

"Good thing you're not worried about falling in love, Dylan," she said lightly, teasing him. "You look a little wobbly there."

And she couldn't say she regretted saying it, precisely. But there was something in the air of the sprawling room, suddenly. Something like grief, raw and encompassing. Powerful and thick.

But she forgot about that when he rose to his feet.

"I told you," he said, his voice low enough to be a growl. "No chance of me falling in love with you."

And she had to wonder why she'd brought up the subject again, when it hurt to hear him say that just as much as it had the first time. More, if she was honest, because she knew better, now. He had been right. He'd been upsettingly right, in fact, about how little she knew about the things that sex could do.

But Jenny still wasn't thinking about that. Not now.

Not while he was stripping off his clothes, tossing them into the chair behind him, and then standing there a moment when he was done, astonishingly naked.

She buzzed a bit, all over, as if her skin couldn't contain all the things her body did in response to the sight of him. It was different to see him naked, even if she'd seen so much of him before. In his running shorts, for instance. And it was certainly different to look at that huge cock, standing away from his body, and understand not only that she'd taken all of that inside of her, but remembering precisely how it had felt.

She heard a greedy little noise, and was only dimly aware that she'd made it.

Jenny didn't intend to move, but she did. And next thing she knew she was kneeling down before him, her hands moving over his strong, muscled thighs.

"Kneeling already, Jenny?" he asked, in that dark, commanding voice that she was sure she'd never get used to. It seemed so unlike the man she'd known for all these years—and then again, it was the man she'd met last night, and he made her shiver, hot and ready, and it was all Dylan. All the sides of the man she knew best. "You're taking to this quickly."

"I want to taste you," she told him, solemnly.

And she kept her head tipped back, so she could watch his face as she reached up and wrapped her hands around his enormous cock. Her mouth watered, but she maintained eye contact as she tipped herself forward, then licked the broad head.

Gently, like the first, sweet taste of an ice cream cone.

He muttered something filthy.

"Is that a yes or no?" she asked. Then she took a moment to suck him, deep into her mouth, so she could play with suction. And the flat of her tongue. Then she grinned at him. "You'll have to speak up."

Dylan laughed, then, a dark and wondrous thing.

She felt him move, though she didn't understand what he was doing for a moment, because the taste of him was rolling through her, male and salty and a hint of what she thought was her, too. The blaze of it surged through her, igniting a new fire and making her pussy clench.

But then his hand was in her hair. He twisted it around, until she realized he was gripping her hair like it was some kind of leash. And something about that made her feel almost sluggish with longing. As if she might not be able to bear it—she wanted this so much.

She dragged her eyes back up the perfect, beautiful length of his body, and found him watching her.

"Hands behind your back," he told her, softly.

"Behind my back?" She didn't understand. "But then I can't—"

"Use them. Or control a thing. I told you I was bossy."

She couldn't tell if it scared her or she liked the challenge of it. Or something in between. But it didn't matter, because when he looked at her like that, with his cock so hard, she rather thought she would do anything he asked. Anything at all.

Jenny let go of his cock, though she didn't want to. And she slid her hands behind her, lacing her fingers together. The position made her arch her back a bit, so her breasts jutted forward, and she saw the appreciative gleam in his eyes.

Worth it right there, she thought.

She liked it even better when he smiled. And Jenny liked it best of all when he tugged a bit on the hair he held in his fist while his other thumb tracked over her mouth.

Not entirely gently. Rude and rough, and it was like a coarse fire consumed her.

"I remember you and Erika trading stories about

the dicks you've sucked." There was a faint, dull ache from how tight he held her hair and that drugging glory of his rough thumb against her lips. "She always loved sex, and we know you didn't, but both of you wielded blowjobs like weapons."

"I wouldn't say that. Exactly."

His thumb pressed over her lips, silencing her.

"I've spent years wondering what it must have been like to be one of those undeserving gobshites, too bleeding stupid to realize you were literally leading them around by the cock." His head tilted slightly to one side as he regarded her, and her stomach quivered. "Is that what you think will happen here? You'll suck me off and reduce me to a blithering mess like all the rest of them? Prepared to follow you to the ends of the earth, desperate for one more lukewarm touch?"

But his thumb was over her mouth, so she couldn't answer. And that was just as well, because she didn't know what she would say. Because he had always talked about her sad love life as if she had all the power when Jenny hadn't exactly seen it that way.

Though tonight she had only the driving need to taste him. That made a stark difference from how she'd treated getting a man off in the past, admittedly.

Men are easy, Erika had declared long ago, dancing with a bottle from the off-license in the street, just begging for trouble. *All you need to do is gaze up at them, beg them for their cock and they're yours.*

Jenny had never done it because she'd found men easy. She'd done it because they were complicated, and wanted things from her she'd had no intention of giving. And because sometimes sex itself didn't do the trick.

Men were visual—wasn't that what everyone always said? They liked a girl kneeling in front of them, or crawling down the length of them on a bed. Until tonight, she'd never really understood the appeal of oral sex. Personally.

She did now.

Back then, however, she remembered giggling wildly with Erika as they'd shared their thoughts on how best to go about handling the boys who'd followed them around. Had they really admitted to that in front of Dylan?

But he was Dylan. He'd always been right there. She might have said anything at all.

"Keep your hands behind your back," he told her, another quiet command. "If you lift them up, I'll stop. Do you understand?"

She nodded, and as she did, he worked his thumb between her lips. It was rude. Obvious. And even so, she sucked on him anyway, and her pussy clenched tight.

"Tell me, Jenny. How's your gag reflex?" Dylan

laughed, with his thumb against her tongue. "That gets you all wide-eyed, does it? I guess we'll see."

He pulled his thumb from her mouth and she felt herself sway, even though that shouldn't have been possible. Not with him holding her like that. A fist in her hair, his cock huge and hard between them and that implacable look on his face.

He made it impossible to remember all the sharp and clever things she'd planned to say. All the ways she'd intended to make him laugh, and remember that she wasn't just another one of his giddy, disposable girls.

But her mouth watered, because his cock was so beautiful, though she had never used that word to describe that part of a man's anatomy before. It was different when it was Dylan. Or maybe because it was so *big*.

"You can have it, Jenny," he promised her, in that low, insinuating way of his. "You'll have to beg me."

And before she'd gotten on that plane, Jenny would have laughed at the idea that she would ever kneel before anyone and beg. For this or anything else. Even earlier tonight, as she'd waited for him by the opera house, she would have rolled her eyes if he'd sauntered up to her and predicted she would beg for the privilege of taking him in her mouth.

But he'd been right about that, too. She felt like a different person. Like a stranger to whoever that Jenny had been.

Because *this* Jenny knew that if she didn't get the chance to taste that cock, to feel him in her mouth, she would die.

"Please," she said, with no hesitation. "Please, Dylan. I want it."

"You want what?"

She gasped a little, but she couldn't have said if it was her breath tangling in her throat or the sudden understanding of what it was he wanted her to say. And she didn't care. She could picture what she looked like, kneeling here on his floor, her head pulled back with his faintly cruel hand in a fist there. And his cock close, but not close enough.

Jenny pictured it, and she didn't understand how that could make her clit ache, but it did. Oh, how it did.

She shifted, trying to get her thighs closer together to give herself some relief. And was somehow not surprised at all when Dylan stopped her, putting his foot between her knees and holding her legs apart.

"You come when I let you come," he told her. "I thought you understood."

"Please, Dylan," she heard herself say again, more frantic this time. It was no longer clear to her what she was begging for, only that he needed to give it to her. Whatever it was.

"Tell me what you want," he said, all dark command.

"I want you to fuck my mouth." Jenny felt her

nipples get even harder at that. Just as her pussy felt soaked. And her clit pulsed with a need like pain, but better. Much better. "Make me come, Dylan. Please."

"You've come a thousand times, by any estimate." As he spoke, he wrapped his own big hand around his cock, then worked it, and it was an agonizing thing to watch. And not only because it was so like that image she'd had of him doing precisely this. "What makes you think you deserve more?"

"Please," she begged him.

His eyes no longer looked green at all. They were black and fierce, and she was all fire and flutter, and she made a sobbing sound she didn't recognize.

Then she didn't care what she sounded like, because he was pressing his cock between her lips at last.

She half expected him to thrust in deep, the way he had earlier, but he didn't.

He wasn't gentle, exactly, but he started slow. He let her taste him. He made a rumbling sound of approval when she used her tongue, teasing that ridge that separated the head from the shaft, then taking him in deeper.

And it was different. It was wildly different from anything she'd ever known, and she couldn't understand why. But her clit kept pulsing, she was soaking wet and as he moved, his thighs brushed against her breasts. That sent delicious spirals of pure sensation arrowing through her. Once again, there was moisture in the corners of her eyes, as her mouth stretched wide to take as much of him as she could.

He used his grip in her hair to guide her, or to hold her still. Whatever he wished. He surged into her, backing off if he went too far, but then—once he knew how far he could go—he did exactly what she'd asked him to do.

And fucked her mouth.

It was a lit match, then a wildfire. It was an ecstatic, glorious thing, so much sensation crashing over her and through her that she almost felt skinless. There was his dark gaze. The implacable wall of his gorgeous body. His hard hand in her hair and the other at her jaw.

There was the ferocity on his face, and in between all of that, part of it and because of it, there was her.

And that was it, she understood as she tipped herself over and gave herself up entirely into his hands. Less a surrender than a becoming.

She wanted to taste him, and she got that, raw and real.

And when he gave a shout and flooded her mouth, she felt her own body convulse, and realized she'd pressed her greedy pussy against his leg. And the sheer joy of tasting him, that intense punch of salt and man, made it go on and on.

He pulled her off his cock, and for moment he stared down at her, his chest heaving.

And she thought she recognized him at last, in that wild expression he aimed at her—

But something in her shied away from naming it.

And then he was lifting her up, hauling her into his arms again, then carrying her into his en suite. He set her down in his shower that was three sides glass, and when he turned the water on it was as if they were standing in the Tasman Sea itself.

The water beat over her, she found herself speechless as she slumped there against the wall, watching him.

She'd had a mouthful of Dylan. And that thought was so wrong and so perfect at the same time that it almost sent her over that edge again.

And maybe she'd made some kind of sound, because he looked over then, and she understood in a flash why it was that sucking Dylan's cock—a sentence she never would have allowed herself to think before in all her life—was so different. She couldn't remember ever doing something like it before.

Because she hadn't.

Because she'd always done exactly what he'd accused her of doing. She'd kept a blowjob in her back pocket to change the conversation. To end a fight. To make unpleasantness go away with a little bit of suction.

This was different, not only because Dylan had taken complete control. In such a masterful fashion that it made her breasts feel heavy and her belly feel unbearably light. Shivery. This was also different because she hadn't thought of what she would gain from it at all. She'd wanted the taste of him, but more than that, she'd wanted to make him happy.

She'd wanted to please him, far more than she'd wanted to please herself.

That struck her as the kind of revelation that if she thought about too closely, might make her curl up into a ball somewhere.

And she was naked in Dylan's astonishingly luxurious shower, and it was no time or place for the fetal position.

"Look at me," she said softly, all too aware of the rough scrape of her voice. "Trapped between the devil and the deep blue sea. Literally."

"Very droll." He moved closer to her, and he didn't ask as he took some of his shower gel and began to lather her up.

He didn't ask, but she didn't mind at all, because that meant his hands were all over her, but extra slippery. And there was a wickedness in his gaze as he tended to her breasts with particular care, until she was rising up on her tiptoes, arching her back, pressing herself even more fully into his palms.

And by the time they were both squeaky clean, she was panting again, with this maddening need for him that only seemed to get worse.

He took her out of the shower, toweled her off and then he led her out into the bedroom again, where it was still night, but barely. And they were both a bit damp as they rolled together on that great bed of his, and Jenny moaned out loud with sheer delight at the feel of his full, naked body stretched out against hers. All the places they were the same, and far more places where they were different.

Dylan brushed her wet hair back, and he took her mouth, and still they rolled this way, then that, as he kissed her with the same raw power he'd done everything else. And she could feel him again, hard and ready.

He pulled back, and then went for his nightstand, but she'd had him in her mouth. She didn't want to feel anything between them. She wanted the full experience.

"I'm on the pill," she panted at him. "I told you already. And I fully trust your test results. We're both gloriously adult, we've had a frank discussion and I really, really want to feel you inside me. Just you, Dylan."

It seemed to take him a long, long time to look back at her. And when he did, she felt everything tremble. The way he looked at her made her quake.

He reached for her, and then pulled her over him, settling her into place astride him.

"Go on," he said as she braced herself against his chest, and looked down at him with delight. "For that, you can play awhile."

"I'm on top. Does that mean I get to be in charge?"

There was a flash of his grin, but it was a sharp, edgy thing. "I said you can play. Make yourself come, however you can. See how long it takes you."

She was in the grip of that fever that never ended, so she didn't waste time asking for clarification. She didn't care. Dylan was sprawled out beneath her and she lifted herself up, canting her hips back so she could find the broad head of his cock with her pussy. Then she began to work him inside of her.

She was wet and slippery, and so hot he hissed a little as he slid into her.

And she had half a mind to tease them both, to draw it out.

But he felt too good. She wanted him too desperately. And his hands were looped around her waist, part of this but not helping her, as she settled herself down and took all of him.

And then she began to rock herself silly.

His cock was a wonder, so big it rubbed up hard against that spot inside of her that made her feel loopy. And every time she rocked herself against him, the hard wall of his abdomen rubbed against her clit.

And she was shaking and sobbing as she moved, faster and faster, using every part of her that she could to make it better. Worse. Whatever those words even meant when it was this good. This hot. This wildly intense.

And then she was coming again, in a great, shuddering, tight wriggle of sensation.

Jenny thought she heard him laughing, dark and low.

She slumped against him, tears streaming down her cheeks again. She was gasping for breath, aware of too many things even as the aftershocks ripped through her.

The way he cradled her head against his chest. The way his other hand tracked down the length of her spine, as if to remind her where she was.

But best of all, he remained hard as steel deep inside her.

When she lifted her head, his green eyes were glittering.

Dylan wrapped his arms around her, shifted slightly and then he took control.

He fucked her, hard.

The harder and wilder he went, the more she felt like liquid gold with the rush of it. She was lost again. She was part of him. Coming and coming, until she couldn't tell the difference between coming and not coming, when there was only him. And the relentless way he drove inside of her.

On and on, until there was no difference between the way she sobbed and the way she shuddered. It was all Dylan.

And when he came again, he shouted out her name.

Then held her there, still sprawled on top of him.

She tucked her face against his chest, and listened to his heart thunder beneath her ear.

Outside, dawn was breaking.

And Jenny knew that she'd gotten exactly what she'd wanted. What she'd asked for.

She'd been properly fucked, finally.

And more than that, she was well and truly fucked, in every other sense of the word.

Because somewhere during that last, abandoned sprint into the deepest joy she'd ever known, the truth had slammed into her along with yet another orgasm.

She'd been keeping this door shut tight as long as she'd known him. And there'd been a reason for that.

Because now that door between them was wide open, and it was far worse than she'd thought it would be.

She was in love with Dylan Kilburn. She suspected she always had been.

But he'd made it clear that he wasn't going to fall in love with her.

And Jenny had no earthly idea how she was going to live with that once she left Australia, returned to her life and married Conrad, as planned.

CHAPTER ELEVEN

He expected her to leave, but she stayed.

She stayed, and they fell face forward into one of those dreams Dylan knew all too well. The dream where Jenny lived here, with him. She slept in his bed and left her things cluttering up his countertop in the bathroom. Bizarre female things that he found fascinating, given the size of her collection and how little she used them. She started to hum again, tuneless little ditties beneath her breath as she moved around the place, and the big, heartbreakingly bright smile she gave him when he joined in made them both laugh.

Dylan knew it couldn't last, that it wasn't real. That was why he didn't do anything truly foolish, like tell his office he would be unavailable for the foreseeable future. And while he thought that his daily forays into reality would make this stolen time with her better, it didn't.

Because if he'd holed up with Jenny on a deserted island somewhere, it would have been a holiday for both of them. And he knew full well that holidays couldn't last. They never did.

Instead, he just…had Jenny. In his life. The way he'd always wanted her.

Sometimes she met him out in the city, and he took her to his favorite restaurants. New flash bars and local dives. His club, when he couldn't make it home without having her. Other nights, he met her back at his and cooked for her, if he had a mind to. Or sometimes, he came in to find her throwing a dinner together for the two of them.

It all made his heart do strange and terrible things inside his chest.

Having Jenny in his bed made it far too easy to imagine what it would be like if this was real. Jenny, there in the mornings. All that texting they did, but with Jenny actually there to pop in for lunch. Or to walk the coastal path with him. Jenny to reach over and hold his hand while they talked, as if that was the most natural thing in the world.

And in between all those sweet, domestic moments he'd never wanted, and yet found he hungered for, he got his hands on her. His hands, his mouth, his cock. And he got to live out every last fantasy he'd ever had involving this woman. From cranky morning sex to long, slow, torture for them both. He got to experiment with tying her up to his bed, bending her over the furniture, and watching how melty and sweet she got when he ordered her about.

He kept waiting for a hitch. For something to change, and ruin this thing they had going on. He expected that sooner or later, the fire would dim a bit.

But it only got stronger. The more he had her, inventive and mad, or intense and quiet, the more he wanted her.

He didn't see how he would ever be over it. The clutch of her pussy on his cock, the eagerness of her mouth. And that virgin ass he'd claimed as his, and his alone.

One night, he came home after a particularly long day filled with irritating meetings and the kind of bad mood that even the thought of his Jenny couldn't alleviate. That was what he thought, anyway, as he came in and saw her curled up in the chair in his bedroom, a book in her lap and her gaze on the sea outside.

And she made his heart flip around inside his chest, but today that made his temper kick in.

Because the longer she stayed, the easier it was to forget that this was only temporary. Dylan couldn't let himself get used to the lift he got when he walked in his house to find her there, because soon enough there would be nothing there but memories. For all the talk they'd had about *proper fucking*, he knew full well who it was who was getting well and truly fucked here.

"You don't look happy," she observed, quietly.

"I don't want to talk," he told her, his voice a low growl. "I want to fuck."

Jenny stared at him a moment, but she didn't snap back at him. Instead, she stood. And as he watched, peeled off the long-sleeved shirt and flowy pants she wore. Then, still holding his gaze, she walked over to the bed with all her natural elegance, and sat there on the foot of it.

Like the bloody queen.

That only made him angrier. Dylan stalked toward her, that raging thing in him a drumbeat against his ribs. When he got to the foot of the bed, he reached out and hauled her toward him. He tipped her back so that her legs were in the air, her head was back on the bed and he could pull her hips to the edge.

He reached down, yanked the zipper of his jeans open, and his cock was already hard. Ready. Because his cock was always hard and ready when Jenny was around. That was the problem.

And she was already wet for him. Because she was always wet for him, and that was one more thing that wouldn't matter when she left him.

Dylan slammed into her with no foreplay and no kind words, just her hips high and her legs splayed open.

She screamed with that same bright joy that lanced through him, arching up off the bed. He gripped her hips and hammered into her, because she was coming already. She was coming over and over, her pussy milking him, hot and tight.

And when she opened her eyes, her gaze was steady. Adoring.

Dylan reminded himself that was a lie, too. Or it wouldn't last anyway, so it amounted to the same thing.

He pulled out and flipped her over, so she was bent there over the bed. And he didn't have to look at those beautiful brown eyes so filled with emotion and pretend he didn't know what he saw there.

Dylan slammed back into her from behind. He watched her dig her fists into the bedclothes as he pounded into her, their bodies making a delirious sort of slapping sound every time he sank himself to the root.

And he could feel it every time she constricted around him, shuddering and shuddering. He went harder. Deeper.

And when he came, he yelled her name the way he always did. He let himself fall down over her back, fully clothed except for his cock. And because she couldn't see him, or what might be written all over his face, he buried his head in her neck.

Dylan tried to breathe. He'd spent all these years fucking other women and pretending they were her. He'd made a hobby out of it. But now he knew better.

Now he *knew*.

And he didn't see how he was going to go fooling his cock into thinking that anyone else was her. That anything else was this.

His breath sawed in and out of him. Everything hurt, and not from exertion. Jenny's lips were parted as she did her own bit of panting, and her eyelashes were dark against her cheeks. He would remember this, too. It would haunt him.

Her lashes fluttered as she opened her eyes, and then she smiled over her shoulder, intimate and soft. Dylan pulled out and turned her over, lifting her up so he could get his mouth on hers.

And he kissed her, haunted already while she was still right here, until they were both a little dizzy. Then they both lay there, breathless again, as the ocean crashed around outside and absolutely nothing changed between them.

Because it never would. Why couldn't he hold on to that the way he should?

"You're going to have to go soon," he said, because not saying it was no longer doing the trick. "Have you sorted out your plane ticket yet?"

He turned his head to look at her, stretched out beside him, and there was something stark and awful on her face. But she looked away before he could look too closely. And Dylan didn't like the fact that she was hiding something from him, or that she was feeling something she didn't want to share.

He wouldn't wish the hurt in him on anyone, especially not Jenny.

But he couldn't say he hated the idea, either.

If she hurt a little more, maybe she'd hurt him less.

And maybe you're a bleeding idiot, a caustic voice in him snarled.

"I keep meaning to do that," she said softly. To the ceiling.

Dylan sighed. "You can't hide forever, Jenny."

"On the contrary." And when she looked back at him, there was something wise and weary in her pretty eyes. It made the ache in him deepen. "It turns out you can hide forever. All you have to do is pretend to be blind."

"People are blind for a whole host of reasons," he countered. He wanted to pull her close. Or jackknife up, then storm about the room, pacing out this *mess* in him. But more than that, he *wanted* to pretend. He wanted to keep on pretending, because that was how this worked. That was how this had always worked. "And those reasons aren't going to go away simply because a person takes a long holiday and engages in a little unexpected intimacy with an old friend."

"It's not unexpected to you," she said quietly. "You told me it would happen."

And there was a part of Dylan that wanted this so badly that he thought he might break out in blisters from the wanting.

But he wasn't made of steel. And he knew what that look in her eyes meant. He was sure it was in his, too—the only grace in that being that it had always been in his eyes and all over his face. She wouldn't see any shift because there hadn't been one.

You'll have to be fine with this as is, he told himself stoutly. Bloody martyr that he'd always been. *You always thought that given the chance, she'd be head over heels in love with you. And so she is.*

But he couldn't celebrate his rightness, because it didn't matter. It changed nothing. She was Lady Jenny Markham. And he might have put a shine on things since he'd left university, but he was still nothing more than one of *those* Kilburns. He'd made a silk purse out of the proverbial pig's ear, but that didn't change what he was. Who he was.

Money would never change where he'd come from.

And a few weeks in sunny Australia, taking in the Tasman Sea, didn't change everything he knew to be true about Lady Jenny. Or, more important, Lord Fuckface himself.

Jenny might not want her arranged marriage any longer, when this was said and done. But when she got away from Dylan and flew back to England, reality would trickle in. She would remember who she was. Who she'd always been. And the complexities of the life she'd planned out long before she'd decided to come down under and see what she was missing.

Dylan knew that all he had to do was give her the faintest signal, and she would tell him every last thing he'd waited his whole life to hear. That she loved him. That finally, *finally*, she loved him.

And there was a part of him that wanted that almost more than he could bear.

He reached over and smoothed her hair back from her face. He saw her eyes get glassy, and he felt that same emotion land on his chest like a block of concrete.

In a way, he'd always known she loved him.

Because she hadn't treated him like all those other boys back when. Because he was the one she called her friend.

Dylan had always held that as a sacred trust.

Because he'd never been one of the wankers. He'd truly been her friend—that part hadn't been pretending. And that meant that now, he had to be a better friend to her than she was to herself. If he bailed on her when it mattered most, he'd be no better than every last one of those tossers who'd tried to use her for their own ends.

Dylan would bloody well love her enough to let her go.

He was sure he'd seen that shit embroidered on a tea towel somewhere.

She was still gazing at him, everything he'd ever wanted right there in her eyes—but he knew it wasn't what *she* wanted. He never had been.

"I told you what would happen," he agreed, and made himself sound *kind*. "It's a byproduct of proper fucking, remember? I did warn you."

Her eyes were glassier, then. And he knew he'd hurt her, he *hated* that he'd hurt her, but it couldn't be helped.

"A byproduct," she repeated, her voice thick. She cleared her throat. "How long does it take for it to go away?"

His hand was still on her face, and he couldn't bring himself to let go. "Not long."

"But what if—"

"There are some people in this life who've always known exactly what role they had to play," he said, gruffly. "And how to play it. You're one of them, Jenny. You've never wavered from the path you're on. As you'd normally be the first to tell me."

"This feels very far away from that path."

Dylan wanted to break things. He frowned at her instead. "If you don't want to marry Conrad, don't. But you and I both know that you should never make decisions that will impact the rest of your life when you're taking a vacation from that life. Go home, Jenny. Figure out what you want there, not here."

"What happens if I go back to my life, marinate in it for the appropriate amount of time and still find that it doesn't fit?"

And he hated the anguish he could hear in her voice. The little crack in it, the darkness in her gaze.

"You have a life already. It fits you perfectly. You're the one who told me you needed to arrange a life around your head. Not your heart. And certainly not what's between your legs."

"Sometimes I think what's between my legs is the most honest part of me."

"Coming feels like honesty," he agreed, gritting the words out. "But in the end, you can make yourself come with a vibrator. With your own fingers. And if it's just wanking in the end, you don't want to make it into something more."

"Dylan." His name was like a sob. "You have to know that I—"

But he moved his fingers to cover her mouth, because there was only so much of this he could take, and he'd passed that mark some time ago.

"I want you to imagine explaining this to your father," he said, his voice stern. And he tried to keep all that fury and hopelessness locked tight inside him. "The honesty of your pussy, for example. Will you sit down in his sodding great hall and tell him that? To explain why you've suddenly changed the whole of your life?"

"No," she whispered. "I certainly will not. And thank you for the...*clarification*."

That last word was a blow, aimed straight for the gut, but he made himself stay where he was. Jenny rolled up, then sat there for a moment with her back to him.

Then she got up and walked away.

Dylan let her go.

Because it was high time he started practicing for the real thing.

CHAPTER TWELVE

JENNY DIDN'T BOOK her ticket home the next day, as Dylan had been certain she would.

Another week rolled by, still glorious in all the same ways, but there was an edge to it now. Something dark in the midst of all that glory. And Dylan found he missed the sheer joy of his fantasy come true, but he told himself this way was better. Because this was the truth.

There was an end coming. He knew that as well as he knew his own name. Better, maybe.

But on some nights it was all too easy to forget.

Tonight, Jenny met him at his office. She smiled politely at his secretary, looking entirely too elegant and pulled together to be the same woman who, a few nights back, had met him in this very same office, and come away with rug burn on her knees.

She'd laughed that heart-stopping laugh of hers, still there on her hands and knees, and called her marks badges of honor.

Tonight it was cold and rainy. Jenny shivered in

the coat she wore as they made their way down the street toward the restaurant Dylan had picked.

"I keep forgetting it's winter here," she said.

"Winter has a way of reminding you it's around," he replied. "Like it or not."

And he was trying so hard to remember different things, now. While she told him stories from her work at her charity, he watched her hands. And that ring she'd never removed in all the time she'd been here. Despite the things they'd done. The ring that told the truth about her intentions no matter how confused she imagined she was.

It's only a matter of time, he reminded himself. *She'll be gone before you know it.*

Still, when their dinner was finished, he had every intention of taking her home, getting her naked and indulging them both. Letting their bodies say all the things he wouldn't let them say in words.

But his mobile chimed in his pocket on the street outside the restaurant, and he swore when he saw the message. "I'm going to have to go back to the office."

"That's all right," Jenny said. With another one of those smiles that killed him. "I'll wait for you."

And once again, Dylan was torn. Because he had to make an unpleasant call—and possibly deal with a whole host of other calls after it—and the part of him that had been ruined for this woman pretty much at first sight loved the idea of her waiting for him. Sitting on the couch in his office like another page out of some sweet, domestic book he would've laughed at, had he ever read such a thing. That she wanted to spend time with him even when it wasn't all about her made his heart seem to thud a little harder.

But on the other hand, it was one more thing he would have to forget when she was gone.

And he was weak, because he took her with him back to the office. And debated making the call he needed to after all, because she was so happy to wave him off and turn her attention to what she told him was a massive library on her mobile. He thought of other women he'd spent time with, and how little they would have understood him cutting a night short. And Dylan really didn't need more reasons to think that Jenny was perfect.

He already bloody knew.

When he checked in on her later, between disasters, she'd fallen asleep. She was curled up on his couch, her pretty shoes kicked aside. He pulled her coat over her like a blanket. Then he kissed her on her temple.

And he wished he was less her friend and more the ruthless bastard he was in every other area of his life. He could take that ring off her finger and smash it. He could spirit her off somewhere and maroon her there, until the next thing she begged for was *his* ring. He could marry her, get a few kids on her and indulge this fantasy of his in every possible way.

A bastard like that wouldn't care how she'd feel some years down the road, when the enormity of how hugely she'd disappointed her father would kick in. He'd weather it, not giving a shit, because he'd have her. Having her would be the only thing that mattered—not how she felt about it.

And not how the world would view it. They would tut and smirk and no doubt get far nastier, if it suited them. No one would ever accept that their beloved Lady Jenny should fall so far, and end up linked forever to a bit of Irish trash.

He couldn't help but wish he cared more about the end result and less about how he'd get them there. It would make everything so much easier.

But Dylan had learned a long time ago that there was no profit in wishing. The only thing that mattered in this world was what a man did.

So he kissed her, then he left her and went back to tend this empire he'd built. Because his business was the only thing that was real. And it was the only thing he would have left when she came to her senses.

He didn't finish until the early morning.

He went into his office again, and woke her this time. As much because he thought he should take her home as for the simple pleasure of watching her blink at him, then smile the way she always did. As if waking up to see him before her was a gift.

God help him, but he was going to miss that.

"Well?" Her voice was foggy as she pushed herself up to sitting position. "Have you staved off disaster?"

"After a fashion."

"I believe in you," she said, still smiling.

Dylan couldn't keep himself from leaning forward and capturing her mouth. And as usual, he didn't know how to kiss her...appropriately.

Because a simple taste of her was never enough.

It got raw, fast. He found his hands in her hair, and he was angling his mouth over hers for better depth. And he didn't know what would have happened if she hadn't pulled back, her eyes dilated and her breath all but gone.

"Are we alone here?" she asked.

Dylan muttered a few choice swearwords. Because they weren't. "No. Half my staff could walk in at any moment."

Jenny smiled again, and maybe he was only imagining that it was more muted than before. Something like sad. She reached over and ran her thumb over his mouth, for a change.

"I'm up for anything," she told him. "It surprises me how true that is, in fact. But I think I'd rather not expose myself to your entire company."

Dylan had a better idea. He stood, pulling her up with him. He grabbed her coat, tossed it to her and then took her hand in his.

"Where are we going?" she asked, laughing, after he hustled her into the lift, and then, when it took them all the way down to ground level, hurried her out the door into the cold early morning street. "Am I going to take a car home?"

And he loved that she called his house home. Just like he loved that her being there made it feel more like a home than it ever had before. Because that was Jenny, really. Always his homecoming, no matter where she was or why. And no matter how soon she might leave him again.

He intended to celebrate that in the most carnal way possible today, and as quickly as possible.

"You're not taking a car home," he said. Shortly.

"You thought a kiss like that was a good precursor for a brisk walk?" But she was laughing as he hurried her down the street, away from his office building.

"Pick up the pace," he advised her, steering them toward the Rocks.

And he could see she understood where they were going the minute they turned into the laneways. She laughed. And she was still laughing when he took her in through that same red door. And when he nodded and murmured something to the man at the desk.

But Dylan couldn't wait to find an open room. He needed a taste to tide him over while he dealt with such practicalities.

He swept her into the first alcove they passed, hoping that the early hour meant that no one *really* saw the way he was kissing her. And maybe also not caring too much if they did.

He pressed her back against the wall, and she wound herself around him instantly. His hand moved of its own accord to get a good grip on the plump curve of her ass, and he loved the greedy little noise she made in return. Lust and encouragement. Need.

It was never enough.

It was never, ever enough, no matter how he kissed her, no matter how tightly she pressed herself against him.

And she was still laughing whenever he pulled away to catch his breath, but he wasn't laughing at all. Dylan had forgotten entirely that he was meant to be her friend first, because she tasted like fire and rain at once. Because she inflamed him and she soothed him, all at the same time, and it only made him want her more. And he had loved her so long now that each new layer was less a revelation and more a confirmation.

She was the love of his life. She always had been. *She always will be,* something in him said, like a dark prophecy.

And at some point he realized that someone was standing there, much too close to their not-so-private alcove. He assumed it was a staff member, come to gently suggest they find a private room, so he pulled away from Jenny. Little as he wanted to stop kissing her.

He automatically twisted to block her, because the staff here might have been paid handsomely to maintain their discretion, but he didn't particularly like anyone looking at his woman.

His friend, he corrected himself acidly.

But when he looked at the man standing there, it was instantly clear that he was no staff member.

He stood tall and faintly disapproving, and he reeked of power and consequence. Though what he wore was not in and of itself particularly telling, it was the way he wore it. Dark trousers. A dark shirt. And the coldest gray eyes Dylan had ever seen.

Something clicked in him. This man was familiar.

Next to him, half behind him, Dylan heard Jenny pull in a sharp breath.

In distress.

And he knew. If he thought about it, he could even see the family resemblance to Erika.

He fucking *knew.*

And in that rush of recognition, he had to face the unpalatable fact that it was a lot easier to think about what a great friend he was in the abstract. Because it felt a whole lot more like dying now that it was happening. Now that he had the opportunity to prove it.

The man before him kept his gaze trained on Dylan for a long, frigid moment. Then he shifted it over Dylan's shoulder, and Dylan could feel Jenny's whole body jolt.

And he wanted to come out swinging. He wanted to teach the rich fuck standing before him exactly why he shouldn't tangle with a man who'd been an

Irish brawler before he'd ponced off to Oxford with the rest of them.

But that was the sort of thing a man who was in love with Jenny would do.

Dylan's job was to be Jenny's friend. Her best friend. That was the promise he'd made.

When that glacial gray gaze tracked back to him, Dylan didn't react the way he wanted to. He made himself stand still.

He forced himself to do nothing at all.

"You must be the famous Dylan Kilburn," the other man said, his voice precise. And frigid. "I believe you were at Oxford with my sister."

"Guilty as charged, mate," Dylan managed to say. And while he didn't strike the easy, friendly note he was going for, he also didn't sound *entirely* like he was chewing on broken glass, so he chalked it up as a win.

"I'm Conrad Vanderburg," the other man said, as if Dylan might not have figured that out already. "And it appears you've already met my fiancée."

"Conrad..." Jenny began, pushing out from behind Dylan's shoulder.

And everything in him demanded that he pull her back. That he handle this. That he do whatever he needed to do—beat his chest, roar. Come over like the raging Neanderthal creature he'd always been, just there beneath his skin.

He *ached* with the need to beat Conrad back, using whatever means necessary to get him away from Jenny.

But no matter what happened here, he knew where this would end. Where it was always going to end.

"If you don't mind," Conrad said, with such scrupulous politeness that it made Jenny flinch and Dylan want to break things—more things—"I'd like to have a word with my future wife."

Jenny took a deep breath, and Dylan could see what she was about to do written all over her face.

And he was the best friend she would ever have. He loved her more than he would ever love anything in this life or the next. Dylan knew that, because, instead of standing there between Jenny and her future, he stepped aside.

Literally.

"Of course," he said.

He nodded at Conrad as if they were exchanging business cards. He forced himself to look at Jenny, and it was worse than he'd expected. She was staring at him, shock and betrayal on her face, because she already knew what he was doing. That was the trouble with all this friendship shit. There was no goddamn mystery, and that was one more thing he was going to make certain to beat out of himself as he got home.

He nodded at her, too. "Take care, Jenny."

Dylan thought he heard her say his name, but he made himself walk away. He imagined them retreating back into texts as the weeks went by. There would be fewer and fewer of those as time went on, he imagined. It would be easier to forget. To pretend. To head back to England and plan her wedding, the way she should have been doing all along. She would invite him, no doubt, and he would go and smile and toast her happiness, because that was what friends did. And in a handful of years it would be like none of this had ever happened. He would be nothing more to her than an old school friend she saw rarely, if at all.

He figured he was already more or less a memory by the time he pushed through the doors, back out into a bright, cold Sydney morning.

And there was nothing he could do about his heart. He'd lost that too long ago now to imagine he'd ever get it back.

But he was a proud Irish man, a saint and a scholar through and through, and well did he know the cure for a spot of heartache. If not for what ailed him, then for what he was going to have to live through now that it was done.

It was finally done.

And Dylan might not find what he was looking for in the bottom of a bottle, but he planned to do a whole lot of asking anyway.

Until what hurt was his head—not that gaping, empty hole where his heart hadn't been since Jenny had claimed it with a happy laugh when they were both eighteen.

CHAPTER THIRTEEN

Conrad ordered tea.

On the list of things that were epically wrong with this moment, this engagement of hers and her entire life, Jenny had to place that at the very top.

The world was ending and Conrad ordered *tea*. As if he was a proper Englishman when she was the one with the British title and the bloodline to match.

And the word *proper* kicked around inside of her, spiked and mean, until she felt more or less bloodied, inside and out.

The tea service arrived, and Jenny had been entirely too well taught to sit back listlessly. Or to slump over and wail, the way she had half a mind to do. So she busied herself pouring out steaming cups, asking muted questions about sugar and cream and then sitting there in the little study Conrad had led her to, staring across a fine antique table at this man there was no possible way she could marry.

He gazed back at her with absolutely no expression on his face.

Clinically speaking, he was a handsome man. Jenny knew that, even if she didn't *feel* the way a prospective wife likely should. Erika had spent the whole of their friendship moaning about how cold her brother was, how cruel, but Jenny had never seen any of that herself. He was simply…expressionless, always.

But what she hadn't understood until now was that he had never truly focused all of his attention on her before.

It was…intense. Something very nearly alarming.

The full force of his attention made her want to squirm. But she didn't.

"This is very awkward," she said instead, because it seemed better to say it than to continue to sit there in silence.

Conrad only gazed back at her, as unreadable as before.

"I certainly never anticipated that you would see…that." Jenny knew she should start apologizing, but she couldn't bring herself to do it. Because she wasn't sorry. If anything, she was sorry that Conrad had interrupted them. "I realize that we never spoke directly about fidelity, but it can't have been pleasant to look up and see…" She blew out a breath and stared down at her tea, not remotely tempted to take a sip. "I take it you're a member of this club?"

"I stay here often when I arrive in Sydney too

early to conduct business," Conrad said, his voice as devoid of emotion as the rest of him.

Jenny lifted her gaze to his. And even as some part of her told her she didn't owe him anything, that theirs was an arranged marriage and surely he couldn't expect anything of her, another part of her cringed in shame. Because she'd promised to marry him, and the promise had meant something to her. And then she'd gone to such lengths to tell herself that promise didn't matter when she was down here in Australia.

Was that really who she was now? Just…a liar?

Once Jenny started questioning the lies she'd told, they all seemed to crowd in on her. Stretching all the way back to a beautiful Irish boy with eyes of the deepest green, who'd appeared in front of her out of nowhere one day when she was barely eighteen.

And had stolen her heart in an instant.

But Jenny had never planned on falling in love. It was the one thing her otherwise indulgent father forbade her—and she'd agreed, because she never again wanted to feel the way she had after her mother had died. She'd done everything she could to make sure she never would.

And yet here she sat, with a cup of tea she didn't want and a sea of grief inside her anyway.

Jenny had ended up right where she'd never wanted to go.

"We have no sexual relationship," Conrad was saying, his voice as remote as the rest of him. "As little as I might enjoy seeing a woman wearing my ring in the arms of another man, I can't claim the sight hurt me in any way. I do not feel betrayed." He studied her for a moment. "I do feel curious, however. Do you plan to continue this affair after our marriage?"

And somehow, that made it worse. She opened her mouth, but nothing came out.

She cleared her throat, then tried again. "I haven't actually given the matter any thought."

One of Conrad's eyebrows rose. "I don't object. In theory. But there's the issue of paternity."

Jenny could remember, so vividly, standing out there near the Opera House Bar, blithely assuring Dylan that this would all be fine. That even if she fell in love, ha ha ha, she would scamper back off into the arms of the husband her father had arranged for her, and all would be well.

How had she ever imagined that she could do that?

She barely knew chilly, controlled Conrad. And she couldn't imagine, now, allowing a man she barely knew to touch her body. To pull out his cock and put it inside of her. The very notion made her feel ill.

Which put rather more of a damper on the issue of the paternity of their potential children than she thought he meant.

And Conrad was a decent man, as she told anyone who dared question her on her choices. Kinder than she'd imagined, if this calm response to finding her with Dylan was any indication. Then again, perhaps that only meant he was significantly more controlled than she'd thought.

But most of all, he was Erika's older brother. And even Erika had softened toward him recently, mostly because she happened to be shacked up with Conrad's best friend.

Whatever the reason, Jenny found herself leaning forward, over the table between them, so she could take his hands in hers.

Something flashed over his face and made those cold eyes of his look silver for a moment. She had the shocking notion that there was a different man in him, too. And one she would likely never see.

"Conrad," she said softly. "Why do you want to marry me?"

"You're Lady Jenny. Who wouldn't want to marry you?"

Jenny could think of one person who didn't want to marry her. One person who'd looked at her with something like torture in his eyes and talked to her about how to let go of him.

"You mean, because of my father," she said, concentrating on the man before her. Not the man she'd already lost.

The faintest shred of amusement moved across Conrad's face. "If you mean your father's money, I have my own."

"Then why?" Conrad's hands were warmer than she'd expected. And a whole lot tougher. "If I'm not mistaken, this is the first time you've ever really looked at me."

Conrad turned her left hand over, and fiddled with the ring he'd put there.

"In the spirit of this sudden attack of honesty," he said, and his voice was so dry that she couldn't tell if he meant to sound that sardonic, or if it was simply a byproduct of the chill, "I didn't need to look at you. You were good on paper. And I wanted to make the right choice. To live up to what was expected of the head of the Vanderburg family."

"Ah, yes," Jenny said. "Expectations."

For a moment, they both stared at her ring.

"You don't seem at all angry," Jenny ventured. She peered up at him. "You don't even seem mildly irritated, if I'm honest."

His gray gaze touched hers and she didn't know how she kept herself from flinching.

"I'm not pleased," he said.

Jenny blew out a breath. She thought about her father and how disappointed he would be with her.

But then, that was all about his fear. And she'd let that fear and her own grief hang over her for so long now that she'd accepted that it was simply…how things were. She'd decided long ago she could never be with someone she loved. And she'd never tried, so she'd assumed she could handle a loveless life.

She knew better now.

Jenny had no idea if she could make Dylan love her, all these years later. What she did know was that she'd never forgive herself if she didn't try.

She pulled off the ring that Conrad had given her, and she met his gaze—and held it—as she placed it back in his hand.

For a moment, he only stared back at her. As unreadable as ever.

"My sister tells me that Dylan has been your best friend as long as she has," Conrad said then. "Though she claims she's your real best friend, because he's not really a friend at all, is he?"

"No," Jenny said. At last. "I'm afraid Dylan has always been a lot more. Even if he did walk away today."

Conrad smiled, then. And his eyes had gone back to that frigid gray. He let the ring roll forward and back in his palm before he closed it up in his fist.

He stood, tucking the ring away in his pocket. And it struck Jenny as funny, almost, that she was yet again in a supplicant position, staring up a man.

But not the right one.

"He wanted to tear me apart with his bare hands," Conrad said, gazing down at her. "I thought he was going to try to put me through the wall. Instead, he walked away. Why would a man do that?"

Jenny only stared up at him as her heart began to pound at her like a battering ram.

"I don't love you, Jenny," Conrad continued. His

voice was matter-of-fact. "If you married me, I never would. Love is not something I have to offer. But even a blind man could see that your friend does not suffer these same restrictions." He inclined his head, cool and unbothered, and she couldn't tell if that made it better or worse. "If you're not content with our arrangement, if you feel even half the things I can see all over your face, go. Find him. I don't think you need my blessing, but you have it."

And Jenny stayed there, still leaning out over the small table, while the man she'd intended to marry turned and walk from the room.

She stayed where she was, there beside a lovely tea service she didn't have the slightest urge to touch.

She thought about all these years since her first sight of Dylan at Oxford. And it was a temptation to think of them all as wasted. But when she set all those years of friendship next to the past few weeks of absolute joy, she knew, somehow, that she couldn't have had one without the other. That it had always been leading here.

What she had to ask herself was whether or not, had Conrad not turned up the way he had today, she would have called off this wedding herself.

Jenny tried to imagine walking down an aisle in the spring, and seeing Conrad standing at the head of it.

And it was wrong. It was just...wrong.

There was only one man she'd ever wanted to

see smiling at her, from the head of an aisle or any-where else.

Her breath left her in a rush. She dug into the pocket of the coat she hadn't managed to take off and pulled out her mobile. Then she called a num-ber she knew by heart, though it was ten o'clock at night there and she knew her father didn't like late night calls.

And in fact, he sounded typically put out when he picked up the phone.

"It's me, Papa," Jenny said. "I know you're asleep or on your way. But I have something to tell you and I know you're not going to like it. I need you to love me anyway."

And when her father sputtered, Jenny told him the news.

Then repeated it when he fell silent.

"Do you love him?" her father asked. He sounded old, for the first time that she could recall. And it made her sad, but it didn't make her change her mind. "Do you really love him?"

"I think I always have, Papa," Jenny whispered. "But I tried not to. For your sake."

"Does he love you?" her father asked, sounding almost severe. As if he couldn't bear to think about it.

"That's the thing," Jenny said with a quiet convic-tion she hadn't known, until now, was there inside her. "I think he's loved me even longer."

And when her father sighed, she knew she'd won.

Or that he would support her, anyway. It felt much like the same thing.

"You don't have to love him," she told her father. "I don't require it."

"I love you, Jenny," her father replied gruffly, and she knew those weren't words that came easily to him. Bringing with them, as they did, the potential for so much loss. So much grief. But she'd never doubted the truth of it, no matter how little he said it. "If this is what you want, I support it. Your mother would have flayed me alive for making you think you couldn't love the man you wanted to love."

And Jenny didn't know when she started crying, but she didn't stop. Not when she ended the call. Not when she sat there a moment, thinking of the mother she'd lost, the father she still had and all these years she'd tried so hard to keep herself from feeling.

But she couldn't cry forever, not even if the tears had more to do with the acknowledgement of emotion—and the sheer relief that she was no longer expected to marry a man she hardly knew and didn't want. She took a deep breath. She wiped at her eyes. She stayed where she was and finally drank her tea.

And then she set off into Sydney to find the love of her life, and convince him that they had never been meant to be friends.

By any means necessary.

CHAPTER FOURTEEN

DYLAN RAN THE coastal path twice, at a speed and intensity he could only call punishing.

It didn't help.

He slammed his way into his house, and it was starting already. Ghosts everywhere he looked. Memories like an assault. It was hard to believe he'd been so careless. So astonishingly reckless. So certain that it would be worth it, no matter what shape he'd find himself in when she left.

The door to the guest room mocked him. He pushed his way past it, down the hall, not sure what he was doing but absolutely certain that he didn't need to go in there. Not yet. He was still too furious about his great bloody sacrifice to tip on over to what waited on the other side of all that black, righteous rage.

He stormed into his kitchen, not afraid to make noise as he rattled his cupboards. He rummaged around in his refrigerator, throwing together the healthy smoothie he normally drank after his runs, barely paying attention to what he was doing.

Because what did it matter?

Congratulations, you pathetic fucker, he growled at himself. *You're a great friend. Lucky you.*

He braced himself on the kitchen bench, but when he looked out toward his million-dollar view, stopped short.

Because a woman was standing there with her back to him, staring out at the same sea.

His heart walloped him one. Then another.

But he was dreaming, of course. He was hallucinating. He'd been up all night, putting out fires and kicking asses all over the globe, and his morning hadn't exactly gone to plan. If he was lucky, he thought sourly, this was actually him in the midst of his death throes. They'd find his body out there on the path somewhere near Coogee, twitching off into eternity.

But she turned around, and the wind picked up the ends of her dark hair. Her eyes were soft and brown; he knew how every inch of her tasted, and it was Jenny.

Of course it was Jenny.

Everything in him lit on fire.

He told himself it was pure rage.

Dylan slammed the glass he was holding down on the countertop, then stormed toward his deck. He flung the glass door open with such force that he was surprised it didn't shatter.

"What the hell are you doing here," he growled.

And he'd seen a host of different expressions on Jenny's face since she'd been here. He could have written a book detailing each and every one of them. But the way she looked at him now, some kind of serenity mixed with defiance, was like a slap.

"I have a key, Dylan."

How dare she look *amused*?

He was too close to her, but he stopped himself before he put his hands on her. Because he couldn't do that anymore, could he? Everything was changed again, and he hated it, and it was a whole lot easier to be noble when she wasn't standing right in front of him.

"Best give it back, then," he said. "And fuck off back to England, as planned."

Jenny didn't snap back at him, which he half expected. Maybe he'd wanted it. And she didn't look upset, either. Instead, she tilted her head to one side, and studied him. "No."

"Sorry?"

"I said no, Dylan. If it's all the same to you, I'm not going to go back to England."

His mind reeled as he tried to figure out how that could be. What it meant. He took a step back from her, because that was the exact opposite of what he wanted to do. And then he raked his hands through his hair, because he couldn't put them on her the way he would have yesterday.

And that meant he had to use his mouth. To talk.

"You're staying in Australia." It wasn't a question, really. And when she nodded, he found he was gritting his teeth. "And your man? He's all right with your relocation? Because that wasn't the impression I got earlier."

"Funny thing about that," Jenny began.

But Dylan couldn't take it. He held a hand up between them, and the truth about all of this, about him, was as clear to him then as the Tasman Sea laid out there before him.

"It doesn't matter," he said, his voice gruff. Deep. "I don't care."

Because he could stand here and pretend to give a shit about whether or not she was engaged. He could pretend that he was in possession of a moral compass when it came to her, but he wasn't.

And sure, he had spent the whole of his life trying his best to be a good man. Because he wanted so badly to differentiate himself from his family. He wasn't an addict. He wasn't a liar. He wasn't a vicious thug, roaming the streets of Dublin and taking out his feelings with his fists. He drank, but never to excess—not any longer.

Dylan had been in control of himself for as long as he could remember.

Except when it came to Jenny.

She was his weakness. She was the one chink in his armor, and if he had to be her dirty little secret, he would do it happily.

Hell, he'd played her toothless buddy for years. What was the difference? At least a dirty secret got to put his hands on her.

"I care," Jenny said, and a different kind of heat flashed across her face.

She stepped forward and, to his great surprise, hauled off and thunked him one. Right in the chest.

He stared down at his chest in astonishment, then back at her. "Why did you thump me?"

"I'm in love with you," she hurled at him, sounding furious.

And that was a far harder hit. It took his breath from him.

"You were absolutely right," Jenny threw at him, in the same voice, crisp with temper. "I had no idea what having sex—or *properly fucking*—would do to me. Because it wasn't the sex, you idiot. It was you. I've been in love with you my whole life."

Dylan had never had auditory hallucinations before. And if this was more of his death throes, he was fine with it. He would die every day to hear her say these things.

"Love was the one thing I was never allowed to do, Dylan. It was the one thing I couldn't allow. Because I was afraid that I would love someone the way my father loved my mother, and I would end up alone. But what good did it do me? All those dates. All those stupid boyfriends. I even agreed to marry a man who I *knew* didn't love me."

Surely by this point, he'd have hurried up and died. The alternative was that he was alive and this was really happening, and he couldn't make any sense of it. "Jenny—"

"I kept telling myself that I was coming to Australia as an experiment, that was all. I knew I wanted you to show me good sex, but I didn't dare hope for *this*." She took the hand she'd used to thump him, hard, and put it over her own heart. "I love you. You're the best friend I've ever had, probably because you were never really my friend at all. You've always been so much more than that to me."

She looked as if she expected him to say something, then, but he couldn't speak. He was frozen solid in disbelief. He couldn't believe that she was saying all the things he'd long since given up on ever hearing from her.

"Now I've seen all these different sides of you," Jenny continued. "And I love them all. And I *am* staying in Australia, and I don't give a toss if that doesn't work for you, because this time your little speech didn't work. I'm not going to wander off with a smile on my face like all those other girls. I'm going to stay right here. I'm going to do whatever it takes to prove to you that you *can* fall in love with me, you really can—"

Her voice began to crack, her eyes had gone glossy, and Dylan couldn't bear it a moment longer. The idea that she believed he couldn't love her felt like it might rip him apart.

"Stop," he ordered her.

In that voice he usually used when she was naked.

And then he smiled, because she gulped back whatever it was she was about to say.

Because she was perfect. And she was here. And when he took a breath, trying to get his heart rate to settle down, he noticed that she was no longer wearing that obnoxious rock on her left hand.

"Where's your ring?" he asked.

"I gave it back to Conrad," Jenny told him. She lifted her chin defiantly. "Then I rang my father and told him that I wasn't going to be marrying with my head, thank you. That after all this time, I finally realized that my heart had been stolen away a long time ago." Her chest heaved, as if there were sobs in there fighting to get out. "Because it was. Because I love you, Dylan. And I don't understand why you think you can't love me back, but I'm hoping I can convince you to try."

"Jenny," he said, because it was all he could say. Because her name had always been his favorite song.

He reached out and tugged her close, so he could look deep into her eyes. And get his hands on her, where they belonged.

"Just try," she was saying urgently. "I promise, if you still can't love me after a reasonable amount of time—let's say six months—I'll accept it." When he didn't speak, because he thought his chest was broken in half, she kept going. "Three months. Okay, a month. Just give me a chance."

And then she fell silent, as if something on his face took her words away.

But that was just grand, because he finally found his voice.

"I told you I couldn't fall in love with you," Dylan said quietly.

He smoothed her hair back from her face and he still couldn't believe that this was happening. That they were standing here, with the Australian sun beating down on them, a world away and all these years later—and it was still the same. It was still so strong.

Stronger, now, than he'd ever believed possible. "Jenny, I've been in love with you all along. I loved you at first sight. And I've loved you since. And I knew that I could never have you, so I had you in the only way I could. Every woman I've ever touched was you. Every woman I've ever seen was you. And yet none of them were truly you, and I'd resigned myself to it. I've been loving you from afar forever."

"But…but…" And she was sobbing then, or maybe she was laughing at the same time, and her eyes were so wide with wonder it was like he fell off the edge of the world and lost himself there. "You walked away. You left me with Conrad. You would have come to my wedding!"

"With a smile on my face," Dylan agreed. "I vowed a long time ago that I would be what you needed, always. It was the only way I got to love you."

"Dylan…" she whispered, and it was like a thousand earthquakes ripped them both open, but only light poured forth.

Then she was in his arms, and she was touching his face.

He was kissing her, or she was kissing him.

And it wasn't about sex. It wasn't about friendship. It was both of those things, wrapped up tight, tangled up as only they could make it, and made new.

Made theirs.

They kept saying it. *I love you.*

Over and over again, as if they were remaking the world every time they said the words. Making all the dark years behind them light, because they'd ended up here.

Out in the light, bathed in love, at last.

That was how Dylan and his perfect Lady Jenny became one.

CHAPTER FIFTEEN

HE DIDN'T GET any less bossy, Jenny reflected a year later, sitting out on that same deck.

In fact, the more time they spent together, the more deliciously commanding Dylan became.

It was winter again, but she still liked to sit outside. She liked to wait for Dylan to finish his early morning run and join her for a coffee before they drove into Sydney's Central Business District together.

She liked the rhythms of this life of theirs. It was more joy than pain, more laughter than tears, and both of them were fully engaged. Committed.

Connected, she thought now.

Jenny had never left Sydney. She'd taken a month or so, what she and Dylan like to call their trial honeymoon, and had simply indulged herself in him. Lost herself in him. With no worries about disappointing her father, this time. And better yet, no fiancé.

Just Dylan. And his wicked imagination. And all the bossiness he could dream up and she could take.

Finally.

Are you ever coming back? Erika had texted a few days after that scene with Conrad. Jenny had doubted very much she knew what had happened. Or are you emigrating?

Jenny had found herself gnawing on her knuckle, so she'd picked up her mobile and called her best friend.

"The short version is that I broke up with your brother and am with Dylan now," Jenny said when Erika answered. "And I guess that's also the long version."

And she didn't know what she expected, but it wasn't Erika's whoop of laughter.

"I knew it!" she crowed.

"I thought you'd be more upset about the Conrad angle," Jenny said after Erika's laughter wound down.

"I probably would be if you'd been marrying each other for the right reasons," her friend said after a moment. "But you never loved him. And Conrad doesn't love anything. And you and Dylan should have gotten together years ago."

Jenny couldn't help but agree. Living with Dylan was easy. So easy, in fact, that they'd had more than a few conversations about whether or not it was *too* easy, and therefore destined to blow up in their faces. Yet as weeks turned to months, and months into seasons, it seemed less and less likely.

They'd been friends for years. And they'd been in

love with each other all of that time. They knew each other's weaknesses already, and then some, which helped. But better still, they were both so *happy*. Finally. Shifting their relationship into what it should have been all along felt like a gift.

The only friction they had they tended to work out in bed. Or with sex, anyway, bed not required.

Dylan didn't have to hide all the different parts of himself any longer.

And Jenny didn't have to pretend that she was endlessly serene.

Sometimes they shouted at each other because they could. Because passion could lead to temper, and neither one of them was perfect. But they always found a way back to laughter. And love.

And the simple beauty of his cock deep inside her, until neither one of them had the energy to fight.

She looked up and smiled when Dylan roamed out onto the deck a little while later. He sat down with her, picking her up and settling her in his lap the way he liked to do. Jenny sighed as his arms came around her. Then smiled as she felt his cock stir beneath her, because a year had passed and if anything, they wanted each other more.

She found new charities here in Australia, and new ways to give back. She and Dylan started their own scholarship program, the better to help kids like the one he'd been, hoping to break the family cycle.

She brought Dylan back to England to meet her father. Or meet him again, and this time, not as a grotty little student upstart, as he liked to call himself, with a chip on his shoulder the size of Ireland. He didn't even call her father Lord Fuckface—to his face.

And her father found a way to fear less, and love more, though he wasn't one to say such things. Not often.

"I expect I'll have to marry you," Dylan said now, playing with her hair.

"I rather like that you haven't made an honest woman of me. I can pretend I'm nothing more than a kept woman. Subject to your every whim if I want to keep my place."

Dylan laughed, but then he was reaching between them, and adjusting her. Lifting up the soft cotton shift she'd worn to sleep in, releasing himself from his running shorts and sliding his cock between her folds.

It always took a little work. There was always that initial stretching, and her body's adjustment to his length and width.

And it was always worth it when he thrust home. Both of them sighed a bit at the fit. The fullness. The feel of him, huge and so hard where she was tight.

Perfect, Jenny thought. *Together, we're perfect.*

"Careful, Jenny," Dylan said, his stern voice in her ear. "You wouldn't want the neighbors to see you acting so dirty in the middle of a bright morning, now would you?"

She shuddered, in that mix of delight and delicious fear that pushed her to the edge of a climax, even though she knew that the deck was more private than it seemed. Or the neighbors would have called the police a long time ago.

"Go on now," he ordered her, as bossy and delicious as ever. "I want you to move, slowly. Very slowly, no matter how good it feels."

Jenny did what he told her, because he was always right when it came to the things they could do when he was buried inside of her. The hotter and deeper, the better.

"What if we'd never—" she began, her eyes dizzy with all that Australian sunshine, and her pussy full of Dylan's enormous, demanding cock.

And better still, her heart so full of love she was surprised it didn't burst.

"We were always ending up here, love," Dylan told her. In that confident, assured way of his, as if he'd always known. "Sooner or later, we were always going to end up right here."

And as she lifted herself, and lowered herself again, so slowly it nearly made her scream, he moved. He picked up her hand, and it took her a moment to realize what he was doing.

Then she understood, and she couldn't tell if she was laughing, or sobbing, because that was the way of it. He made her feel too much for it to be contained into any one thing. It was all the things, always.

And now he'd slid a diamond onto her hand.

And this ring made her heart ache. It was simple, with a beautiful, understated elegance and a deep, sweet shine. It was endless and clear, and it felt like this.

Like him.

Like them, forever.

"Marry me," he said, as she rocked herself on his hard cock, making them both whole. Keeping them connected the way they liked best. "You've been my best friend. And my lover. I want you to be my wife. The mother of my children. My everything."

"Dylan," she managed to gasp out as sensation clambered inside of her, her clit throbbed with need and her heart felt a part of that same sobbing thing that wrecked her and remade her with every deep thrust. "Oh, Dylan, I love you. I'll marry you. I'll be anything you want me to be. Forever and ever."

And he took control then, hammering into her, and then taking the hand he'd just put his ring on, and guiding it to her own clit.

And there he pressed her own fingers against the place where they were joined, so they both exploded into bliss.

Together.

The way they always had been.

And always were, forever after.

* * * * *

DIRTY WORK

REGINA KYLE

MILLS & BOON

To Jeanne-Marie, my road trip buddy, sommelier, Lindt truffle supplier, and plot partner extraordinaire (the penis party is all yours, babe). Come for the cheap wine, but stay for the good chocolate.

CHAPTER ONE

Ainsley

I'VE SEEN A LOT of strange things in my line of work. Manhattan is full of oddballs, and I seem to be a magnet for them. I've taken each and every one of their, shall we say, eccentric requests in stride. You know what they say. The customer's always right. Well, almost always. I do have some hard limits.

And this may be one of them.

I get down on my knees and look my newest prospective client in the eye. The trendy Tribeca loft is big by Manhattan standards, but he seems to dominate the space, his massive frame making the *Mad Men*–style furniture look like it belongs in a dollhouse. He's impeccably groomed and sleekly muscled, coiled and ready to pounce like a jungle cat at the slightest sign of weakness.

Honestly, I'm a little afraid of him. He's more than a tad overwhelming. I'm not sure I can handle that much raw, unadulterated power. I wonder not for the first time what he's doing here, in this apartment. With his bulk and brawn, he seems more suited to country living than city dwelling. I can't help feeling he'd be happier somewhere with more room to roam.

"So what do you think, Ainsley? Can you do it?" an uncertain female voice asks from over my shoulder.

Brie Lawson. I'd almost forgotten she's there, that's how uncharacteristically rattled I am. In truth, she's the prospective client, not Roscoe. We met at a spin class in the Village. I made the mistake of telling her what I do for a living, and she insisted I was the only one who could help her.

And Roscoe.

"Please, Ainsley. I don't know what I'll do if you don't say yes."

"I don't know, Brie," I answer, not taking my eye off Roscoe, who's been surprisingly quiet throughout this whole ordeal. "This is totally out of my comfort zone."

"I'll pay double your usual rate. Triple. Well, Jake will. Lord knows he can afford it."

That's right. It isn't even Brie who'll be my client if I accept her crazy proposal. It's her mysterious, heretofore unseen brother who'll be footing the bill for my services.

The very exorbitant bill.

I make one last head-to-paw assessment of the

Irish wolfhound sitting on his haunches in front of me, then get back to my feet with a crisp nod. This may be an exercise in insanity given my spotty history with dogs, especially large ones, but three times my going rate is too damn good to pass up. Odds & Errands—the concierge service I started out of my apartment a little less than a year ago—needs the business. And mama needs those Louboutin striped leather sling-backs she saw in the display window at Saks.

"Deal."

Brie starts to squee, but I rise, cutting her off with a hand held palm out, Supremes style. "I'll walk him twice a day. Make sure he's got food and water. That's it. No snuggle time. No cleaning up any of his little—or not so little—indoor messes. No hauling fifty-pound bags of dog chow up five flights of stairs."

"The building has an elevator."

I arch a brow at her. "Do you want me to take this job or not?"

"I want, I want." Brie throws her arms around me and I instinctively tense up. Such effusive displays of affection aren't the norm in my family. Hell, any displays of affection aren't the norm for the emotionally stunted Scott clan, and I'm still getting used to my new friend's tendency toward over-the-top exuberance. I make a conscious effort to relax as she continues to sing my praises. "You're a lifesaver. Se-

riously. I was dreading telling Jake I was dumping
Roscoe on him. But he won't take it half so bad now
that you'll be around to share the burden."

I don't like the sound of those words. *Share the
burden.* But it's too late now. I've already given my
word, and that's not something I take lightly. Besides,
those Louboutins aren't going to buy themselves.

The aforementioned burden trots on over and tries
to worm his way between us, clearly wanting to get
in on the action. I disentangle myself from Brie and
take a step back from the pair.

"How did you get stuck with him anyway?" I ask.

She reaches down and takes hold of Roscoe's collar, keeping him blessedly beside her and away from
me. "My parents won a three-month cruise in some
raffle fundraiser. They figured since I've been staying with Jake while making the audition rounds, we
could take care of Roscoe together. I don't think
anyone—least of all me—considered the possibility I'd book something while they were gone. And
certainly not something that was going to take me
out of town for so long."

Brie's practically bursting with excitement, and
I'm reminded what brought me here in the first place.
I push aside my aversion to PDA—and Roscoe—and
step back toward her to give her a quick squeeze.
"Have I told you how jealous I am? Six months doing
my absolute favorite musical—*Les Misérables*—in

one of my favorite places, sunny San Diego? You're going to kill it, girl."

She totally is. Brie may be one of my newest friends—I've known her only a few months—but I had the pleasure of catching her semi-autobiographical one-woman show at Studio 54, and she's damn good. I've seen enough Broadway musicals to know she's got what it takes to make it on the Great White Way. That was one of the few perks of being a junior associate at Dwight, Kearns & Goodwin, attorneys at law. Free theater tickets when the partners didn't need them to wine, dine and entertain clients. Yankees and Rangers, too, which Dale sure didn't seem to mind.

No. I'm not going to think about Dale. And I'm not going to think about DK&G. I've left all that in the rearview mirror, on the side of the highway covered in road dust.

Brie blushes and returns the squeeze, pulling me back to the present. "Thanks, but I'm only in the ensemble. If it's anything like either of the Broadway productions, the lighting will be so subdued I'll be in shadow the whole time."

"You know what they say." I shake my finger at her. "There are no small parts…"

"Only small actors," Brie finishes, and we bump fists. That much PDA I can deal with. Although I'm not sure fist-bumping in front of a dog counts as public.

She lets go of Roscoe's collar and gives his head

a pat, and he flops down onto the floor like a drag queen doing a death drop. He's way more chill than I expected. Maybe not all big dogs are high maintenance. I'm going to have to read up on the breed. Research is key to everything we do at Odds & Errands. Like I always tell my army of two—Aaron and Erin, and yes, I really did hire two people with pretty much the same name, albeit different spellings and different sexes—preparation is more than half the battle.

"So." Brie rocks back and forth on the soles of her Vans pink glitter high-tops. "What happens now? Is this a handshake agreement or is there some sort of paperwork we have to sign?"

This is the part I hate. The business part. At least with friends. It's awkward and icky and it's why I tend to shy away from mixing work with my personal life. But Brie seemed so desperate when she asked—no, begged—me to bail her out. She'd had a mini-freak-out worrying how her brother would react when she told him she was leaving him with the responsibility of caring for a dog the size of a small pony. Made him seem like a borderline tyrant.

Unfortunately, since the tyrant is the one paying my tab, he's the one I need to be dealing with.

"There's paperwork, but since I'm on your brother's dime, he's the one who has to sign."

"Well…" Brie rocks faster, twisting the hem of

her Florence and the Machine T-shirt in her fingers. "That might be a problem."

Great. Not five minutes in, and already a wrinkle in this half-baked plan.

I plop myself down on a retro-chic chair that's more comfortable than it looks, figuring this has the potential to be a long, drawn-out discussion. Roscoe takes this as an invitation to join me, lumbering over and sprawling across my feet. Christ, he's heavy. He must weigh close to two hundred pounds. Still, I humor him, scratching behind his ears, which earns me a tail thump.

"How so? You said your brother's a grade-A workaholic who doesn't have time to deal with a dog on his own, right? And money's not an issue for him."

Brie perches on the arm of an equally uncomfortable looking sofa. "Yes and yes, but he's in South Beach scouting a location for a new club. He doesn't get home until late tomorrow night, and I have to be on a plane to California first thing in the morning."

I frown. This definitely throws a wrench into the works. "I thought your contract didn't begin for another couple of weeks."

"The girl I'm replacing is leaving earlier than expected. They want me there as soon as possible."

She at least has the good graces to look apologetic.

"So your brother's just going to...what? Walk in and find me here with his dog?" Brie starts to correct me, but I whip out my "Stop! In the name of love" hand gesture again and the words get stuck in her throat. "Yeah, yeah, I know. Your parents' dog."

"Of course not. I'll call him and explain everything before I go. And it if helps, I can take care of the paperwork. I'm an authorized user on his credit card in case of emergencies."

"I'm not sure he'll see this as an emergency."

Brie rolls her eyes dramatically. Everything she does is dramatic. She's what Erin would call extra. Part and parcel of being an actress, I suppose. I admit, it was a bit much at first, but now that I'm used to it, it's more entertaining than exhausting.

"Trust me, if the alternative is him scooping dog poop in Hudson River Park, he'll think it's an emergency."

I'm not entirely convinced, but Brie does her best impression of a damsel in distress, her amber eyes going wide as dinner plates and her full lower lip jutting out in a pathetic pout, and I cave.

Sucker.

"Okay."

Stepping over Roscoe, I make my way to the kitchen area of the open floor plan, where I left my Kate Spade tote, one of the few holdovers from my DK&G days. Fortunately, I always keep a folder in there with a few blank copies of the standard Odds & Errands contract. When you're in business, especially a business like mine, everyone you meet is a prospective customer.

I pull out a blank contract and a pen, make a couple of quick changes to the standard terms to reflect the specific services and higher rate we agreed on, then slide pen and paper across the mammoth marble-topped kitchen island to Brie. "Read it, print your name and credit card information in the spaces provided and sign on the line marked 'client.'"

She grabs her ever-present messenger bag, whips out a credit card and fills out the form, signing her name with a flourish that's as extra as she is. Then she pushes the paper back toward me. I tuck it safely in my tote and hold out my hand. "Pen?"

I hate asking, but I've lost so many it's become a running joke with my employees. I'm almost positive Aaron and Erin have some kind of bet going. The loser probably has to buy the winner Starbucks for a week.

"Oops." She hands it over.

"Thanks." I drop it into my bag. "And I'll need a key. Do you have a spare?"

"Jake keeps one in here somewhere." She rummages through drawers until she produces a leather key chain with a pair of shiny silver keys dangling from it. She beams, holding it up like she's found the holy grail. "The long one's for the entrance to the building, and the short one's for this apartment. Heads up."

She tosses it to me, and I make a sweet one-handed catch. Ten years of tae kwon do as a kid, and I still haven't lost my lightning-fast reflexes. I add the key chain to the growing collection in my tote, making a mental note to tag it later so I remember whose apartment it goes to. "That should do it."

I give her a brief, semi-awkward parting hug. "Have a great time in San Diego. Work hard. Play hard. And don't forget to slay."

She laughs and hugs me back. "I'll do my best."

I start for the door, then remember one more thing and turn back to her. "Oh, I should probably have your brother's cell number, since you'll be like three thousand miles away."

She nods. "I'll text it to you."

"Great." I open the door, step through, then turn back one last time.

"But if this blows up in our faces, I'm totally throwing you under the bus."

CHAPTER TWO

Jake

NORMALLY, I LIKE coming home after a too-long business trip. Sleeping in my own bed. Never running out of hot water in the shower. Binge watching the latest Marvel series on Netflix. My Tribeca loft was one of the first things I bought when Top Shelf started raking in the dough, and I spent a small fortune—or what seemed like a small fortunate at the time—making it the ultimate man cave, a place where I could relax, unwind and escape from the pressures of owning Manhattan's trendiest nightclub with my best friend and business partner, Connor Dow.

So why the hell am I standing at my door, key in hand, afraid to go in?

Brie, that's why.

Don't get me wrong—I'm hugely proud of my baby sis for going after her dream and grabbing it with both hands. When she texted to tell me the news about her new gig, I let out a war whoop in the middle of a tense negotiation. And when I talked to her later, the excitement in her voice put a shit-eating grin on my face. It's just that it couldn't have come at a worse time.

I'm in the middle of trying to find the perfect spot for our new club in Miami. We're looking at doing some substantial renovations in New York, expanding our square footage so we can add another VIP section and a first-run screening room for major motion pictures and live-streamed concerts. All of which requires us to secure some serious financing. The last thing I need is to be responsible for taking care of the giant, hairy, slobbering beast my parents think passes for a dog. I was counting on my sister and her way more flexible schedule to do the lion's share of the Roscoe-related duties while they were on their cruise.

Odds are he's destroyed my loft by now. By my calculations, he's been alone for like eight to ten hours straight, depending on when this pet sitter person Brie hired was there last. More than enough time for him to have shredded my couch, peed on my bed and chewed my cross trainers to shreds.

I steel myself for whatever I might find inside and insert the key in the lock. Might as well face the music sooner rather than later. What damage has been done is done, and postponing the inevitable will only make it worse.

The lock clicks, and I push the door open, wheeling my carry-on in behind me. At first glance, nothing seems out of place. The couch is still in one piece. My cross trainers are intact, in their usual spot on the shoe rack by the front door. I can't see my bed, but Roscoe's lounging like the King of fucking Siam in front of the gas fireplace, snoring softly, so my best guess is that's undisturbed, too.

Then I see her.

She's on her hands and knees in the middle of the hand-knotted Persian area rug my decorator insisted was the perfect piece to "tie the room together," scrubbing furiously and muttering something under her breath. I catch the words "damn dog," "I swear to God," "kill Brie" and "shouldn't be doing this."

But it's not her words that have my cock doing a little happy dance. It's the swaying of her perfect ass in those figure-hugging jeans as she continues to scrub away, blissfully unaware I'm watching her. Either she's a hot burglar with a cleaning fetish or she's Brie's friend the dog walker.

Obviously, I'm hoping for the latter.

I clear my throat to let her know I'm there, and she jumps, almost spilling the pot of soapy water next to her. She wheels around on her knees, blue-gray eyes blazing.

"Jesus Christ." She throws the sponge into the soapy water, sending up a spray of suds that float to the carpet, and stands, hands on her shapely hips.

"Don't you know you're not supposed to sneak up on someone like that?"

Roscoe lifts his head, surveys the situation, lets out a loud doggie yawn and promptly goes back to sleep. Good move, staying out of the fray. Maybe there's hope for him after all.

"In my defense, this is my apartment. And I wasn't expecting anyone to be here this late." My flight was delayed, and it was almost eleven by the time we landed. It must be after midnight now. I set my messenger bag down and stick out my hand. "Jake Lawson. I assume you're the pet sitter my sister hired to help with Roscoe."

"Ainsley Scott, executive concierge and owner of Odds & Errands," she says, ignoring my hand. "I don't usually deal with dogs. I'm doing this as a favor to Brie."

I pretend she didn't just diss me and casually shove my hands into the pockets of my jeans. "And for a pretty hefty fee, so she tells me."

She shrugs. "Fair compensation if you ask me. Plus, from the looks of this place, you're not exactly hurting for money."

I fold my arms across my chest and look down at her. The top of her head comes up to my chin, putting her at about five-two in her ballet flats. My mind quickly calculates how we'd fit together in bed, in the shower, against the wall. Complex calculations are more Connor's thing, but this kind of assessment

I can more than handle. It doesn't take an actuary to figure out how fucking good it would be with her, wherever, whenever, however.

"So the richer the customer, the more you gouge him?" I ask. "Doesn't sound like a smart business model."

She glares at me like she can read my dirty thoughts. Which is impossible, of course. But even if she were the Long Island Medium, I'm not going to feel guilty. Any red-blooded male who found her in the middle of his living room on her hands and knees, her J.Lo booty undulating like she's starring in a hip-hop video, would be thinking the same damn thing.

"I don't gouge my customers, Mr. Lawson," she says all stiff and formal, and fuck if that doesn't turn me on even more. My filthy mind goes down a dom/sub wormhole, and I'm not sure which fantasy is hotter, her standing over me in leather and latex or me with her blindfolded and bound, at my mercy. It takes me a second to realize she's still talking. "I'm good at what I do. I'm prompt, reliable and discrete when called for. My clients appreciate what I have to offer, and they're willing to pay top dollar for it."

She bends down to pick up the pot, which draws my eyes back to her butt. I've never considered myself an ass man—boobs have always been my personal kryptonite—but for this girl, I could change. Not that her tits are bad, either. From what I can see under her T-shirt, they're pert perfect handfuls, not too big and not too small. Like in that bedtime story with the three bears—hers are just right.

She breezes past me to the kitchen area. Naturally, I follow, like she's the Pied fucking Piper and I'm a rat, under her spell.

"I suppose you'll expect extra for working after hours," I say, leaning against the counter.

Christ. Why did every word out of my mouth sound like I was in a low-budget porno?

"No." She dumps the soapy water into the sink and rinses the sponge. "My fee is negotiated up front. I never charge overtime unless agreed upon in advance. I only stopped by tonight because your sister texted me that your flight was delayed. She was worried about Roscoe being alone for so long. With good reason, it turned out. But now that you're here, you can finish up."

"Finish up?"

"Your dog peed on the rug. I soaked it up with paper towels and used dish soap to clean it. This should help neutralize the ammonia."

She fills the pot with fresh water and adds a splash of vinegar. Where the hell did she find that? I feel a little violated knowing she's been through my cabinets. Not that I've ever really been through them. It's not like I do much cooking, and what little I do need my once-a-week housekeeper makes sure to stock.

"He's not my…"

"Save it." She cuts me off, tossing the sponge back into the pot and shoving the whole thing at my chest. I have no choice but to take it, warm water sloshing onto my Henley. "I know. He's not your dog. But he's your responsibility for the next three months. Which means you're on cleanup duty."

"I don't know." I scrub a hand through my hair and fight back a yawn. The adrenalin of walking in on my sexy pet sitter—correction, executive concierge—is starting to wear off and the fatigue of flight delays, a packed plane and what had to be the slowest Uber driver in the tristate area is settling in. "It seems to me if you had walked him like you were supposed to, he wouldn't be peeing on my Persian rug. Which, in a way, makes it your responsibility."

"Two times a day," she says, holding up two fingers in case I'm a slow learner and need visual reinforcement. "That was my agreement with your sister. I walked him this morning at eight and this afternoon at four."

"Hey, I couldn't help it if my flight had mechanical trouble."

"I know." She grabs a denim jacket from one of the high-backed stools flanking the kitchen island and shrugs it on. "That's why I rushed over here when I got your sister's text. This was your one freebie. In the future, I'd appreciate a heads-up if you're going to be out late. That way I can adjust Roscoe's schedule. My number's on a sticky note on the fridge, along with a copy of our service contract."

She slings a purse that looks big enough to hide a body in over her shoulder and starts for the door, turning as she reaches it to throw one last parting jab. "And trust me, if I have to come over here at this hour again, you will pay extra."

I watch her sassy ass sashay out of my apartment and sigh, my body finally giving in to exhaustion and collapsing onto the closest stool.

I have to hand it to her. She's right about one thing, that's for sure.

I'll be paying. For the next three months. In spades.

CHAPTER THREE

Ainsley

"OKAY, SO ERIN, you'll drop off Mrs. Harris's dry cleaning, return Mr. Albertson's cable box and pick the Barton kids up from rock climbing at Chelsea Pier at three."

She gives me a mock salute. "On it, chief."

"And Aaron…" I scroll down to the next page of the beautiful color-coded spreadsheet that's our virtual bible at Odds & Errands, keeping us organized and running smoothly. "You're waiting for Hästens to deliver the Stillwaters' new mattress. They should be there sometime between ten and two. And don't forget to make sure they take away the old one. When you're done with that, you can take Mrs. Vincent's Mercedes to be detailed."

"Can I switch with Erin?" He wrings his hands together and pouts, hitting me with his best puppy dog eyes. "Pretty please? I'll pick up the Barton kids if she takes the Mercedes. I hate driving in the city. And Mrs. Vincent gives me the creeps. She's always looking at me funny."

"It's okay with me if it's okay with the boss lady," Erin offers, ever the amenable employee. "I like to drive. And Mrs. Vincent's not looking at you funny. She probably just misplaced her glasses again."

"Done," I say, forestalling any further debate on something that should have been settled the second Erin uttered the words "it's okay." Doesn't matter to me who does what, as long as it all gets done. I make the appropriate changes to the spreadsheet, hit Save and review it one more time. "That leaves me with picking up groceries for Mr. Perkins, standing in the TKTS line for the Ackerman twins and…shit."

The dog.

"What's wrong?" Erin asks.

I look up from my computer. "We have a new client."

A white lie. Truth be told, I've been taking care of Roscoe for the better part of two weeks now. I just haven't had the stomach to add him to my spread-sheet, which would mean explaining to the Bobbsey Twins why I broke my absolutely-no-dogs rule. But I can't keep it a secret forever. And now seems like as good a time as any to confess.

Aaron frowns. "Since when is that a problem?"

Since our new client found me on all fours on his living room carpet.

I've dealt with all kinds of customers without losing my cool, but something about Jake Lawson—all manly and broody and judgey—had run me off the rails. Maybe it was the way he'd made me feel, hot and bothered and defensive as hell at the same time. I cringe inside remembering how rude I'd been to him, shoving the pot of water at him and waltzing out the door. So much for the customer is always right.

I blame Brie. She should have warned me her brother was pantie-meltingly gorgeous. Tall and dark-haired, with piercing russet brown eyes, a strong, square jaw dotted with sexy eleven o'clock stubble, and a build that made my mouth water—perfectly sculpted, like he'd earned his muscles through manual labor and not hours at the gym, even though logic told me it was probably the latter. Just the way I like my men. Well, except for the whole broody, judgey thing.

Then again, Jake is Brie's brother. She probably doesn't think of him that way. At least, I hope she doesn't. So I guess the blame rests solely on me and my overactive hormones.

"Since I forgot to add him to the spreadsheet," I lie again, crossing my fingers behind my back and keeping my long internal monologue to myself.

"You? Forgot something?" Aaron rushes to my side, feels my forehead with the back of his hand, then turns to Erin. "She's not running a fever."

"Maybe not, but she looks pale." Erin joins him,

grabbing my wrist, and pretending to search for my pulse. "I think she needs medical attention. Should we call a doctor?"

"Very funny, Key and Peele. Sit back down and give me a second."

They take their seats opposite the repurposed five-panel door that serves as my desk as I type, making a few hasty mental calculations while I amend the almighty spreadsheet. Thinking on your feet is an essential skill in the concierge business. Things are always changing, often with little to no notice.

Let's see... Mr. Perkins is on the Upper West Side, TKTS is in Times Square, which is in Midtown, and Jake's down in Tribeca...

I snap my fingers. "Got it. I'll take care of Mr. Perkins's groceries first, grab the tickets at TKTS, then shoot down to Tribeca to take care of Roscoe."

With any luck, I'll be done by noon and on time for my lunch date with Mom in the Meatpacking District. Her treat, natch. The only way you'll catch me at Fig & Olive is if someone else is paying the tab.

"Who's Roscoe?" Erin asks. "Our new client?"

"His dog." I give the new and improved spreadsheet a final once-over before hitting Save. "Or his parents' dog, to be more accurate."

"A dog?" Aaron practically screeches. I swear, he could give Brie a run for her money. His picture should be next to the word *drama* in the dictionary.

Well, his and Brie's. "I love dogs. But I thought you said pets were off limits."

"That's right," Erin chimes in. "You said we were a concierge service, not pet sitters."

"It's a favor for a friend." I don't bother telling them about the hefty fee we're getting. If things keep looking up, I'd rather surprise them with a nice Christmas bonus.

"A friend, huh?" Aaron waggles his eyebrows. "Let me guess. Is this friend a male?"

"Maybe a tall, dark and eligible male?" Erin throws in for good measure.

Nope. So not going there with these two. I knew hiring grad students as my part-time labor force was going to bite me in the ass. They're both way too interested in my love life.

Or lack thereof.

"I think we're done here." I close the cover on my laptop. "Unless either of you has actual work to discuss, this meeting is adjourned."

We agree to regroup back at my place at four and go our separate ways. I catch an uptown 1 train and take care of Mr. Perkins's grocery shopping without incident—his list isn't too long, and I've got his fridge stocked by ten. I'm not so lucky with TKTS, though. The app tells me the wait at the discount ticket booth is already over an hour and a half. Damn summer tourists. There's no way Roscoe's going to

wait that long before going out, and I'm sure as hell
not risking another accident.

I do a little more of that quick thinking, decide
I'll have to try to kill three birds with one stone, and
stick out an arm to hail a cab. Pricier than the subway, especially since I've got a monthly pass, but
I'm pressed for time, and I figure with what Jake's
paying me I can swing it. Plus, like everything else
work-related, I'll write it off as a business expense.

I slide into the back seat and give the cabbie Jake's
address, simultaneously whipping out my phone so I
can shoot my mother a quick text to push our lunch
date back to one and let her know we'll need sidewalk seating. I don't dare tell her why. She'll freak
if she finds out I'm bringing a *d-o-g*. Pets were
strictly verboten in the Scott household, especially
large, hairy ones. Too much fur on the stuffy French
Regency-style furniture.

Text sent, I dump my phone back in my bag and
lean forward so the cabbie can hear me. "There's
an extra ten spot in it for you if you get me there in
under fifteen minutes."

He does, and there's a big smile on his face as he
drives off. I fish Jake's key chain out of my bag, trying to remember which key I need first. Is the long
one for the building, or the apartment? I get a temporary reprieve from having to figure it out thanks
to the Boho-chic chick in a floppy hat, white eyelet

dress and cowboy boots who bursts through the door at just the right moment.

I catch the door and slip inside. The doorman gives me the evil eye until I flash Jake's keys and explain that I'm there to walk Roscoe. Then his suspicion changes to sympathy and he waves me up.

Forty-five minutes, one epic battle to get Roscoe's leash on, and a harrowing cab ride later—the first three that stopped bailed once they realized how damn big the dog was, and I had to bribe the fourth with the promise of a twenty-dollar tip—and Roscoe and I are in Times Square, an area of the city I usually avoid like the plague. It's crowded, touristy and as an added disincentive Dale's office is half a block away. Not that I'm likely to run into him in the throng of Broadway lovers lining up for discount tickets at the TKTS box. Dale is to theater as my mother is to the discount rack at Bergdorf Goodman. A total no-go.

Or at least he was when he was with me. Lord knows what he and Una do for shits and giggles. I mean, she was his secretary, for God's sake. Excuse me. Administrative assistant. Either way, a total freaking cliché. But at least he can't complain he never sees her because she spends too much time at work. Lord knows I heard that refrain often enough. The fact that it was true didn't make it any easier to hear. Long office hours are a given when you're trying to make partner at a prestigious New York law firm.

I give myself a mental bitch slap for letting my mind wander back down the Dale-and-DK&G road as Roscoe and I take our place in line. My life has taken a complete one-eighty in the year and a half since Dale dropped his bombshell on me, breaking our engagement. And while I'd be lying if I said it doesn't still sting a little, I don't regret it one bit. Getting unceremoniously dumped on the eve of my wedding was exactly the wake-up call I needed.

Despite what my bitterly disappointed parents think.

"Can I pet your dog?" the girl in front of me in line asks. She looks to be about eight or nine, her *Aladdin* T-shirt a dead giveaway as to what show she's hoping to see. A woman who's obviously her mother hovers over her shoulder.

"She loves dogs," the woman says. "But I've taught her always to ask before petting one. You can't tell just by looking if a dog is friendly, right Hannah?"

"Right." The little girl—Hannah—nods vigorously, her pigtails bouncing.

"Go ahead." I step to one side and nudge the dog forward with my knee. He's almost as tall as she is. "Roscoe's as friendly as they come."

Sure, I haven't known him long. But it doesn't take a rocket scientist—or the hours I've spent on the internet researching Irish wolfhounds—to figure out this guy wouldn't hurt a flea. My first impression was way off. He's more of a gentle giant than a vicious beast.

"Hey there, Roscoe." Hannah holds her hand out to him, palm flat. Her mother really has taught her well. He sniffs it, then licks, and the next thing I know the two of them are thick as thieves while Hannah's mom and I chat about shows we've seen and want to see. It makes the hour or so we wait to get up to the ticket window—during which another fifteen or twenty people stop to pet my big, slobbery, overly friendly companion, drawn in like flies to honey by his dopey doggy grin and fiercely wagging tail—fly by.

I have definitely underestimated the power of the pooch. I start thinking of other errands that might be more enjoyable with Roscoe along. Going to the farmer's market in Union Square for Mrs. Black. Dropping off Mr. D'Ambrosio's library books. Depositing Mrs. Matos's Social security check. (No matter how many times I try to convince her, she refuses to sign up for direct deposit. Says she doesn't trust computers. I don't have the heart to tell her I usually go to the instant teller machine.) Maybe it won't be so bad having a dog in our care after all.

When I'm ten people from the head of the line, I text one of the Ackerman twins, and she rushes over from Restaurant Row, where she works as a hostess, to take my place. I say goodbye to Hannah and her mom, check my phone and see I've got about forty-five minutes before I'm due to meet my mother. Rather than risk another cab ride, I decide to walk the High Line. Yet another one of Manhattan's many pleasures I hadn't had the time to experience when I was chained to my desk at DK&G. The elevated park on an abandoned freight railway, with its lush greenery, historic buildings and quaint overlooks, never fails to calm my nerves and soothe my senses.

The feeling doesn't last long. At least not for me. I can't speak for Roscoe, who doesn't seem to be phased by much of anything.

"You're late." My mother purses her perfectly painted lips—Casablanca by Tom Ford, her day shade—and crosses her legs, not bothering to do anything so drastic as to, say, get up and give her own flesh and blood a hug.

"I'm right on time." I pull out the chair opposite her and sit, not needing to check my phone since I've kept meticulous track of the time throughout our walk, doing my level best not to upset Mommy Dearest. Like I stood a chance of that happening. I think my mere existence pisses her off. She swears I wasn't an "oops" baby, but it sure seems that way sometimes.

"On time is late." She takes of sip of her sidecar— all she ever drinks, and only after noon—and ges- tures to Roscoe, who's made himself comfortable at my feet under the table. "What is this monstrosity? And why are you so sweaty?"

I flag a waiter. I don't usually drink on the job, but one beer won't hurt. There's no way I'm getting through this meal without a little liquid courage, especially with my mother already well into her first drink. "It's good to see you, too, Mom."

She doesn't say anything, just gives me a judgmental stare over the rim of her glass. Eventually, I give in. Like I always do.

Well, almost always. I'm not going back to my old way of life, no matter how much she and my father guilt trip me.

"This is Roscoe." I reach down to scratch the top of his big ole head. "He's a who, not a what. I'm helping take care of him for the next few months. Or Odds & Errands is. And if I'm sweaty, it's because we walked here from Midtown on the High Line."

"Ah, yes. Your father and I donated to that project when it was first getting started." Guaranteed that was the closest she'd ever get to it. My mother and the great outdoors did not mix well. Her idea of roughing it was staying in a hotel with fewer than five stars. "You couldn't have left him at home?"

Yeah, I could have. I had time to get him back to Tribeca. But a little, rebellious part of me wanted to bring him to our lunch date, knowing it would get under my mother's skin. Not that I'm admitting any of this to the woman sitting across the table from me, her judgey stare still intact. "You know how it is. Busy morning. I had a to multitask."

The waiter finally makes his way over to us. I order a craft beer I've never tried—I like to experiment—and we both order our meals, kale and quinoa salad for Mom, naturally, and a thick, juicy burger with a side of fries for me. Her lips form an all-too familiar pout, making her disapproval evident. I ignore it and take a slice of warm, crusty bread from the basket in the middle of the table, dipping it liberally in their signature basil-infused olive oil. If I'm feeling really rebellious, maybe I'll even order dessert. The crème brûlée cheesecake here is fantastic.

"Your little gopher business is going well, then?" my mother asks.

It's the same conversation we've had hundreds of times. I tell her—for the hundredth time—that Odds & Errands is doing just swell, thank you, fend off the rest of her questions with the most banal, general answers I can give and make the expected polite inquiries about my father, aunts, uncles and cousins— all doing heaps better than me, of course—until our meals arrive and we eat in silence.

"So," I say, sneaking the last bite of my burger to Roscoe, who thumps his tail in appreciation. "Was there a reason you summoned me here?"

"I did not summon you." My mother sets her fork down, leaving half her salad uneaten, and dabs her mouth with her napkin. "I merely thought it would be nice if we spent some time together."

Right. My mother never does anything without some sort of ulterior motive.

"It's just that Martin Fletcher—you know Martin, he's the president of our co-op board—well, he thought you might want to come to one of our tenant meetings," she continues. "Talk up your services. I know you say you're doing fine, but some new business couldn't hurt, right?"

And there it is. My mother the white knight, swooping in to save what she perceives as my pathetic failure of an ass.

"Thanks for lunch. I've got to go. Roscoe should have been back home by now." I push my chair back and stand, unraveling the dog's leash from the table leg, where I'd tied it to keep him secure.

My mother lowers her napkin. "What about Mr. Fletcher's offer? I can text you his number so you can set something up."

"I'll think about it," I toss over my shoulder, already halfway down 13th Street.

Spoiler alert: I won't. Not one little bit.

CHAPTER FOUR

Jake

FOR THE SECOND time this week, I'm standing in the doorway of my apartment, shitting bricks. Only this time I'm inside, not in the hall. And I'm not freaking out because I'm afraid the monster my parents call a dog has wreaked havoc on my apartment. I'm freaking out because, as far as I can tell, he's not there. He's nowhere to be seen, and the place is as quiet as Grant's Tomb. No whining. No tail thumping. No obnoxious, window-rattling canine snores.

Roscoe and I may not be best buddies. On good days, we tolerate each other. But the parental units are inordinately attached to him—a fact I find especially ironic seeing as they refused to get a dog when Brie and I were kids, no matter how much we begged. The thought of telling them their pride and joy has been dognapped or is lost in the big, bad city gives me the willies.

I drop my gym bag on the floor next to the couch

and walk through the loft, calling his name. The silence is deafening. Where the hell is he? Sexy pet sitter—and yeah, that's what I put Ainsley in my phone as—texted hours ago to let me know she was taking him for his morning constitutional. She should have had him back by now.

I pull my cell from my pocket to make sure I haven't missed another text from her. Nothing. I'm about to call her when the door opens and Roscoe bursts through, dragging Ainsley behind him. She kneels down next to him to take off his leash, obviously unaware of my presence, and I take the opportunity to study her unobserved.

She's beautifully bedraggled in one of those short, strappy denim one-piece things women seem to love and classic white Converse Chuck Taylor high-tops, her hair half-escaped from its ponytail and her cheeks flushed and shiny with a thin sheen of sweat. My cock surprises me by standing at attention. I adjust the waistband in my thankfully roomy gym shorts, wishing I still had my bag in hand to use as a shield, and fight the sudden, overwhelming, irrational urge to cross the room and kiss the ever-loving shit out of her until we're both desperate, panting and ready to fuck like oversexed monkeys.

My reaction is like a virtual smack upside the head. Don't get me wrong. I'm not a damn saint. I like women, and they sure as hell seem to like me. But this instant, visceral, almost primal attraction? This burning need to be inside Ainsley, who I've known all of fourteen days, to hear her scream my name as I make her come again and again? That's something entirely new—and more than a little bit unsettling—for me. So I shove it way, way down deep and adjust my shorts again, thanking my lucky stars that the object of my fantasies is preoccupied with the damn dog.

It takes her only a few seconds to free Roscoe. She gives him a pat on the head and shoos him into the living room area, toward the hideous corduroy doggie bed he seems determined not to sleep in, preferring to sprawl his gigantic body across my California king. Then she stands, our eyes meet, and she lets out a cock-teasing little gasp that has me wondering why I'm not following through with my initial instinct and kissing the shit out of her.

"Is this going to be a regular occurrence, you sneaking up on me?" she asks, breathless. One hand flutters to her chest, drawing my attention to the dark shadow of her cleavage. "Because if it is, maybe you could put a bell around your neck or something. Give a girl a little advance warning."

"Are you saying you want to collar me?" I quirk a brow at her, unable to pass up the opening she's unwittingly given me. "I never would have guessed you're into that kind of stuff, but I'm game if you are."

She rolls her eyes. "Why am I not surprised you went there?"

She spins on her heel to go hang Roscoe's leash

on the hook by the door where, until he showed up, I kept my keys. Her hair swirls around her face as she turns, and I catch a whiff of her. Even hot and slightly sweaty from being dragged around mid-summer Manhattan by the quadruped from hell, she smells fucking fantastic, like sunshine and straw-berries, with a dash of vanilla. The urge to lean in and inhale—or devour—her is strong, but I marshal all my powers of resistance and retreat behind the kitchen island, hoping a three-hundred-pound slab of marble between us will be enough to keep my hands to myself and my dick in my pants.

"Um, because I'm a guy?" I yank open the stain-less steel sub-zero fridge and pull out a Gatorade. Cool Blue, my favorite. I crack it open, take a long swig, then catch Ainsley's eye. My mouth engages before my brain, making me instantly regret what comes out of it next.

"Want one?"

It's official. I'm a fucking moron. I'm supposed to be hustling this girl out of my apartment, not inviting her to stay for goddamn tea and crumpets. Or elec-trolytes. I mentally cross my fingers, hoping she's got some superimportant engagement to run off to. Like getting her nails done. Or watching paint dry.

She pauses, then shrugs, pulls out a stool and takes a seat at the island, resting her forearms on the Calacatta marble my designer had flown in from Italy at a cost of I-don't-want-to-know. "Why not?"

Fucking A.

I grab another Gatorade out of the fridge and slide it across the counter to her. "I hope blue's okay. It's all I've got."

Another shrug as she twists the cap off. "I'm not picky."

"Where were you?" I ask, finally getting around to the question that's been nagging me since I opened my door and found my apartment dogless. "I thought you took Roscoe out hours ago."

I sneak a glance toward the living room and see the dog in question occupying most of my designer leather sofa. Not the doggie bed, but at least it's better than my California king. He's out cold, his head lolled back and his eyes closed. Wherever Ainsley took him, she sure ran him ragged. I should probably be thanking her for wearing him out, not giving her the third degree.

"I did." She tips her head back to take a sip, and I'm riveted by the curve of her lips and the long line of her throat as she drinks. Fuck, I'm turning into some sort of pervert, getting off on the simple but suddenly strangely seductive act of a woman swallowing. Fortunately for me, the sip is a quick one. Unfortunately, her next action—licking her lips—is no less sexually arousing. "My schedule was jam-packed this morning, so I took him along with me on a few errands. I hope you don't mind."

"You took him along with you?" I repeat like a

robot. My brain seems to have short-circuited, stuck on the image of her downing that Gatorade.

"Yeah. He was a big hit with the crowd at TKTS. My mother was less enthusiastic, but that was fun, too."

I don't want to dig into what's obviously a less than perfect relationship with her mom, so I opt for the next worst thing—guilt tripping her. "Next time shoot me a text and let me know if you're going to have him out that long. I was about to call 9-1-1."

Her face falls. "Seriously?"

"Okay, maybe I'm exaggerating a little." I lean against the counter and swig my Gatorade. "But I'd be lying if I said I wasn't concerned. My parents would kill me if anything happened to Roscoe. I'm convinced they like him better than me."

"I'm sorry." She sets her drink down. "I didn't mean to scare you. I didn't think you'd be back so soon. Brie says you work pretty much 24/7."

So she's been talking to Brie about me. Interesting. I throw caution to the wind and take the stool next to her, sitting so close we're practically touching from shoulder to thigh, her strawberry vanilla scent threatening to pull me in and drag me under. "Really? What other lies has my beloved big-mouthed little sister been spreading about me?"

Her breath hitches ever so slightly and her nipples look like they could poke holes through her romper, living proof that I'm not the only one feeling this crazy chemistry between us. When she speaks, her voice is a notch lower, huskier than before, confirming my not-so-scientific hypothesis. "You're saying you don't work all the time?"

"I work hard." I lean in suggestively. "But I like to play hard, too. Did Brie tell you that?"

"Not exactly." Ainsley wraps her fingers around the neck of her Gatorade bottle, which, naturally, has me picturing them fisting my semi-erect cock. "Just that on the rare occasions when you're not working, you like to play the field. I think she was trying to warn me away from you."

I'll have to remember to kill my sister when she gets back from the left coast. But right now I've got more pressing concerns. Like my dick pressing against my boxer briefs.

"Did it work?"

She lifts the bottle to her lips and takes a deliberate, slow sip, almost as if she's stalling for time, not sure whether she wants to continue our verbal foreplay. Because make no mistake, that's what this is. And both of us know it.

"Did what work?" she asks finally, setting the bottle down.

"Her warning."

With only inches between us, I find myself noticing new, intriguing details about her. The spray of freckles across the bridge of her nose. The gold flecks in her blue-gray eyes. The silvery glint of a stud in her tongue. And here I thought she couldn't be sexier. Just the thought of her giving me head, that little silver ball flicking against my shaft... Damn. It's almost enough to make me shoot my load.

She lifts her chin defiantly. "I'm here, aren't I?"

Completely tossing what little good sense I have left into the goddamn trash can, I reach out and trace her lower lip with my thumb. To my surprise, she doesn't pull away. Instead, her lips part, giving me another glimpse of that sexy stud. The need to kiss her, to suck her tongue into my greedy mouth and play with that naughty piercing, is overpowering. I don't even try to fight it this time, lowering my head to hers.

"What are you doing?" Her words come out on a whisper, her warm breath dancing across my thumb.

"Kissing you." I slide my hand to the back of her head, anchoring it in place. "Unless you tell me to stop."

"I should."

Her ponytail is a distant memory now, and my fingers mesh into the silky strands of her free-flowing hair. "Give me one good reason."

"Roscoe."

"Sound asleep."

"Your sister."

"Thousands of miles away." My gaze drops to her parted lips, plump and pink and practically begging for me to make good on my promise. That fucking stud provokes and entices me, making my already stiff cock impossibly harder. If she walks away from me now, I'm going to have to take the world's longest, coldest shower just to be able to walk straight. "Is that the best you've got?"

A deep blush colors her cheeks and her eyes darken to a midnight blue. She puts a manicured hand to my chest, freezing my breath in my lungs. "You haven't begun to see my best."

"Show me," I demand when I'm able to breathe again.

She hesitates, then leans in, brushing her mouth over mine in a move that's more tease than kiss. But I'm not letting her get away that easy. Now that I've got her where I want her, I want more than a taste. I want that pierced tongue tangling with mine. I want her teeth nipping at my lips. I want her arms around me, her chest smashed against mine, her fingernails digging into my back.

Like that pain in the ass chick in *Willy Wonka & The Chocolate Factory*, I want it all. And I want it now.

I bury my fingers deeper in her hair and stand, moving so fast I kick my stool over. It lands with a thud on the hand-scraped hardwood floor. Roscoe stirs but thank fuck doesn't wake from his sleep of the dead. Even if he had, it wouldn't have mattered. I'm not getting cockblocked by a damn dog.

"You call that a kiss?" I ask, wedging my leg between hers. "This is a kiss."

I lower my head and slant my lips over hers. The kiss starts as a slow burn. I tease her with soft nips and light licks, stoking the fire, building up to the inferno I know is only moments away because there's no way I'm going to last longer than that without losing control.

She moans into my mouth and wraps her arms around me, grinding against my thigh. Fuck that's hot, the way she takes what she wants without asking, without apology. That's all the license I need to take my foot off the brakes and go all in, kissing her harder, deeper. She tastes icy cool and raspberry sweet from the Gatorade, and her soft curves fit perfectly to my harder edges. I let my free hand roam up those curves to her breast, and she moans again as I find her nipple through the thin fabric of her romper and roll it between my thumb and forefinger.

I break off the kiss but only to slide my mouth down her neck, leaving a hot, wet trail to the hollow of her throat. I'd like to explore even lower, to discover if she's a basic bra or lacy lingerie kind of girl. Unfortunately, skilled as I am in the art of getting a woman out of her clothes, I can't for the life of me figure out the thingamajig she's wearing. There's a row of buttons down the front, but when I try to undo the top one it doesn't budge.

"You're driving me crazy," I groan. I try the next button. No dice. I'm ready to rip the fuckers off. "These goddamn buttons are driving me crazy."

"They're for decoration only," she pants, arching into me. "There's a zipper. In back."

I reach around her, find the tab, and inch it down, my fingers grazing her bare skin on the journey. A line of goose bumps sprouts in their wake and I get a thrill knowing I did that to her, that she's as into this as I am. I push the straps off her shoulders and down her arms, and the torture device drops to her waist, leaving her in only a pretty pink bra that barely contains her pale, perfect breasts.

Lacy lingerie. Score.

"Please." Her slow grind picks up steam and her eyes drift shut. Her arms band around me like a vice, my fantasy about her nails digging into me becoming reality. She's hot and wet against my thigh even through a layer of denim, and my sexual Spidey sense tells me she's seconds from coming.

"Fuck, yeah. That's it, baby," I murmur against her neck, encouraging her. I tweak one nipple through the lace of her bra, and she sucks in a sharp breath. "Let go."

A few more hip rolls and she does, throwing her head back and calling out my name. She continues to spasm for a few seconds until her arms loosen their iron grip on my midsection and she collapses against me, spent.

I pull the edge of one bra cup down and free her breast from its frilly prison, hopeful she's up for another round where we both get off. Those hopes die a quick and painful death when an bone-rattling thump from the living room startles us. Because I'm the guy with the worst luck in the five boroughs, Roscoe, back from doggie dreamland, has chosen that exact moment to fall off the couch. He lifts his head and lets out a low, mournful howl that pierces my very soul.

Shit. This has the potential to be almost as bad as if the beast had been dognapped. My parents are going to flip out if their precious baby has a boo-boo.

"Don't move." I peel her arms from around my waist and step back, planting a hard, fast kiss on her bee-stung lips. "He's probably fine, but I should at least check on him. I'll be right back."

I sprint to Roscoe's side, and the howling stops as I do a quick head-to-tail exam. I'm no vet, but nothing feels broken. My diagnosis is confirmed when the big drama queen gets effortlessly to his feet and trots off toward my bedroom, presumably to take up residence on my bed.

"See?" I stand, wiping my hands on my shorts. "No harm, no foul. Now how about we pick up where we left off?"

But when I turn back to Ainsley, expecting to find her half-dressed and ready for more, my door swings shut with a hollow, ominous click, and she's gone. I tunnel my hands through my hair and glare in the direction of my bedroom, swearing under my breath.

Fucking dog managed to cockblock me after all.

CHAPTER FIVE

Ainsley

"YOU DID WHAT? With a client?" My bestie Mia gapes at me, her glass of prosecco stalled halfway to her lips. We met in contracts class first year of law school at New York University, and even though I'm no longer practicing we've stayed close. She's one of the only holdovers in my life from my legal-eagle days—and one of the few people who didn't think I was crazy for chucking it all and starting over.

"Who are you?" she asks, her cherry lips twisting into an impish grin. "And what have you done with my best friend?"

I knock back the rest of my drink and plunk the glass down on the table. I knew it was a huge risk going out on the town with Mia tonight. Two rounds in, and my tongue's already as loose as my morals were in Jake's apartment earlier. But it's too late to take the words back now. As my great-aunt Elizabeth used to say, in for a penny, in for a goddamn ton.

"I dry humped his leg like a bitch in heat." *And came so hard I saw stars. Without even taking off my clothes.*

Mia lets out a low whistle. "Damn, girl. You sure know how to break a sexual drought."

I stare her down. "Who said I was in a sexual drought?"

"You did. The last time we were here."

Here is Tammany Hall, our favorite Greenwich Village dive bar. The drinks are cheap, the floor is sticky and the decor is a cross between a bordello and a hunting cabin, with an odd yet somehow soothing combination of red velvet and taxidermy. But the atmosphere is always friendly and on game days you can catch the Yankees and Mets on the dueling flat screens above the scarred oak bar.

I decide to ignore the issue of my heretofore virtually nonexistent sex life and plow on. I've started this story. I might as well finish it.

Unlike Jake, who didn't get to finish. At least not with me. Who knows what he did after I cut and ran? Or came and ran.

I slam the door on the image of Jake with his dick in his hand, sliding his fist up and down his impressive length until he shoots his load all over those washboard abs I felt under his T-shirt, and signal the waitress for another drink. "That's not all."

"There's more?" Mia lifts her now-empty glass, indicating she's ready for a refill, too. "Please tell me that after the dry humping, you ripped his clothes off and rode him like a polo pony."

I wish. "Not exactly."

"Then what?"

She flips her long inky-black hair over her shoulder, and I swear two guys at the table next to us start visibly drooling. That's Mia. Everywhere we go, she attracts attention, with her Cher-inspired locks, flawless olive skin and statuesque figure. The chart at the doctor's office says I'm average height and weight, but next to her I feel like a bridge troll. If she wasn't so stinking nice, and so oblivious to her effect on the male of the species, I'd have to hate her just on principle.

The waitress comes with round number three, and I hand off our empty glasses before taking a sip from my new one. "Let's just say it wasn't my finest moment."

"Come on," Mia whines. "Spill. You can't leave me hanging."

"Well, since you put it that way…" I let my words trail off, hoping she gets the general idea without me having to fill in the dirty details.

She cocks a perfectly shaped brow at me. "Stop being so evasive and spit it out."

So much for subtlety. I try again, still tiptoeing around the subject but a little less delicately this time. "Leaving people hanging seems to be my MO today."

"You did not get your jollies and leave him all hot

and bothered, did you?" She takes one look at my face, which must have guilt written all over it, and knows the answer. "Oh my God, you totally did. You filthy little tease."

"Hey, I told you it wasn't my finest moment." I take a hit of prosecco. This conversation definitely requires more alcohol. "Roscoe fell off the couch, and when Jake went to check on him, I bolted."

"Roscoe?"

"The dog." I bury my head in my hands with a groan. "It was humiliating. I couldn't look him in the eye after grinding on his thigh like it was a stripper pole."

"The dog?" she teases.

I lift my head long enough to shoot daggers at her. "Very funny."

"Hey." She takes my hands and pries them away from my face. "If I know men, you have nothing to be ashamed about. I guarantee he enjoyed it as much as you did."

I'm starting to feel a tad bit better about my porn star performance when she throws in a zinger. "Of course, he probably would have enjoyed it more if you stuck around for an encore."

"Thanks for reminding me." I reach for my drink. I seriously don't know how I'm going to face Jake again. Maybe I can pass this job off to one of my assistants. Aaron loves dogs. He'd probably jump at the chance to hang out with Roscoe.

"I have idea." Mia whips out her cell phone. "You said this guy Jake owns a club, right?"

"Yeah. Some high-end place in Chelsea." Not my scene, for sure. Mostly celebs and artists, mixed with a smattering of uptown girls and downtown finance boys. Too crowded. Too noisy. Too stuffy. I prefer joints like the one I'm in now. Quirky. Cozy. And quiet enough to have an actual conversation.

"What's it called?" she asks, tapping her screen to open her internet browser.

I try to dredge the name up from the recesses of my memory. Brie must have mentioned it a million times. She's inordinately proud of her brother and his pull-himself-up-from-his-bootstrap success. "Top… something. Drawer, maybe. Or Shelf. Why?"

"We're going there. Tonight."

It's a good thing I'm not mid-sip, or I would have spit prosecco all over Mia's brand new chili-red Kate Spade canteen bag. "Why in hell would I want to do that?"

"So you can apologize." She taps away on her phone, presumably Googling the name and address of the club.

"That is so not going to happen."

"This must be it," she says, continuing to stare at the screen as if she hasn't heard me. "Top Shelf, 455 West 17th Street. I'll order us an Uber."

"Earth to Mia." I reach across the table and snatch her phone. The woman is a force of nature once she gets rolling, so it's imperative I stop her before this crazy idea of hers becomes a full-fledged plan of action. "I'm not Ubering anywhere."

She stands and slings her purse over her arm. "Fine. We'll catch a cab. Or take the subway. It's only a few stops."

"You're not hearing me." I don't budge from my seat, hoping Newton's first law will work in my favor. A body at rest tends to stay at rest, and here's where I'm staying.

"I hear you perfectly fine. I'm just not listening. There's a difference." She holds out a hand for her phone, but I pull it out of her reach. "Seriously, Ainsley. Trust me on this. You'll feel better once you've cleared the air."

She may have a point. But it's not one I'm willing to concede just yet. "I'll text him."

"Nice try, but I'm not letting you get off that easily. There's too much room for ambiguity and misinterpretation in a text. Face-to-face communication is best."

"Who says he's even there?" Brie does. According to her, her brother practically lives at the club, so the odds are pretty strong he's there now. Not that I'm admitting that to Mia.

"It's a chance I'm willing to take. Besides, the Yankees are losing, and I'm in the mood for something more than cheap prosecco and stale nachos."

She waves a hand at the half-eaten basket of chips on the table.

I look down at my outfit. Mia, as always, is fine and fresh and totally fierce in a little black dress that's far from standard and five-inch, fire-engine red heels that match her purse and jewelry. But there's no way my nacho-stained tank top, skinny jeans and flip-flops are getting past the bouncer manning the velvet rope.

"I'm not dressed for the club scene." It's my half-assed, last-ditch effort to get out of this, but if I know Mia, she'll have some solution at her fingertips. The girl is a never-ending fount of can-do. I don't think the word *no* is in her vocabulary.

She doesn't disappoint.

"My place is closest. We can stop there first." She pulls two twenties from her purse and plunks them down on the table to cover our tab, waving off my protest. "You can borrow my Armani shift dress. You know, the navy one with the beaded-fringe hem."

I palm my breasts, which are at least two cup sizes bigger than hers. "Like anything in your closet can contain these puppies."

"It's very forgiving. And a little cleavage will make your apology go over that much smoother."

More like a lot of cleavage, but it's clear there's no point arguing with the force of nature that is Mia Hadid. I hand over her phone, the battle lost. The best I can hope for now is that by some miracle workaholic Jake has come to his senses and taken a night off. Or if he hasn't, he's too busy to deal with an insignificant errand girl with a tendency to hump and run, and I can convince Mia it's socially acceptable to revert to my original text message plan.

I push my chair back and stand, snatching my wristlet from the table. "Fine. You can dress me up and take me out on one condition."

She lets out a high-pitched squee, but I hold a hand up to stop her.

"Not so fast, Henry Higgins. You haven't heard the condition yet."

She frowns, creasing her perfect, normally wrinkle-free forehead. "Henry Higgins?"

"You know, from *My Fair Lady*." She's still staring at me like I have two heads, so I go on. "It's a musical. Based on the play *Pygmalion*. He takes a lowly flower girl and turns her into a lady."

"Figures. You and your show tunes." She grimaces, but I know she's not serious. She's been my date to the theater more times than I can count in place of my Broadway-boycotting ex-boyfriend. "So what's the condition?"

"By twelve o'clock I'm home and snug in bed."

"But it's almost eleven now," she says, twisting her wrist to check the diamond-studded Patek Philippe she bought herself at Tiffany when she made partner last month. I brace myself for the flood of regret, the deluge of could-have-been-me's, but they don't come. All the confirmation I need that I made the right decision walking away. As if I needed more proof that my life is ten thousand times better as the owner of a boutique concierge service than it was as an overworked, overstressed attorney.

I link my arm through Mia's and steer her toward the door. "Then we'd better get going. Because at midnight this lady turns back into an errand girl."

CHAPTER SIX

Jake

"YOU CAN GO HOME, you know." Connor's voice comes from over my shoulder as I stare at the bank of computer screens that dominates my enormous chrome-and-glass executive desk. "You don't have to be at the club every waking hour."

"I could say the same thing to you," I shoot back, tapping a button on my keyboard to flip from one security camera to another. It's been a fairly uneventful night so far, but that could change at the drop of a hat. Or a beer bottle. It doesn't take much to set tempers flaring, especially when alcohol is involved.

Connor rests his butt on my desk and waves a manila folder in my face. "I had to get the quarterly payroll taxes done. I was heading down the hall to drop them on Diane's desk so she can double-check my math in the morning when I saw your light on. What's your excuse?"

"Just keeping an eye out for trouble." I switch screens again. "It's a full moon. And the city's in the middle of a heat wave, with no end in sight. All the crazies will be out tonight."

"We have people for that. I believe they're called bouncers."

"I know that. I hired them."

"Then what are you really doing here?" Connor folds his arms across his chest and cocks his head to give me the hairy eyeball. "Afraid to go back to your empty apartment now that your sister's gone?"

"Are you kidding? The man cave's all mine again. I can walk around buck naked. Leave the toilet seat up. Drink milk straight from the carton." Not that I do any of that stuff. Much.

"Even assuming I buy what you're shoveling, that doesn't tell me why you're still here."

I shrug. "You know how it is. People like to rub shoulders with the club owners. Makes them feel special. And you hate that shit, so…"

He waves a hand at the bank of computers. "Shouldn't you be down there, then?"

"I was about to head out when you waltzed in."

One eyebrow arches upward, making it obvious he still doesn't believe me. "You sure that's the reason you're working late, and not that you're obsessing over the Miami deal?"

"I'm not obsessing," I insist, even though he's half right. The Miami deal's never far from my thoughts, even when I'm focused on something else. Making this thing happen means everything to me. If we can successfully expand into one new market, the whole world's ours for the taking.

And I want the whole world, dammit.

"If you say so," Connor says, his tone skeptical.

"I do."

He reaches out and puts a hand on my shoulder. "You know, there's no rush on this Miami thing. We're going to have our hands full with the New York renovations. Maybe it wouldn't be such a bad idea to hold off on any other big projects until they're done."

"You worry about the renovations, and I'll handle Miami. The market's the softest it's ever been in South Beach. Trust me, now's the time to jump in."

"I've trusted you since we were in Garanimals."

"You were the one in Garanimals, dude. I was perfectly capable of matching my own clothes without the help of jungle creatures."

"Right. Like that puke green and florescent orange striped shirt you liked to wear with those hideous plaid pants."

"Stripes go with everything."

He rolls his eyes. "Okay, Tommy Hilfiger. Just keep me up to date on Miami. And let me know if you need anything on my end."

"Will do."

I tap a key to check one last live feed before I go

down to the club floor and swear under my breath,
my mouth going as dry as Central Park's Great Lawn
in August. Two women stand just inside the entrance,
but it's the petite blonde with the killer curves who
has my undivided attention. She's traded her normally casual attire for a flimsy little cocktail dress
that hugs those curves like a jealous lover and a pair
of spiky heels that make her legs look like they go
on for miles.

Fuck me sixty-nine ways to Sunday.

"What's wrong?" Connor's hand drops from my
shoulder and he swivels his head to study the monitors. "Trouble brewing?"

You can say that again.

"Nah." *Liar.* "Just see a familiar face."

His eyes stop on the screen with Ainsley and her
gal pal. One quick keystroke and they're gone, but
it's too late. He flashes a superior, knowing, smile.
"The blonde or the brunette?"

I stand and stretch. The sooner I get out of here,
the sooner this conversation can end. "What makes
you think it's one of them? There's like six computer
screens. It could be anyone, anywhere."

"I don't know." He hauls his ass off my desk and
follows me out the door and into the hallway. "Maybe
because that's the screen you practically fell all over
yourself to change so I wouldn't see it."

"Did not."

"Did too."

"Not."

"Too."

We're at the elevator, and I punch the down button. "What are you, seven?"

He nudges me in the ribs with his elbow. "If I was, I'd be doing your homework."

He's half right. He may not have done my homework for me, but there's no way my sorry academic self would have graduated high school without a lot of help from Connor. The day Mrs. Nielson paired us together for the second grade science fair was the luckiest damn day of my young life. Of course, I didn't know then that I was dyslexic. No one did. That diagnosis wouldn't come for another year, after a boatload of questions and tests.

The elevator dings and the doors slide open for me to step inside. Connor starts to come in after me, but I stick an arm out, blocking him and preventing the door from closing in one fell swoop. "Don't you have some tax forms to deliver?"

He stares at the folder still clutched in his hand. "Right. Damn."

"I guess this discussion will have to keep until tomorrow, then. Unless you want to join me on the floor when you're done dropping those off."

Connor flinches like he's been struck and steps back. "Thanks, but I'd rather eat a shit sandwich."

No surprise there. Crowds aren't his scene. That's why he's the quiet genius behind Top Shelf and I'm the pretty boy front man. It's like high school all over again. Connor the shy, studious bookworm. Me the cocky jock who loved the spotlight. We've always been an odd pair. Like Felix and Oscar on that old sitcom my dad loves to watch in reruns. But it works.

"That's what I figured." I lower my arm and the elevator doors start to close. "Don't forget, we're meeting with the architect to go over the plans for the renovations at nine."

"I'll be there."

He touches two fingers to his forehead in a mock salute. It's the last thing I see before the doors come together and the elevator starts to move.

Alone, my thoughts turn to the woman waiting downstairs. Ainsley doesn't strike me as the club rat type. So why tonight? And why Top Shelf? Did she come here looking for fun? Or looking for me?

The elevator bumps to a stop, and I know I'll have my answer in a few minutes. But when I step onto the floor, it's wall-to-wall partiers, and Ainsley's nowhere to be seen.

"Hey, boss." Brandon, the former Force Recon Marine who's my head of security, comes up behind me and claps me on the shoulder, yelling over the techno pop tonight's guest DJ is spinning. "How's things?"

"You tell me," I shout back.

He lifts an unconcerned shoulder and lets it fall, like being responsible for the safety of a nightclub full of millennials in various states of intoxication is no big deal. And I guess maybe after spending two tours in Afghanistan doing covert ops, it's not. "Busy, but so far nothing major. A guy who was a little too handsy with one of the waitresses. Some teenagers with bad fake IDs. Two women doing meth in the bathroom. My guys took care of it, no problem."

The drug shit pisses me off, but it's an occupational hazard in the nightclub biz. I've got a good crew, though, and if Brandon says they handled it, that's good enough for me.

Now that I'm reassured everything is business as usual, I decide to cut right to the chase. "I'm looking for someone. Female."

"Business or personal?"

"Business," I lie. My business. Not his. "She's about five-three, maybe five-four. Shoulder-length blond hair. Wearing a little black dress—or maybe it was dark blue—and high heels. Which probably put her at more like five-seven or five-eight."

Brandon smirks. "You realize you just described half of the women in this joint, right?"

"Never mind." I scrub a hand through my hair and scan the bar area. Still no Ainsley. I should have known it wouldn't be that easy. Nothing worthwhile ever is. And I have a growing suspicion this woman is more than worth my while. "I'll find her myself."

He eyes me suspiciously. Not that I blame him. I'm not in the habit of stalking our female clientele.

Top Shelf is my company, not my personal dating service. I don't dip my wick in the company ink.

But you know what they say about rules. They're made to be broken.

"Well, good luck on your quest, Frodo." Brandon claps me on the back. "I should check on the guys working the door."

He ambles off, the crowd parting for him like the Red Sea. I circle the dance floor a few times, my eyes pausing on every tiny, curvy blonde. But none of them are the tiny, curvy blonde who's got me tied in knots.

I'm about to abandon the dance floor and try my luck in the VIP section when I spot her. She's across the floor on the fringe of the action watching her friend, who's at the center of it all, surrounded by a cadre of male admirers, shaking her booty to Ariana Grande's "Thank U, Next." And yeah, sue me. I know who Ariana Grande is. And the names of all of her songs. Although I wish I didn't. Truth be told, I'm more of an old school, classic rock kind of guy. Led Zeppelin. AC/DC. Black Sabbath. But that stuff doesn't go over well with the club set.

I find an empty spot against the wall and take up residence, prepared to wait for the right moment to make my move. But my ass has barely touched the painstakingly restored exposed brick when that moment arrives, courtesy of the jackass who sidles up next to Ainsley and starts gyrating against her like Channing freaking Tatum.

Not. Gonna. Happen.

I'm off like a shot, pushing through the crowd with none of my usual finesse, not caring who's in my way or what they're speculating about the crazy club owner plowing through their ranks. I'm a man on a motherfucking mission, and nothing—and no one—is going to stop me from stopping the creep creeping on Ainsley.

It seems like hours, but it's probably only a few seconds before I've got my hand on the creep's shoulder and I'm pulling him backward, away from Ainsley.

"Hey." He tries to pry my fingers off his Brooks Brothers button-down, but that only makes my grip tighten. "I'm dancing here."

Dancing's a generous term for whatever the hell it is he's doing, but I let it pass. Ainsley doesn't, however.

She stands up straighter in her high heels and plants her hands on her hips. The combined effect makes her already generous chest stick out even farther, a fact that doesn't go unnoticed by the creep, whose eyes zero in on her breasts. I'd like to gouge them out of his smug face with a spoon. If I had one. And if my eyes hadn't done the same damn thing.

"You call that dancing?" She lifts one perfectly

shaped brow. "Looked like you were getting elec-trocuted to me."

"You didn't have any complaints until he showed up." The creep jerks his head at me.

"Really? What did you think it meant when I threatened to knee you in the crotch?"

"I dunno," he says, swaying back and forth drunk-enly. "Foreplay? Some girls like it rough."

Oh, for fuck's sake. This guy's seen *50 Shades* one too many times. Not that I've seen it. At least not all of it. My sister may have forced me to watch a scene or two on cable before she took off for California.

"Tell you what." I grab his other shoulder to steady him. "You agree to leave the lady alone, and I agree not to throw your ass out of here."

He scowls up at me. Up because I've got a good four inches on him. And about thirty pounds, all muscle. "You and what army?"

"That army." I nod to Brandon, who's making his way back through the crowd, trailed by two of his crew. Don't get me wrong. I can more than handle this douchenozzle by myself. But it'll be easier with some backup to help convince wannabe Magic Mike to move along peacefully. And if that doesn't work, Brandon and company can drag him out by the col-lar of his designer shirt, and I won't have to get my club owner hands dirty.

"Hey, Zach."

"This guy giving you trouble?"

"Want us to take him out back and beat the shit out of him?"

I let go of Magic Mike and swing around to find myself surrounded by three khaki-clad yuppies who can only be his friends. *Dammit*. One drunk, over-confident asshat I can take care of solo, but four? I'd have to be really lucky. And they'd have to be really drunk.

Out of the corner of my eye I see Brandon and his boys rushing toward me, barreling through the dancers like they're bowling pins. Looks like the cavalry's coming to the rescue. Now I've just got to stall for time until they get here.

I hold my hands up, palms out, in an I-come-in-peace gesture. "Listen, guys…"

Those are the last words I utter before I'm sucker punched in the head, and I fall to the floor.

Hard.

CHAPTER SEVEN

Ainsley

"I CAN'T DO THIS," I hiss into the phone as I stand paralyzed outside Jake's apartment, staring at his door like it's the portal to an unknown world. Which, in a way, I guess it is. Because I have no clue what's waiting for me on the other side. After last night, I wouldn't be surprised if Jake took one look at me and barked at me to get out.

"Don't be ridiculous," Mia snaps back. "You're a professional. You have a job to do. Get in there and do it."

"Did you see Jake's face when they loaded him into the ambulance?" I shudder at the memory. I've never seen anyone so pale, his skin the color of chalk, his lips pressed into a harsh, thin line, his whiskey-brown eyes squeezed shut. "He was obviously in a lot of pain. I heard one of the EMTs say his shoulder was dislocated. Thanks to me."

Now I have two things to apologize to him for. I should start a list.

"The only one to blame is the entitled prick who coldcocked him." Mia pauses, and I can almost picture her lost in thought, twirling a lock of long dark hair around her finger. "And maybe me. If I hadn't left you alone…"

"Stop. This is not on you. I'm a big girl. I can take care of myself." Usually.

Mia's dry laugh cuts across the phone line. "Funny how easy it is for you to let me off the hook. Too bad you can't do the same for yourself."

She's got a point. Time for me to pull up my big girl panties and face the music, whether the tune's "Get Back" or "Let's Get It On." Truth be told, I don't know which one I'm more afraid of hearing.

With my free hand, I pull Jake's keys out of my bag. "Okay, I'm going in. Wish me luck."

"Trust me, you're not gonna need it. That boy's got it bad for you."

It's my turn to laugh now. "You're dreaming. Or smoking something funny."

"You're the one who's delusional. The guy practically broke the land speed record racing to your rescue."

"Now you're making me feel guilty again."

"Totally not what I intended. I just don't want you to miss what's staring you right in the face."

I hear something crinkle, then what sounds like

chewing. Figures. Mia's always hungry. In law school she'd eat an entire quart of Ben & Jerry's New York Super Fudge Chunk after every exam. She was always trying to get me to join in. With my own quart, of course. Sharing hers was out of the question. But unlike her I don't have the metabolism of a hummingbird.

She takes another bite and speaks through a mouthful of whatever she's gorging on. "Now quit stalling and go get your man."

"He's not…"

The line clicks off, and I let the rest of the sentence trail away. No point protesting to deaf—or AWOL—ears. Stuffing the phone in my bag, I insert the key in the lock, turn it and push the door open a crack.

"Jake? Roscoe?" There's no answer from man or beast, so I give the door another shove and I take a step inside. "It's Ainsley. I'm here to walk the dog."

Still no response. I'm starting to wonder if Jake's done something stupid like try to take Roscoe out himself when the furry monster pokes his head out of one of the bedrooms and comes lumbering toward me.

"Hey, boy." I kneel down to rub one of his ears. He likes that. Another of the things I've learned about Roscoe in our getting-to-know-you period. "Where's Jake?"

As if on cue, a loud crash comes from what I assume is the master bedroom at the far end of the loft, followed by a flurry of swears in Jake's throaty, masculine voice. My brain is instantly swamped with images of him lying on the cold, hard wooden floor in a puddle of blood. Or close to losing consciousness in the tub, his injured arm twisted awkwardly underneath him, the pain too much for him to bear. Don't most at-home accidents happen in the bathroom?

I jump up and sprint toward the source of the commotion, Roscoe at my heels. But when I burst through the door into Jake's bedroom, I immediately feel like an intruder. There's too much of him here. His minty, soapy, supersexy scent. The half-open book he was reading—the latest Jack Reacher mystery—on the nightstand. The imprint of his body on the massive memory foam mattress. What's nowhere in sight, however, is the man himself.

Another crash and a second barrage of profanity shifts my attention to the master bath. I shove down the feeling that I'm trespassing, drop my purse on the bed and sidle up to the partially open door. Some things are more important than privacy. Like personal welfare.

"Um, Jake," I call awkwardly through the space between the door and the frame. "It's Ainsley. Everything okay in there?"

Roscoe, who hasn't left my side, adds a concerned bark.

"Everything's fine." Jake's voice is clipped, strained. He's obviously in pain, but too damn stubborn to admit it. Typical tough guy. "Go walk the dog. I don't want him peeing on my rug. Again."

I'm about to clap back with a snappy rejoinder—something about how the first time wasn't my fault—when I hear crash number three, followed by some even more creative swearing.

"Doesn't sound fine to me." I grab the doorknob, ready to pull it the rest of the way open. "I'm coming in. Cover your naughty bits."

"My naughty bits?" He chuckles.

Laughter. That's got to be a good sign. Still, I'm not leaving without checking on him. "You know what I mean. You've got three seconds to hide the family jewels."

"Are you sure that's what you want? We could pick up where we left off yesterday."

No, I'm not sure. But I'm not letting him know that. "That's a bit cocky, isn't it? From out here, it doesn't sound like you're in any condition to get it on."

"I'm a man. Where there's a will, there's a way."

"Ah, so that's how that little thing works. Mind over matter."

"Who are you calling little?" he asks with a laugh, but this time it morphs into a groan.

"That's it. I'm coming in, whether you're decent or not."

I shove the door open and step into the biggest freaking bathroom I've ever seen. It's like a palace, all shiny and sterile and manly with pale gray tile, polished brass fixtures and a rich walnut vanity. A glass shower big enough for a four-person orgy dominates the far wall. It would be a picture fit for *Architectural Digest*—if it wasn't for the man slumped against the vanity, with what looks like the contents of one—or two—of the drawers strewn on the floor around him.

The very nearly naked man. Jake's naughty bits might be covered by the towel loosely tied around his waist, but not much else is. And when I say loosely, I mean that sucker's hanging on for dear life. At any moment, the poor excuse for a knot could let go.

I stare at the scrap of terrycloth, not sure if I'm willing it to stay up or fall down. I don't know if I'm ready for Jake in all his fully nude glory. My poor, palpitating heart can hardly handle what I'm seeing now. The guy's like the poster child for masculine perfection. Firmly muscled biceps. Broad chest with just the right amount of fine, dark hair. Washboard abs. My fingers itch to trace their ridges and valleys before following his happy trail down his abdomen, to his belly button, and under that damn towel to his...

Stop. This is your friend's brother. And your client. You came in here to make sure he wasn't in mortal peril, not ogle him like a side of Kobe beef.

I tamp down my runaway sex drive and close the door behind me, making sure Roscoe's on the other side. He whines for a hot second, then I hear his nails tapping on the floor as he trots off, hope-fully not to pee on Jake's precious carpet. But I can't worry about that now, not when Jake's obvi-ously hurting.

I cross to him, stepping over and around all the crap on the floor. Up close, I notice a bloody scrap of tissue stuck to one cheek. It should send his sex appeal into a nosedive, but instead it somehow in-creases it tenfold. I try my best to ignore the flash flood of lust coursing through my veins and wave a hand at the mess at his feet. "You call this fine?"

He glares at the contraption on his right arm. "This stupid fucking sling is making everything dif-ficult. Why couldn't I have landed on my left shoul-der?"

"Here." I bend and start picking stuff up. Tooth-brush. Razor. Hair gel.

He snatches a tube of shaving cream from my fin-gers with his good hand. "I can do that."

"Can you?" He bristles at the jibe, and I decide to change tack. Like my mother always says, you get more flies with sugar than vinegar. I don't usually pay much attention to her pearls of so-called wis-dom, but in this case, she might be on to something.

I dump the toiletries in the open drawer and lay a palm on Jake's good shoulder. "I get it. You're frus-trated. You're used to doing things for yourself. But it's okay to ask for help once in a while. Especially when you're hurt."

He stares at the tube of shaving cream in his hand. "It's humiliating. I'm a grown-ass man, and I can't even shave myself."

I pat the toilet seat. "Sit. I'll do it."

His gaze shoots to mine. "You can't be serious."

"Do I look like I'm joking?" I retrieve the razor from the drawer and hold it aloft like it's the sword of Gryffindor.

"You look like Sweeney freaking Todd." He eyes me skeptically but lowers himself gently onto the toilet, peeling the tissue off his cheek and tossing it into the garbage. "I'm not sure I should let you near my face with a sharp object."

"Sondheim?" My lips curl into a smile. "I'm impressed."

"You can't grow up with a theater geek without a little of it rubbing off on you, no matter how much you resist."

He smiles back, and my heart, which had almost regained its normal rhythm, starts racing like an Indy car again. It's those damn dimples. They should be illegal.

I hold out my hand for the shaving cream, and his fingers brush mine as he places it in my palm. A zing of awareness buzzes from the point of contact straight to my girly parts.

Great. Now my heart and my hormones are out of control. This is going to be harder than I thought. I'm trembling inside and out, anticipation of what I'm about to do making me shiver. I'm going to wind up either cutting him or kissing him.

Maybe both.

But it's too late to back out now. I'll have to take my chances and hope for the best. Whatever that is.

I set the razor down on the vanity and squirt a dollop of shaving cream into my palm, rubbing my hands together to work up a lather. "Sit still."

"Yes, ma'am," he says with a smirk.

But the smirk disappears when my hands cup his cheeks. He sucks in a breath that echoes in the cavernous room as I spread the cool, sweet-smelling foam on the lower half of his face. His skin is hot under my hands, his stubble tickles my palms and I don't know how long I can last without giving in to temptation, climbing into his lap and planting a kiss on those full, firm lips.

After a few seconds of torture, I stand back to admire my handiwork and reach for the razor.

"Are you ready?" I ask shakily.

"Are you?"

His eyes meet mine, and the raw, carnal need I see in their chocolate depths stuns me to the core. I'm almost positive it's reflected back in my own. I've never been so turned on in my life. If you don't count yesterday in his kitchen.

"Sit still," I pant. I'm having trouble catching my breath. You'd think I just finished a triathlon.

"You said that already."

"R-right." I stammer. "I just don't want to cut you. You've been injured enough for one twenty-four-hour period."

"You won't." He takes my free hand in his and squeezes. I expect him to release it, but he laces his fingers with mine and holds tight, his thumb tracing distracting patterns on the back of my hand.

I lean against the vanity to steady myself and lift the razor to his face, running it slowly, carefully down one cheek. For the next few minutes, the only sounds in the bathroom are the soft scrape of the blade and our increasingly ragged breathing. It's the most intimate, sensual, erotic thing I've ever done. Counting yesterday in his kitchen.

"Turn your head," I order when the side of his face closest to me is clean-shaven.

He does, but on the way around his gaze snags mine again, piercing me with white-hot shards of desire. "I'm starting to think dislocating my shoulder is the best thing that's ever happened to me, Nightingale."

"Nightingale?" I've been called a lot of things but a bird known for its powerful and beautiful song isn't one of them. I'm guessing that's because I'm tone deaf. The only thing you'll catch me singing is "Love Shack" on the occasional karaoke night with the gals in my darts league, and that's only after a minimum of two drinks and a whole lot of prodding from my posse.

"As in Florence," Jake explains, mischief waring with the desire in his dark eyes. "My own personal, private duty nurse."

"Executive concierge," I correct, my voice so thick with need I barely recognize it.

Tentatively, I rinse the razor, then silently slide it down his stubbled cheek. The air between us is hot and heavy with sexual tension as I continue the process— rinse, scrape, rinse, scrape—until his skin is smooth.

"There." I trade the razor for a towel and hand it to him. "All done."

"Not quite." He pats his face dry and tosses the towel into the sink.

"Do you need my help with something else?"

"You could say that."

He stands, and I try but can't suppress a little gasp at the huge erection tenting the towel still miraculously clinging to his waist.

"So you see the problem."

I'd have to be blind not to.

He hooks a thumb under the towel, and it slips down a little lower. Seriously, at this point it has to be divine intervention holding that thing up.

"Any idea what to do about it?" he asks, his voice as rough and needy as mine.

Oh, I've got a few. All of them delicious and dirty. The question is, will I stick around long enough to do any of them? Or am I going to chicken out and run away?

Again.

He must sense my hesitation, because his expression gets all serious and he takes a step back, putting some space between us. "Look, I don't want to pressure you. But unless I'm way off base, I'm not the only one who's horny as hell right now."

I think about lying. But he's not blind, either, and my body's telling a different story. I glance down at my chest. My nipples are practically poking holes through my Keep Calm and Be a Unicorn T-shirt. There's no way he's missing that.

"You're not way off base," I rasp. "But…"

He closes the gap between us and touches a finger to my lips, silencing me. "If there's one word I hate almost as much as *no*, it's *but*. We're two consenting adults who want to jump each other's bones. What's wrong with that?"

I shoot a worried glance at his sling. "What about your shoulder?"

"The last time I checked, that's not the appendage I need for what I have in mind."

As if to prove his point, he uses his good arm to pull me to him, the evidence of his arousal pressing against my belly. I let myself relax into him, my reasons for resisting becoming dimmer and dimmer by the second.

"Does that mean what I think it means?" he asks, the hand on my back dropping down to cup my ass.

"That depends." I'm hot everywhere, the ache between my legs sharpening into a persistent, almost painful throbbing. "What do you think it means?"

"I think it means you want me to do this."

But before I can find out what "this" is, the tinny tones of Men at Work's "Who Can It Be Now" ring out from the bedroom, making me tense in his arms.

Or, more accurately, arm.

"Shit. My cell phone."

"Ignore it," he growls, splaying his fingers across my ass cheek and squeezing.

"I can't. It might be work." The second the words are out of my mouth, I want to suck them back in. When I left DK&G, I swore I was done letting my job control my life. But I should have walked Roscoe and been back at the office—aka my apartment— for our morning meeting by now. Aaron and Erin are probably camped out in the hallway outside my door, picturing me lying in the gutter somewhere.

Reluctantly—and gently, being careful not to jar his injured shoulder—I worm my way out of Jake's embrace and make a beeline for my purse, managing to fish out my phone and swipe the screen to answer before it stops ringing.

"Hey, Aaron. Or Erin. Sorry I'm late. I got held up with Roscoe. But I'll be there as soon as I can."

"Held up?" Jake mutters with a smug smile as he breezes by me on his way to the dresser. "Is that what the kids are calling it these days?"

I wave him off with my phone-free hand, using all

my Jedi mind powers to brainwash him into keeping his big mouth shut. If my coworkers find out
I've been playing house with him, I'll never hear
the end of it.

He yanks a pair of boxer briefs from one of the
dresser drawers, and I turn my attention back to the
phone. Sure, I'm tempted to watch him drop the towel
so he can get dressed. What woman with a pulse and
half a brain wouldn't be? But I'm afraid the sight will
render me speechless, and then Aaron—or Erin—
will definitely think I've gone off the deep end.

"Why don't you guys go to the Starbucks on the
corner and get a couple of lattes," I suggest. "On me.
I'll text you when I get off the subway at 28th Street."

That ought to keep them happy. I grab my purse
from the bed, ready to make yet another quick exit.
It's becoming a pattern with us. At this rate, I should
just have little sympathy notes printed up. *Sorry for
giving you a case of the blue balls, Jake. Better luck
next time.*

"Thanks for the offer," the voice on the other end
of the phone says. "But seeing as I'm almost three
thousand miles away in San Diego, I'll have to pass."

"Brie."

Shit. I was in such a hurry to answer, I didn't
bother to check the screen before I swiped right, just
assuming it was one of the Aarons. Or is it Erins?
Whatever. The point is, if I had seen it was Jake's
sister, I would have let the call go to voicemail. It's

majorly uncomfortable trying to have a casual conversation with her brother in my peripheral vision,
wearing only those damn boxer briefs. The way they
hug his tight ass and muscular thighs…

Damn.

Nevertheless, I persist.

"Hey, girl." My voice sounds unnaturally high,
even to my ears. I clear my throat and make a conscious effort to sound less like Minnie Mouse on he-
lium. "How's things on the West Coast?"

Jake catches my eye and mouths, "My sister?"

I nod.

"Are you okay?" Brie asks, completely bypassing
my question. "You sound funny. Like you're at the
bottom of a well or something."

"I'm fine," I lie. "Just busy. Lots of errands on
the schedule today."

"Well, I hope you have time to squeeze in one
more as a favor to a friend. Have you walked Roscoe yet today?"

"No…" I hedge. "I'm, uh, on my way there now."

"Good. I'm worried about my brother. Connor
told me he got hurt last night."

"You talked to Connor?" My gaze flicks to Jake,
who's struggling to pull on a pair of sweatpants one-
handed.

"Shit," he mutters.

I hold the phone away from my mouth. "He told
Brie about your…accident."

Jake scrubs a hand over his freshly shaved jaw. "I should have known he couldn't keep his trap shut. I didn't want her to worry about me."

"Are you still there?" Brie asks as I bring the phone back up to my face.

"I'm here," I assure her. "What do you want me to do?"

I know what I want to do. Jake. But I doubt that's what his sister has in mind.

"I've been trying to reach him, but he's not answering his phone. Can you check on him for me? Make sure he's okay on his own? Connor said the doctor recommended someone stay with him for a few days until his shoulder was feeling stronger, but my brother, in typical alpha male fashion, nixed that idea. Connor even offered to get him a home health aide, but he said he didn't want some stranger in his space."

I look over at him. He's sitting on the corner of the bed, fighting to get a T-shirt on over his sling. Stubborn idiot. "Yeah, that sounds like Jake."

"What sounds like me?" he asks through the shirt that's now covering his face.

"Tell you what." I speak into the phone, ignoring him. "I'll do better than that."

What I'm about to propose is either the most brilliant idea I've ever had or the most dangerous. Or both. I take a deep breath and plunge forward.

"I'm not a stranger. I'll stay with him."

CHAPTER EIGHT

Jake

"Are you sure this is everything?" I eye the stack of bags by the door. "You don't have another, say, ten suitcases with the doorman downstairs?"

It's the day after Ainsley announced that she's moving in with me, and now I understand why it took her twenty-four hours to get her stuff together. Hell, I'm surprised she was able to do it that fast.

"It'll do for now." *For now?* "If I need to, I can always grab more stuff from my place."

"You mean there's more where all this came from?" The bag on top of the pile starts to teeter, and I reach out my lone remaining functional hand to steady it. "I find that hard to believe."

She cocks her head and shoots a meaningful glance my way. "It's nice to see being an invalid hasn't made you lose your sense of humor."

"I'm not an invalid," I protest. "I can take care of myself. Even with one hand strapped to my chest."

"If that's true, then why did you agree to let me stay?" she asks.

"Because if I didn't, my sister would have been on a plane to JFK faster than you could say overprotective."

And because if we're living under the same roof, maybe there's a chance we'll finally finish what we started in the kitchen. And the bathroom.

She gives me a saucy smirk. "Funny, that's not the way I see it. If it wasn't for me, you'd have a face full of way-past-five-o'clock-shadow right now instead of that sexy stubble you're sporting."

I see her smirk and raise her a cheeky grin. "You think my stubble is sexy?"

If she says yes, I'm keeping it, no matter how goddamn itchy it is.

But she doesn't say yes. Then again, she doesn't say no, either. Instead, she snatches up one of the bags and blows past me into my apartment. Roscoe, who's snoozing on the sofa—even though his dog bed is mere feet away in front of the fireplace—lifts his head to see what all the commotion is about. He looks around briefly, then lets it fall back down onto the cushion with a loud whoosh, apparently not interested enough in what's going on to stir from his slumber.

Lazy fuck.

"Where do you want me to put my stuff?" Ainsley asks as she descends the three steps that lead from the entryway into the living area.

"I'll show you your room." With my good arm, I grab the suitcase on top of the stack and follow her. "Then you can settle in while I go make sure things are running smoothly at the club."

I'm expecting a call from my contact in Miami. We're close to signing on the dotted line for ten thousand square feet of rental space in the heart of South Beach. Then I've got to approve the new drink menu, order supplies for our first Big Apple Bollywood Blowout at the end of the month, hire a new bartender to replace the one who quit without notice last week...

Ainsley stops so short I almost plow into her. "Not so fast, Speed Racer. I'm under strict orders not to let you anywhere near Top Shelf."

"Let me guess," I drawl, sarcasm dripping from every word. "My sister?"

She shakes her head, whipping her loose ponytail from side to side, and the scent of her shampoo wafts over me. Summery, like coconut and fruit salad and sunshine. And so damn tempting. I want to rip out her hair band and bury my face in her sweet-smelling curls.

Christ. What the hell is wrong with me? This woman is turning me into a hair-sniffing horn dog.

"Nope." She turns to face me. The smirk is gone, replaced by a cat-that-ate-the-canary smile. "Connor."

A shard of white-hot jealousy pierces my midsection. What the hell is my best friend and business partner doing with my dog walk—er, executive concierge? How do they even know each other? Unless they met the other night at the club. I'm almost positive Ainsley stayed with me until the ambulance came. Somewhere in the dim recesses of my mind are fuzzy memories of her squeezing my hand—the one at the end of my uninjured arm, of course—and murmuring faint but firm reassurances in my ear as I lay on the edge of the dance floor. But I don't remember Connor being there until later, at the hospital.

But who knows? Anything's possible. I was in too much pain to pay much attention to what was going on around me. And once the EMTs got there, they drugged me up so good I was practically comatose.

My grip on the handle of her suitcase tightens. I know if I look down I'll see the whites of my knuckles, but my eyes are locked on hers. "Since when are you and Connor having heart-to-heart chats?"

"Since Brie gave him my number. He figured you might try something like this."

"Like what?"

"Ignoring doctor's orders. I have it on good authority you're not supposed to go back to work until he clears you."

"I manage a nightclub. Ninety-nine percent of what I do is talk on the phone and push paper. It's not particularly physically demanding."

She eyeballs my sling. "It's the other one percent

that's the problem. Connor says this isn't the first time you've thrown yourself in the path of danger. He thinks you have a hero complex."

Another stab of jealousy claws at my gut. "Oh yeah? What else did my ex–best friend have to say about me?"

"Just that he felt a lot better knowing I'd be staying with you."

"So that's what this is. You're supposed to babysit me. Keep me away from Top Shelf and out of trouble."

She traps her bottom lip between her teeth and looks up at me, her wide, storm-cloud eyes laced with amusement. "Think of me as more of a roommate than a babysitter. Someone to bake cookies and binge-watch *Game of Thrones* with."

Not the activities I have in mind. But they'll do. For a start.

"Fine. No club." Lots of people work from home. I'll keep tabs on things remotely, after she's gone to bed. She's got to sleep sometime, right?

I head for the bedroom closest to mine. Because I'm a glutton for punishment, obviously. Ainsley trails after me and deposits her suitcase and purse on the bed, looking at me like I've sprouted a second head. Or like she can read my mind.

"That was way easier than I expected. What gives?"

"I know a losing battle when I see one," I lie, hoping it's convincing.

I set the bag I'm carrying down next to hers. She unzips it and starts pulling out clothes and organizing them on the bed. Tiny tank tops. The shortest of shorts. I catch a glimpse of something pink and lacy, and she slams the suitcase shut before I can see more.

"I can unpack later. I'm starving. Why don't we go grab something to eat? I'd offer to cook, but I've been known to burn water."

"Don't you have other clients to take care of?"

"Not today." She snags a pale gray Yankees cap from one of the piles on the bed and plunks it on her head, pulling her ponytail through the opening at the back. "Today I'm all yours."

All yours. Her words have my cock pressing against the zipper of the jeans it took me an hour to get into one-handed, but my brain's stuck on something else.

"If you're here with me, who's minding the store?" I ask, curious. One entrepreneur to another.

"Aaron and Erin. The grad students who run errands for me. They've got everything under control. And if they have any problems, they know how to get in touch with me."

Grad students? Is she fucking serious? If they're anything like the ones I knew when I was an undergrad at the City College of New York, they're more into booze than business. "Are you sure you can trust them?"

"Sure, I'm sure." She waves a hand, like the company she's built from the ground up is a fly she can shoo away and forget. "They're totally reliable. Been with me since I started."

Connor's been with me since the beginning. Since before the beginning. We took a seedy strip club and turned it into one of the hottest nightspots in Manhattan. I know Top Shelf is in capable hands with him. But that doesn't mean it's not killing me taking a step back, even if it's only temporary. The club isn't just my livelihood. It's my life.

I stare at her, slack jawed. "I don't get how you can be so unconcerned."

She lifts a shoulder nonchalantly then lets it drop. "I'm not unconcerned, I'm delegating. Besides, it's just work. It'll still be there when I get back."

I don't tell her that's what my father thought, too. But when he returned to the consulting firm that bore his name after his heart attack, the business was in shambles. And less than six months later, it was gone, along with our home and most of our savings, including my college fund. It took years for our family to recover, financially and emotionally.

Years I don't particularly want to rehash with Ainsley.

"So, food," I say, figuring that's a safe change of subject. "What do you feel like? We can go out or order in. I have a bunch of menus in the kitchen. Burning water's my specialty, too."

Hell, I don't even know whether my housekeeper

stocked the fridge this week. I haven't looked in there since I got back from the hospital. For all I know, there's nothing on the shelves but craft beer and condiments.

"Let's get out of here. You need a change of scenery." She scoops up her purse and slings it over her shoulder. "And I know just the place."

We take Roscoe for a quick walk to do his business then catch the C train at Chambers Street. Half an hour later, we're sitting on vinyl-upholstered chairs in a fifties-style diner, surrounded by drag queens in poodle skirts and saddle shoes belting out show tunes while serving burgers and milkshakes. Or, in our case, root beer floats.

"What do you think?" Ainsley takes a sip of her float and eyes me over the top of her glass. "Pretty great, huh?"

A Cher wannabe finishes crooning "If I Could Turn Back Time" and hands the mic over to a queen in a tiara, feather boa and elbow length gloves who launches into a rendition of "Diamonds Are a Girl's Best Friend" that sounds more like Marilyn Monroe than genuine article. The crowd—impressive for a weekday lunch—is totally into it, laughing and clapping as Marilyn ruffles the hair of an unsuspecting diner and drapes herself seductively across his lap.

"Great? It's fucking genius." I snag a napkin from the stainless steel dispenser, borrow a pen from a passing waitress and start scribbling. The wheels in my head are spinning fast and furious. Drag karaoke nights. A stage show. Maybe even a monthly Sunday drag brunch. There's a whole market just waiting for us to tap.

"What are you doing?" Ainsley asks.

"Jotting down a few notes," I answer without looking up. "I want to talk to Connor about doing some stuff like this at Top Shelf."

Before I realize what she's up to, she snatches the napkin out from under my fingers and holds it out of my reach. "No work. Not today. Today is for celebrating."

She turns a blinding pearly white smile on me, and my dick twitches. "What are we celebrating?"

"Whatever you want." She folds the napkin and tucks it safely away in her purse. "The sun in the sky. The leaves on the trees. The best root beer float in the five boroughs. And the fact that we're here enjoying it all instead of wasting this beautiful day slogging away at work."

She sips her drink, leaning forward to take the straw between her lips. She toys with it as she sucks, and my dirty mind replaces the red-and-white-striped cylinder with my cock, which hardens predictably, pressing against my fly. I take a sip of my own float, hoping it will act like a splash of ice-cold water to my libido, and reach under the table to surreptitiously adjust my jeans. When she finishes, she sits back and pushes her glass away with a satisfied sigh.

"What do you have against work?" I ask as a waitress drops off our entrées. Big, juicy cheeseburgers with thick-cut steak fries. Ainsley insisted on ordering for both of us, and I'm man enough to let her take the lead if that's what she wants. I'll have to put in some extra time at the gym to work off the carbs once my arm is out of this sling, but judging by the mouth-watering smells wafting from the plate in front of me, it'll be worth it.

"I don't have anything against work," she insists. "But some people don't know when to give it a rest. You know what they say. All work and no play makes Jake a dull boy."

She crosses her legs, letting one sandal dangle from her prettily painted, cotton candy pink toes, and gives me a playful, come-hither stare over her burger that's enough to make me forget we're in the middle of a crowded restaurant. I'm about to haul her across the table, onlookers be damned, and remind her how not dull I can be, but I don't get the chance. Marilyn's on the prowl, looking for her next unsuspecting target, and she's heading my way. The next thing I know, she's got her boa wrapped around my neck while she sings in my ear about Tiffany and Cartier and rocks that are square cut or pear-shaped.

Some guys might feel threatened by having a drag queen hang all over them, but not me. I'm secure enough in my masculinity to laugh and play along. Marilyn finishes the number with a flourish, thanks me for being a good sport, and moves on, and I turn my attention back to Ainsley, who's munching on her burger with a bemused smile on her face.

"Still think I'm dull?" I ask, popping a fry into my mouth.

"I never said you were dull." She dabs at the corner of her mouth with her napkin, mischief dancing in her eyes. "Exactly."

Her phone chimes from the depths of her purse, and she reaches inside to dig it out.

"Shit," she mutters as she reads the screen, her face suddenly serious, all traces of amusement gone. "I have to take this."

"Let me guess. Work."

She nods, at least having the good grace to look ashamed.

"Who's the dull one now?" I tease as I take a bite of another steak fry. I haven't braved the burger yet. The thing's the size of a small car. I'm still trying to figure out how I'm going to manage it one-handed.

"I'm sorry. It'll just take a second."

She ducks outside to take the call. When she returns a few minutes later, a worried frown creases her forehead.

"Is everything all right?" I ask as she slides back into her seat.

She shakes her head. A lock of hair escapes from

her ever-present ponytail, and she tucks it behind her ear. "I have to cover for Erin. She's stuck on the subway. I hate to eat and run, but I've got to get downtown before three to pick up a penis cake."

"A what?" I must have heard her wrong. There's no way she just said what I thought she said.

"A penis cake."

Nope. I definitely heard it right the first time.

"It's for a bachelorette party," she explains between bites of her burger. "They've got a penthouse suite at the Soho Grand. I'm supposed to pick up the cake, bring it there and get started on the decorations."

"Decorations?"

"More penises. The maid of honor's seriously obsessed with them. She had us order penis lollipops, penis confetti, penis shot glasses, even a six-foot blow-up penis that I don't know and don't want to know what they plan on using for."

"Sounds delightful." And by delightful, I mean scary as shit. A six-foot penis. How's a guy supposed to compete with that?

Ainsley polishes off the last of her burger and pushes her plate away. "Sorry for cutting our lunch short. But don't worry. I should be able to get to your place in time to take Roscoe out before it gets dark."

She stands, and I follow suit. My parents' dog is the last thing on my mind right now. It's hard for me to concentrate on anything at the moment except the woman across from me. She's doing something with her mouth that's damn distracting.

"Hold up. I'll go with you."

The words escape my lips before I can stop them. I tell myself it's because I'm curious. I've never been to a penis party before. But that's horseshit. Truth is I don't want this date—if that's what this is—to end. If that means dick decorating for a bunch of bawdy bachelorettes, then I'm willing to swallow my male pride and take one for Team Spend the Day with Ainsley. And if I play my cards right, maybe the night, too.

"You don't have to do that," she protests, unhooking her purse from the back of her chair and slinging it over her shoulder.

I signal to our waitress for the check and a doggie bag for my burger. "I know I don't have to. I want to. Besides, I'm guessing you could use an extra hand. I may only have one working, but it's all yours."

I pat my sling and wince. Damn shoulder hurts more than I want to admit. I probably should have taken the doctor up on his offer to prescribe me something stronger than ibuprofen. But I hate the way the hard-core stuff makes me feel. Woozy and wobbly, like I'm in a brain fog. Or a M. Night Shyamalan movie.

Ainsley studies me. She's way too perceptive. Sees everything. No doubt she's figured out I'm in pain and is getting ready to send me packing. I'm gearing up for a fight, but she surprises me and gives me a resigned shrug. "Have it your way. You can help. But you're on light duty. No lifting boxes or climbing ladders."

I cross my heart and hold up three fingers. "Scout's honor."

"You were a Boy Scout?" she asks, her tone suspicious.

"Cub Scout. I only made it to Webelos," I confess. "But we Webelos take the Scout's oath very seriously."

"From what I've seen, you take just about everything seriously. But we're going to change that." She takes a pair of sunglasses out of her bag and slips them on. "Come on. Let's go play with some peckers."

CHAPTER NINE

Ainsley

"WHAT THE HELL is this?"

I look up from the penis wine charms I'm fastening around the stems of eight wine glasses—one for the bride and each of her seven bridesmaids—to see Jake holding a box like it's about to bite him. I suck in a giggle when I see the picture on it. Two women whacking each other with inflatable dicks strapped around their waists.

"That's one of the party games. Dueling Dickies."

He shudders. "Please tell me I don't have to blow them up."

"So you're okay with being serenaded by drag queens, but putting your lips on a plastic penis is where you draw the line?"

"I am not giving a blow job to a four-foot phallus."

This time I can't fight the laughter, and it bubbles out. "No worries. If it threatens your precious manhood, I'll do it. You can fill Willy Whack-It."

"Willy what?"

"The party pecker piñata."

I hand him a bag of individually wrapped penis gummies and point him toward the fully stocked bar, where the piñata lies face up, its taunting, cheeky smile on full display. He approaches it cautiously, like it might jump up and attack him if he moves too fast.

"You weren't kidding when you said the maid of honor is penis obsessed. This thing's creepy. What kind of dick has a face? It's looking at me like it wants to stab me in my sleep."

I put a charm on the last wine glass, open a bag of brightly colored confetti shaped like tiny, adorable, nonmurderous penises, and start scattering them across the dining table.

"Don't be such a wimp. It's all in good fun." I should stop there, but I can't help baiting him. It's too easy, and I like getting a rise out of him. In more ways than one. But for now, I'll settle for the one. "You know what fun is, right?"

He fixes me with those piercing, brandy-brown eyes. "You mean like our shaving session? That was fun. Or how about when you rode my leg like a bucking bronco? I really enjoyed that. And based on your screams and moans, so did you."

My face goes instantly hot and tingly. My girly parts, too. I decide to ignore it for the time being and focus on the task at hand. We have to get this place decorated before the bride and her entourage show up. Then I can get Jake home, where I can jump his bones. And this time, there's no stopping until we both get off.

"You got that thing filled yet?" I gesture to the piñata.

"So that's how you want to play it." He finds the sticker marked Fill Here and peels it off. "Fine. I'll let you off the hook for now. But don't think the subject is closed."

"What subject?" I ask, feigning innocence.

"You. Me. Trust me, Nightingale. This—" he waves a hand between us "—is happening, whether you want to admit it or not."

Admit it? I'm counting on it.

"Just finish stuffing the piñata so we can hang it up."

I scatter the last of the penis confetti, crumple up the empty package, and toss it into the heavy-duty garbage bag I mooched off housekeeping. Normally I'd bring one with me. We've got a no-mess-left-behind rule at Odds & Errands. Another way we try to stand out from the competition. But since I'm pinch hitting today, I'm not as prepared as I usually am.

Jake rips the bag of gummies open with his teeth, dumps them into the papier-mâché penis, then puts the sticker back on to seal it up. "There. All done. Where do you want it?"

"Hmm…" I scan the large, open loft, looking for a safe place to hang a piñata. Somewhere the ladies can swing away at it without fear of damaging any of the Soho Grand's pricey decor. "How about over there?"

I point to the archway that separates the dining area from the living space. He nods and starts to pull a chair over.

I stand in his path, blocking him, hands balled on my hips. He may be bigger and stronger than me, but there's no way he's more determined. "Not. Gonna. Happen. Remember our deal. No heavy lifting. No climbing."

He steps aside with an elaborate bow. "As you wish."

"*The Princess Bride*. Impressive."

"You can thank my sister for that, too. She made me watch it a least a hundred times. Even tried to get me to dress as the Dread Pirate Roberts one Halloween, but that's where I drew the line."

"Too bad," I say, dragging the chair beneath the archway. "You would have made a cute Dread Pirate Roberts."

"The Dread Pirate Roberts is not cute," Jake huffs. "He's feared across the seven seas for his ruthlessness and skill with a sword."

"Wow, you weren't kidding when you said you'd seen the movie a hundred times." My eyes dart around the room until they spot what I'm looking for. "Can you bring me that box of tools on the couch?"

I'd had them delivered directly to the hotel along with the decorations. A tad more expensive, sure. But also way more efficient. And it's not like my clients can't afford to pay a little bit extra. They're clearly not hurting for money. From the looks of this place, it's costing them a pretty penny.

Jake crosses to the couch, picks up the box, and looks inside, but he doesn't bring it to me. Instead, he just stands there and stares at me like I'm about to take a sledgehammer to the *Venus de Milo*. "The Soho Grand isn't going to be too thrilled with you making holes in their ceiling."

"Hole," I correct him. "Singular. And I've already cleared it with the management. I've got someone coming in to patch it up after the bridal party checks out on Sunday."

This isn't my first rodeo. Or my first bachelorette party. I know how to grease the wheels and smooth things over to get my clients what they want, within reason. Just another perk of our personalized service.

He lets out a low whistle and crosses back to me with the box. "Now I'm the one who's impressed."

"I may not be a workaholic like some people—" I give him a pointed look over my shoulder as I climb up on the chair "—but that doesn't mean I don't care about doing my job and doing it well."

"I can see that."

I glance down at him, and I'm shook. Where's the sarcastic smirk? Or disdainful frown? I mean, he's got to be messing with me, right? I'm totally cool with how I run my business, but there's no way it's up to Mr. I-Live-At-The-Office's impossibly high standards.

But he's not messing with me. He's standing there holding the stupid box to his stupid side with his stupid, uninjured arm, gazing up at me with an earnest expression and nothing but sincerity in his eyes.

My heart and stomach do a simultaneous flip-flop, like synchronized swimmers executing a perfectly choreographed routine. It's ridiculous, I know, but this seems like a big moment somehow. Significant. Meaningful. It dawns on me that it's because Jake's opinion matters to me, and I'm shook all over again. I'm not used to giving a rat's ass what anyone thinks about how I live my life, especially not a guy I met only a few weeks ago.

It must show, because his earnest expression turns to concern.

"Are you okay?" he asks, his brows knotting together.

"Uh, sure." I gesture to the box, which he's set down on the floor next to him. Now is not the time for introspection. It's the time for hanging this piñata and getting the heck out of here. I can sort out my jumbled emotions later. "There's a pack of nails in there. Can you hand me one?"

For the next few minutes we work together in silence like a well-oiled machine, Jake anticipating my needs without me having to say a word. He gives me a nail. I position it in the center of the beam. He hands me the hammer. I use one end to tap the nail in and the other to pull it out so I can screw in the eye bolt he puts in my palm. He hands me a length of rope. I run it through the bolt.

I give the bolt one last turn to make sure it's in there good and tight, then bend down to grab the piñata Jake's already retrieved from the bar. The chair wobbles, and I feel myself losing my balance. One second I'm upright, the next I'm in a nose dive that lands me sprawled on top of Jake, the piñata tossed aside and fluorescent neon penis gummies scattered all around us on the floor.

"I'm so sorry. Your arm…" I try to scramble off his chest, but the arm I'm not freaking out about locks me to him like a vice. At least I didn't break that one, too. That's some small consolation for knocking him down like a bowling pin.

"My arm is fine," he assures me, his breath warm on my cheek, stirring the hair that's come free from my sad mess of a ponytail. He chuckles, and the low rumble reverberates through me, making my nerve endings tingle. "Well, technically it's not fine. But it's not any worse than it was before you fell on me. My left side took the brunt of the impact."

I try to wriggle out of his grasp, but he's too strong, even with only one arm. "Um, we should probably get up."

"Uh-uh." He shakes his head, and unruly dark hair flops over his forehead. My fingers itch to push it back, to feel the slip and slide of the thick locks as I smooth them away from his face. "Not so fast."

"But I'm squashing you." I'm not a heavyweight, but I'm not petite, either. He can't be comfortable with me spread-eagled over him.

"Right. I've got you exactly where I want you." His hand drifts from the middle of my back down to the curve of my ass and squeezes.

I let out a thin, breathy exhale. "You want me crushing you like a grape?"

He rolls us so I'm beneath him. He looms above me like some wild pagan god, propped up on his good arm, his chest heaving and a thin sheen of sweat dampening his brow. "There. Now you can stop worrying about squashing me and start concentrating on more important things."

"Like what?"

Please, please, please let him mean what I think he means.

"Like this."

His lips come crashing down on mine, and my heart wants to sing. He does mean what I think he means, and then some. I like to kiss as much as the next gal, but this is more than kissing. It's kissing on steroids. Jake's mouth is moving against mine like the world is seconds from ending, like this is the last time we'll get to do this and he doesn't want to hold anything back.

He coaxes my lips apart with his tongue, and my eyes flutter closed. I wrap my legs around his and reach up to rake my fingers through his hair. I'm drowning in him, being dragged under by his touch, his taste, his smell.

But what a way to go.

I forget where we are. I forget that we've got a job to finish. I forget that at any minute a bride-to-be and her seven bridesmaids could waltz in here and discover us on the floor, making out like a couple of horny teenagers.

Until the click of a lock shatters the silence and I freeze.

"Ainsley? You here? The front desk gave me a key. I know I'm super late, but I thought you might still need some help getting everything set up for the party."

I roll off Jake, but it's too late. Erin's startled gasp tells me she's already seen us, and what she's seen is more than enough for her to know we weren't playing tiddlywinks.

"Sorry," she says, but she sounds more amused than contrite. "I guess I should have knocked. I didn't realize you had company."

I scramble to my feet, hastily and futilely trying to tame my flyaway hair and smooth my rumpled T-shirt. Jake, in contrast, takes his bloody sweet time getting up. When he does, he ambles over to my assistant and sticks out his left hand.

"You must be Erin. I'm Jake."

"It's nice to meet you, Jake." Erin shakes his hand and immediately launches into the Spanish inquisition. "How do you and Ainsley know each other?"

I try to interrupt their little heart-to-heart before Jake can spill the beans about how we met, but he's too quick.

"She's helping me take care of my parents' dog while they're on vacation."

"So you're the guy who got Ainsley to break her no pets policy." Erin shoots me a knowing glance.

"You have a no pets policy?" Jake asks.

"Had," Erin clarifies. "Past tense."

"I made an exception for a friend," I insist. "That's it. No big deal."

"A friend." Erin puts air quotes around the last word. "Right. Now I understand why she's been hiding you."

"I have not been hiding him." I haven't. Not really. Although right now that sounds like a freaking fantastic idea.

"Really?" Erin says, echoing my thoughts. "Then how come you've never asked me or Aaron to walk Roscoe?"

Jake cocks his head and squints at me. He's enjoying this way too much. "That's a good question."

One I don't have a good answer to. So I do what any rational person in my situation would do.

Punt.

I pick up the piñata and start shoving packs of gummies back inside. "We're almost done here. We just have to finish hanging Willy Whack-It and get rid of the garbage."

Erin takes the piñata from my hands. "I can handle that. You and Jake should get out of here."

I glance at the clock above the trendy white stone fireplace. "The bridal party will be arriving soon. I should stay and meet the maid of honor. Make sure everything gets her stamp of approval."

"What's not to approve? This is gonna be a kick-ass penis party."

Jake waves a hand around the room, and my eyes follow it, landing on penis straws, penis balloons, penis headbands. Yep. These crazy broads are actually going to wear tiny dicks on their heads. And around their necks, too. I know for a fact there's a package of necklaces with little pink plastic peckers around here somewhere. The place is packed with penises. I don't think there's a schlong-shaped favor in the tristate area we haven't got.

"Jake's right. You guys have done a great job. I doubt anyone will have any complaints, especially once they've had a drink or two or three, but if they do, I'll deal with them." Erin sets the box down on a chair and shoos us toward the door. "Go have some fun. You know what fun is, right?"

My eyes practically roll to the back of my head. There's nothing more infuriating than having your own words used against you, even if the person using them doesn't know you said the same thing not ten minutes ago.

I sneak a glance at Jake to see if he's picked up on it. Yep. He's eating this up, the smug bastard. He winks at Erin and snakes his good arm around my waist, steering me to the door.

"Fun?" His hand sneaks lower, daring to cop a not-so-discrete feel of my left butt cheek. "That's my middle name. Right, Nightingale?"

CHAPTER TEN

Jake

IT'S AFTER FIVE when Erin springs us from the penis party and we walk out of the air-conditioned Soho Grand into the stifling, sticky heat of late afternoon Manhattan in July. I call an Uber Black to take us back to my apartment, figuring I'd rather be comfortably cool and alone with Ainsley in the back of a luxury automobile than have to share her with hundreds of rush hour commuters in a crowded, smelly subway car.

But about two minutes into the ride, I realize that was a huge ass mistake. And not because we're stuck in traffic on Broadway. I'm in no hurry to get anywhere. And it's not exactly a hardship being trapped for a little while longer in the back of a BMW 7 Series with the star of all my most recent late-night sex fantasies.

Or it wouldn't be a hardship, if Ainsley would stop staring out the damn window and talk to me. You'd think she'd never seen Midtown before.

My attempts at conversation have all been met with grunts. And pitying glances in the rearview mirror from our driver, a guy about my age who clearly thinks I've got zero game in the romance department. He's probably plotting how to slip Ainsley his number without me noticing. Like that's gonna happen.

I sneak a peek at her in my peripheral vision. Ramrod posture? Check. Crossed arms? Check. Pursed lips, locked jaw and hands clenched into fists on her shapely thighs? Check, check and double check. Her body language screams, "Back the hell off." She's obviously upset about something. Probably still smarting over what went down with Erin.

Don't get me wrong. I'm not all that thrilled about getting caught with my pants down, either. Metaphorically speaking, that is. Although a few minutes more and who knows what the poor girl would have walked in on.

Instead, here I sit, a BMW's width away from the woman who was on top of me not half an hour ago, still hard as a goddamn steel pipe, apparently destined never to turn my late-night fantasies into reality. So yeah, I'm frustrated, too.

But I get the feeling Ainsley's more mad at me than the situation, and I don't have a freaking clue why. I may be too stupid to figure out what I've done to piss her off, but I'm not stupid enough to get into it with her while Mr. I've-Got-More-Game-Than-

You listens in on us from the front seat. So I bite my tongue until we're safely alone inside my apartment, out of earshot of any potential eavesdroppers.

Unfortunately, the second the door clicks shut behind us Ainsley's clipping Roscoe's leash on, muttering something about taking him for a quick walk to do his business. When they return a few minutes later, things aren't any less strained, and she disappears into what will be her bedroom for the foreseeable future to "settle in."

Even more frustrated than before, I head to the fridge and crack open a double IPA from my favorite Brooklyn brewery, which takes longer than usual with my dominant arm in a sling. After a few restorative slugs, I trade the beer for my cell phone and call the guy who's been my wingman since puberty hit and we discovered girls were good for more than just teasing.

"How's the convalescent?" Connor asks, picking up on the first ring.

"Convalescing." I collapse onto one of the stools at my kitchen island and stare longingly at my beer. Having one working arm sucks donkey balls.

"I hear you've got a house guest." His smirk is almost audible.

"My sister has a big mouth. You two must be beside yourselves. You got your way. You wanted someone to stay with me, and my dog walker—" executive concierge, I mentally correct myself "—is moving into the spare room as we speak."

"Excuse me while I play the world's smallest violin for your pity party," Connor scoffs. "I was thinking more along the lines of Nurse Ratched. Yet somehow you manage to convince your superhot pet sitter to be your personal Clara Barton."

"Florence Nightingale," I mutter. "And how do you know my pet sitter is hot?"

"I saw her on the monitors at the club, remember? Or are all those painkillers they gave you messing with your head?"

"Very funny. You know I hate that shit."

"So what's the problem? The legendary Jake Lawson charm not working on this one?"

"Who says I'm trying to charm her?" I'm glad we're not FaceTiming. One look at my guilty expression, and Connor would know I'm lying my ass off. I've never been able to hide anything from him. It's why I stopped playing poker with him.

"I saw the way you were stalking her on the security monitors. And if the rumors flying around this place are true, you hurt your shoulder riding to her rescue. If you're not trying to tap that, then I'm the king of England."

Damn. He's good. Even across town, I can't bullshit my best friend.

"England doesn't have a king," I say, ignoring the

elephant in the room. "Queen Elizabeth's reigned for like a million years."

"Sixty-seven, if you want to get technical, but that's beside the point."

"What is the point, exactly?"

"The point," Connor says with an exasperated sigh, "is that the woman you're jonesing for is unpacking her unmentionables in your spare room. And you're wasting time on the phone with me."

"She's pissed off at me," I admit, giving up the pretense that I don't want Ainsley to tend to more than my injured arm. "I'm giving her some space."

"What if she doesn't need space? What if what she needs is for you to show her you're sorry."

I crane my neck so I can see the door to Ainsley's bedroom. Still closed. I lower my voice anyway, to be on the safe side. "How can I show her I'm sorry if I don't even know what I'm sorry for?"

"Did you dislocate your brain along with your shoulder?" Connor asks. "If the apology's good enough, she won't care whether you actually understand what put you in the doghouse."

I've got my doubts about his theory, but seeing as I don't have any better ideas, I decide to go along with it for now. "How do I make sure it's good enough?"

"Actions speak louder than words. You need some sort of grand apologetic gesture."

"Like what?"

"Haven't you ever watched any rom-coms?"

I grimace. "Not if I can help it."

There's a moment of stunned silence before Connor speaks, and when he does, his tone is incredulous. "Not even *Pretty Woman*? Or *Sleepless in Seattle*? Or *Bridget Jones's Diary*?"

"Dude, you're scaring me. Name one more movie, and I'm gonna have to ask you to turn in your man card."

"Be that way. But don't blame me when you crash and burn with your dog walker."

"Executive concierge," I correct him.

We sign off, but I can't stop thinking about our conversation. Maybe Connor's right. Maybe I need a grand gesture to win my way back into Ainsley's good graces.

But what?

My stomach rumbles, reminding me that it's been hours since lunch. A lunch I hardly ate. I'll bet Ainsley's hungry, too. And the way to a person's heart is through their stomach, so…

I scroll through my contacts until I find the number for my favorite Asian fusion place. I've got no clue what she likes, so I order a little bit of everything—Thai, Chinese, Japanese. I even throw in some Korean barbecue for good measure. Then I break out my rarely used dinnerware, set the dining room table—also almost never used—light a couple of candles my sister must have left behind to com-

plete the picture and wait for the doorman to ring
and tell me the food's here.

I'm sorting through takeout cartons—opening
each one, checking the contents, sticking in serving
spoons—when Ainsley comes wandering out of her
room. Her hair is down, blond waves swinging around
her shoulders with every step, and she's changed into
floppy pajama pants with llamas all over them—or
are they alpacas? I never could tell the difference—
and a tiny tank top that leaves no doubt she's braless.
Either she's purposely torturing me or she's letting her
guard down. I've got my fingers crossed it's the latter.

"Do I smell pad thai?"

"And kung pao chicken. And bulgogi. And shrimp
teriyaki." I stick a spoon into a carton of rice and pull
out a chair for her. "I covered all the bases. I wasn't
sure what you liked."

"I like it all, unfortunately." She sits down, her
eyes flicking from the cartons to the china, to the
candles. "It looks great. Thanks."

I pick up a bottle of Château Bauduc sauvignon
blanc I picked out earlier from the wine cooler—
screw top, because there's no way I'm wrestling with
a corkscrew in my current state. "White okay?"

"Perfect." She looks up at me sheepishly through
long pale lashes as I pour her wine. "I'm sorry I was
such a bitch before."

I fill my glass and take a seat opposite her. "I
think that's supposed to be my line."

"Well, you didn't help matters any with Erin. All that winking and ass grabbing. I'm sure she's told Aaron all about it by now over a couple of chai lattes. I'm never going to hear the end of it at the office."

Shit. I hadn't even thought of that. Now I really am sorry. I was trying to play it cool, like what Ainsley's assistant walked in on was no big deal, but all I did was make a bad situation even worse for her.

"What can I do to fix things?" I ask. "I'll do anything. Talk to Erin and Aaron. Tell them—I don't know. Whatever you want me to tell them."

She shrugs and reaches for the kung pao chicken. "What's done is done. At least you didn't tell her I'm staying here. That would have been a disaster."

Logically, I know she's right. Her employees can't know she's shacking up with a client. But that doesn't make the karate chop her words deliver to my gut any less painful.

I push the feeling aside and shovel shrimp onto my plate. We enjoy a leisurely meal—leisurely because it takes me forever to eat with my left hand. The chopsticks they sent with the food are totally out of the question. Even with a fork, I'm constantly spilling stuff on myself, the table, the floor.

On the plus side, my crappy table manners leave us plenty of time for conversation. We talk about our jobs, our families, the new season of *Stranger Things*. Nothing's off limits, and I'm surprised how much we have in common. Big things, like our pride in our work, even though she's way more chill about hers than I am about mine. And small stuff, like how we both despise black licorice and white chocolate.

When we're done eating, we clear the table together and put the leftovers away in the refrigerator. It's all very *Leave It to Beaver*—thank you, MeTV, for giving my sister something else to force me to watch with her—if Ward had ever deigned to help June with something so mundane as the dishes instead of sitting on his ass, smoking cigars and reading the daily newspaper. But unlike ole Ward, I'm a modern male. I've got no problem doing so-called women's work. My parents made sure of that. Chores weren't divided by sex in the Lawson house. Brie and I got equal time inside—cooking, cleaning and folding laundry—and outside, moving the lawn and taking out the trash.

I lean against the counter and watch Ainsley stack the last of the plates in the dishwasher. Sharing space with someone is easier than I expected. Comfortable. Almost effortless. But maybe that's because of the particular someone I'm sharing space with.

I'm about to suggest we retire to my private rooftop terrace with an after-dinner brandy—hoping to set the mood for some sexy time—when Ainsley lets out a little squeal.

"Is that a Scrabble board?"

I follow her gaze to the card table Brie and I set up in the corner. Family game night was a staple growing up. Something we could continue to enjoy even when the purse strings were tight. And Scrabble was a perennial favorite. A fun way to help me manage my dyslexia. Not that I realized my parents' ulterior motive at the time.

My sister and I resurrected the tradition when she moved in. We were in the middle of a particularly cutthroat contest when she left for San Diego, and I haven't had the heart to break down the fancy board she bought me as a thank-you for letting her crash at my place, even though we've got a long-distance game going thanks to Words With Friends.

"Yeah. Wanna play?" I move closer to Ainsley and throw my arm around her shoulder. It's not exactly the after-dinner entertainment I had in mind, but the night is young. We can play Scrabble now and do the wild thing later.

"Sure," she says. "But can we move it to the coffee table? I was looking forward to relaxing on your amazeballs retro couch."

There's a number of things I'm looking forward to doing with her on my couch. Relaxing being among the most innocent.

"My couch is amazeballs?" I ask. I like that she likes it. Her approval gives me an irrational sense of accomplishment. It's not like I picked the damn thing out.

"It's surprisingly comfortable. Roscoe likes to sit and snuggle with me after our walks."

On cue, the hound, who's passed out in front of the fireplace, on his back with his legs splayed like a porn star, lifts his head and howls.

"He's not supposed to be on the sofa." Not that I've been able to keep him off any better than she has. "And I thought snuggling wasn't part of your job duties."

"I know. And it wasn't supposed to be. But I'm a softie. I can't say no to him. And I always brush off the cushions afterward. Part of Odds & Ends's no-mess-left-behind promise."

Roscoe stands, stretches and trots over to his empty food bowl.

"Tell you what. I'll feed the beast. You set up the board. But I'm warning you, I'm a Scrabble junkie. And I hate to lose."

"Bring it, word boy."

I feed the dog, pour us a couple of brandies and carry them on a tray back to my amazeballs couch, where Ainsley's made herself at home with her knees tucked under her, her pink-tipped toes peeking out from beneath the hem of her llama pants. She's got the board ready to go and her tiles all picked out and neatly arranged on one of the racks.

"Impressive," she says, nodding to the tray I'm balancing one-handed.

"I was a waiter before I was a club owner. And a bartender, and a bouncer and a booking agent. I even did a short but memorable stint as a DJ. My dad always said it was a good idea to learn a business from the ground up."

"He sounds like a smart man."

"He is." I don't elaborate. I don't want to talk about my father now. Or business.

I set the tray down a safe distance from the board, pull up a chair and sit across from her with the coffee table between us. Can't have her peeking at my rack, or accusing me of peeking at hers. Although from here, I've got a sweet view of the only rack I want to see. Her tank top doesn't hide much. I'm getting an eyeful of her breasts, tight against the thin, clingy fabric, the outline of her dusky nipples clearly visible. My fingers twitch with the need to peel it off her, but I resist the siren's song of immediate gratification in favor of the more tempting idea that's beginning to form in my sex-obsessed brain.

She thinks I don't know how to have fun? I'll show her what fun is.

I drag my gaze from her perfect tits and carefully select tiles from the drawstring bag on the table. "How about we make this a little more interesting?"

She reaches for her brandy. "What did you have in mind? A wager?"

"Of sorts." I lift my drink to my lips but stop short of sipping. "Have you ever played strip Scrabble?"

CHAPTER ELEVEN

Ainsley

JAKE GLOWERS AT me as I come back into the living room. "What the hell are you wearing?"

I glance down at my outfit. I've thrown on a sweatshirt, plus two pairs of socks, a pair of Converse high-tops and my Yankees cap. I almost put a bra on, too, but the thought of harnessing the girls back up again was too much to bear. "I told you, if we're playing strip Scrabble, I'm starting off with more than a tank top, pajama pants and underwear."

He gives me a quick once-over then studies his own attire. "Swap tank top for T-shirt and pajamas for sweats and that's all I'm wearing."

"That's your problem." I plunk myself back down on the sofa, stretching out this time instead of curling up like a human pretzel. This thing was made for lounging. I get why Roscoe's so attached to it. Fortunately, I don't have to fight him for space tonight. Jake's shut him away in the master bedroom, where he's probably taking up most of the king-size bed, so he won't disturb our game. "I've never played strip Scrabble before. What are the rules?"

"For every fifty points your opponent scores, you lose an article of clothing. If you challenge a word and win, you get to put one thing back on. But if you lose, something else comes off."

"Sounds easy enough." I twist the simple sterling silver pinkie ring I always wear on my left hand. "Does jewelry count as an article of clothing?"

His forehead creases, and I know he's counting the piercings in my ears—two in the right, four in the left. I'm not sure if he's spotted my tongue stud. And he sure as hell hasn't seen the tiny silver chain hanging from my belly button. I went a little body-bling crazy when I escaped the repressive big-city-law-firm atmosphere of DK&G. I've contemplated getting a tattoo or two to go along with the multiple piercings, but I haven't figured out what I want yet. Or where. If I'm going to get something permanently inked on my body, it has to be meaningful. And someplace it won't hurt like—

"Hell, no," Jake declares, unknowingly completing my thought. Apparently the six—or seven—piercings he can see are six or seven too many for strip Scrabble. "I'm already at a big enough disadvantage."

"Chicken."

He shrugs and makes a show of rearranging his tiles. "I prefer to think of it as pragmatic."

"You can think of it any way you want. That doesn't change the fact that you're afraid of getting your ass kicked by your dog walker."

"Executive concierge," he corrects, smirking at me over the rim of his brandy snifter. He gestures to the empty board with his glass. "Ladies first."

"Nice try." I smirk right back. Jake's not the only one who's played this game before. With my clothes on, that is. But still. "Official Scrabble rules state that we each draw a tile, and the player with the letter closest to *A* starts the game. Technically, we should have done that before picking our tiles, but I'm willing to let that minor infraction slide."

Sure, I'd love the advantage of making the first move on a clean board—and earning the double word score that comes with it for covering the pink square at the center. But I'm planning on winning this game fair and square. Pun intended.

He sips his drink and leans forward, resting his strong, sinewed forearm on his thigh. Is forearm porn a thing? Because if it is, Jake could make a fortune off his. Not that he's hurting for dough. "I thought we were making up our own rules."

I don't know if it's the alcohol, the late hour or something else—like maybe he's as turned on by this erotic, pretty-please-precoital dance we're doing as I am—but his voice seems to have dropped an entire octave. It's rough and slow and smoky, sending hot little pinpricks of desire shooting through my nervous system.

I adjust the pillow behind me and cross my ankles. "Only for the stripping part."

He leans in closer, and for a long moment we just stare at each other across the board, the air thick with sexual tension. Finally, he takes another sip of brandy, sets his glass down and sits back. A Cheshire cat smile spreads across his handsome face, dotted with stubble that's sprouted in the I-can't-keep-track-of-how-many hours since I shaved him this morning. I don't know what's got me more hot and bothered, the damn sexy stubble or the thought of shaving it off him again.

"Okay. We'll do it your way," he says, that whole rough-slow-smoky thing making him sound like Idris Elba and ramping the pinpricks up to a steady, persistent ache.

Get a grip, girl. Focus. If you play Scrabble with your hormones and not your head, you'll be naked in no time.

Although that might not be such a bad thing...

I pick a tile out of the bag, then hold the bag out to him.

He reaches inside, pulls out a tile, and holds it close to his chest. "You show me yours, and I'll show you mine."

I turn my tile around to face him with a dramatic flair. "*D*. As in damn hard to beat."

He lays his tile face up on the table, and my heart sinks. "*B*. As in better luck next time, Nightingale. Because I'm up first."

I grab his tile and toss it back in the bag with mine. Then I sit and wait as he sorts through the tiles on his rack, scowling and shuffling until he finally picks six tiles and lays them down in a horizontal line in the center of the board.

"Laytex. Double letter score for the *X*, and double word score for going first. That makes—" He does a quick mental calculation, his brow furrowing adorably with the effort of counting in his head. I give him credit, though. I'd be using my fingers. Maybe my toes, too, after the socks came off. "Sixty-four. Lose the sweatshirt."

"Not so fast, word boy." I hold up a finger. "Number one, there's no *Y* in latex. And number two—"

I add another finger. "I decide what I'm taking off, not you."

"Fine. I'll give you number one." He takes away the *Y* and moves the *LA* over a square. "But my place, my rules. And I say winner gets to tell the loser what to take off. So I repeat."

His eyes darken to an almost inky black. "Lose. The. Sweatshirt."

"And I repeat. Not. So. Fast." If the intense, hotly appraising way he's looking at me is anything to go on, I have a pretty good feeling how this night's going to end. But I want to enjoy the journey. I add up the remaining tiles on the board, as predicted with the help of my fingers. "You've only got forty points. I'm not taking anything off."

"Not yet," Jake adds with a seductive eyebrow waggle. "But soon."

Unfortunately—or is it fortunately?—his prediction turns out to be correct. After I score a pathetic six points with my first word—*loner*, built off the L in *latex*—he tops a hundred points with *squeeze*. My sole consolation is that Jake relents and lets me pick what I'm stripping off, so all I lose is one of my two pairs of socks.

Half an hour later, that consolation is like a distant speck in the rearview mirror. I'm in my skimpy tank top and lemon yellow lace panties, the rest of my clothes in a heap on the floor. Jake's not wearing much, either. He's down to his butt-hugging boxer briefs. But considering that he started with only those and his sweats and T-shirt, he's doing way better than me on the board.

Truth is, the more skin that's showing—his and mine—the less I'm focusing on the game and the more I'm wishing it's over already and we're naked, entwined and sweaty. I study my tiles, then the board, then back to my tiles again, seriously contemplating throwing in the towel—and off my few remaining clothes—journey be damned.

"Times up," he announces after long seconds have

ticked away without me making a move. "Either pass your turn or exchange tiles."

I reach into the bag and do a quick count of what's left in there. "There are only two tiles. Scrabble rules require seven for an exchange."

"Then I guess you're passing your turn."

Using the *Z* in *zone*, he lays down the rest of his tiles to make the word *whizbang*. "Boom. Fifty points for using all my tiles. Plus double word score. That's another hundred and two points for me. And two less pieces of clothing for you."

I bite my lip and try to steady my ragged breathing. "That's all I'm wearing."

"I've noticed. Which means I'm the winner of this game. And as the victor, I get the spoils."

His eyes rake me up and down. I can feel my nipples hardening, rubbing against the soft cotton of my tank top.

"The spoils?" The words come out on a puff of air. I surprised they come out at all, to be honest. My brain's ability to form coherent thought has been severely compromised by the miles and miles of toned, tanned flesh on display across the table.

"You."

The owner of said toned, tanned flesh crooks a finger, beckoning me to him. I stand on shaky legs and cross to him, almost naked, totally vulnerable.

"You've got me." My arms dangle awkwardly, like a department store mannequin. I pop a hip and put a hand there, striking a pose I hope reads more shy seductress than deer in headlights. "What do you plan to do with me?"

"Anything you want. But I'd like to start with a little striptease. Shirt first. I want to see those beautiful breasts."

Jake polishes off his brandy and smiles up at me. Yep. The Cheshire cat grin is back. I'm on fucking fire, and he's sitting there cool as a goddamn cucumber, issuing orders like a drill sergeant.

A dirty drill sergeant who knows exactly what to say to make me cream my pretty panties.

I reach for the hem of my tank top and yank it over my head, quick, like pulling off a Band-Aid. It might not be the most seductive striptease, but I'm afraid if I wait too long, if I think too much, I'll remember all the reasons why this is bad idea.

Instinctively, my hands go to my chest, covering my more than generous boobs. I've never felt so exposed as I do at this moment. Physically and emotionally.

Jake shakes his head and motions for me to lower them. "Don't hide from me, Nightingale. I want all of you."

All of me. That's what I'm afraid of. That this man will wind up possessing not only my body, but my heart and soul, too.

Still, I can't seem to resist him. And I don't want to. I let my hands drift to my sides. He sucks in a harsh breath and strokes his growing erection through his boxers. It's the sexiest damn thing I've ever seen.

"Now the panties," he growls.

I push aside my self-consciousness and slide the scrap of lace over my hips and down my legs, kicking it off when it reaches my ankles.

"Fuck, you're gorgeous." The hand on his cock picks up speed.

I mentally will him to ditch the boxers so I'm not the only one in my birthday suit. Okay, I confess. That's not the only reason. I want to see him touch himself without a layer of cotton between his fingers and his dick. No, *want*'s not a strong enough word. I need it, like I need air and water.

But my Jedi mind trick skills must be rusty, because instead of losing his briefs he takes his hand from his cock and grabs my wrist, pulling me closer.

"I like this." He releases my arm and flicks my bellybutton chain.

"And this." His finger moves lower, through the neatly trimmed patch of curls above my pussy, making me shiver.

"I showed you mine," I say, echoing his words from earlier. "Now you show me yours."

With agonizing slowness, he lifts his hips and hooks a thumb under the waistband of his boxers.

"Tease." I let out a low moan as I watch him drag his underwear down his powerful thighs and perfectly muscled calves. It should be awkward with only one hand, but that somehow manages to make the agonizingly slow journey even more sexy.

After what seems like an eternity, the briefs hit the floor. He kicks them aside and spreads his legs invitingly. "Straddle me."

My clit swells at his hotly whispered command. I do as he asks, brushing my warm, wet, center against his equally warm, wet cock as I climb on top of him. The brief contact makes me want more. More skin on skin. More friction and heat. I brace my palms against the back of the chair and lower myself onto him, but he grabs my waist, stopping me.

Something inside me cries out in protest. I'm panting. Desperate. I don't have time for slow kisses or soft touches. I need him inside me. Now.

I suck in a breath, working up the courage to ask for what I want.

"Please," I gasp. "Fuck me."

CHAPTER TWELVE

Jake

IT'S NOT LIKE me to say no to a beautiful woman. Especially one who's in my lap, naked and begging me to fuck her.

But there's a first time for everything. And this is that time.

"What's your hurry, Nightingale?" I tease, planting an openmouthed kiss in the hollow at the base of Ainsley's throat that makes her moan. "Somewhere else you need to be?"

"No, but there's somewhere else I need you to be. Like inside me."

She tries to wriggle her way down onto my cock, but I shift my weight so she winds up riding my thigh. It brings back images of her in my kitchen, grinding against me until she came, her cheeks flushed and her lips rounded into a perfect O. I'm half tempted to fuck taking it slow and give her what she wants. Like the last time she rode me.

Her eyes close and she lets out her breath on a long, low hiss that's equal parts exasperation and entreaty, mirroring my own feelings. My dick is screaming for release. But my head—the other one— is telling me it'll be even better if we take our time getting there.

Putting on the brakes with this woman might just be the end of me. But man, oh man, what a way to go.

"We've got all night," I tell her, running my hand up her side, loving the feel of the curve of her hip, the dip at her waist, the swell of her breast. "And I fully intend to use every last second of it."

There's not a whole hell of a lot of talking after that, unless you count our indistinct moans and groans. I touch and taste her everywhere. Palm those tremendous tits. Nibble on her earlobes. Trail hungry kisses from her mouth, to her jaw, down her neck to her shoulder and lower.

She's just as adventurous, exploring inch after inch of my body with her hands, lips, teeth and tongue. I was right about that naughty tongue stud. The way it feels when she flicks it against my nipples is everything I imagined and more. I'm dying to have it on my cock.

When she gets there, though, it's not with her mouth but with her hand, reaching between us to encircle me. She slides her thumb through the bead of moisture gathered at the tip, and I jerk back, muttering a string of curse words.

Jesus. If my dick was screaming for release before, now it's leading a goddamn please-let-me-come parade.

Through some feat of superhuman strength, I manage to ignore the ache in my groin and prolong the torture a few minutes longer. Only when we're both clutching and grasping at each other like overeager teenagers, panting and past the point of no return, do I give in and push the hand on my cock aside, thrusting upward and burying myself in her sweet pussy.

"Yes."

The one word—a single syllable, three letters, uttered on a sigh as she rests her forehead against mine—wrecks me. Then she wraps her arms around me—slowly, softly, even in the heat of passion remembering to be careful of my dislocated shoulder— and I'm not just wrecked. I'm fucking shattered.

I've been with women who were more—how do I put this?—sexually resourceful. Women who could bend and twist themselves into myriad positions. Even one woman who'd been on the United States Olympic gymnastics team. But none of their fancy moves or complicated contortions can compare to this. This small, simple, softhearted gesture that's struck me like a lightning bolt to the soul.

I seat myself deeper inside her, and she rocks back against me with sexy, breathy little gasps. Christ, she's so wet and hot and tight, her juices soaking my bare cock…

I freeze midthrust.

Shit. No condom.

The fact that I'm so far gone I neglected to wrap my willy speaks volumes. I've never not worn a condom before without first making sure my lady's protected and we're both clean. And when I say never, I'm not exaggerating. I mean never. As in not ever.

I feel like a total heel. Here Ainsley's doing her best to look out for me, and I can't even remember to suit up.

"We have to stop." My one-armed grip on her loosens, but I don't release her completely. If I do, she might wind up on the floor. "We—I mean, I forgot protection."

"I'm on the pill," she assures me. "And I'm clean."

"Same here. That is, I'm clean, too," I clarify.

"Then there's no reason for us to stop, is there?" Her hands explore my back and move down to my ass, pulling me tight to her.

I still feel like a heel for forgetting the condom, but she has a point. No harm, no foul, right? Besides, there's no way I can resist when she's touching me like that.

So I don't bother trying.

I start to move inside her again, hard and fast. The time for sweet and slow is long, long gone. She moans my name into the crook of my neck as her nails dig into my ass. When I snake my hand between us to thumb her clit, she goes off like a Fourth of July firecracker, bucking and writhing against me, her soft sex sounds building to a kind of high-pitched wailing that shouldn't torque me up even more but somehow does.

Her release signals my cock that it's okay to let go, and it does, in spades. I flood her until I'm empty, and we cling to each other sweaty, sated and spent.

We stay that way for I don't know how long until I'm semirecovered and able to stand, easily managing to take her with me despite the fact that I've got one arm strapped to my chest.

"What are you doing?" she asks, her legs coming up to wrap around my waist.

"Taking you to bed. I'm not through with you yet." Not by a long shot.

I head for her room, remembering there's an overgrown, overly affectionate canine in mine. Not because I have an aversion to women invading my inner sanctum. At least, that's what I'm telling myself.

"I thought kitchen stools and 1960s-inspired armchairs were where we did our best work," Ainsley jokes.

"Nightingale," I say, shouldering my way into the room and depositing her on the bed. "You haven't even begun to see my best work."

Consciousness comes slowly the next morning, courtesy of what sounds like an army of orcs banging on my front door. It takes me a few seconds to get my bearings. This isn't the master suite. I'm in one of the spare bedrooms, Ainsley's soft, warm, fabulously naked body draped deliciously across mine.

Memories of last night come flooding back—the strip Scrabble, the down-and-dirty cowgirl chair sex, the slower, sweeter, more traditional but no less intense missionary bed sex, not once, not twice, but three times—and my dick stirs to life, ready for round five. Maybe a little soapy shower action.

Then the banging starts up again, joined by an unfortunately familiar howl from my bedroom, and I have no choice but to extricate myself from Ainsley's embrace. She stretches, moans and rolls over, burying her beautiful face in one of my luxury goose down pillows.

Damn. Looks like I wore her out. A kernel of pride plants itself in my sternum and swells to the size of a soccer ball, puffing out my chest.

I drop a kiss in the sex-mussed hair at the top of her head and make my way toward the living room to find my long-ago discarded sweats. On the way, I spot my sling, tossed aside after round one—or was it two?—of bed sex. The doc said I can sleep without it, although there wasn't a whole lot of sleeping going on in here last night. I consider taking the time to wrangle my way back into the damn thing, but the banging and the howling are picking up speed and volume. Leaving the sling where it is, I continue on my way, closing the bedroom door behind me so I don't disturb Sleeping Beauty.

"Hold your horses, I'm coming," I shout, not sure if it's directed at Roscoe, whoever's at the door or both. I decide to deal with the dog first. I crack my bedroom door open to let him out, and he practically bowls me over on his way to the kitchen to check out the food and water situation.

After a quick peek inside to make sure he hasn't peed on my designer bedspread or chewed up one of my Gucci loafers, I head for the door. I'm halfway there when Connor's voice rings out through the banging.

"I know you're in there, Lawson. The doorman's working a double shift. He said you haven't left since last night."

I've got to have a word with that guy. He's not supposed to let anyone up without calling first.

"How did you con your way past him?" I ask, opening the door.

"I'm on your emergency contact list." He brushes past me into the kitchen, stopping to pet Roscoe, who's sitting mournfully next to his empty food bowl. "I've been trying to call you for over an hour."

I dump a couple of scoops of kibble from the wholesale club–size bag on the floor next to the refrigerator into Roscoe's bowl and lean against the counter. "What's up?"

Roscoe wedges his big body between me and Connor, buries his face in his food and starts chowing down like he hasn't eaten since there was a Bush in the White House.

Connor steps around the dog and pulls out a stool to sit down. "Your guy in Miami faxed some documents for you to go over. Said it's time sensitive. He wants you to get a hold of him as soon as you've read them."

"Why didn't he fax them here?"

"Beats me. You'll have to ask him."

He hands over a large manila envelope, then frowns. "Where's your sling?"

"Relax, Dr. House. I'm allowed to take it off to sleep."

"You're not sleeping now."

I toss the envelop onto the counter. "I just woke up. Cut me some slack."

Connor's eyes dart to the digital clock on the microwave above the stove. "Jake Lawson, sleeping past seven? What's wrong? Are you sick? Hung over? Or did you stay up all night playing hide the cannoli with your new roommate?"

It takes everything I have not to smack the smirk off his smug, pretty-boy face. He may be my best friend, but right now he might as well be Draco Malfoy to my Harry Potter. I've got to get him out of here before Ainsley stumbles out of bed, all morning-after sleepy and sexy and clearly well fucked. One look at her and Connor will know exactly what went down last night.

Or who went down on who.

I scrape a hand across my five o'clock–shadowed jaw and eye the Keurig. Connor's self-congratulatory, superior, I-told-you-so is the last fucking thing I need without caffeine in my system.

I start to open the cabinet next to the sink where I keep the coffee mugs, then abruptly slam it shut. I don't want Connor to get any ideas about staying for a cup of joe, no matter how bad I'm craving a hit of caffeine right about now.

"Documents delivered. Was there something else you wanted?"

He cocks his head and raises an eyebrow. "Can't a guy check in on his injured friend and business partner?"

"You've checked. I'm fine. Thanks for stopping by. Don't let the door hit you on the way out."

"If I didn't know better, I'd suspect you were hiding something." He stands. "But best friends since second grade don't keep secrets from each other, right?"

Wrong. Whatever is going on with me and Ainsley, I'm not ready to talk about it yet. Even with Connor.

I pat the envelope on the counter.

"I'm just in a hurry to get these papers read so I can call Alex. We're this close—" I hold two fingers about an inch apart "—to inking a deal for a sweet space right on the strip in South Beach."

Although I'm starting to worry that the landlord is jerking us around. Every time it looks like we're getting close to signing on the dotted line, he changes up the terms. I wonder what new wrinkle he's thrown at us now.

Connor considers me for a long minute, then nods and starts for the door. "I'm still not convinced this is the right time for us to expand, but I'm trusting your gut on this one. Keep me in the loop, and let me know if there's anything you need."

The door swings shut behind him, and I move at light speed to lock it. My gaze strays to another door, the one where I left Ainsley tucked fast asleep in my spare bed, looking like a rumpled, fallen, hot-as-fuck angel. My cock twitches, letting me know exactly what I need, and I check the lock one last time before going for it.

Paperwork and Miami and Alex—hell, even Roscoe, who's whining to go out—can wait. Time for round five and that soapy shower action.

CHAPTER THIRTEEN

Ainsley

"WHAT ARE YOU hauling me off to today?" Jake grumbles as I lead him across the artificial turf at Hudson River Park's Pier 46. "Another drag show? A museum? Shakespeare in a parking lot?"

We've done all of those things—and more—in the seven stupendous sex-filled days I've been staying at Jake's. Usually he's not so surly about our little excursions. Sure, Mr. All-Work can take some convincing to switch to play mode. But he comes around pretty quickly. Especially when I sweeten the deal with the promise of a late-night excursion between the sheets. Or in the shower. Or on the kitchen counter…

Today, though, he's moodier than usual. But I have a feeling I know what's bugging him. I'm hoping this not-so-impromptu picnic will get him out of his funk. Then—fingers crossed—he'll be in the mood for another late-night excursion when we get back to his place.

Maybe this time we'll christen the balcony, me holding tight to the railing while Jake pounds me from behind with the New York City skyline, illuminated at night, as our backdrop.

Sweet zombie Jesus. My panties are getting damp just thinking about it.

"It's a surprise." I heft the basket in my right hand and tighten my hold on Roscoe's leash with my left. The big lug's been a prince all day, tagging along with me on errands like he's done all week. But I don't want to risk losing him in the crowd that's starting to set up chairs and blankets in front of the giant inflatable screen at the far end of the lawn. "We're celebrating."

"Celebrating what?"

"Your good news from the doctor." I gesture with my head to his right arm, newly sans sling.

Jake frowns. He's been a grump since he met us after his follow-up appointment with the orthopedist. "If you call another week out of work good news. I don't see why I can't go back. My arm feels fine."

"I'm sure the doctor's just erring on the side of caution. He doesn't want you playing bouncer again until it's a little bit stronger. And he let you ditch the sling, didn't he?" I stop at what looks to be a good vantage point, close but not too close to the screen and off to one side, so we won't get crushed in the mob of moviegoers. "Baby steps. It's all about the small victories."

I ignore the voice at the back of my head telling me that this small victory has big implications for me. For us. With Jake back to two mostly usable arms, there's really no reason for me to keep shacking up with him.

Well, except for the multiple orgasms.

"Small victories suck," he mutters, taking Roscoe's leash from me so I can put the basket down and pull out the blanket I've packed. "I have to get back to work. Shit's going down on this Miami deal. The architect we hired is finishing up the preliminary drawings for our New York renovation. And we're short two bouncers, thanks to the stupid summer cold that's going around. They need me."

"No one's indispensable. Connor can handle things until you're able to return."

He flinches a little. Understandable. No one likes being told they're an easily replaceable cog in the corporate machine. But my words aren't meant to be hurtful, just truthful. Jake lives for his job. He needs a wake-up call, before it's too late and one day he looks around and finds that's all he's got.

Like me.

I spread out the blanket, take a seat and pat the space next to me. "In the meantime, why not stop and smell the roses? Or eat dim sum from Wo Hop and watch an iconic '80s movie."

He lowers himself to the ground, staring at me openmouthed the whole way down. "You went to

Wo Hop? I've loved that place since college. Their roast pork chow fun got me through freshman year."

"I know." Roscoe flops beside Jake, his big canine body taking up a good two-thirds of the blanket. I drag the picnic basket closer to me, open the flap and pull out a rawhide bone to keep him occupied. "Connor told me."

Jake takes the bone from my hand and passes it to Roscoe, who immediately begins gnawing on it with the enthusiasm of a two-year-old who's been given his first lollipop.

"You and Connor seem to be getting awfully chummy," he mutters, not looking at me.

I stretch up on my knees to kiss the corner of his mouth, this spark of jealousy in him making me bold. "Don't get your knickers in a twist. All of our conversations revolve around one subject. You."

He seems satisfied with that and moves on to another subject. "So what's the movie? Please tell me it's not *The Princess Bride*."

"That's next week." I start pulling dinner out of the basket. Steamed dumplings. Egg rolls. Roast pork buns. The aforementioned chow fun. Both forks and chopsticks, since I don't know how adept Jake is with the latter. "Tonight's feature is *Ferris Bueller's Day Off*."

He unwraps a pair of chopsticks and reaches for the dumplings. "Cool. I've never seen that one."

Now it's my turn to gape openmouthed. "Are you

kidding me? You've never seen *Ferris Bueller*? It's a coming-of-age classic."

"Nope." He pops a dumpling in his mouth. "Never."

"Then it's a good thing I brought you here so you can pop your *Ferris Bueller* cherry. There's a huge hole in your pop culture education that needs filling. You're in for a treat once dusk rolls around."

We've got about an hour before that happens, which we spend chowing down, chatting, people watching, trying to keep Roscoe from eating our neighbors' meal—fried chicken, clearly more appetizing to him than rawhide and MSG—and listening to the tunes DJ 2-Tone is spinning until the spectacular reds and golds of the Hudson River sunset fade and it's dark enough for the movie to start. Once Jake and I have destroyed the dim sum, I pack up the remnants of our dinner and head over to the concession stand under a tent at the edge of the water to grab us some free popcorn. Not that either of us is particularly hungry after consuming half our weight in Chinese food. But hey, free is free.

"What's this flick about anyway?" Jake asks when I return with the popcorn—extra butter, of course, because popcorn without extra butter is barely worth mentioning, let alone eating.

I sit criss-cross applesauce next to him and glance at the screen, where the opening title sequence—the one with Ferris in bed, faking sick—is beginning to play.

"Don't tell me you're the kind of person who likes to ruin movies by talking all the way through them." I hold his bag of popcorn just out of reach. "Because that's a deal breaker. I may have to go sit with that group of nuns over there. I'll bet they'll be quiet."

"I'm sure they will." He puts a hand on my ass and gives it a playful pinch. "But they won't be nearly as much fun. And I know how much you value your fun."

He makes a grab for the popcorn, and I jerk it away from him, spilling a few kernels, which Roscoe promptly inhales.

"This is a cult classic. You have to experience it for yourself. I don't want to spoil the surprise."

He gives in with a resigned shrug and lies back on the blanket, propping himself up on one elbow with his long legs stretched out in front of him, bare beneath the hem of his khaki shorts and unfairly tan for someone who spends most of his waking hours working. He's probably one of those guys who gets a perfect, golden tan in the blink of an eye. Whereas no matter how hard I try, the result is always either fire-engine red or pasty white.

"If you say so." He crosses his legs at the ankles and looks up at the screen. Ferris is up and out of bed and quoting John Lennon. "I just hope it lives up to the hype."

"It will. Now shut up, watch and learn."

I hand over the popcorn, and we munch contentedly, tossing an occasional kernel to Roscoe, as Ferris, Cameron and Sloane cavort their way through Chicago. Jake seems to be enjoying it. He's smiling, laughing at all the right parts, looking more relaxed than he's been since he left the apartment for his doctor's appointment.

"So," I ask when the movie is over and we're packing up and trying to rouse Roscoe, who dozed off about the time Ferris was twisting and shouting on a float in the middle of Chicago's Von Steuben Day Parade. "What did you think?"

"I liked it." He nudges Roscoe off the blanket so he can pick it up.

"You liked it?" I echo, incredulous, grabbing the blanket from him and stuffing it in the picnic basket. "You just witnessed almost two hours of John Hughes's genius, and that's the best you could come up with?"

"I'm no movie critic." He takes hold of Roscoe's leash and tugs the dog to his feet. "But it was okay."

"Okay?" I sound like a damn parrot, but I can't believe what I'm hearing. "What part of cult classic did you not get?"

"All right, if you want the truth—"

"I do." *I think.*

"I found Ferris kind of—" He pauses, and I'm not sure if he's searching for the right word or if he's afraid to spit it out and say what he's thinking. "Annoying."

He. Did. Not. Just. Say. That.

"Did we even watch the same movie?" I snatch the basket up and sling it over my arm. "Ferris is not annoying. He's the complete opposite of annoying. He's a freaking inspiration."

"He's a slacker. And a hedonist. His whole life is devoted to the pursuit of pleasure, at the expense of everything else. Schoolwork. Chores. Family relationships. I don't find that particularly inspirational."

"Did you miss the part about life moving fast, and if you don't stop and look around once in a while, you'll miss it?"

"That's no excuse for blowing off your responsibilities."

This conversation is starting to piss me off bigtime, so I guess it's a good thing we're interrupted by a voice cutting through the crowd noise, calling my name.

"Hey, Ainsley. Over here."

I swivel my head and spot her easily. Mia stands out in just about any crowd. But she's even easier to pick out here, tall, dark and striking, wending her way through the throng of moviegoers with an easy grace even in skin-tight jeans and four-inch heels, a slightly older salt-and-pepper-haired man who I vaguely recognize as one of her fellow junior partners at DK&G following in her wake.

"I was right. It is you," she says as she gets closer. "I didn't expect to see you here."

"I could say the same thing about you. How'd you get out of the office before midnight?" I tease, giving her a quick, one-armed hug.

"Summer associate outing," Salt-and-Pepper chimes in. "We thought it would be a nice change from the stuffy cocktail parties and dreary dinners."

"Who thought it would be a nice change?" Mia arches a brow at him.

"You did," he concedes with a smile.

"You remember Paul, don't you? He's in Mergers and Acquisitions." Mia lays a possessive hand on his arm.

"Of course," I fib. Now it's my eyebrow that's lifting. Mia hasn't mentioned that she's seeing anyone. Then again, I haven't said anything to her about whatever it is I'm doing with Jake, either. I give Paul a polite nod. "It's good to see you again."

"Same," he says. "How's the errand girl business treating you?"

"Executive concierge," Jake corrects him.

Shit. I almost forgot he's here.

"Who's your friend?" Mia asks before I can gather my wits and introduce him.

"Jake Lawson." He reaches down to scratch Roscoe between the ears. "And this is Roscoe."

Mia shoots me a we-are-so-talking-about-this-later look before refocusing her attention on Jake. "I thought you looked familiar. Top Shelf, right?"

"And you're Mia's friend. The one who was with her the night I got hurt."

"How's your arm?"

"Getting better, thanks." He steps aside to avoid being crushed by a pack of teenagers barreling across the lawn, pulling an oblivious Roscoe, who's too busy scarfing up stray popcorn to pay attention to his surroundings, with him. "We're blocking traffic. How about we walk together?"

We head out of the park, Jake and Paul leading the way and making small talk as Mia and I lag a few feet behind.

"I'm happy to see you took my advice," she says smugly.

"What advice?"

"To quit stalling and get your man."

"Lower your voice." I do a quick take to check on Jake. Fortunately, he's far enough ahead and deep enough in conversation with Paul not to have heard my none-too-subtle ex–best friend. "And he's not my man."

"Oh, really?" She leans in and at least does me the courtesy of turning down the volume. "Do you go on movie dates with all your clients? Or only the superhot ones with asses you could crack an egg on?"

I sneak a peek at Jake's butt. She's right. The damn thing's so tight, you probably could crack an egg on it. Or bounce quarters. Too bad the guy's wound tighter than the expensive, ultrathin Piaget watch he's wearing, too. Still, I'm tempted to try the egg thing—or the quarter thing—or both—later. Purely for purposes of scientific research, of course. For the good of womankind.

I sigh. "He does have a nice booty, doesn't he?"

"Nice doesn't begin to describe it. He's got some serious junk in that trunk."

We dissolve into giggles like a couple of tweens at a boyband concert, and I promise to fill her in on everything the next time we get together for a girls' night, as long as she does the same. When we reach Charles Street, the four of us part company, since Mia and Paul are going uptown while Jake and I are heading downtown to Tribeca.

It's a nice night, not as unbearably hot as it's been lately and with a light breeze coming off the river, and we've got Roscoe with us, which makes taking the subway out of the question, so we decide to backtrack and walk the Hudson River Greenway rather than catch an Uber back to Jake's.

"I had an interesting conversation with Paul," he says as we enter the greenway. The waterfront walkway and bike path is packed with people, many of them clearly moviegoers with the same idea as us, based on the blankets and baskets they're carrying.

"Did he hate the movie as much as you?" I quip.

"I told you, I didn't hate it. I liked it. The scene in the police station with Ferris's sister and that biker dude was hysterical. And the principal was a riot, too. I just have a different take on the whole Ferris-as-hero-or-antihero thing than you do, that's all."

"I guess we can agree to disagree," I concede. I'm not going to let a stupid movie—even a childhood favorite—ruin an otherwise pleasant evening. One that's hopefully going to get even more pleasant once we get back to his place and get naked. "What did Paul have to say that was so interesting?"

"He told me you used to work with him and Mia."

"Oh, that." I roll my eyes. If you asked me, my too-long stint at DK&G is just about the least interesting thing about me.

"Why didn't you tell me you were a lawyer?"

"It wasn't important. It still isn't."

"Not important? It was a huge part of your life for a long time. Paul told me you were on the verge of making partner when you quit to start Odds & Errands."

"Emphasis on the 'was.'"

"What happened?"

I shoot him a side-eyed look. "What do you mean what happened?"

"Something must have happened for you to give all that up."

Something did, but it's not something I'm ready to discuss with Jake. Especially not in the middle of a public park surrounded by strangers. When—if—the times comes for this discussion, it's going to between me and Jake, not me, Jake and a horde of walkers, joggers, cyclists and the occasional Rollerblader.

Besides, my breakup with Dale may have been the catalyst for my professional about-face. But if it wasn't that, it would have been something else. Looking back, with the wisdom of hindsight, I can see that it was only a matter of time before my career imploded. I'm not cut out for the life of a high-powered, big-city lawyer. I was just waiting for the axe to fall.

"Give up what?" I ask. "All the late nights at the office? The weekends? The takeout food, eaten at my desk?"

I'm on a roll now. "Should I go on? Because I can."

"Hard work takes sacrifices. But weren't they worth it? You were on the edge of achieving everything you worked so hard for. And now you're—"

"I'm what?" I stop dead in my tracks. "An errand girl?"

Paul's words from earlier still rankle. But the thought that Jake's thinking them too hurts even more.

He stops with me, pulling Roscoe up short and forcing a late-night jogger to veer around us. "I didn't say that."

"No. But you were about to. Or something pretty damned close to it."

All my anger from before comes flooding back.

He doesn't understand Ferris, and he doesn't get me, either. Just like my parents, judging me for jumping off the white-collar hamster wheel and redefining success on my own terms.

We're at the intersection of West Houston Street. And there's a subway station a few blocks away. Just like that, a plan takes shape.

"I need some space." The traffic light's red, so I start to cross.

"Wait," Jake calls after me. "Where are you going?"

"I'm hopping on the 1 train. You can keep walking or take an Uber, I couldn't care less."

And with that not-so-original parting shot, I'm gone.

CHAPTER FOURTEEN

Jake

IT'S QUIET AND dark when Roscoe and I get back to my place, and my first thought is that somehow we beat Ainsley there. Or worse, she's not coming back except to pick up her stuff, probably when I'm not here. I mean, she does have a key.

I bend down to unhook Roscoe's leash. That's when I see it. A sliver of light coming from under her door.

She's here. Thank fuck.

A sense of relief floods through me like a glacial thaw. And while I'm reassured, I'm also scared shitless. The former because, well, she's here. The latter because I care so damn much about the whereabouts of a woman I've known less than a month.

But fear's never stopped me before, and it's not going to stop me now. There's something about this woman that calls to me on virtually every level. Not just physically, although—duh—it's no secret what she does to me in that department, thanks to my disobedient dick. What I feel for her goes deeper than that. How much deeper, I don't have a clue. Yet. That's something I plan on figuring out.

If she'll talk to me.

I give Roscoe a pat on the back, hang up his leash and head for Ainsley's room, leaving custody of the couch to the dog. Her door's open a hair, but I knock anyway. I'm already on thin ice with her, although I'm not completely sure why. I was just trying to get to know her better. Figure out what makes her tick. We're obviously cut from different cloth. But that's not a deal breaker. At least, not for me.

Still, now is not the time to risk poking the bear.

"Ainsley," I call softly, knocking again. "You in there?"

Stupid question. Of course she's in there. Her or an extremely efficient burglar.

"You can come in," she answers after a beat. "I won't bite your head off. Much."

She sounds defeated. Resigned. Broken. My heart breaks a little for her, too. And for me, knowing I'm responsible for her bad mood, even if I'm not exactly sure how.

I push the door open, and the crack in my heart widens. She's sitting on the bed, surrounded by piles of clothes, her open suitcase on the floor at her feet.

"Going somewhere?" I ask, pushing aside a stack of her frilly underthings and sitting next to her.

"It's not like you need me here anymore." She picks up a T-shirt and drops it into her bag. "As long as you don't try to play hero again, you should be fine."

"What if I need to lift something heavy? Or change a lightbulb? Or just get lonely?"

"You've got my number. Feel free to use it. Except for the lonely part. You'll have to find someone else for that. I'm an errand girl. Not a call girl."

She picks up another T-shirt, but I pluck it from her fingers before she can add it to the suitcase and toss it back onto the bed.

"There you go again, putting words in my mouth. I never called you an errand girl." Or a call girl, but I don't go there.

"You didn't have to. You made your opinion of my change of career perfectly clear. And if you think I haven't heard it all before, you're dead wrong. I just didn't think I'd hear it from you."

She grabs a pair of shorts and throws them into her bag before I can stop her.

"Heard what all before?"

"You were so close to making partner at one of Manhattan's top law firms," she says, her tone mocking. "And you threw it all away. For what? So you could do other people's dirty work? What kind of career is that?"

Shit. Is that what I sounded like? A judgmental prick?

She reaches for a pile of socks, and I grab her wrist, stopping her. "If I sounded like that—"

"You did."

I flinch and let go of her wrist, her confirmation that I was a complete jackhole as painful as if she'd slapped me. "Then I'm sorry. I was trying to understand you. Not judge you."

"Sure seemed like you were judging me."

She blinks, and I get the sense she's fighting back tears, making me feel like I've been slapped again. Harder.

"I guess I shouldn't be surprised that a guy as successful as you looks down on me and my insignificant little business," she continues, pretending to be occupied with a loose thread on her sleeve. "It's not like I'm hitting the Fortune 500 anytime soon, or making the Forbes 30 Under 30 list. Hell, even my own parents are ashamed of me."

"Hey." I hook a finger under her chin, forcing her to look at me. "Stop doing that."

"Doing what?"

"Talking shit about yourself. It's not a competition. I don't look down on you. And I doubt your parents are ashamed of you, either."

She rolls her beautiful, sad eyes. "You haven't met my mother."

"I'd like to." The words roll off my tongue before I can stop them. But once they're out, I realize I don't want to take them back. I want to go all in with her.

"I'd like to meet your whole family. I want to get to know you better."

And I want her to get to know me, too. Which is why I go where I go next, opening a metaphorical vein and spilling a little of my soul.

"I'm sorry I was such a dick," I say, cupping Ainsley's cheek. My thumb strokes slow circles on her soft skin. She doesn't pull away, giving me the courage to continue. "I'm used to work being the center of my life. It's hard for me to step back. That doesn't mean everyone's wired the same way, or that everyone should be."

"Why?"

My thumb freezes midcircle. "Why what?"

"Why is it so hard for you to stop and smell the daffodils?"

"Daffodils?" I echo, letting my hand fall to her thigh.

"Roses are so cliché." A faint smile plays about the corners of her lips, one that has hope blooming in my chest. "And you get what I mean."

I do. But where to start? The dyslexia? My dad's heart attack? The collapse of his business?

For the next ten minutes or so, it all spills out. My struggles with reading. How I had to work twice as hard as my fellow students to get half as far. How our family lost everything—including my college fund—when my dad's company went under, and how I swore I'd never be in that position again.

Ainsley listens patiently, understandingly, even giving the hand on her thigh a sympathetic squeeze when I get to the part about watching Connor head off to Columbia while I went to City College. When I'm done, she tilts her face up to plant a quick kiss on my jaw.

"Thank you."

"For what?"

"For trusting me enough to open up to me. I was wrong to assume you were no different from my pain-in-the-ass parents."

She flattens a palm against my chest, right over my heart. There's no way she doesn't feel it banging around my rib cage like a blindfolded bird. The effect she has on me is impossible to hide. In more ways than one, I think, as my cock picks that exact moment to spring to life, making my cargo shorts suddenly uncomfortable.

I pull her in—with both arms, thank you very much—and fold her against me. "Does that mean you forgive me for being an insensitive jerk?"

She sucks her lower lip between her teeth and looks up at me with those stormy gray eyes, the intensity I see there stealing my breath. "On one condition."

"That I fuck you until you come so hard you forget your own name?" I ask hopefully, brushing back her hair and kissing her temple.

She laughs, the vibration traveling through me

like a warm, smooth shot of Macallan 1926. "Two conditions, then."

"What's the second one?"

"That you go twenty-four hours without working. That means no cell phone. No iPad. No computer. Just you, me and Roscoe."

"Can we spend them all in bed?" I lay her down, covering her lush, lithe body with mine. "Without the damn dog?"

Clothes fall to the floor, but she doesn't seem to care, all thoughts of packing apparently in the past. "He might have something to say about that."

"I'll deal with him later. Buy him off with some of those apple bacon treats he likes. Or a new stuffie. Maybe a duck, since he seems to enjoy tormenting them in the park so much."

"So is it a deal?" Her hands find their way into my hair. "No work for a whole day?"

She arches into me, making her full, round, fucking flawless tits even more prominent. And more appetizing. I can't help myself. I lower my head, sucking one nipple into my mouth through her shirt. When I draw back, I admire my handiwork, her pale pink nipple and rosy areola clearly visible through the wet white cotton.

"Not only is it a deal, Nightingale. How about we sweeten the pot with a little bet?"

"You mean like strip Scrabble?" She rolls me onto my back, straddles me and whips off her top, leaving those beautiful breasts covered only by a lacy lavender bra. "News flash. You don't need a bet to get me out of my clothes."

"Duly noted." I like this playful, take-no-prisoners Ainsley. I run my hands up shapely calves, over smooth thighs, to her hips, where I hold on for dear life. Now that I have her where I want her, no way am I letting her go. "But I was thinking more winner gets to decide where we go on our next date."

"Date?" she asks, her voice husky.

"I don't know what you think we've been doing, but movies, museums, theater in the park, even that damn drag diner—they all qualify as dates in my book. Especially when they're followed up by wall-banging sex."

Hell, now that I think about it, this is the most time I've spent with a woman in ages. Maybe ever. I'm more of a serial dater. I haven't been serious about anyone in a long time. Work's made that impossible.

Which proves she's got a point about stopping to smell the daffodils. It's only one day. What could happen in twenty-four hours? Negotiations have stalled on the Miami deal. And Connor can handle anything else that comes up.

"Okay." Ainsley's eyes flash with amusement as she rolls her hips, moving against me. "You're on. The clock starts—"

She reaches behind her back to unhook her bra.

The straps slide down her arms, and she takes it off, dropping it to the floor with the clothes we knocked off the bed earlier. "Now."

Not one to waste time—or a set of tits as spectacular as hers—I switch our positions again, shifting us to our sides so I can shuck off my T-shirt, shorts and boxer briefs. Once I'm naked, I concentrate on her, peeling off her denim cutoffs and pretty panties— lavender, the same shade as her bra—and leaning over to kiss her other nipple.

"Again," she says, and she doesn't have to ask me twice. I trace a damp circle around her nipple with my tongue, then draw it into my mouth and suck. She lets out a sexy, throaty moan that goes straight to my cock, making it leak on the ridiculously expensive eighteen-hundred-thread-count sheets.

She tastes good. Damn good. Like honey and lemon. But I'm a greedy bastard, and I want more. I want to taste her everywhere. So I kiss my way down to the neatly trimmed landing strip above her sex.

Ainsley digs her fingers into my hair and yanks hard, stopping me. "Not that. Not now. I want you to fuck me."

"Taste first." I untangle her fingers from my hair and settle between her legs. "Fuck later."

"But—"

I kiss the sensitive skin of her inner thigh, then turn my attention to her sweet pussy. At the first long, slow lick her protests fade and her head falls back on her pillow.

I've always enjoyed going down on women, but this is different. My dick is hard as a steel spike, and I swear I could come just from eating her out. But I ignore that horny fucker because it's all about her pleasure right now, not mine.

Her hands clutch at the sheets and her breath is coming in quick pants that have her breasts heaving. When I sense that she's close, I slow down. Her back arches and she grinds against my face with a frustrated groan. I chuckle into her folds, which only makes her groan louder and grab my head, pushing it deeper into her.

Who am I kidding, thinking I'm in control here? The woman wants to come, and I'm not strong enough—or stupid enough—to deny her. I follow her not-so-subtle suggestion, increasing the pressure and speed of my licks and kisses until she climaxes on my tongue.

"Wow," she says when her body finally stops spasming and she's lying limp and satisfied on the bed. "That was—"

"Just the beginning." I press a kiss to the spot where her hip meets her thigh and roll her to her stomach, positioning my still dripping, iron-hard cock at her entrance. "We've got twenty-three more hours to fill."

CHAPTER FIFTEEN

Ainsley

WHO SAID THAT the greatest danger is underestimating your opponent? Sun Tzu? General McArthur? Lady Gaga?

Whoever it was, they were right.

"I can't believe I lost," I say, covering my head with my pillow.

"Believe it, Nightingale." Jake pulls the pillow away and points to the clock on the nightstand. "Read it and weep. Twenty-four whole hours, and I haven't checked my cell phone or email once. Longer than that, if you want to get technical, since we slept through the deadline."

He tosses the pillow onto the floor and rolls on top of me, his morning wood nestling between my butt cheeks. "Or fucked through it."

"Nobody likes a sore winner." I wriggle out of his embrace so I can sit, taking the sheet with me. He may be ready and raring to go again, but I need a breather.

He follows me up, pushing my hair to one side and kissing my neck. "Something tells me I'm not the one who's sore this morning."

Smug bastard. But he's right. I am a little sore you-know-where. Twenty-four hours of almost non-stop sex—we took breaks to eat, use the bathroom and feed and walk Roscoe—will do that to a girl.

"I need a shower." And to brush my teeth. Shave my legs. Pluck my eyebrows. It's a testament to Jake's sex drive that none of that shit seems to bother him.

I let the sheet drop, swing my legs over the side of the bed and stand, completely unselfconscious in my nudity. No point in being modest with a guy who's had his head between your thighs. Multiple times.

Jake's eyes darken to chocolate pinpoints as they rake my naked body from head to toe, lingering a little longer than necessary on my breasts. Figures. He's a total boob man. Not that my nipples mind. Predictably, they perk up under his heated gaze. I may be sore down there, but apparently they don't care.

"Mind if I join you?" He throws off the sheet, and his raging hard-on springs free.

My nipples are tight little pebbles now, but my pussy is throbbing in protest. "Um, sore. Remember?"

He lifts his huge frame out of bed and comes up behind me, banding his arms around my waist and cupping my breasts in his beefy hands. "I can take care of that."

I want to resist, but my traitorous body has other

ideas, and I lean back against him with a sigh. "Even your penis isn't that magic."

"No." He nips at my neck, then soothes the spot with a kiss. "But my tongue is."

He's right, as usual. An hour later—after we've gotten really, really dirty and then soaped and scrubbed each other clean—Roscoe's been walked and fed and we're on our way to the mystery destination Jake, as the winner of our little contest, has chosen for our date.

I've tried getting him to spill the beans, but no dice. I think he's getting a kick out of keeping me in the dark. Either that or he thinks I'm going to flip out when I find out where he's taking me. All I know is one, he told me to dress comfortably but leave my flip-flops at home. And two, we're taking the Q train, so it's somewhere in Brooklyn.

As we ride down in the elevator, I pull out my phone to text Aaron and Erin. They've been rock stars, picking up the slack at Odds & Errands while I play house with Jake. I owe them both a huge bonus in their next paycheck.

When I'm done giving them today's rundown and letting them know I'll be back at the office tomorrow—a little part of me dies as I type that last part—I stuff my phone back in my I Swear Because I Care drawstring bag and glance at Jake. He's resting against the bar that runs along the back wall of the elevator, arms folded across his broad chest, a shit-eating grin splitting his face.

"What's so funny?" I ask, trying hard to ignore the way the sleeves of his polo shirt pull taut at his biceps.

"You. On your phone. Maybe you should take your own advice and stop and smell the—" He taps a finger on his chiseled jaw. "What was it?"

"Daffodils," I answer. "And I'm surprised you haven't busted yours out to check your messages. Or call Connor."

"Left it upstairs. Didn't even bother to power it up this morning."

Wait—what? I must have heard him wrong. "You turned off your cell phone?"

"Figured that was the easiest way to avoid temptation."

"And you don't have it with you?"

He shakes his head, still smiling. He looks unnaturally calm for a man who, just a couple of days ago, would have rather watched *The Princess Bride* on an endless loop than give up his lifeline.

"You realize the bet's over, right?" I ask. "And you won."

He shrugs. "I figure what's a few more hours of radio silence. Besides, I want to enjoy this day without interruptions."

Sweet zombie Jesus. Can a woman orgasm from words alone? Because I'm pretty sure I just did.

I feel like I'm living in a cheesy rom-com. The ones I love to watch but can't help poking a little fun at, too, with the kind of sappy love story—complete with an embarrassing meet cute, a handsome hero, a playful pup and oodles of witty banter—that you think is fantasy, not fact.

Until it happens to you.

Jake's eyes lock with mine, and the sincerity in their dark depths makes my heart skip like ten beats. The pull he has on me is hard to put into words. It seems crazy. I met him barely a month ago. But my head can't deny what my heart's known almost since the first time I saw him.

I'm falling for this guy. Hard.

"Thanks," I say, standing on tiptoe to kiss the corner of his mouth.

As a thank-you, it leaves a lot to be desired. Ditching his phone is epic rom-com grand gesture material. It deserves an equally epic response. Definitely something more than a measly "thanks" and a pathetic peck on the kisser.

In a show of solidarity, I fish my phone out, power it off and drop it back in my bag. "There. No interruptions."

He snakes an arm around me and pulls me flush to him. I can feel every peak and valley of him, every hard edge and smooth ridge.

"You know," he says, his breath ruffling the hair behind my ear. "We can always forget about the bet and head back upstairs."

Damn, this man. My body's gone from zero to

take-me-now in less than six seconds. It should be illegal what he does to me.

"But you won," I remind him for a second time. "Don't you want to claim your prize?"

"You are the prize, Nightingale."

The nickname started as a joke, but the way he says it now is like liquid sex, all rich and warm and gooey.

As if his words aren't enough of an aphrodisiac, his lips are sliding down my neck now, dropping soft, wet kisses all the way to my collarbone. Then they retrace their path, traveling up to my mouth and claiming it in a hot, determined kiss that has me clinging to his shoulders and salivating for more.

When we come up for air, I manage to summon up the willpower to shake my head and push at his chest, creating a sliver of space between us. "You're not getting out of this that easily. I'm dying to find out where you're taking me."

The elevator dings, and the doors slide open to reveal an elderly woman with an enormous orange tabby cat on a harness. Seriously, the thing must be almost half Roscoe's size. Which is saying something for a feline. Jake and I share a secret smile and start to pull apart as she steps into the car, the monster cat following obediently beside her.

"Don't mind us," she says, a twinkle in her rheumy eyes. "Far be it from me to stand in the way of young love. And Prince Harry here is the soul of discretion."

"Thanks, Mrs. G." Jake reaches down to pet

Prince Harry, who arches into his hand, no more than immune to his charm than I am. "You too, Harry."

"Will we see you at the building-wide ice cream social this week?" the older woman asks, looking from him to me and back again. "You can bring your friend."

"Wouldn't miss it," Jake says with a smile that's as genuine as they come. It's obvious he has a fondness for his elderly neighbor. And her cat. "I've got a little something for Harry. I'll bring it with me."

"Ooh," Mrs. G. squeals. "Is it one of those catnip mice he likes so much? I gave up looking for the last one you brought him. I don't know what he does with them. I think he swatted it behind the refrigerator."

Jake puts a finger to his lips. "Shh. We don't want to spoil the surprise."

The elevator dings again, signaling that we've reached the lobby. Mrs. G. says her goodbyes, and she and Prince Harry take off in the direction of the park.

"You're full of surprises, aren't you?" I ask Jake as we walk the other way, toward the nearest subway station.

He spreads his arms wide, like Jesus on the freaking cross. "I don't know what you're talking about. I'm an open book."

"If you're so open, why won't you tell me where we're going?"

"Because patience is a virtue. And good things come to those who wait."

"You sound like a Chinese fortune cookie," I

grumble. With that line of conversation officially at a dead end, I decide to try another tack. "How long have you known Mrs. G.?"

"I met her a couple of months after I moved in. She was struggling with an armful of groceries, and I helped her bring them upstairs to her apartment. Rumor has it her late husband was some kind of mafia boss. She's got a son, but he's a big-shot Hollywood producer, so I try to look out for her when I can."

Work-is-my-life Jake taking time out of his busy schedule to look after a little old lady? I study him out of the corner of one eye as I digest this new piece of information. Every time I think I've got him pegged, he changes the game.

I playfully shoulder bump him. Well, my shoulder, his bicep, since he's so much taller than me. "Has anyone ever told you you're a nice guy, Jake Lawson?"

"My mother," he answers easily. "And my fourth-grade teacher, Miss Traylor. She saw me give Annie Pulaski my cherry popsicle when Annie dropped hers. What she didn't know was that the gesture wasn't totally altruistic. I was angling for a kiss."

"So that's why you're sucking up to Mrs. G.," I tease. "Or is it Prince Harry you want to smooch?"

"Very funny." We're at the entrance to the Canal Street subway station. Rather than go down the steps that lead to the tracks, he stops and pulls me roughly into his arms. "But there's only one person I'm interested in kissing right now. And she's right here."

As if to prove his point, his lips lock on mine. He tastes like his minty toothpaste, mixed with the quick cup of coffee he downed while we walked Roscoe and raw, masculine need. His strong hands frame my ass, gripping and kneading until I'm moaning into his mouth. This being New York, our PDA goes virtually unnoticed, pedestrians ebbing and flowing around us like we're rocks in a river.

"Any more questions?" he asks when he's done turning me into a quivering mess. "Or can we get this party started?"

The subway ride is uneventful. We stand at first because it's crowded, Jake with one hand on the strap overhead and the other around my waist, steadying me each time the train lurches to a stop. As we go farther into Brooklyn, the car empties out, and we're able to find seats next to each other.

With each stop, I look questioningly at him, silently asking, "Is this the one? Do we get off here?" He just shakes his head and smiles until we're almost at the end of the line and it begins to dawn on me.

"We're going to Coney Island, aren't we?" I say just as a disembodied voice comes over the loudspeaker to announce it as our last stop.

He's thrown me for another loop. I love the beautifully, marvelously, gloriously tacky feel of the place once known as America's playground. The boardwalk. The carnival games. The rides. The arcade. The air thick with the smell of fried fair food.

But I thought Jake's speed was more sampling cuisines of the world at Time Out Market, or even hunting for treasures at Brooklyn Flea. Not wooden coasters and Whac-a-Mole.

"Beach or amusement park?" I ask, hoping it's the latter. I'm not wearing a swimsuit, and it's not like we brought any towels or beach chairs.

"Amusement park." Jake stands and holds out a hand, pulling me up with him. "If that's okay with you."

"Are you kidding?" I hitch my drawstring bag over my shoulder and stand next to him, waiting for the doors to open. "It's better than okay. It's awesome. I can't wait to kick your ass at Skee Ball."

"I wouldn't be so sure about that, if I were you," he says with an overly confident grin. "I happen to be a Skee Ball champion."

I tilt my head up to meet his gaze. "Good. That will make it even more satisfying when I kick your ass."

The doors slide open, and we head up the stairs into the sunshine and smells of mustard, sauerkraut and beer-battered onion rings. My stomach grumbles, reminding me that we skipped breakfast.

I pull my sunglasses out of my bag and slide them on, searching for the familiar iconic yellow building with the green-and-white-striped awning. "But first, I'm starving. What do you say we stop at Nathan's for one of their famous hotdogs?"

CHAPTER SIXTEEN

Ainsley

"THAT THING IS not sleeping with us."

I laugh and plop the giant Day-Glo green inflatable alien in a place of honor in the dead center of the bed. "You're just mad because I won it instead of you."

"I'm not mad, I'm repulsed." Jake grimaces. "That thing is hideous. Couldn't you have picked something useful, like an iPad? Or a jar opener?"

"He's useful. Put him in the passenger seat, and you can drive in the high-occupancy vehicle lane during rush hour. And I think he's kind of cute, in an ugly sort of way."

"I live in Manhattan. I haven't owned a car in years. Hell, I don't even have a driver anymore. I'm fine with Uber, taxis and the subway." He sits on the foot of the bed—as far as he can possibly get from the alien, I note—and kicks off his Vans, giving the alien a side-eyed glare. "How do you know it's a he?"

"Lucky guess."

I toss my bag on the dresser and start to shed my clothes like they're on fire. It's been a fun day—we rode every ride and played every arcade and carnival game in Luna Park—but it's been a long and hot one, too, and I'm in serious need of a shower. With a little encouragement, maybe we can have a repeat of this morning, and I can get Jake to join me and scrub my back.

And my front.

The shirt goes first, then the bra. When I pop the button on my cutoffs and start to lower the zipper, Jake lets out a low growl.

"Are you trying to torture me?"

I slide the zipper down another inch. "If I were, would it be working?"

"Fuck, yeah." He strokes his already growing erection through his shorts. "Put me out of my misery and lose the Daisy Dukes. And whatever's underneath them. I want you naked."

"What about you?" My voice is a breathless whisper, my heart's racing like a subway train—express, not local—and my damn nipples are standing at attention again. Knowing how I affect him is the biggest turn-on going.

"What about me?" he asks right back, stroking faster.

"Shouldn't you be naked, too?"

"That can be arranged."

He stands, grabs the hem of his polo shirt with both hands, and lifts it slowly, teasingly, like in a cheap porno. But way better, because unlike most of those guys—yeah, I not ashamed to admit I've watched a few, my trusty vibrator at the ready— Jake's got a body that's worthy of a Marvel superhero. I take the time to appreciate each abtastic inch of fine, firm flesh as it's revealed before the shirt is over his head and on the floor.

Way, way better than PornHub and my rabbit.

"On the count of three," he says, unbuttoning his shorts and reaching for the zipper tab. "One."

Our zippers slide down.

"Two."

Our thumbs hook into our waistbands.

"Three."

We're naked and on each other faster than you can say nymphomaniac, our clothes strewn carelessly around the room. We smash into each other, everything—lips, chests, legs—coming together like a perfect, frantic puzzle. It's more than a kiss. It's an erotic dance, a prelude to fucking.

Or something more than fucking.

Without warning, he slows things down, removing his mouth from mine and hoisting me into his arms, cradling me against him as he starts to move toward the bedroom door.

"Where are you taking me?" It's the second time I've asked him that question today. I hope his answer is as perfect as it was last time. This day has been the most fun I've had in ages. And the most fun I've had with a member of the opposite sex—in or out of bed—in, like, ever.

And it's not over yet. Not by a long shot.

"My room." His eyes shoot daggers at the alien, still holding court front and center on my bed. "I'm not making love to you with that thing staring at me."

Making love. Something more than fucking. Another perfect answer from a guy who's turning out to be pretty perfect, too.

"Shower," I blurt out, suddenly remembering my initial reason for getting naked. Well, one of the reasons.

"Later." He shoulders his way through the door into the hallway. "Why get clean when we're just going to get dirty again?"

He's got a point, so I don't argue. Besides, I kind of like him all hot and sweaty. I bury my face in the crook of his neck and sniff, then lick. It's like I'm back at Coney Island. He tastes and smells of salt water, fried clams and Italian ice.

I press my lips to his jaw.

Delicious.

It takes only a few steps for him to reach the master bedroom. His man cave. The one room I haven't set foot in since I started staying here.

Until now.

It's not like he's got a lock on the door. Or a No

Girls Allowed sign. I've just never had a reason to go in there. He keeps the door closed, and we've been using my room for sexy times. Whether that's out of habit or something deeper on Jake's part, I don't know. I've tried not overthink it and live in the moment.

Just like I'm trying to live in this moment and not attach too much significance to our change of venue.

Fortunately, I don't have time to dwell on it too much because we've crossed the threshold into the inner sanctum. Jake lays me down on the California king that dominates the room and stretches out beside me. I expect him to get right down to business, but he surprises me yet again, propping himself up on one elbow and staring at me with a reverence in his eyes that makes my heart flutter and my stomach flip.

This isn't about sex anymore. If it ever was. This thing between us—this connection—is more than physical.

It's new. And exciting. And more than a little bit scary. No man has made me feel this strange combination of exhilarated and anxious. Not even dickweed Dale. And I wasted three years of my life with him.

Well, I'm done with that shit. Life's too short. I'm not wasting another second.

I slide down his body, positioning my head between his legs. His thick erection stares me in the face, and I swear I'm practically salivating.

"No." Jake winds his fingers through the hair at the nape of my neck. "I won't last long if you do that. You know how I love it when you use that naughty tongue stud of yours on my cock."

Yeah, I know. That's why I'm doing this. And I'm not taking no for an answer. Jake's made me feel so good in so many different ways today. Giving up his phone. Taking me to Coney Island. I mean, is there anywhere on earth that screams fun more than a freaking amusement park? Now it's my turn to do something for him.

And a little bit for me, too, if I'm being honest. Giving my man head isn't exactly a chore.

My. Man. I know it's fast, but that's what he is. In my mind, in my heart and in my soul.

"I know you love it," I say, my mouth hovering over him. "That's why I'm doing it. You might as well just lie back and enjoy it."

I curl my fingers around the base of his shaft, and he hisses.

"Fuck, Nightingale."

His hands leave my hair and fist in the comforter. I've won this battle. Not that he put up much of a fight. My lips haven't even touched his dick, and he's so turned on he's already wet with precum.

For that matter, so am I. My pussy's dripping just from thinking about what's coming next.

And who's coming next.

I bring my lips to his tip and lick away some of the moisture. It's thick and sweet and slightly salty. I lick again.

"Oh, yeah," he moans. "That's it. Tease me. Drive me crazy with your wicked tongue and that fucking stud."

He doesn't have to tell me twice. I flick my tongue up and down his length, like I'm licking an ice cream cone. Savoring every inch of him. With each flick, my stud brushes his hard, hot flesh.

He shudders and lets his knees fall open, making more room for me. I move in closer and take him into my mouth, wrapping my lips around him and sucking him in.

"Holy fuck." Jake's knuckles are white, that's how tightly he's gripping the comforter. "That feels incredible."

His admission spurs me on. I bob faster, swirling my tongue around him, making sure he can feel the stud he loves so much. The hand circling the base of his cock moves lower, to his balls. Cupping them. Squeezing them. Teasing them with my fingertips.

His hips jerk upward and he swears under his breath. "I wasn't kidding about not lasting, Nightingale. I'm about to blow."

He means it as a warning, a signal for me to pull off him. Instead, I double down, open wider and suck him in.

All. The. Way.

He's balls-deep in my throat now, and I'm going down on him like a pro. He mutters incoherently as I flatten my tongue and make my lips tight so I can suck him harder, but every third word or so I catch a "yes," "fuck" or "more."

It's only a few seconds before he comes hard. I stay with him until he's done, swallowing every last drop. Then I give him one last, long, lingering lick and let go.

He drags a hand through his hair and makes a sound that's somewhere between a sigh and a groan. "Have I told you how fucking fantastic you are at that?"

"Only after every blow job I've given you," I say, laughing as I crawl back up his big, beautiful body. "But don't stop. A girl can never get too many compliments."

He pulls me in to him, hooking his leg over my hip and kissing my forehead. "Give me a few minutes, and I'll be ready to go again."

I snuggle closer, my head burrowing into his chest. The soft, fine hair sprinkled across his pecs tickles my nose. "No rush."

I mean it. The sex—no, lovemaking—is great, but this is pretty great, too. Just being together. Skin to skin. Our chests rising and falling in unison. His heart beat slowing to a steady rhythm under my cheek.

After about five minutes, I feel his hand snake between us and move down my belly, toward my clit.

"So soon?" I ask, sucking in a ragged breath as he finds his target. "Are you sure you're up to the challenge?"

He rocks his hips, pressing his resurgent cock against my stomach and showing me exactly how up he is.

"Challenge accepted."

CHAPTER SEVENTEEN

Jake

I WAKE THE next morning with Ainsley wrapped around me like boa constrictor. Par for the course these days. What's new is the bed we're occupying.

Mine.

I wait for the panic to set in. Bringing her here last night was a spur of the moment decision. I don't usually have women in my master suite. With enough spare bedrooms to accommodate the Knicks' starting front court lineup, keeping my personal space just that—personal—has never been a problem.

The realization dawns that I could have done the same thing last night. Taken Ainsley to any of those other spare bedrooms. Or just shoved the hideous plastic alien off her bed and taken her right then and there.

But I didn't. I brought her here because I wanted her here. It might have seemed spur of the moment, but my subconscious was telling me something.

It was telling me that this woman is different. Special. Someone I want in my life—and my bed—for more than a night or a week.

Instead of panic, a tidal wave of calm floods through me. Her, me, together like this—it feels right. More right than anything's felt in longer that I can remember.

I brush her hair off her neck and leave a trail of kisses down her spine. She stirs but doesn't wake. Unlike my cock, which is wide awake and raring to go.

But as good as a slow, sweet session of morning sex sounds right about now, that's not what Ainsley needs. She needs to know how I feel about her. And what better way to start than by showing her, not telling her.

It's like that old saying. Actions speak louder than words. And I want my actions to scream. I don't want Ainsley to have any doubt about what I'm saying.

As carefully as I can, I slide out of bed, doing my best not to disturb her. I hold my breath as her eyelids flutter open, but they drift shut just as quickly and she rolls over, back in dreamland.

Although if her dreams are anything like mine—and Christ, I hope they are—she'll wake up horny as hell with her hand down her pants.

Figuratively speaking, of course. Because when we sleep together, clothing is less than optional. It's forbidden.

Remembering that Ainsley's naked under my expensive sheets makes it that much harder to leave her, but somehow I manage to throw on a pair of boxer briefs and get my ass out the door. I pad barefoot into the kitchen and practically trip over Roscoe, who's lying in front of his food bowl looking mournful. I give him a quick scoop of kibble and some fresh water so he'll stop mooning like a sick calf and yank open the subzero fridge.

My initial plan was to start my actions-speak-louder campaign by cooking her breakfast—you know, the whole way-to-the-heart-is-through-the stomach thing. But one look inside my empty refrigerator—my housekeeper's on vacation, and Ainsley and I have been too busy fucking like sailors on shore leave and ordering takeout to food shop—kills that not-so-brilliant idea.

Good thing I can think fast on my feet, a skill I've honed at Top Shelf. You can't own a business and not have to make split-second decisions when things don't go according to plan.

I close the fridge and do a quick pivot to the counter, where my cell phone's charging. I can call Bubby's and have sourdough pancakes, cheddar grits and crab cakes Benedict at our door in less than an hour.

But when I power up my phone, the damn thing goes crazy with email, text messages and voicemail alerts, most of them from Connor and Alex, my contact in Miami. My heart drops to my stomach as I click on the most recent voicemail and hear a clearly panic-stricken Connor.

"Hey, man. I don't know where the fuck you are or what the fuck you're doing, but you need to call Alex ASAP. He's been trying to get in touch with you. The landlord on that property you've been looking at in South Beach is ready to pull the trigger, but he wants an answer by end of day or he'll go to the next highest bidder. And when you're done with Alex, call me, asshole. As your friend, not your business partner. It's not like you to fall off the face of the earth like this. I'm worried about you."

Shit, shit, shit, shit, shit.

I don't even bother to listen to the rest of the voicemails or read any of the text messages. Instead, I hit Alex's number on my speed dial.

"Finally," he says when he picks up, not even waiting for me to identify myself. "Where the fuck have you been?"

I skip the niceties and cut right to the chase. "Is it too late? Did we lose the property in South Beach?"

"Gone with the wind, pal. Sorry. That's what happens when you don't answer your phone. Or respond to your messages. I must have left you twenty voicemails and at least as many texts and emails."

"Shit," I say, out loud this time. It's no use making excuses. "This is on me. I'm sorry."

"It's your loss. Just let me know how you want to

proceed. I can start looking for another location. But I don't know how long it will take to find something that meets all your specifications. You're a tough man to please."

I slump onto a stool, resting my elbows on the hard cold marble of my kitchen island. "Yeah, I know."

"And you have to promise me you won't go AWOL again."

"I promise."

He signs off, and I take a deep breath before making the next call. When Connor picks up, I fall on my sword before he can chew me out.

"I fucked up. Big time. We lost the Miami property."

"I figured as much. What happened to you? Did you lose your phone or something?"

My phone? No. My mind? Yes.

"Temporary insanity," I mumble, eyeing the Keurig enviously. I could use a cup of coffee. Or something stronger. Like lighter fluid.

"What?" Connor asks.

"Never mind. I'll tell you about it later. Right now, my priority is straightening out this mess I've gotten us into."

"How? The landlord's rented the property to someone else. You said so yourself. We've got a lot of time and money invested in this already. This could set us back months, if not more."

He isn't saying anything I haven't told myself in

the past five minutes, but that doesn't make his words any easier to hear. He's had my back since we were seven, and this is how I repay him. What kind of a dick does that?

My kind, apparently.

"I know." A heavy weight lands on my thigh, and I look down to see Roscoe's head resting there, his soulful brown eyes looking back at me pityingly. Great. Even the damn dog feels sorry for me. "Like I said, I fucked up. You trusted me with this project, and I let you down."

I'd let us both down. Lost focus. Taken my eye off the ball. The one thing I'd sworn never to do. Well, that stops. Now.

"I'll fix this somehow. I swear. I'm taking the first flight I can get to Miami. I'll talk to the landlord. See if there's any way he can back out of the deal and give us the space. And if that doesn't work, I'll stay down there until I find another location. A better one."

"Look, Jake, you don't have to—"

"Yeah." I cut him off. "I do. I'll text you with my flight information."

I hang up before he can try to convince me to stay. Or whatever he was going to try to convince me to do. I shoot off a quick text to my secretary, asking her to book my flight and hotel, and I'm about to go hop in the shower when I see Ainsley hovering at the other end of the island. Roscoe abandons me and trots over to her, flopping at her feet.

"You're leaving."

She doesn't yell. Or call me any of the names I definitely deserve. Her voice is soft and steady, but it guts me nonetheless.

"You heard."

She steps over Roscoe, crossing her arms in front of her chest. Her hair is still all sexily mussed from sleep, but at least she's put some clothes on. I don't know if I could have stopped myself from fucking her against the counter if she marched out here naked. One last hurrah before I have to head to Miami for who knows how long.

"What did you mean when you said you were temporarily insane?" she asks.

Fuck. Fuck. Fuuuuck. She heard that, too?

"How long have you been standing there?"

"Long enough to know you think the past forty-eight hours were a huge mistake."

"A mistake that cost me the Miami deal."

She flinches like I've slapped her. "So I was right. You do think it was a mistake."

Shit. I'm screwing things up. Again.

I take two deep breaths to try to collect my thoughts, but it doesn't help. This morning has gone completely off the rails. I'm supposed to be feeding her goddamn breakfast, not fighting with her.

"That's not what I meant."

"It's what you said."

"Did you not hear me?" I slam my hand down

on the marble so hard my fingers ache. So much for collecting myself. The noise makes Roscoe raise his head and whine, but I ignore him. I've got enough problems. I don't have time for his shit right now. "The Miami deal is dead."

"I get that you're disappointed—"

"Disappointed doesn't even begin to cover it."

"There will be another opportunity, Jake." She moves in closer, reaching out a tentative hand to touch my shoulder. "There's always another opportunity. What there won't be is another me."

I hear her, but I don't. No matter how hard I try, I can't stop the anger, the frustration boiling up inside me. It drowns out everything else. Hope. Reason.

Even her.

I shake her hand off. "I had people counting on me, Ainsley. And I instead of doing what I was supposed to be doing—my goddamn job—I was off playing carnival games and screwing the dog walker."

She flinches again, my words striking another, deeper blow. I've gone too far, and I know it. But some stupid, inexplicable force is preventing me from backing down.

She draws herself up to her full five feet something, fortifying herself, like she's preparing for battle.

"Executive concierge," she corrects me, her words clipped and brittle.

My phone dings. It's a text from my secretary. She has me booked on a flight leaving JFK in a few hours.

I stand abruptly and let out a long breath. "I can't do this now. I have to catch a plane to Miami. We can settle this later."

Maybe by then I'll be able to get my head out of my ass and my foot out of my mouth. But Ainsley's got other ideas.

"I think we settled it already." She grabs her drawstring bag from the floor by the door, where she dropped it last night in our haste to get to the bedroom.

Christ, that seems like a lifetime ago now.

"I'll be back to get the rest of my stuff later," she says, not bothering to hide the little catch in her voice. "When you're not here. And don't worry. Odds & Errands will take care of Roscoe while you're gone. For an additional fee, of course."

She's out the door before I can respond, and I'm left standing in my boxers, watching my parents' annoying, freakishly large dog lick his balls and trying to figure out how my entire life went to shit before breakfast.

CHAPTER EIGHTEEN

Ainsley

"EARTH TO AINSLEY." Erin reaches across the desk and taps my head with the eraser end of her pencil. "Are you even listening to me?"

"Of course I am," I lie. "You were saying something about the Bartons' grocery order."

"That was so five minutes ago," Aaron says with an impressive eye roll. "We've moved on to Mrs. Vincent and her Mercedes. Which I still don't want to drive."

I tap my keyboard, and a tick appears in the appropriate box of my trusty computerized spreadsheet. "Noted."

"Are you sure you're all right?" Erin sits back and studies me from across my desk with a worried frown. "You haven't been yourself since—"

"Can we stick to business, please," I say a little too harshly.

The problem is Erin's right. I haven't been myself lately. It's been two weeks since I walked out on Jake, and I swear I'm barely functioning. Without him, everything feels empty. Blah. Beige. It's like I'm moving through a thick fog of melancholy that I can't shake, no matter how hard I try.

I wasn't half this bad when Dale pulled his disappearing fiancé act. I felt betrayed, sure. And abandoned. After years of being part of a twosome, I was alone.

But I didn't ache for Dale like I do for Jake. Losing Dale was like giving up Diet Coke. Once I kicked the habit cold turkey, I didn't really miss it. Losing Jake is like having a limb cut off. The pain may ebb and flow, but it never fully goes away.

What makes it hurt even more is that I thought we were really connecting. And not just in the bedroom, although that part was pretty spectacular. That thing Jake did with his tongue on my clit...

Nope. Not going there. What was I thinking before my mind went down dirty memory lane? Oh, right. Connecting. Outside the bedroom.

It seemed like Jake was starting to relax and loosen up with me. Having fun with the drag queens at the diner. Filling a penis piñata. Screaming his head off on the Cyclone at Coney Island.

But one phone call from the office, and he was back to Mr. All-Work-No-Play. The angry words he hurled at me ping-pong in my head, fresh pain stabbing my gut with each ping, ripping at my heart with each pong.

A mistake that cost me the Miami deal.

I was off playing carnival games and screwing the dog walker.

I blink back tears—it's bad for office morale to let your employees see you cry—and do the same thing I've been doing for the past fourteen days—tell myself no matter how much it hurts, it's for the best. If there's one thing I learned from my last breakup—and from Ferris Bueller—it's that life is short, and spending it worrying about work is a waste of valuable time. I can't be with someone who's not down with that philosophy.

No matter how occasionally fun and always fuckable he is.

"Uh, boss?" Aaron says softly, nudging me out of my depressing daydream. "The schedule?"

I clear my throat and focus on my computer screen.

"Right. So Erin—" I point to her. "Will take care of Mrs. Vincent's Mercedes. And Aaron—"

I point to him. "You've got the Bartons' groceries. Okay?"

They both nod, and I make another tick in the spreadsheet.

"Good. Now which one of you wants to feed and walk Roscoe today?"

"That's another thing." Erin tucks her pencil behind her ear and eyes me again. She's way too suspicious. Then again, she's the only one of my assistants who's met Jake. No doubt she suspects he's the tall, dark and handsome cause for my mood swings. "Why don't you walk him anymore?"

"Yeah," Aaron chimes in, depositing his long, lanky frame into the seat next to her. "You're the one who insisted we break our no pets policy. Besides, I thought you liked the hairy beast."

"I do." And his temporary caretaker. A little too much. "But my schedule's full today."

"With what?" Erin asks.

With whatever keeps me far, far away from Jake's apartment. I'm not ready to go back there. I may never be ready. Too many memories, good and bad. It's hard enough having to answer his daily texts about Roscoe.

"I'll take the morning shift," Aaron jumps in, rescuing me. Bless his clueless little heart. "If she'll do the dinner run."

I turn to Erin. "That okay with you?"

She shrugs. "Sure."

I send them on their respective ways, grab my I Drink Coffee Because Adulting Is Hard mug, and head into the kitchen for my third cup of dark roast. It's shaping up to be another long, depressing day. And it isn't even nine o'clock yet.

I just manage to get a K-Cup in the machine when my intercom buzzes, telling me someone's downstairs. I shove my mug under the spout and hit the brew button before heading into the living room to answer it. A girl's gotta have priorities. Whoever's down there, they can't be more important than coffee.

The buzzer goes off again, three times in rapid succession. My mystery visitor is an impatient little fucker.

I puff a stray lock of hair off my forehead and hold down the talk button. "Hello?"

"It's your mother." Her voice makes me shrivel like I've been doused by a bucket of ice water.

"Mom." I'd sink to the floor if I could, but my arm's not long enough for my finger to stay on the stupid intercom button. I settle for leaning against the wall for support. "What are you doing here?"

"Can't a mother visit her daughter?"

Not my mother. Not in this lifetime.

Hell, I wasn't even sure she remembered where I lived. Or maybe I was hoping she forgot.

"Ainsley?" I can almost see the look of haughty disdain she's worked years to perfect. "Are you still there?"

I sigh and stab at the intercom button. "Come on up."

It's not like I have much of a choice. As much as I'd like to, I can't very well leave the woman who gave birth to me in the lobby.

I glance around my studio apartment, my eyes lighting on all the things she's sure to find fault with.

The dirty dishes in the sink. The piles of papers everywhere. The basket of laundry I haven't gotten around to folding yet.

I fleetingly consider doing a quick cleanup, but fuck it. She's the one who showed up unannounced. If she doesn't like my housekeeping skills—or lack thereof—that's her problem.

From down the hall, I hear the elevator ding, followed by the staccato click-clack of my mother's ever-present designer pumps—I don't think the woman's worn anything with less than a three-inch heel since grade school. I open the door and step aside to let her in.

"Darling." She brushes past me, striding into my humble abode like she owns the damn place. Not that she'd ever lower herself to live south of Central Park. "I've been worried sick about you. You haven't returned any of my calls or texts."

"Yeah, I'm sorry about that. Things have been crazy."

I cross my fingers behind my back at the lie. Not the sorry part, the crazy part. I really do feel bad for giving her reason to be concerned. And not just because I know how much she hates the worry lines she gets around her eyes and mouth.

She pushes aside a stack of magazines, daintily brushes off the couch cushion and sits, crossing her legs and smoothing her perfectly tailored pencil skirt over her slim thighs. I have to hand it to her. For a woman over fifty, she's in damn good shape. My mother has always prided herself on her appearance.

Unfortunately, she doesn't feel the same way about me.

"You look terrible," she says, pursing her lips.

"Gee, thanks." I stare down at my respectable but pedestrian outfit—boyfriend jeans, a V-necked top and a white blazer. I guess I should be thankful. If she had come an hour earlier, I'd have still been in my Hello Kitty pajamas. "If I knew you were coming, I would have put on my Sunday best."

"That's not what I mean." She clucks her tongue at me like I'm a rebellious teenager. Or one of her staff. "You're pale. And the circles under your eyes are getting darker by the minute. Are you sleeping? Eating? Have you been taking the multivitamins I suggested?"

Not enough, too much and what multivitamins? I must have tuned out that lecture. Something I did frequently when my mother got on a roll. It was a matter of self-preservation.

"I'm fine. Like I said, I'm just busy." I remember my coffee and head for the Keurig. "Can I get you anything to drink? Water? Coffee? Tea?"

Or I could open a vein and let you drink my blood.

She waves me off. "Work is going well, then? Business is booming?"

I sip the sweet, caffeinated heaven, taking my time to savor it before answering, and flop into the bean bag chair I've had since college. It was the first piece of furniture I ever purchased, and I don't have the heart to get rid of it. Plus, it's more comfortable than it looks, and my mother despises it. She says bean bag chairs are for children, and if it doesn't have a frame, it's not supporting hers. That's bonus points in its favor in my book.

"We've got more than we can handle," I admit, not too modest for a little humble brag. "I'm considering hiring another assistant."

If I can stop mooning over Jake long enough to put a job posting up on ZipRecruiter.com.

My mother arches one perfectly tweezed brow. "I take it that's why you haven't called Martin."

I rifle through my mental Rolodex but come up empty. "Martin?"

"Fletcher," she supplies with an exasperated huff. "The head of our co-op board. I texted you his number. He's been expecting your call."

Dammit. This again?

"Yes, this again. Although I wish you wouldn't swear. It's not ladylike."

Shit. I didn't mean to say that out loud. But now that I have, maybe it's the perfect time to get this out in the open. Maybe that's what my subconscious was after all along.

I take another sip of coffee, wishing I'd thought to spike it with a shot of something stronger, and dive right in. "The truth is, Mom, I haven't called Martin—

Mr. Fletcher—because I don't want to come speak at any tenants' meeting. I'm not looking for pity clients."

She frowns, creasing her Botoxed forehead. "Who said anything about pity clients?"

"Why else would you be trying to throw business my way?" I down the rest of my coffee then deposit the mug on the floor next to me, earning me another disapproving glare. I ignore it and plow on. Now that the floodgates are opened, there's no stopping the tsunami of truth spilling out of me. "It's obvious you think I'm struggling."

"I don't know where you get these ideas." My mother shakes her head. Her impeccably coiffed signature bob barely sways gently then falls back into place, not a hair out of line.

"Hmm, let's see." I tap my chin like I'm deep in thought. "Could it be the countless times you've mentioned that it's a good thing I have my legal degree to fall back on? Or maybe it's how you call Odds & Errands my 'little gopher business.' You've always treated it like it's some sort of hobby, a passing fancy I'm dabbling in until I get bored and go back to practicing law. News flash, Mom. I don't need anything to fall back on, and even if I did, it wouldn't be anything even remotely connected to the law. I am not getting sucked into that live-at-the-office, eat-breathe-and-sleep-work world again."

Now that the words are finally free and out in the

ether, I feel lighter somehow. More at peace. Whether it's with myself or with my mother, I'm not sure. But I'm not sure it matters, either.

I risk a glance at her. Not that I'm expecting much in the way of a reaction to my outburst of verbal vomit. My mother doesn't do emotions. With her it's all logic and reason and careful control.

So when I see her wiping away what can only be a tear with the back of her hand, it's an understatement to say I'm shocked.

"I know I'm not the best at showing emotion," she says, making me wonder for not the first time whether the woman can read minds. Then again, if she could, we wouldn't be having this discussion. She would have known what I was thinking ages ago. "Saying how I feel isn't easy for me."

Her voice wavers, the careful control she prides herself on slipping a notch. I'm tempted to jump in. To do what I've done in the past when we've come close to this reckoning. Lie, tell her it's okay, relieve her of any guilt she might have over our strained relationship.

But I don't. Instead, I bite my lip and sit back, ears—and heart—open to what she has to say. Because maybe, like me, she needs to get something off her chest. And maybe this time it will be what I need to hear.

She takes a handkerchief from her vintage Hermès alligator bag—seriously, who carries a handkerchief anymore except stuck-up suits and elderly grandmothers? Or an alligator bag for that matter?—dabs at her eyes and continues. "I understand that you're perfectly capable of taking care of yourself. But I'm a mother. Mothers worry. Even the worst of us."

Okay, it's not exactly what I was hoping for. But it's close. And I've got to give the woman credit for trying.

"I appreciate that. But I don't need your help." Emotional support would be nice. But I don't want to push my luck. Maybe we can work toward that once we get past this hurdle.

"It wasn't you I was trying to help," my mother insists, carefully folding her handkerchief and putting it back in her bag. Apparently, the threat of more waterworks has passed. "Well, not only you. Our doorman is swamped with requests he can't handle. I thought if he could refer tenants to you, or if they knew about your services so they could contact you directly, it would save everyone a lot of time and trouble. And Martin agrees. It was his idea to have you come to one of our meetings. I suggested putting your business cards in the lobby, but he thinks the personal approach will work better."

Damn. I hadn't considered the possibility she might be coming at this from a completely different angle. I just assumed she was looking out for me, not her neighbors.

"Like I said, we're pretty busy, but tell Mr. Fletcher I'll give him a call this week. Maybe we can set something up." I make a mental note to start drafting that ZipRecruiter ad ASAP. We're definitely going to need another body if this pans out.

"Thank you. He'll be relieved to hear that."

She stands and loops her purse over her arm, signaling that she's reached her limit of mother/daughter bonding for today. I follow her to the door, only mildly disappointed that she's cutting our conversation short. We've made progress. More than we have in years. For now, that's enough.

"How about we have lunch sometime next week," I offer, figuring it couldn't hurt to extend the olive branch a little further.

"I'd like that," she says, and for the first time in a long time I believe her. "I'll check my schedule and get back to you."

I swallow a laugh. She sounds like she's scheduling a dentist appointment, not lunch with her only child. But I remind myself that this is about progress, not perfection, and wrap my arms around her in an only semi-awkward hug that she returns slightly less stiffly than usual.

"But not Fig & Olive," I add. "We should expand our horizons, try someplace different."

Translation: less pretentious. I wonder how she'd feel about being waited on by a drag queen singing show tunes. The thought brings up memories of Jake with a boa around his neck and Marilyn Monroe crooning in his ear. Somehow, I doubt my mother would be as good a sport as he was. But then I remember why I walked out on him, and the bad memory sours the good.

"If that's what you want," she agrees somewhat reluctantly, pulling me back to the present. I'll take it as a win. I open the door for her, and she steps through then turns back to me with an expression even more serious than her typical resting bitch face. "Can I give you one last piece of motherly advice?"

I doubt it will be the last, but I nod.

"Maintaining a balance between work and your personal life is a delicate thing, no matter what profession you're in. I've watched your father do it for years. It's like a seesaw. It won't always be perfectly parallel. Sometimes it has to tilt one way or the other. The key is to make sure it's not always to one side."

She gives me a kiss on the cheek and click-clacks down the hall toward the elevator, leaving me with more questions than answers. If I was wrong about her, could I be wrong about Jake, too?

Or what if it's not him that I'm wrong about? What if it's me? Is it possible I'm the one with my seesaw stuck in one direction? In my quest for balance, have I swung too far to the opposite extreme?

I step back into the sanctuary of my apartment and close the door, my head pounding with the pressure of all the riddles my mother's left in her wake. I need to solve them. And as much as I hate to admit it, I know just the person to help me.

Dickweed Dale.

A phone call's out of the question. There's no way I want to hear that douche canoe's voice again. Besides, I blocked his number after he called to invite me to his goddamn wedding. To his secretary. I mean, administrative assistant. Like, who the hell does that? Invites their jilted fiancée to their fucking wedding?

But a carefully worded email trying to get to the bottom of our breakup? Was it really all work-related, or was there something else? Did I overcorrect for something that wasn't a problem—or at least not the real problem—in the first place?

That I can do.

CHAPTER NINETEEN

Jake

"So what do you think? It just came on the market and my guess is it's going to go quick, so if you want it, we're going to have to act fast."

I take a look around the latest rental property Alex is showing me. What is this, the tenth? Twentieth? I've lost track. At some point, they all start to look the same.

But this one is the most promising space we've visited in the three weeks I've been in Miami. Lots of square footage to work with. Open floor plan. High ceilings. And a great location, right off the main drag in South Beach.

I can picture a bar running along the wall to my right. Dance floor in the center. DJ at the back. There's even a raised platform on the left that could easily be used as a stage or roped off for VIP seating, plus three more floors above for whatever else we want. Office space. Private VIP suites. Or maybe a screening room like the one we're planning for New York.

It's as close to perfect as we're going to find. As good as, if not better than, the place we lost out on, if I'm honest. I should be over the moon. But when I answer him, my voice is flat. Emotionless.

"Draw up the papers. I need to run it by my partner, but I can't imagine he'll object."

Half an hour later, I'm back in the air-conditioned bliss of my hotel room with nothing to do but think or watch the highlights of last night's Yankee game on ESPN. Since the Bombers lost in a blowout that's too painful to relive, I'm stuck with thinking. Which sucks, because these days, my mind's got one track.

And it leads to Ainsley.

It's not a path I want to go down, so I grab one of the local craft brews from the minibar—a decision I know I'll regret when I get the ridiculously exorbitant bill—and pick up my cell to call Connor.

"What's the word?" he asks when he answers on the first ring.

"I think I've found our new Miami digs."

"That's good news." He pauses, probably to save whatever spreadsheet or tax form he's working on. "Isn't it?"

"Sure." I kick off my shoes, pop the top on the beer and stretch out on the bed. "My guy's drawing up the paperwork. I'll have it to you by tomorrow."

"Then why do you sound like your dog just died?"

The word *dog* naturally leads to thoughts of Roscoe, which of course brings me back, painfully, to Ainsley. Fuck. Maybe calling Connor wasn't such a good idea after all.

I swig my beer—a little on the hoppy side, but not bad—and adopt a tone that I hope sounds more I-haven't-got-a-fucking-care-in-the-world than I'm-sitting-here-all-alone-crying-in-my-beer. "The last I heard, Roscoe's happy and healthy, unless you count eating an entire roll of toilet paper and then puking it up all over my Timberlands."

"Heard from who?" he not-so-gently prods. "Your sexy pet sitter?"

Yep. Definitely a mistake calling my former best friend.

"She's not a pet sitter," I correct him for the thousandth time. "She's an executive concierge."

"I notice you didn't dispute the sexy part."

"I've got eyes." And a brain that works. Most of the time.

"Is she still staying at your place?"

I lift the beer can to my lips and tip it back, letting the crisp, amber liquid slide down my throat and buying me a few seconds to come up with an appropriately nonresponsive response to Connor's prying. "What is this, twenty questions?"

"If it is, I've got a long way to go. I'm only up to four so far."

"Five," I amend after doing a quick mental tally. "But who's counting?"

"You are, apparently." I hear shuffling, then the soft click of a laptop closing that tells me he's shut down his computer, leaving him with nothing but me to focus on.

Fan-fucking-tastic.

"So are you going to answer me or not?" he continues.

"I forgot the question," I lie.

"Is the sexy pet sitter—sorry, executive concierge—still squatting at your place?"

"One, her name is Ainsley. Two, she wasn't squatting. She was there to lend me a hand—pun totally intended—until my arm got better. And three, no. She moved out before I flew down here."

"Trouble in paradise?"

Yes. "No trouble. I didn't need her anymore, so she left. Simple as that."

Even as they leave my mouth, the words feel wrong. Stupid. Pointless. Flat-out false. Because I can't imagine a time when I won't need Ainsley. Who else would take me to a diner full of drag queens? Or play strip Scrabble with me? Or kick my ass at Skee Ball, win a fucking florescent green alien and give me the best goddamn blow job of my life, all in one day?

She's like the yin to my yang. The sparkle to my seriousness. The Yoko Ono to my John Lennon, without all the adultery and breaking-up-the-band crap.

Then what are you doing alone in a Miami hotel room, drinking already warm beer and lying your ass off to your best friend? my subconscious screams at me. *Get on the next plane to New York and make things right with her.*

I dismiss my subliminal musings as the ramblings of a pathetic, lovesick fool—there's no use pretending, at least to myself, that I haven't fallen hard for this woman—and polish off what's left of my warm beer, crushing the can in my fist and tossing it at the garbage can. It bounces off the rim, the hollow, tinny sound echoing the emptiness inside me.

It doesn't matter that I want her more than my next breath. Ainsley's made it perfectly clear with her tersely worded responses to my texts that all I am to her now is a client. Roscoe's temporary fur daddy. Any shot I had at something more with her—like maybe a real, romantic relationship— has sailed.

"Come on, man," Connor scoffs. "You can't bullshit a bullshitter. Especially one who's known you most of your life."

"I don't know what you're talking about." Another lie. It's getting easier. Although I'm not sure it's any more convincing.

"You expect me to believe you shared an apartment with her and didn't get it on? Or at least do some heavy petting?"

I shrug, even though he can't see it. I need this

conversation to be over. "Last time I checked, it's a free country. You can believe whatever you want."

"You know, I saw her last week," he says out of the blue as I'm about to make some excuse to hang up.

"Ainsley?" I ask, trying to sound disinterested, which is pretty much the furthest thing from what I'm feeling at the moment. So much for hanging up. I'm gripping my phone so hard I'm afraid the screen might shatter. "Where?"

"At Le Bernadin," he says, naming one of Manhattan's most exclusive—and most expensive—restaurants. "With another guy. Wall Street type. Impeccably tailored three-piece suit. Trendy haircut. Rolex Yacht-Master."

"Are you kidding me?" I snap, bolting upright. My free hand fists in the thin hotel bedspread. The image of Ainsley being wined and dined by some Wall Street wolf makes me wish I had another beer can to destroy.

"Gotcha." I can almost hear the smug smile spreading across Connor's face. If I could, I'd reach through the phone and smack it off. "I knew that would smoke you out. You hooked up with Ainsley, and now you're jealous."

"Did you or did you not see her with another dude?"

There's a long pause, during which I contemplate no less than fifteen ways to murder Connor and hide the body, before he answers, "Not."

My fingers slowly unclench, releasing the bedspread. "You're a real asshole. You know that, right?"

"You say asshole, I say friend. Someone had to force you to face facts."

"And what facts are those, exactly?"

"You've finally found something—or someone—more important to you than the art of the deal. And it scares the shit out of you."

He's right, I realize suddenly. Why else would I be sleepwalking through the past three weeks in South Beach, going through the motions without any of my usual cutthroat enthusiasm for business negotiations?

"Fine, I have feelings for her," I admit. "But I let them almost cost us…"

"Nothing," Connor interrupts. "They cost us nothing. And even if they had, so what?"

"So what?" I echo incredulously. "Do you remember what happened to my father's business when he got sick? That's what happens when you take your foot off the gas pedal. And I don't want that to happen to Top Shelf. To us."

"I remember what happened," Connor says, his voice low and serious, any hint of teasing gone. "Do you?"

"Of course I do. I was there."

"You were, what, eleven? Twelve? Have you ever talked to your father about it? Asked him how he feels?"

"No." I shake my head, forgetting again for a second that Connor can't see me. "It was a pretty painful period in our family's history. I can't imagine it's something he'd want to revisit."

"Well, I have," Connor says, surprising me. "And do you know what he told me? He said that as hard as it was to watch the company he built from scratch go down the tubes, it taught him that what's really important isn't money or status or success, whatever the hell that means. It's the people who stick with you through the ups and downs."

I force myself to think back on the months after my dad's heart attack. Not just the shit parts, like I usually do. The together times. Like our family game nights. Watching movies borrowed from the library on the worn secondhand couch my mom found at the Salvation Army. Stringing microwave popcorn and making salt dough ornaments to decorate the Charlie Brown Christmas tree my dad brought home from the local hardware store.

We may have had to sell most of our belongings and downsize to an apartment not even one-quarter the size of our house, but my parents made sure we found ways to laugh. To love.

"Yeah." I swallow the lump that's suddenly lodged in my throat. "That sounds like something my dad would say. But what was I supposed to do? I had to come down here. I screwed up. I had to fix it. And being here was the best way I knew how to do that."

"Christ, you're a stubborn son of a bitch." Connor sighs. "I've been telling you all along, but you just won't listen. Miami isn't make or break for us. Hell, I'm still not convinced it's a good idea for us to be expanding with renovations set to start in New York. There will be other clubs. Other cities. Other opportunities."

Other opportunities. It's almost exactly what Ainsley said. Right before she walked out.

I tip my head back and stare at a water stain on the ceiling, quietly cursing my own stupidity. "I think I screwed up. Again."

"You think?" Connor jibes at me.

"Fine. I know."

"So what are you going to do about it?" he asks.

"I don't know, man." I stand and pace the room. I think better when I'm in motion. And I need all my brain cells firing at full capacity to come up with a way to win Ainsley back. "She was pretty pissed at me."

"Understandable, given her last breakup."

His words stop me in my tracks. "What about her last breakup? And how do you know more about her love life than I do?"

"Brie," he explains simply.

"You've been talking to my sister?" No. Not going there. I can't worry about why my best friend and my baby sister are suddenly getting all chummy when I've got my own shit to straighten out. "Never mind. Just tell me what you know."

"Her fiancé dumped her right before their wedding."

Her what? "She never mentioned that she was engaged."

"Yeah, and the guy was a total dick. Left her for his secretary. Said Ainsley was already married to her work."

Ouch. "Let me guess. That was when she quit her job at the law firm."

"Yep. She started her errand—uh, executive concierge business a few months later."

Holy shit. It all makes sense now. Ainsley's laid-back attitude toward work. Daring me to go a whole day without electronics. Her admiration for Ferris Bueller and his life-moves-fast-and-if-you-don't-stop-and-look-around-you'll-miss-it mantra.

I start pacing again, my synapses firing at warp speed as a plan begins to take shape. An outrageous, impracticable, so-over-the-top-it-just-might-work plan.

"You still there?" Connor asks. "Or did you finally grow a pair and hang up so you could get your ass on a plane to New York and grovel in person?"

"I'm here," I say, ignoring his put-down. I'm a man on a mission, and petty insults aren't going to distract me from my game plan. "Do you have a pen and paper handy? Or better yet, boot up your computer."

"Why?"

"Because I have an idea. And I'm going to need your help to make it happen."

CHAPTER TWENTY

Ainsley

IT TAKES ALMOST a week for Dale to respond to my email. Not that that surprises me. He always did things at his own, leisurely, the-world-will-wait-for-me pace.

What surprises me is that I've been staring at my computer screen for ten minutes without opening the damn thing.

I'm not sure what I'm more afraid of. That he'll give me the answer I'm hoping for. Or that he won't.

Before I can overthink this anymore, I pull up my big girl panties and click on the email. It's another minute before I work up the nerve to focus on the screen and read what he's written.

Ainsley,
Sorry it's taken so long for me to get back to you. Una and I are in Fiji, celebrating our anniversary.

I wince. Way to rub it in, Dale. Once a dickweed, always a dickweed, I guess. I say a silent prayer of thanks that I dodged that bullet.

I scroll down and read on.

You asked if your work was really the cause of our breakup, and the answer is yes—and no. Yes, the demands of your job made it hard for us to spend quality time together, and our relationship suffered because of it. And no, despite what I said at the time, that wasn't the reason I broke off our engagement. Or at least not the only reason.

The truth is, if you were the right woman for me, I would have been willing to compromise on the work thing. Maybe even been a stay-at-home dad to our eventual kids. But love is like the tide, it comes and it goes, and the tide ran out on my love for you.

I know this is hard to hear, but the least I can give you now is honesty. I hope this gives you the closure—or whatever it is—you're looking for, and that you can move on like the rolling ocean waves, with strength and purpose.

Gotta go. Una has us scheduled for a couple's massage at the hotel spa. Maybe the three of us can get together for drinks or something when we get back to the city.
Dale

I stare at the screen for a hot second, trying to make sense of the what-the-fuckery I've just read, then burst into hysterical laughter. The tide ran out on my love for you? Move on like the rolling ocean waves? Who does Dale think he is, Walt freaking Whitman? Hell will freeze over before I meet him and his not-so-blushing bride for drinks or anything else.

Still, I appreciate his honesty. No matter how painfully saccharine. And I'm talking acute physical pain here, like I've got a stomach bug. Or food poisoning. But he did make one good point—being in a relationship requires trade-offs. Compromise, not sacrifice. Bending, not breaking.

Am I willing to meet Jake halfway? Is he willing to meet me?

I know my answer—hell to the yes. Sure, Jake went a little off the deep end when his deal fell through. But so did I, dropping ultimatums like atom bombs and storming out without giving him a chance to calm down. We had a good thing going, and I let it go without lifting so much as a finger, never mind putting up a fight.

No more. Time to lace up my gloves and get into the ring. Metaphorically speaking, of course.

I open a new browser tab and I'm deep into an Expedia search for last minute deals on flights to Miami when someone knocks—no, pounds—on my door. I glance at the clock on my computer screen. 8:59. My worker bees are right on time.

"Come on in, door's open," I call, minimizing

my browser. Strategizing my next move with Jake will have to wait. You know the saying, "little pitchers have big ears?" Well, nosy assistants have big eyes. And long necks, perfect for reading over your shoulder.

"What's so funny?" Erin asks as she barrels into my apartment like she's got the NYPD hot on her heels. But no, it's just Aaron, balancing a tray of cardboard coffee cups with a familiar green logo.

"Yeah." He hands me one of the coffees and takes his usual place for our morning meetings in one of the chairs across from my desk. "We could hear you laughing all the way down the hall."

"Funny meme on Facebook," I lie, taking a sip of my coffee—light and with more artificial sweetener than I care to admit, just the way I like it.

"Ooh, can I see?" Erin comes up behind me, craning her neck over my shoulder to peek at the computer screen.

See what I mean? Big eyes. Long neck.

I point to the empty chair next to Aaron and open up my almighty spreadsheet. "Sit. No time for social media this morning. We've got important new business to discuss."

It's not a lie. I met with Martin Fletcher and the tenants in my parents' building last week, and my mom wasn't kidding when she said they were a needy bunch. We've got three new clients already, and I have an inbox full of résumés to cull through from prospective additions to the Odds & Errands team.

Of course, the sooner I send these two on their way, the sooner I can concentrate on Operation Get Jake Back. No, that makes me sound like a bounty hunter. Operation *Miami Vice*? I grimace. Not much better.

Never mind. I'll figure out the name later.

"Okay, first on the agenda—"

"What's that?" Erin's head swivels to the open window across the room.

Aaron's eyes follow her. "What's what?"

"That music." She crosses to the window. "Can't you hear it?"

I can, now that she mentions it. It sounds like…

"'Twist and Shout,'" Aaron confirms, unfolding his lanky body from the chair and joining Erin. "The Rolling Stones, right?"

I wince. He's only a few years younger than me, but sometimes it seems like an eternity.

"Beatles, you idiot," Erin corrects him, smacking him on the shoulder. "Haven't I taught you anything?"

She turns her attention back to the commotion outside, which is growing louder by the minute. "Holy shit. Is that what I think it is?"

Aaron waves me over behind his back, not taking his eyes off whatever the hell is happening on the other side of the window. "Boss, you've got to come over here and see this."

I glance longingly at my spreadsheet. Every second wasted is a second farther away from Jake. "Is it more important than our morning meeting?"

"I don't know about important," he says, still not tearing his gaze away from the window. "But it's a lot more interesting."

"If I indulge you, will you both quit goofing around so we can get back to business?"

"Trust me." Erin turns to face me, her eyes wide and a shit-eating grin splitting her face. "You don't want to miss this."

"Fine." I can't imagine what has my coworkers so amped up, unless someone's down there handing out free lattes and warm chocolate chip cookies, but I might as well give in and do what they're asking. The sooner I get this over with, the sooner I can give them their assignments and send them on their way. And the sooner I can send them on their way, the sooner I can get back to Operation Jake in the Box.

I cringe at my own bad pun. Strike three. Naming covert ops is definitely not my superpower.

As I approach the window, Aaron and Erin part to make room for me, like I'm Moses and they're the Red Sea. The music is deafening now, the final strains of "Twist and Shout" shaking the glass.

"Ladies and gentlemen," a familiar voice booms

over a loudspeaker as the Beatles give way to Wayne Newton and the opening bars of "Danke Schoen."

"You're such a wonderful crowd. We'd like to play a little tune for you. It's one of my personal favorites. And I'd like to dedicate it to a young woman who thinks I don't know how to have fun."

I slowly lower one butt cheek to the windowsill, needing something to keep me vertical since my legs, which have turned into overcooked spaghetti, are threatening to collapse out from under me. It can't be him. It can't. No matter how much I want it to be. I must be hearing things. The Jake I know would never make a spectacle of himself on a busy New York City street in broad daylight.

Or would he? Maybe I'm not the only one who's had a change of heart. Maybe this is his way of telling me he's willing to bend, too.

I flatten my palm against the glass and look down. All those classic, clichéd symptoms of shock—slack jaw, shortness of breath, pulse racing like a hummingbird on heroin—come at me with the force of a ten-ton truck. Or a two-ton SUV pulling a flatbed trailer. Because that's what's stopped in the middle of 31st Street, almost directly below my window.

But this is no ordinary trailer. It's covered in electric blue Astroturf, fake pine trees and tacky plastic flowers. At the back are three wide, semi-circular steps leading to a platform packed with dirndl-wearing women—no, wait. Are those the drag queens from the diner? I'm almost positive that's Cher with the accordion. And Marilyn Monroe on her left, holding Roscoe's leash as he dozes at their feet, totally unfazed by the music blaring from the two huge speakers behind him.

And in the center of it all is Jake, wearing gray pants, a white T-shirt and a strangely patterned black-and-gold vest. My heart does its predictable flip-flop. He looks damn delicious, even from forty feet up and in clothes that can only be described as dorktastic.

He lifts his head and his eyes scan the facade of my building. When they find me in the window, he brings the microphone closer to his sinful mouth and smiles.

That's when it hits me, what he's doing. The music. The outfit. The dirndl-wearing drag queens.

It's the parade scene from *Ferris Bueller.*

My hand flies to my mouth and tears burn the backs of my eyelids. I blink them back and dig the heels of my hands into my eye sockets to make sure I'm not hallucinating. Nope. Still there, all of it, down to the last drag queen.

"Ainsley Scott," Jake says, his voice thick with emotion and conviction. "This one's for you."

"How does that guy know your name?" Aaron asks.

Erin moves to his side and smacks him on the

arm again. Harder this time, from the sound of it. "Do us all a favor and just stand there, be quiet and look pretty."

"Ow." He rubs his shoulder and pouts at her. "Was that really necessary?"

"You're still talking, so I'd say yes. Do I need to hit you again?"

They continue to squabble, but I ignore them. Jake has my undivided attention. He's in full Ferris mode now, lip synching along with Wayne and hamming it up with everything he's got.

"What are you still doing here?"

Erin's question is met with silence, and it takes a second for me to realize she's talking to me and not Aaron. I pry my gaze off Jake and stare at her, confused. "Should I be somewhere else?"

"Yes." This time it's my arm she smacks. And yeah, it's hard and it hurts. She gestures out the window to the street below. "Down there. Unless you're playing hard to get or something."

Hard to get is definitely not the message I want to send. More like take me, I'm yours.

I make a mad dash for the door, but somehow Erin gets in front of me.

"Wait a second." She reaches up, pulls out my ponytail, and fluffs my hair. Then she pinches my makeup-free cheeks, unbuttons the top button on my blouse, and stands back to examine her handiwork, nodding approvingly. "There. That's better. Now go get him, tiger."

"Thanks," I croak as Aaron opens the door and ushers me into the hall with a dramatic sweep of his arm.

"Break a leg," he calls after me. "That means good luck."

"Only in the theater," Erin corrects him. "In normal, everyday life, good luck means good luck. Or you got this. Or knock 'em dead. Although I admit that last one's probably not the best in this particular situation…"

The door clicks shut, cutting her off, and I race down the hall to the elevator. The damn thing is slow as fuck, so I wind up taking the stairs. It's only four flights, but by the time I reach the bottom, a crowd is gathered on the sidewalk, traffic is backed up and people are hanging out of their windows to get a better view.

But just like in the movie, no one seems to mind the disruption to their daily routine. Instead, everyone's cheering and clapping and whipping out their cell phones to record it all for posterity. And YouTube, no doubt. Jake will be plastered all over the world wide web by lunch, if not sooner.

"Ainsley."

I whip my head around to see the driver's door of the SUV swing open. A guy almost as criminally good-looking as Jake steps out and waves at me.

"Hang on," he yells, working his way through the crowd. "I'm coming to get you."

Jake has spotted me, too. His eyes lock with mine as he mouths the last lines of the song.

Danke schoen.

Auf Wiedersehen.

Danke schoen.

But this isn't goodbye, it's hello. The sweetest, wackiest, most elaborately orchestrated hello of my life. When I think of what Jake must have gone through to set this whole thing up...

A loud, involuntary sob escapes from somewhere deep inside me, and happy tears stream down my cheeks.

"Are you all right, dear?" the woman beside me asks, patting my shoulder.

"Oh my God, Marsha," her friend exclaims, grabbing my arm. "It's her."

"Who her?" Marsha asks.

"The girl he's singing to. Ashley. No, Ainsley. You are her, aren't you?"

I nod—no use denying it when everyone will know who I am in a matter of minutes—and as-of-yet-unnamed woman number two sighs. "Isn't it romantic?"

"I wish Hank would do something like this for me," Marsha laments. "But I'm lucky if he remembers to put the toilet seat down."

"Ainsley." SUV guy appears in front of me, holding out his hand. "Connor Dow. Nice to finally meet you face-to-face."

So this is the infamous Connor. I take his hand and shake it. "Likewise."

Jake lets out a very un-Ferris-like growl into the microphone. Connor chuckles and throws an arm around my shoulders, making Jake growl even louder. "Let's get you on that float before my best friend threatens to kick my ass. As if he could."

"Hold on to that one, honey," Marsha tells me, and her friend nods in agreement. "Any man who's willing to risk public humiliation in the name of true love is a keeper."

"Thanks," I toss over my shoulder as Connor steers me toward the trailer. "I will."

Word of my identify must have spread because the crowd gives us a clear path from the sidewalk to the street. When we reach the float, Connor gives me a quick squeeze and whispers in my ear.

"He can be a jackass sometimes, but he's one of the good guys. Take care of him. And if you can get him out of the office and off my back every so often, I'd be eternally grateful."

"I'll try."

I squeeze him back, and he hands me over to Jake, who passes the microphone off to one of the drag queens. Then he bends down, wraps strong fingers around my upper arms, and hauls me up onto the trailer.

"You're crazy," I say, echoing Cam's line to Ferris.

"Yeah," Jake agrees. "For you."

He swallows hard, making his Adam's apple bob in his throat. Now that I'm up close to him, I can see other telltale signs of nervousness. The thin line of sweat at his brow. The clammy hands. The slight twitch in his left eye.

It's fucking adorable.

I shake my head and smile, a big, dopey grin that makes my cheeks ache. "That line's not in the movie."

"I know. Neither is this." He pulls me closer to him and takes me into his arms. "It's called artistic license."

"Well, if we're going off script…"

I grab the collar of his vest and yank his mouth down to mine. I pour everything into this kiss. Passion. Promise. Loyalty.

Love.

After a moment of stunned inaction, Jake's an active participant, his hands tangling in my hair, his lips parting, his head tilting to deepen the kiss.

Roscoe howls. The crowd whoops and hollers. The drag queens do some sort of celebratory dance behind us. But it all fades into the background as we kiss like there's no one watching. Like we don't have a whole host of cell phones trained on us, ready to share on social media with just a few clicks so even more people can watch us later.

So much for my aversion to PDA.

"Hey," Jake says when we finally come up for air. "This is supposed to be my mea culpa. I'm the one who messed up. You were right. Top Shelf can live without Miami. But I can't live without you. You make me a better man. One who's not afraid to channel his inner Ferris and stop and look around once in a while."

I burrow my nose into the crook of his neck, letting his sweaty, soapy scent permeate every cell of my body. God, I've missed his smell. "Your inner Ferris, huh?"

"Yeah. I'm through letting life pass me by. I want to live it to the fullest. With you. I want us to go to drag queen diners and decorate for penis parties and play strip Scrabble and have wild, wall-banging sex and slow, soft, sweet sex as much as you want for however long you'll have me." He cups my face, one thumb tracing tender circles on my cheek. "I love you, Ainsley."

My heart's beating so fast I swear it's going to burst free from my rib cage. "I love you, too. And we both messed up."

I'll explain about Dale later. My ex is the last thing I want to think about right now. I want to get back to the good stuff.

The kissing.

I go for his vest, my greedy hands eager to drag

him back down to me. He takes them in his, holding me off.

"We'll probably mess up again," he says. "At least I will."

"I'm sure I will, too. But we'll work through it. Meet each other halfway. Make sure the seesaw doesn't tip too much one way or the other."

His brows furrow. "Seesaw?"

"I'll explain later." I loop his hands around my neck and lean into him, enjoying the way his hard body feels against my softer one. "Now I need you to kiss me."

He does. This time it's less frantic, less hurried. This kiss is a leisurely dance, a slow exploration. His lips are everywhere, trailing soft, teasing nips along my collarbone, under my chin, over my shoulders.

Someone—I think it's Aaron from on high—yells for us to get a room, and a horn honks, starting a symphony of discordant beeping. We break apart, breathless and laughing.

I rest my head against Jake's chest. Beneath my cheek, his heart beats a rapid rhythm that matches my own. "Looks like our time's up."

He brushes my hair back from my face and runs a finger along my jawline. "More like it's just beginning."

Jake signals to Connor, who gives him a thumbs-up and hops back into the driver's seat of the SUV. It inches forward as someone fires the music up again and the Beatles blast from the speakers. The drag queens start twisting and shouting, and Marilyn hands Roscoe's leash to Jake so she can join in on the fun without a one-hundred-and-eighty-pound canine holding her back.

"What are we going to do now?" I ask, not really caring. As long as we're together. Although a little privacy would be nice so we could get started on that wall-banging sex he talked about. Followed by the slow and sweet variety.

He reaches down to pet Roscoe—the dog that started it all—then brings his mouth inches from mine, a confident, sexy smile curving his lips. "The question isn't what are we going to do. It's what aren't we going to do."

* * * * *

COMING SOON!

We really hope you enjoyed reading this book.
If you're looking for more romance, be sure to
head to the shops when new books are
available on

Thursday 28th May

To see which titles are coming soon, please visit
millsandboon.co.uk/nextmonth

LET'S TALK
Romance

For exclusive extracts, competitions
and special offers, find us online:

f facebook.com/millsandboon
🐦 @MillsandBoon
📷 @MillsandBoonUK

Get in touch on 01413 063232

For all the latest titles coming soon, visit
millsandboon.co.uk/nextmonth

MILLS & BOON

THE HEART OF ROMANCE

A ROMANCE FOR EVERY KIND OF READER

MODERN

Prepare to be swept off your feet by sophisticated, sexy and seductive heroes, in some of the world's most glamourous and romantic locations, where power and passion collide.
8 stories per month.

HISTORICAL

Escape with historical heroes from time gone by. Whether your passion is for wicked Regency Rakes, muscled Vikings or rugged Highlanders, awaken the romance of the past.
6 stories per month.

MEDICAL

Set your pulse racing with dedicated, delectable doctors in the high-pressure world of medicine, where emotions run high and passion, comfort and love are the best medicine.
6 stories per month.

True Love

Celebrate true love with tender stories of heartfelt romance, from the rush of falling in love to the joy a new baby can bring, and a focus on the emotional heart of a relationship.
8 stories per month.

Desire

Indulge in secrets and scandal, intense drama and plenty of sizzling hot action with powerful and passionate heroes who have it all: wealth, status, good looks...everything but the right woman.
6 stories per month.

HEROES

Experience all the excitement of a gripping thriller, with an intense romance at its heart. Resourceful, true-to-life women and strong fearless men face danger and desire - a killer combination!
8 stories per month.

DARE

Sensual love stories featuring smart, sassy heroines you'd want as best friend, and compelling intense heroes who are worthy of them.
4 stories per month.

To see which titles are coming soon, please visit

millsandboon.co.uk/nextmonth